Painted
DESERT

Painted
DESERT

Love Flourishes in the Picturesque Desert

NANCY J. FARRIER

BARBOUR
PUBLISHING

Published by Barbour Publishing, Inc., P.O. Box 719, Uhrichsville, Ohio 44683, www.barbourbooks.com

Our mission is to publish and distribute inspirational products offering exceptional value and biblical encouragement to the masses.

ecpa Member of the
Evangelical Christian
Publishers Association

Printed in the United States of America.

Dear Readers,

Arizona. From low desert covered with cacti and mesquite to mountains wrapped in stately pine trees, Arizona is a vast area of changing scenery. From the Grand Canyon and the Petrified Forest to the many ancient Indian ruins, there is much to see in this beautiful state.

Painted Desert will treat you to some of the popular sights of Arizona, plus a few that aren't as well known. These are places that I have enjoyed, either on my own or with my family on our various jaunts.

In *An Ostrich a Day*, Blaire and Burke will visit the Reid Park Zoo in Tucson and the Gila River outside of Winkelman, Arizona. Jazmyn and Thor see some of the wildlife habitat found in the White Mountains of Arizona as they spend time together in *Picture Imperfect*. Maddy and Jason walk the back roads of what was once my hometown of Dudleyville, Arizona, and get together at the renowned Arizona-Sonora Desert Museum in *Picture This*.

Thank you for choosing to spend time with each of these couples as they learn of God's plan for their lives and their need to trust Him with all their hearts. As you read this book and share their stories, consider God's infinite love for you, and how He cares about each step you take.

God's Blessings,
Nancy J. Farrier

An Ostrich a Day

Dedication

To my Lord, who gave the gift of laughter and the Bible, His Word, that guides my steps.

Thank you to my daughters, Anne and Abigail, who love to edit my books.

To Steve and Mitzi Stumbaugh. Thank you for sharing your knowledge of ostriches and for all the fascinating stories.

Chapter 1

Blaire Mackenzie stepped from her rental car and frowned at the barren Arizona hills surrounding her newly inherited piece of desert. *Barren, just like my life.* She sighed. *Well, not as desolate as the Sahara.*

Prickly cacti, standing stiff and erect like sentinels, marched across the hills, and scrub brush of some sort covered the ground. Blue lupine and California poppies dotted the hillsides. What had the man at the gas station said? The spring flowers were in full bloom, making the desert a garden? Obviously, his idea of a garden didn't agree with the lush flowers found in the Midwest where Blaire hailed from.

An ostrich ranch! Blaire shook her head. Why in the world had her uncle thought she would want to live in this desert and raise ostriches of all things? Who wanted to live around a bunch of overgrown chickens that laid such huge eggs you couldn't even eat them? She'd read an article about these birds. One ostrich egg equaled twenty-four chicken eggs. Who could eat that much for breakfast? How many pound cakes would you have to make to use one egg? The thought boggled the mind.

A strong afternoon breeze whipped Blaire's hair across her face and pulled at her full skirt like a mischievous child. Taking a deep breath, Blaire had to admit there were some advantages to being in the middle of nowhere. The absence of exhaust fumes and the utter quiet gave her the feeling of stepping into another time. At least March in southern Arizona shouldn't bring surprise snow flurries or constant rain.

She wiped a wavy strand of hair off her face, while her other hand tried to smooth her blowing skirt. Was Arizona always this windy? Blaire watched in amazement as a miniature brown tornado moved across the nearby pasture, heading toward the hills. The sandy cyclone picked up bits of debris, distributing dust and plant fragments in another area as the turbulence wound down.

God, I don't know how this could be the place You planned for me to live. There must be a mistake here somewhere. Blaire's gaze wandered across the pens of ostriches. The long-necked birds peered over the fence at her with their comical faces. *How could anyone be happy here, Lord? There isn't even a shopping mall within fifty miles.*

Stepping aside, Blaire swung the car door shut. A young man approached, and Blaire took the opportunity to study him. Would this be the foreman, Burke

Dunham? No, she decided. A foreman would be older. The dark-complected youth walking toward her looked like he could still be in high school.

Blaire straightened her shoulders and took a deep breath. "Okay, girl," she muttered softly to herself. "Time to make a good first impression."

"Hello, may I help you?" The young man smiled as he greeted her. His warm brown eyes and white teeth sparkled in the afternoon sunlight. Windblown black hair framed his youthfully handsome face.

"Hello." Blaire attempted a nervous smile as she raked the blowing hair back from her face. Thankfully her skirt wasn't trying to fly off over her head anymore. "I'm looking for Burke Dunham. I'm Blaire Mackenzie, Ike's niece."

"I'm Manuel Ortega. My mother and I worked for your uncle. I'm sorry about your uncle Ike. He was a good man." Manuel grinned and extended his hand. "We've been looking forward to you coming."

Blaire relaxed and stepped forward to shake hands with Manuel. In midstep she realized why her skirt wasn't blowing anymore. Caught in the car door, the material tightened around her legs, clamping them in its cottony embrace. Blaire swung forward. Her foot slipped in the sandy dirt. Her arms flailed like an out-of-control windmill. She fought to regain her balance. With a gasp, Blaire realized her face was about to meet the Arizona sand.

A large hand gripped her arm like a vise, and Blaire, pulled upright, found herself looking into a pair of eyes the color of the sea on a moody day. Aqua. Sea green. Her favorite color. Blaire pushed back from the man and his wonderful eyes only to be caught once more by the confines of her trapped skirt.

"Let me help." The deep, rich voice echoed with a tinge of amusement at her predicament. With one hand still on her arm, he reached over and did what she should have done two minutes earlier. He opened the car door, releasing her skirt to play with the wind once more.

Immediately, Blaire stepped back and reached down to keep her skirt from becoming a head scarf. She could hear Manuel chuckling and felt the heat of a blush as she watched her rescuer grin in amusement. A worn gray cowboy hat shaded his incredible eyes.

He stretched out a hand to her. "Hi, I'm Burke Dunham, the foreman here. I believe I heard you tell Manuel you're Ike Mackenzie's niece."

Blaire nodded. "That's right. I guess I own this ranch now." She lifted her chin, trying to regain a little confidence in front of this much-too-handsome man she would be required to work with. He lifted his hat and brushed his hand over short, straw-colored hair. The cleft in his chin reminded her of her mother's favorite movie star. He settled his hat, and his muscular arm dropped to his side as she stepped away. Standing back a little, she found it easier to look at him without having to tilt her head back so far.

"Well, Miss Mackenzie." Burke spoke seriously. "I know Manuel's a good worker, one of the best, but you don't have to throw yourself at his feet."

Manuel laughed, and Blaire knew her face must be bright red. She wanted to do something totally childish such as slap the smug look from Burke's face or give him a swift kick in the shins. Instead, she heard the voice of her mother saying, "Pride goeth before destruction, Blaire," and she remembered her resolve to make a good impression.

Swallowing her pride, Blaire managed a small smile. "Thank you for helping me out, Mr. Dunham."

A truck pulling a long trailer rumbled down the driveway, road dust boiling out from under the tires. After it ground to a halt, Manuel and Burke both waved at the driver, who stepped down from the cab. "Excuse us for a minute, Miss Mackenzie." Burke nodded at Blaire. "This truck is here to pick up some ostriches. I'll help Manuel get started with the loading, then I'll come and show you around. I'll only be a few minutes."

Blaire watched as Manuel and Burke greeted the driver of the truck like an old friend. They gestured down a side lane, then headed that way as the man climbed back in the vehicle. The truck and trailer clattered down the road, following Manuel and Burke like an overgrown puppy dog, obscuring the two men in the windblown dust.

Blaire sighed, blinked away the image of mesmerizing aqua eyes, and looked across the top of her car at the ranch house. The one-story adobe building sprawled beneath several stately trees. Their branches draped gracefully over the house in an apparent attempt to ward off the sun's heat. A covered porch ran the length of the house, complete with a swing to enjoy on balmy evenings. Trumpet vines covered the latticework at the ends of the porch, their orange blossoms making a bright pattern in the green leaves.

Six months ago Blaire would have laughed uproariously if anyone had suggested she move to the middle of nowhere and take over her uncle Ike's ostrich ranch. Blaire had intended to continue her career with Bennett and Sons, an accounting firm. Of course, her engagement to Richard Bennett, the son of the firm's founder and its current owner, had meant she would someday be quitting her accounting career to begin another one as a wife and mother. Blaire had looked forward to that time.

Then four months ago that world fell apart. Richard left town with the firm's secretary—and they weren't traveling on business. He sent Blaire an e-mail telling her the engagement was off. An e-mail of all things. He didn't even have the courage to tell her his decision to her face. Without returning home, Richard closed the firm just after Christmas, putting all the employees out of jobs. Blaire had cried until she could barely see out of swollen eyes, feeling as if her life were over before it even began.

O God, only You know how much he hurt me. Blaire blinked her eyes to clear the tears as she remembered the sidelong glances of the office workers and the whispered conversations that ended as soon as she entered a room.

For the last three months, Blaire had worked non-stop for a tax preparer, doing taxes for senior citizens who were homebound or in nursing homes. Blaire prayed constantly for the Lord to show her where He wanted her and what He wanted her to do with her life.

When she'd learned of Uncle Ike's death and of the ranch she'd inherited, Blaire was positive that this was her answer to prayer. She'd made arrangements to have her things shipped to Arizona, tied up all the loose ends, and fled the Midwest, where all her hopes and dreams lay scattered. But when she met with the lawyers in Phoenix, Blaire discovered her dreams of cows and grass-carpeted hills didn't match the reality of her inheritance. Uncle Ike had left her a dry, dust-covered ranch full of giant birds.

Turning from the house, Blaire walked toward the nearest pen of ostriches. Three birds stood in the pen. Two were lighter in color. The third ostrich was the largest. His dark-feathered wings waved slightly as he stalked regally around the pen as if trying to impress the world with his importance.

"You must be named Richard," Blaire said to the strutting, dark-feathered ostrich. "You swagger around like you're God's gift to the human race and everyone should be impressed. Well, I'm not awed by you, your majesty."

The female ostriches moved closer to the fence, and Blaire grimaced. "Well, here's Vanessa, the secretary. Yep, same long eyelashes, except these might be real." Blaire leaned forward to get a better look. "My, my, Vanessa, you sure do have knobby knees. Maybe you should wear your feathers a little longer." Shaking her head, Blaire sighed. "I must be going batty. Here I am talking to a bunch of stupid birds."

Blaire strolled on, finding a pen with young ostriches stalking around in miniature imitation of the regal adults. Their feathers looked as soft as down, and Blaire reached through the fence as they came close, trying to see if they felt as soft as they looked. "Ouch!" Blaire jerked her hand away and rubbed her thumb where the young bird had snapped at it. "You guys don't have any teeth," Blaire said, glaring at the young ostriches, "but you sure do have some strong jaws. I guess it's a good thing you're toothless."

The birds crowded close to the fence, tilting their heads from side to side as if trying to understand exactly what Blaire was saying. She smiled and held one hand up in the air. All the little heads followed her hand, reaching toward it with their beaks. With her other hand, Blaire quickly reached through the fence and gently touched one of the ostriches. The stiff, prickly outer quills poked her fingers. Slipping her hand farther through the fence, Blaire could reach the soft, downy under-feathers of the baby ostrich.

"Ah-ha!" Blaire grinned. "I gotcha that time. At least this proves I'm smarter than an ostrich. I guess you guys don't care too much, do you?" The little heads all tilted to one side in unison as if considering whether they cared or not. Blaire laughed and walked back toward the pens of adult ostriches.

Manuel grinned at Burke. "The new boss sure is a pretty one."

Burke laughed. "I have to agree she's better looking than Ike. We'll see how she works out. I don't know if someone from the big city will enjoy living here in the middle of the desert."

As Manuel moved toward the pen of ostriches, Burke stood momentarily lost in thought about his new boss. Once again he could see her clear blue eyes. Wide as the Arizona sky on a summer day, those eyes and her heart-shaped face were perfectly framed by thick waves of ash blond hair. Despite her slender frame, Blaire exuded confidence and an air that left no doubt about her ability to handle herself in just about any situation.

"Well, maybe not any situation," Burke chuckled as he remembered a blue-flowered skirt trapped in a car door. *Looks like she may fit in here after all,* he thought.

Blaire studied the huge birds with their beautiful long-lashed eyes and slender, graceful necks. She assumed the dark-feathered one was the male. He slowly waved his black-brown wings tipped with white and strutted proudly around the pen, eyeing Blaire as she watched him. The smaller females, with their lighter, grayish-brown coloring, hovered near the nest on the far side of the pen.

Blaire stepped back as the male ostrich stalked past the fence where she stood. He paused, tilting his head to one side, and watched her intently as if warning her not to come too close to his domain.

"Who do you think you are, Buster?" Blaire drew herself up to her full five foot two inches and tried to stare the ostrich down. "I happen to be in charge here now, so you'd better mind your manners." Blaire grinned in triumph as the ostrich moved on, continuing to strut around the pen toward the females.

He slowly fanned his wings as he walked. Blaire watched as one of the long, grayish-white under-feathers drifted to the ground. She moved around the fence and knelt down, hoping to reach the long plume and pull it to her. Unfortunately, the feather remained out of reach, and the wind appeared to have died down for the moment.

Keeping an eye on the ostriches, Blaire moved to the gate and lifted the latch. All three birds were across the pen, apparently ignoring her as they silently discussed something among themselves. Perhaps she could slip inside the pen, retrieve the feather, and be out before they even noticed her.

She slipped the gate open and stepped through, her heart pounding. The silky feather beckoned to her as it lay on the ground only a few feet away. Blaire inched across the pen, then bent to pick up the long downy plume. As she stood, she looked up once more to check on the ostriches before she made her escape from the enclosure.

To her horror, the male ostrich was racing toward her at an incredibly fast pace. His wings were spread and his mouth opened as if sounding a silent battle cry. Blaire stood frozen, unable to take her eyes from the enraged bird bearing down on her. Time slowed. She knew she wouldn't be able to escape this ostrich and his malicious intentions.

A strong arm grasped Blaire around the waist and jerked her off her feet. In a wild dance, someone whirled her around and waltzed her through the gate of the pen before she knew what had happened. Tilting her head back, Blaire looked up into aqua eyes, noticing for the first time how they faded to gray-green at the edges. The eyes flashed with anger, and she flinched despite her resolve to always be strong.

"What do you think you're doing?" Burke exploded as he slammed the gate shut behind them. "Are you trying to get yourself killed?"

Chapter 2

Blaire tore herself from Burke's arms. "Of course I wasn't trying to get myself killed," she retorted, waving her hand in a futile attempt to clear away the cloud of dust stirred up by the ostrich's flying feet.

"Then just what were you doing in that pen?" Burke glared at her through narrowed eyes. "Don't you know a male ostrich that size could kill you with one kick?"

Blaire felt faint at the thought of being so close to death. "I. . .I only wanted the feather." A mixture of guilt and anger washed over her, and she stalked across to a pen containing three female ostriches. The curious birds stood near the fence, watching closely as Burke followed her. Blaire feigned interest in the ostriches, hoping Burke would drop the subject and remember his promise to show her around.

Burke took a deep breath and rapped his hat against his leg to knock off the dust. He raked a hand through his short-cropped hair before slamming the hat back on his head. "The ostrich was only defending his territory and his mates. He didn't stop to consider whether you intended to harm them." Softening his tone, he continued. "Until you learn the ropes, ask before you go into a pen, please. Once you get to know your way around, you'll be fine."

Blaire glanced up at him, nervously running the soft feather through her fingers. Her breath caught in her throat as she met his mesmerizing aqua eyes. The intensity of his gaze bored right through her as if he could read her thoughts. She looked down without speaking, chiding herself for acting like a tongue-tied teenager. She wanted to feel anger, yet she knew he was right. She shouldn't have been in the pen.

God, what is happening here? You know I didn't want to ever be attracted to a man again after Richard. I don't even know Burke, and yet he has me stammering and feeling like a fool.

Blaire backed a few steps away from Burke, trying to distance herself from him, hoping to regain her composure.

"Miss Mackenzie." Burke stretched out a hand toward her, and Blaire stepped away even farther, her back coming up against the fence of the ostrich pen.

A sudden pain in her scalp caused Blaire to gasp and blink back tears. Again and again the jolt of pain shot through her. She lifted her hands to her head in an effort to figure out what had grabbed her hair and tried to step away, but something held her in place. Burke moved closer and reached his hand toward her. She wanted to dodge but remained helpless to move her head as it snapped tight against the fence. It felt as if her scalp were being pulled in several directions at once.

"Owww!" Blaire yelled.

Once more Burke came to her rescue, the corners of his mouth struggling not to tip upward in a smile. Reaching above her head, Burke grabbed an ostrich and forced it to release Blaire's hair from its beak. A hunk of ostrich-gummed hair fell in Blaire's face, but once more her head was jerked back.

"Shoo now! Get out of here," Burke yelled at the ostriches, waving his hands to distract them. The others loosed their hold on Blaire and moved back into the pen.

"Are you okay?" Burke's mouth quivered. His jaw clenched as if he were trying not to laugh at her.

Blaire imagined the spectacle she must make. Her hair would be sticking out in all directions, ostrich slobber, if they did such a thing, shining on the dark blond waves. Her face must be as red as a candy apple. *O God, I certainly made an impression here. I'm so glad I won't be staying long.*

As Blaire looked at Burke, who fought to keep from laughing, she glanced over at the ostriches and swore she could see a smirk on their silly bird faces. It was too much. First she grinned, then chuckled, and before she knew it she was grasping her sides, doubled over with laughter. Burke joined her as he led her a safe distance from the pen.

"Are you okay?" Burke gasped again when they'd calmed down enough to talk. "They pulled your hair pretty hard." At that they both dissolved into giggles again.

Finally, Blaire could control her laughter enough to be able to admit, "I'm fine. My head is a little sore, but at least I still have some hair left." She rubbed her scalp and ran her fingers through her hair in an attempt to get it back in a semblance of order. "Thank you, once again, for rescuing me. I'm not sure how I'll manage here. I don't know what Uncle Ike was thinking, leaving this place to me."

"I think Ike knew exactly what he was doing." Burke's low, rich voice still held a hint of amusement. "Ike used to talk about you a lot. He always wanted you to come to visit. He said you stole his heart when you were a baby and would crawl on his lap and fall asleep. He talked about your blond curls and blue eyes and said you could get him to do anything for you. Is that right?"

Blaire smiled, remembering how Uncle Ike always treated her like a queen. "Before Uncle Ike traveled, we were very close." Blaire frowned. "Then he started moving around the country, going from one job to another. We didn't see much of him because he barely gave us his new address before he moved to another place. A couple of times he showed up at our house for a short visit. I always missed him."

"He was a good man," Burke agreed. "Come on, I'll show you around the ranch. Ike bought this place five years ago and worked hard to build it up. He's done a remarkable job considering the opposition he faced and the state of neglect the place was in when he bought it."

"Opposition?" Blaire questioned.

Burke shrugged. "Oh, you know, raising ostriches in cattle country just isn't done. But your uncle did everything with such grace that he won a lot of friends in a short time. Come on, let's start over here with the hatchery."

Burke led the way to an oblong shed and unlocked the door. Blaire followed him into a small room equipped with several pairs of clean sandals and a sink for washing. "Ostrich eggs are easily contaminated, so if you ever handle them, you must wash your hands first. If your shoes are dirty, slip them off and put on a pair of these sandals."

Blaire nodded, then peered through the glass of the door leading into the next room. Several large metal incubators lined the walls. She could see the huge, cream-colored ostrich eggs resting side by side, waiting to hatch out.

"What are all the lights on the wall by the door?" Blaire indicated a panel of lights with digital numbers glowing beside them.

"Those show the temperature of each incubator. We check these several times a day. We have to maintain the temperature at 97.5, and if it dips too low or goes too high an alarm sounds outside and in the house."

"How many eggs do you get every day?"

Burke frowned in thought. "Well, we have forty-two breeders—females that are laying fertilized eggs—and they each lay an egg every forty-eight hours. We get approximately twenty-one eggs a day and put most of them in the incubators. The infertile eggs are blown out and sold to a lady in Tucson."

"What does she do with the eggs?"

"She decorates them, does etchings, then sells them. She makes some beautiful lamps out of the eggs."

"So about how many eggs are fertile?"

Tilting his head back, Burke frowned for a moment. "I think we get an average of eighteen fertile eggs a day."

Blaire's eyes widened. "That's a lot of eggs—almost five hundred and fifty a month. There weren't that many ostriches out there. What do you do with them all?"

"You haven't even seen any of the ranch yet. Come on, I'll take you on a little tour."

Burke led Blaire to a fairly new dark blue pickup and opened the door for her. He flipped the door shut and walked around the truck. Blaire started to pull her skirt out of the way so she could fasten her seat belt. As Burke climbed in on the driver's side, she sheepishly opened her door and pulled the skirt inside the truck. She made a face at Burke. "I guess my skirt just likes doors."

Burke chuckled with her as he drove down a lane between ostrich pens. "We only keep the breeders close to the house. That makes it easier to gather the eggs. Your uncle's property, now yours, extends out through these hills."

They rounded the base of a hill. Blaire gasped. Fenced pastures stretched before her, filled with ostriches of various sizes. "How many are there?" she asked in an awed tone.

"We currently have over twenty-eight hundred birds, not counting the breeders up by the house."

Blaire looked at him in shock. "What did Uncle Ike do with so many ostriches?"

Burke grinned, and she quickly looked back out the window at the fields dotted with ostriches. "Over there," Burke said, pointing out the window, "is our processing plant. There's a growing market for ostrich meat, so a lot of our birds are raised for slaughter. We do sell some of them, too, especially the ones that look like they will be good breeders."

Burke pulled the truck to a stop and climbed out. "Come on," he said as he opened Blaire's door. "You can walk in with these ostriches. The only ones that are really dangerous are the breeders. These are juvenile females."

"They all look big to me," Blaire murmured as they walked toward the pasture gate.

"Just remember to stay out of the pens with males in them, and you'll be fine. Watch out!" Burke grabbed her arm and pulled her toward him. A tingle raced up Blaire's arm, and she tried to pull out of his firm grasp.

"Watch out for what?"

"The cactus." Burke pointed to the prickly plant she had nearly walked into. "This is the desert, and many of the plants here are very unfriendly. It's the only way they can survive. That one, the cholla, is particularly nasty."

Blaire leaned over for a closer look and shuddered at the miniature branches covered with vicious-looking curved barbs. It wouldn't be pleasant to get stuck with those. She glanced back up at Burke. "It seems all I'm doing today is thanking you for saving me from one thing or another." Burke smiled warmly, but before he could say anything she hurriedly added, "I'll be glad when I can get back to the city where life is safer."

Burke's warm smile faded. He turned to open the pasture gate, waited for Blaire to step through, then followed, clicking the gate closed behind them.

The pasture stretched before her, barren of growth, picked clean by hundreds of curious beaks. They were standing in a long valley between low hills. Blue-tinged mountains lifted high in the distance, meeting a skyline that appeared to extend forever. A few white, puffy clouds scudded across the azure sky.

Blaire looked around slowly. There were no tall buildings here, no freeways or bus routes. She couldn't even hear a car engine. The utter quiet could be peaceful, she supposed, if one adjusted to the silence. Blaire didn't think she would ever adapt, and she didn't want to anyway. This wasn't for her. She wanted the excitement of city life, shopping, and the ease of getting anywhere she wanted in a matter of minutes on the convenient freeways.

Blaire closed her eyes for a moment and pictured her favorite mall. Throngs of people crowded through, chattering to one another as they made their purchases or just window-shopped. The hum of voices. The smell of cookies, caramel corn, and candies. The mouth-watering aroma of various ethnic foods. Blaire could almost smell her favorite Mexican dishes.

The smile blossoming on Blaire's face faded as she recalled her last trip to the mall. She and Richard had walked arm in arm as she chattered nonstop about their wedding. Richard had been unusually quiet that day. Later Blaire realized his thoughts weren't on her and their upcoming wedding; he was thinking only of his plans to dump her and run off with Vanessa.

"Miss Mackenzie?" Blaire jumped as Burke touched her arm. She blinked back tears and fought to clear her memories.

"I'm sorry." She blushed, thinking how stupid she must appear. "I was just comparing the quiet openness of the desert to the city life I'm used to. I don't know how you survive without. . .I mean, where do you shop around here anyway?"

A low, hearty sound rumbled in Burke's chest. "We have peddlers who come by every couple of months and show us their wares. If we get too desperate, we can send out a distress signal and have food air dropped so we don't starve."

Blaire rolled her eyes. "Okay, I deserved that, but you have to remember I'm used to having a grocery store or mall within fifteen minutes of where I live."

"Well, we are a little farther from shopping, but it isn't hopeless. There are stores in Winkelman and Kearny where you can pick up a few things. For major shopping, most people go to Globe, Tucson, or Phoenix. They even have movie theaters and malls, just like they do back East."

Blaire's melodic laugh floated across the quiet pasture. "I guess you adjust to this life, but I'm not sure I ever could."

"Come on." Burke led the way across the pasture. "I want to show you something." They walked toward the largest group of ostriches, dust from the barren ground swirling up around their ankles. "These are all young females around ten months old."

Blaire wrinkled her nose as the dust from shuffling ostrich feet drifted up around them. She fought a losing battle to stop the sneeze that was building. As she lifted her hand to her nose, Burke pulled a brightly colored handkerchief from his hip pocket and handed it to her with a flourish.

In unison the ostriches lifted their long necks to stare at them. They tilted their heads to one side and circled uneasily, then began to edge away. Blaire's sudden sneeze echoed across the pasture.

As one, the young birds stretched out their long legs and ran. More and more of the ostriches joined the first group racing around the barren field, dust flying around them in a cloud. Blaire jumped as Burke leaned close and said, "Just stand still, and we'll be fine. They can reach speeds of up to forty-five miles per hour and can continue at that pace for about twenty minutes."

"Do they do this very often?" Blaire stared in amazement at the racing birds, their strong legs pushing hard and giving them the appearance of floating above the ground. Their wings fanned uselessly beside their bodies.

"Once in awhile something spooks them, and they take off for a run. Then again, sometimes they don't get spooked. Perhaps running feels good."

Once more the young birds raced around the far end of the pasture heading back toward the gate. As they ran opposite Blaire and Burke, the lead bird pivoted and headed straight for them. The other birds followed their leader, and to Blaire's horror, the whole flock of ostriches rushed at breakneck speed toward her. This time the gate was too far away to dash through to safety.

God, help us, Blaire silently pleaded as she flung herself at Burke, hiding her face against his chest and trembling in anticipation of being trampled by hundreds of gargantuan chickens.

Chapter 3

Burke's arms closed around Blaire, pulling her close against his chest. A lemony scent wafted up from her, and for a moment he felt the temptation to bury his nose in her hair. His jaw clenched in an effort to avoid being affected by this attractive woman.

A swirl of dust drifted over the pair as the young ostriches skidded to a halt. Nosy beaks tugged at their clothing. Burke made himself release Blaire as she pushed away from him. Her widened eyes and open mouth told him more than words of her surprise to still be standing and not squashed under ostrich feet.

"They stopped," Blaire gasped.

Burke chuckled. "I wouldn't bring you anywhere you'd be in danger. These young ladies won't hurt you, although if you're not careful they can get a little rambunctious with your clothing."

Blaire firmly pushed away an ostrich who was trying to remove her skirt. "Stop that."

"This is worse than the wind, huh?"

Blaire nodded, her sky blue eyes twinkling. "Perhaps she thinks she'll look better in this skirt than I do. I have to admit I'm a little selfish, though. I don't plan to exchange my skirt for her feathers no matter how beautiful they are."

"Before she gets too disappointed, maybe we should continue our tour." Burke led Blaire through the crowd of ostriches. Like a group of nosy schoolgirls, the ostriches followed them to the gate, looking disappointed at being left behind.

Back in the truck, Burke and Blaire rattled over the rutted dirt road as he pointed out the fields filled with various age groups and sexes of ostriches. He showed her the hayfields where they raised much of their own feed and the processing plant where the ostriches were butchered.

"What do you do with all the meat?" Blaire asked as they walked out of the cool building that housed the processing plant.

"We have several markets for the meat across the country. We also sell the skins. Ostrich hides make good leather. In fact, there's a better market for the leather now than the meat. That could change with the problems in the European meat market." He shrugged. "Who knows what will happen there. Now, I'd better show you to the house and get you settled in before Isabel tans my hide."

"Who's Isabel?" Blaire asked as Burke closed her door, walked around the front of the truck, and climbed in on the driver's side.

"Isabel is Manuel's mother," Burke answered as he started the truck and slowly headed back toward the house. "She worked for Ike when he first came here, and Manuel was an ornery high school student. Her husband died in an accident at the mines. I guess Ike was an answer to prayer for her."

"Why is that?"

"Well, she didn't have much family here, and she'd never worked outside the home. Ike not only gave her a job and a home, but he took Manuel under his wing and helped him get straightened out. I sometimes wonder how Manuel would have turned out if Ike hadn't come along. He sure ran with a rough crowd back then."

Blaire leaned her head back against the truck seat, obviously tired. Burke glanced sideways at her, wondering at his attraction to this woman he had just met yet felt he'd known for years. Of course, Ike always bragged about Blaire and showed every picture of her like she was his favorite daughter instead of a niece.

Lord, Burke prayed silently, *You know she says she's not staying. Help me not to get attached to her. I don't want to be involved with a woman. They're just trouble, and I don't need that.*

Burke thought of his years growing up. He remembered his mother mostly from her pictures. She'd died when he was eight years old. Sometimes a certain fragrance or phrase she used to say would remind him of how she loved to hold him on her lap and read to him. Mostly, he recalled her leaving him. He could still remember the old feelings of rejection as he stood beside her casket and looked at her still, white face.

His grandmother tried hard to fill in. Burke loved her and slowly trusted her with his deepest hurts and fears. However, just before he turned twelve, he came home from school to find his grandmother lying cold and quiet in the middle of the living room.

Then there was Julie. His jaw clenched until his teeth hurt. He refused to think about Julie.

Since that time Burke hadn't trusted another woman. They all left right when you learned to love them. He didn't want to get involved with a woman and risk the vulnerability that came with it. After experiencing the feelings Blaire evoked, Burke sincerely hoped she would go back to the city as fast as she had arrived.

⁂

"Come on in." Burke set the suitcase down and opened the door for Blaire. She stepped up beside him, carrying her smaller case and her purse. Gazing in awe at the double doors, Blaire admired the colors in the stained-glass panels at the side of each door. Beautiful lavender irises glittered in the midst of the design of green grasses and blue sky. Tiny yellow-and-orange butterflies hovered over the flowers.

"Your uncle Ike said irises were always his favorite flower." Burke pointed to the glass panels. "He figured this was the best way to have irises all year round."

"They're beautiful," Blaire said. "You can almost see the butterflies' wings moving and hear bees buzzing. Whoever made these stained-glass windows did an excellent job."

Blaire turned to go through the doorway, still thinking of Uncle Ike and his love for flowers, not seeing the step up into the entryway. The toe of her sandal caught on the edge of the step, and she stumbled forward, unable to catch herself because her hands were full. The blur of tile flooring rushed up to meet her before she could even think about what to do.

"Whoa, there." Blaire felt Burke grab her arm, stopping her just as her knees met the floor. "There you go throwing yourself on the ground again." Burke's voice held a hint of amusement.

As Burke helped her to her feet, Blaire could feel the heat of a blush spreading up her face. She turned to look at him. "I guess I have a confession to make." She bit her lower lip, trying to hold back the hysterics. "I'm a complete, total, hopeless klutz." Unable to hold back any longer, she burst out laughing.

Burke joined in her laughter as he reached back outside for her suitcases. "We'd better get you into the living room. At least it has a padded carpet if you feel an urge to throw yourself down again."

Still giggling, Blaire turned to look through the entryway into the long living room. Mexican tile covered the foyer in a half moon shape that led to the rich, brown, variegated living room carpet. Blaire's shoes clicked a loud tattoo as she crossed the tile and turned silent as they sank into the thick carpeting.

The living room was definitely a man's room, complete with polished wood and brown cushioned furniture. A smattering of wildlife prints decorated cream-colored walls. Old-fashioned lanterns and branding irons trimmed the mantel above the fireplace. Heavy wooden beams graced the vaulted ceiling. The room created a down-home feel, and Blaire wanted nothing more than to sink into one of the couches, kick off her shoes, and prop up her feet.

"What is that heavenly smell?" Blaire breathed deeply. Her stomach rumbled, and she realized how hungry she was. After learning the exact nature of her inheritance that morning, she'd been so upset that she'd only managed to eat a little soup and salad for lunch. Now her appetite had returned, and the enticing aromas drifting from the kitchen drew her like a magnet.

Burke took in a long breath, a slight smile lighting his handsome features. "I believe you've gotten a whiff of Isabel's famous enchiladas."

Blaire forced herself to look away as his sparkling eyes met hers. *He works here*, she thought. *I can't be attracted again to someone I work with*. She did her best to ignore the prickle of electricity racing through her.

"Isabel," Burke called. "Miss Mackenzie is here."

A small, stocky woman hurried into the living room, brushing a strand of gray-streaked dark hair from her face. A sheen of sweat lit up her face along with a smile that made Blaire feel more than welcome.

"Miss Mackenzie." Isabel bubbled with excitement. "I've been looking forward to meeting you. I loved your uncle Ike so much." A tear threatened to fall from her warm brown eyes, and she swiped it away with the back of her hand. "I hope you are hungry. The lawyer called and said you were on your way, so I made a special Mexican supper for you."

Burke grinned and leaned over to give the excited woman a quick kiss on her cheek. "Slow down, Isabel, and let me introduce you."

Isabel frowned at Burke and said loftily, "We do not need such formality here. I know who Miss Mackenzie is. She is part of my family. Right, *mija?*" Isabel's friendly smile warmed Blaire in a way she couldn't describe. She knew she would enjoy getting to know this friend of her uncle.

"Well, I'm not sure what a me-ha is, but I agree we don't need formality. I'm so glad to meet you, Isabel, and yes, I'm starving." Impulsively, Blaire bent down and gave the diminutive woman a quick hug.

"*Mija* is a Spanish term of endearment meaning 'my daughter,' " Burke informed Blaire. "Now if you ladies will excuse me, I'll put these suitcases in Blaire's room and help Manuel with the chores. We should be done in about an hour. Is that okay?" He looked at Isabel.

"That will be fine, *mijo.*" Isabel smiled and patted him affectionately on the cheek. "Why don't you show Miss Mackenzie her room, and she can come to the kitchen when she's ready."

Burke led the way to a door to the right of the living room. He set the luggage down inside the doorway and stepped aside for Blaire to enter. "This was Ike's room, so it isn't very feminine. We didn't redecorate because we didn't know what you would like. I hope the decor is okay for now."

"I love it. Besides, I won't be staying long," Blaire said, turning away from the sudden anger apparent in Burke's green eyes. She turned to gaze in awe at the huge room, mentally comparing it to her small apartment in Illinois. Thick forest green carpet covered the floor and set off cream-colored walls. The king-size bed in the middle of the room looked more like a twin. A stone fireplace in the outer wall was lined with reminders of her uncle, including a row of pictures on the mantel.

"There's a bathroom through this door." Burke gestured to the left. "The door on the other side of the bathroom leads to the office. Ike recently had a computer installed to keep track of all the ostriches and accounts. I'm afraid he didn't get things caught up. He wasn't the best at doing the book work."

Peeking through the door into the bathroom, Blaire turned back and smiled at Burke. "Maybe I can be useful here for a while, anyway. As an accountant, doing the books will be my specialty. At least, if I don't fall on top of the computer."

Blaire could hear Burke chuckling until the hall door closed behind him. She sighed as she looked at the huge room that was now hers. *O Lord, I would love to live in a room like this. I love this house, and the people here are so friendly. Why does it have to be in the middle of a desert? I know You don't mean for me to live in a place this desolate.*

Stretched out across the huge, soft waterbed, Blaire sighed in delight as the mattress cradled her tired body. For the first time in weeks she relaxed, nestling on top of the brown striped comforter. Her body grew heavy, and she drifted off to sleep. Twenty minutes later she groaned as she forced herself up off the bed, knowing if she stayed there any longer she would be asleep for the night.

Crossing to the mammoth fireplace, Blaire began to study the pictures on the mantel. Most of them were snapshots of her by herself that her mother had sent to Uncle Ike over the years. The photos were arranged chronologically. In the middle were shots of Blaire and Uncle Ike together before he left on the road, Blaire and her younger brother and sister, and a picture of her family taken for the church directory just before Blaire graduated from high school.

Shrugging off a feeling of melancholy, Blaire unpacked and hung her dresses in the closet. She wanted to visit Isabel in the kitchen. Perhaps talking with Isabel would help her forget the confusing feelings she struggled with. Blaire knew God didn't want her to stay in a place like this, somewhere so foreign to everything she'd grown accustomed to. What she didn't understand were the feelings of contentment that crept in, the desire to settle into this beautiful old house and stay forever.

Following the enticing aromas drifting through the house, Blaire had no trouble finding Isabel. The kitchen, easily as large as Blaire's bedroom, included a dining alcove with a beautiful oak table and matching chairs. Isabel bustled from the rich walnut cabinets to the triple stainless-steel sink. A large pot of something bubbled on the stove, and Blaire could see a couple of cheese-topped dishes baking in the oven.

"Hello," she said hesitantly.

Isabel turned quickly, perspiration shining on her brown face. "Oh, *mija*, come in and sit down. Can I get you something cool to drink?"

"No thanks, Isabel, I'm fine. Is there something I can do to help with supper?"

"I think the food is about ready. Burke and Manuel should be about done with the chores. I hope you like Mexican food."

Blaire crossed to the stove, peered into the large pot, and breathed in the fragrance. "I love Mexican food, but something tells me I've never had the real thing in Chicago."

Isabel laughed. "Mexican food varies from state to state. We'll have to wait and see if you appreciate Mexican food from this area. I tried not to add too much chili, knowing you were from back East. Did you enjoy your tour of the ranch?"

Blaire leaned against the counter and groaned. "I loved seeing everything, but I'm afraid I made a complete fool of myself today." She sighed and recounted for Isabel all the embarrassing incidents—catching her skirt in the car door, getting her hair pulled, being terrified of the racing ostriches, and finally falling through the doorway to the house.

Isabel laughed and handed Blaire a bowl of jalapeño peppers to set on the table. "I'm sure no one thought you a fool," Isabel assured her.

"I'm positive Burke thinks I'm nothing but a clumsy oaf."

"I don't think that at all." Burke's low voice near her ear startled Blaire.

"Ahh!" she yelled, throwing her hands in the air. Jalapeño peppers flew from the dish like tiny green missiles, scattering across the kitchen floor.

Chapter 4

For the next few days, Blaire worked hard at learning her way around the ranch. She wanted to discover the full scope of her inheritance so that she could put the property on the market soon. She quickly realized the number of ostriches and the extensive operations made the operation a sizable legacy from Uncle Ike. Before listing the property with a Realtor, she wanted to know its value—even if that meant staying longer than a few weeks.

Blaire tilted her head and listened to the rumble of a large truck lumbering down the driveway, the vibrations drumming through the floor of the house. Almost daily a variety of vehicles arrived to haul off meat or pick up ostriches sold to other ranches or individuals. The noisy trucks were the one intrusion into an otherwise quiet existence. *Thank You, God, for that bit of noise. Otherwise, the quiet would drive me crazy.*

A knock sounded on her bedroom door. Blaire sighed and set her Bible on the small table next to her. "Coming," she called, as she padded across the soft, thick carpet.

"Good morning, *mija*." Isabel's smile lit the room as Blaire opened the door. "There is someone here to see you."

"Me?" Blaire stepped out of the bedroom, wondering who her visitor could be.

"Some men with a big truck say they have brought your belongings." Isabel grinned. "I am so glad that you will be able to make the house more like your own now."

Blaire walked out onto the verandah. Two men were disgorging the contents of the truck she'd heard coming down the driveway. Cardboard boxes of various sizes and a few pieces of furniture were piling up on the porch, neatly balanced one on the other. Movement caught her eye. Over by the ostrich pens Burke and Manuel were walking toward the house, probably wondering what was happening.

"Wait," Blaire called to the movers. "Why did you bring this here?"

The stocky young man closest to her shifted uncomfortably and shoved a hand in the pocket of his coveralls. "We're just following orders, ma'am. We were told to deliver these goods to this address."

"But I told the lawyers I wanted to keep my things in storage in Phoenix until I decided what to do about the ranch. Can't you take them back?"

"If we take it back and store it, you'll be charged extra." The man scratched his head and gave his partner a bewildered look.

"Mija," Isabel said, "why don't you go ahead and keep your things here? It would be a waste of money to send them back to Phoenix."

Just then, Burke and Manuel arrived. The intensity of Burke's gaze weighed Blaire down. She glanced at him, and like an animal trapped in a glare of light, she couldn't look away. Burke's mouth tipped up, softening his clean-cut features. Released from his magnetic pull, Blaire nodded. "I guess we'll put everything in the spare bedroom until I know where I'll be staying."

Blaire tried to ignore the way Burke's half-smile turned to a scowl. For the past few days he'd seemed to avoid her. Now he looked almost angry as he and Manuel joined in helping unload the boxes.

Before long, the delivery truck was lumbering back down the driveway and out of sight, leaving her precious belongings in a pile for the entire world to see.

"Well, we could form a bucket brigade to get all this stuff in the house." Burke grinned at Blaire as if trying to present a peace offering.

Blaire forced a smile and nodded. "Either that or we could put up a yard-sale sign."

"I'm sure you have some beautiful things in here, *mija.*" Isabel peered at all the carefully marked boxes. "I think we should just start carrying these in and line them along the bedroom wall."

Manuel picked up a couple of boxes as Burke reached for a small one on top of a stack. "Here's one you can carry, Blaire. It's marked 'personal clothing,' and is it ever heavy," Burke grunted as he slowly lifted the box, his back slightly bent from the effort. "Here, you take it," he called as he heaved the box toward Blaire.

"Wait," Blaire squealed as she reached for the box flying through the air toward her. She braced herself and took a step back as the box thumped against her. Instinctively, she closed her arms tightly around the cardboard carton. Her mouth dropped open in surprise. The box wasn't heavy at all.

Suddenly, she felt something brushing against her legs. She looked down, and her cheeks burned. The bottom of the box had popped open from the force of her hold, and a kaleidoscope of colored underwear and bras had tumbled to her feet. A lacy bra dangled from the bottom of the box, the pink satin bow in the middle of it twinkling in the sunlight. *Oh, please, let this porch open up and swallow me.*

Blaire glanced up to see Manuel biting his lip to keep back the laughter. Burke stared wide-eyed, his mouth hanging open and his cheeks flushed. Horrified, she watched as he lifted his gaze to hers. His mouth snapped shut and his eyes sparkled. Leaning against the boxes, Burke threw back his head and began to laugh.

The heat of embarrassment surged through Blaire as she watched him. She started to turn but stumbled and grabbed a post to catch herself. The mashed box flew through the air and thumped against the house. Colored underwear and lacy bras scattered across the porch. Burke leaned over, grasped his sides, and howled at the sight of the dainty clothing dangling from the swing.

"Here, *mija*, let me help with that box." Isabel reached for the crumpled box. Her lips twitched, and her eyes flashed with humor. Blaire glanced again at the embarrassing bits of clothing perched haphazardly around her. Unwanted laughter welled up inside. One chuckle slipped out followed by another, and soon they were all in hysterics as Blaire and Isabel rescued the wayward underwear from various perches around the veranda.

After repairing and refilling the box, Blaire carefully carried it into the house and added it to the growing stack. "Well, at least I didn't air my dirty laundry." She grinned. "Those were all clean."

Isabel chuckled. "I know you didn't plan for your things to be shipped here, but why don't we unpack a few boxes? Maybe it will help you feel more at home."

"No." Blaire frowned. "I don't plan to stay longer than needed. I don't want to have to pack again."

Burke straightened from depositing the last of the boxes, his smile vanishing. "What do you plan to do with the ranch?"

"I plan to sell it." Blaire tried to ignore the hurt and anger in Burke's eyes. "I can use the proceeds to open my own accounting firm in Chicago or maybe Phoenix. I've always wanted that."

Burke's eyes were devoid of humor, and his mouth set in a stern line. "What about Isabel and Manuel? If you sell the ranch they won't have a home anymore. Don't you care that they will have nowhere to go when you leave?" He took a deep breath, lifted his hat, and raked his hand through his hair.

"Of course I care. I didn't think about that." Blaire tried to look away to avoid the discomfort of Burke's gaze. "Uncle Ike was wrong about me. I'm not cut out for country life."

"I guess Ike didn't know you as well as he thought he did." Burke's eyes reflected the sadness of his tone. "Come on, Manuel. We need to finish our other chores." With that he stalked out of the room, followed by Manuel.

Silence settled around her as Blaire stared after Burke's retreating back. She turned to look into Isabel's teary eyes. "I'm sorry, Isabel. I didn't realize your situation. I'm just trying to find out what God wants for me to do."

Isabel squeezed Blaire's arm. "It's okay, *mija*. You have many decisions to make."

Blaire gave Isabel a quick hug, and the older woman smiled, reaching for the repaired box. "You should at least put these underwear in a drawer where they can't get away again."

Blaire looked at the boxes lining the bedroom wall. All her worldly possessions were packed in them. Studying the labels, she walked along the row and picked out three boxes from the stack.

"Help me carry these over next to the bed, and we'll unpack them," she said, handing one of the smaller boxes to Isabel. She picked up the other two and crossed the bedroom.

"This is my collection of giraffes," Blaire explained. "I've been collecting them since my twelfth birthday when Dad and Mom got me this stuffed one." Blaire pulled a well-loved fuzzy giraffe from the box and laid it on her pillow.

"Oh, this one is beautiful." Isabel pulled a carved mother and baby giraffe from the box. The dark wood gleamed. The mother giraffe's long, graceful neck circled over her young one as she bent toward it.

"My sister sent me that one last Christmas. She and her husband are missionaries in Africa. One of the men in her congregation carved it."

"I didn't know your sister is a missionary." Isabel beamed her approval. "Ike once told me your brother is a pastor."

Blaire nodded, relaxing. For the first time in months, she felt a longing to talk to someone. "My family always went to church. Everyone assumed I would marry a pastor or missionary like my sister." She sat down on the bed, fingering a small glass giraffe. "You know, I knew all the Christian lingo from the time I could talk. I went to church, helped with the nursery when I got older, sang in the choir, and did everything a good Christian should do."

"But you weren't really a Christian, were you?" Isabel sat close to her on the bed.

Blaire glanced up, tears in her eyes. "I wasn't. Everyone thought I was, and they all had such high expectations for me. I let them down." Blaire wiped the tears from her eyes with the side of her hand. "I wanted to be an accountant. I dreamed of having my own business. Then when I went to work at Bennett and Sons and met Richard, I thought my dreams were coming true."

"What happened, *mija?*"

"We planned to marry. I floated through life those days not seeing the other side of Richard. He charmed me. Blinded to his faults, I didn't realize what was happening until too late. He ran off with the secretary, then closed the firm, putting us all out of work." Blaire continued to talk, telling Isabel of the whispers behind her back and the shame she had suffered.

"The only good thing that came of it was a realization of my need for Jesus. I can remember all the hurt. It was a physical pain." Blaire drew in a shaky breath. "One night I lay on the floor and pictured myself at the foot of the cross. I gave all of myself to Jesus, even though my life wasn't much. I'm trying hard to live as He wants me to live."

Isabel hugged Blaire to her. "Oh, *mija,* you are all Jesus wants. There is no greater gift you can give Him than your love and your life."

Burke pressed his fingers against the corners of his eyes, trying to stop the moisture threatening to overflow. He eased out of the padded chair in front of the computer in the office, praying it wouldn't squeak and reveal his presence. A high-pitched squeal echoed in the office. He hoped Blaire and Isabel were too distracted to notice. He hadn't meant to eavesdrop on them. He'd only wanted to run in and try to straighten out some of the accounts. Now, all he wanted was some fresh air and the space to distance himself from the hurt in Blaire's voice. No wonder she wanted to get away, to lose herself in the city.

Crossing to the hatchery, Burke wondered at the emotional pain Blaire had endured. How could that cad justify treating her so callously? Anger burned within until he recalled the good that came from the shame. *Lord, I guess sometimes we have to fall flat before You can get our attention. Thank You for reaching out to Blaire. Please heal her wounds. Help her to see that You brought her here for a reason. I don't believe Ike made a mistake.*

Burke washed his hands with disinfectant, donned a pair of clean sandals, and slipped through the heavy door of the incubator room. Checking temperatures, he moved around the room, looking over the oval, ivory-colored eggs. He smiled as he looked in the last incubator. Several of the eggs were cracked, shaking from time to time as the occupants demanded their release. Burke hurried from the room, slipping on his shoes again and heading for the house.

"Blaire." Burke strode through the kitchen door. "Isabel, come here."

The two women stepped out of Blaire's bedroom, their eyes slightly reddened. "What is it, *mijo?*" Isabel asked.

"It's time." Burke's grin widened at Blaire's look of confusion.

"Time for what?" Blaire asked.

Burke winked conspiratorially at Isabel. "Come with me and find out." He gestured toward the back door.

Isabel nodded in understanding. "You two go ahead. I'll be along shortly."

Blaire followed Burke out the door. Entering the hatchery, Burke pulled off his shoes, slipped on sandals, and told Blaire to do likewise as he began to wash his hands.

"What is going on?" The mystified tone in Blaire's voice made Burke want to laugh.

"I have something to show you." He chuckled as he opened the door to the incubator room. "This is the most exciting time of the year."

Burke stopped in front of an incubator. He reached back, pulling Blaire closer. She leaned forward, gazing at the eggs. Suddenly she gasped and turned to look at him, her blue eyes wide with delight. "The babies are hatching."

"Yep," Burke agreed. "This is the first hatching of the year. It's always my favorite. Help me move the eggs to the hatching area."

For the next few hours, Blaire watched mesmerized as the baby ostriches pecked their way bit by bit through the tough shells housing them. She gasped in awe when the first little bird tumbled free, a piece of shell sticking to his bottom like a diaper. Its wet feathers made it look like a porcupine body with spindly legs and a long neck. In the heat of the lamp, the newly hatched chick dried, its feathers fluffing out.

Aware of Burke close beside her, Blaire couldn't help giving him a smile of delight. His answering grin warmed her, making her long to always share such moments with him. His green eyes glowed with warmth and humor. She almost felt a sense of tenderness and concern for her coming from him.

"Do you think I could hold the baby?" she whispered, as if it wouldn't be right to speak loudly in the presence of new life.

"Here, I'll pick him up for you." Burke cradled the small bird and placed it in her cupped palms. The outer feathers prickled. The ostrich looked at Blaire, its long curled eyelashes accentuating the big eyes. Blaire felt her heart melt as she contemplated this miracle of new life.

"Enjoy holding him now," Burke said. "You won't be able to hold this baby for long. Within six months he'll be taller than me."

Blaire shook her head. "It's hard to imagine they can grow that fast." Suddenly she remembered she wouldn't be here in six months. "I don't want to get attached to these birds." Blaire held the baby toward Burke. "Here, take it back."

The door to the hatching room opened. Isabel peeked in. "You've got a visitor, Blaire."

"Another one?" Blaire gaped, pulling the small, warm, moist bird close to her again.

A tall, broad-shouldered man stepped into the room, looking out of place in a pair of their sandals. His jeans, denim shirt, and deep tan spoke of outdoor work. Light brown hair sprinkled liberally with gray peeked out from under a cowboy hat. His features looked somehow familiar, but Blaire knew she hadn't met him before.

Burke and Blaire stood at the same time. "Hey, Dad." Burke held out his hand to the man. Blaire gaped open-mouthed from one to the other. No wonder the man looked familiar. He was an older version of Burke except for his light brown eyes.

Burke turned to Blaire. "Blaire, I'd like you to meet my dad, Jed Dunham. He owns the cattle ranch that borders yours. He and Ike were good friends."

Jed smiled, his leathery face crinkling. "I'm sorry to be so long getting over here, Miss Mackenzie. I've had quite a bit to do." He held out a hand toward Blaire.

Blaire balanced the warm ostrich chick on one hand and reached out to shake hands. As Jed Dunham's hand closed over hers, she realized her mistake. Shock registered on his face as his eyes dropped to their linked hands.

Blaire pulled her hand away, willing the bird dropping on her hand to disappear. The quiet room, once cozy, now felt suffocating. She looked up at the stern rancher contemplating the goo smeared between his fingers. "Well, at least we know his parts are working." The words popped out before she thought. Blaire could feel the red-hot blush spreading over her face.

At her side Burke burst into laughter.

Chapter 5

A few days later, Blaire followed Isabel into church. They were running late, and the swell of voices lifted in a familiar hymn drifted out to them. Burke walked close behind Blaire, but Manuel had hurried ahead to find a seat with his friends.

Blaire had visited this church two times, and she wasn't at all sure she liked it. In Chicago she'd found anonymity in a large congregation. Here everyone knew everyone else. Oh, they were friendly enough, smiling and nodding at her as she walked through the door, greeting her with hugs and handshakes when she arrived early enough. Blaire had discovered that even though she loved crowds, she wasn't sure how comfortable she could be in such personal relationships with other Christians. For the first time, she felt expected to share her life and faith with people outside her family.

Blaire's stomach roiled as various members turned to look or gave discreet waves of their hands. At her home church she rarely shared eye contact with anyone. The people gathered for the worship service and didn't greet anyone other than the members of their small group of family or friends. The first time she'd attended church with Isabel, however, people had asked about her life history before she'd had the chance to sit down.

An older couple smiled and edged to one side, making room as Isabel moved into the pew, followed by Blaire. Burke sidled in beside her, filling the pew to capacity. His shoulder brushed against Blaire's as he reached for a hymnal. Blaire's hand grazed his as she reached to support one side of the book. She gripped the back of the pew in front of her with her left hand, feeling the padding squish stiffly beneath her fingers.

The singing ended, and Blaire sank to the pew, wedged between Isabel and Burke. She forced herself not to lean into Isabel in an effort to avoid contact with Burke. What made her so aware of this man? Even his regular breathing matched her rhythm. Burke shifted and moved his arm to rest along the back of the pew behind Blaire's shoulders. The change didn't help. Instead, the muscles along Blaire's back tensed. She wondered what it would be like to lean a little to the right, resting against Burke's side while his fingers trailed down along her shoulder. She gave herself a mental shake and opened her Bible to the Psalms as the pastor directed, praying for the ability to focus.

The pastor's deep voice filled the sanctuary. " 'The Lord is my shepherd, I shall not want. He maketh me to lie down in green pastures. . . .'" His even bass tones rolled over Blaire. She felt herself relax, the tension washing out of her.

Pastor Walker paused, taking the time to look out over the congregation. He leaned forward, his fingers curled around the edge of the podium. "For the last two weeks we've discussed the first verse of Psalm twenty-three." He grinned. "I'm sure you all have perfect recall of my messages on the Lord being our shepherd or caretaker and how we want for nothing because of that." A ripple of merriment passed over the room. Pastor Walker grinned. "Today I want to talk about green pastures." He released the podium and stepped to the side.

"How many of you grew up where the winters were fierce?" A small showing of hands waved in the air. "I grew up in Wyoming. We had frigid winters I thought would never end." He hugged his arms around his middle. "But although the winters were long, hard, and dreary, I remember the excitement and anticipation of spring." He gestured to an older man seated toward the front of the church. "Paul, I know you lived in the Northeast. Do you recall the color of the first green of spring?" A faint smile dimpled Paul's cheeks, and he nodded.

Pastor Walker stepped down off the dais. "I'll never forget the wonder that special color of green brought each year. I wanted to touch each blade of grass. As the pastures became covered in green, I would often lie on my back, watching the clouds overhead, smelling the damp earth, completely content. Did any of you do that?" Several heads nodded.

He stepped back up behind the podium and stared down at his Bible. " 'He maketh me to lie down in green pastures.' He maketh me." Pastor Walker's piercing gaze seemed to rest on each person for a moment as his gaze swept the room. "Why do you suppose God has to make us lie down in green pastures? Wouldn't we want to be there? Don't you think we would anticipate God's green pastures like we waited for the first green of spring?" He paused. " 'He maketh me. . . .'" He shook his head and was silent for a moment.

Blaire leaned forward, hanging onto his every word.

In words so soft the whole congregation seemed to lean closer to hear, Pastor Walker continued. "What if God doesn't see the color green in the same manner we do?" Silence stretched across the crowd. "What if our idea of green pastures is totally different from the one God truly means for us? What then? Has God made a mistake and put us in the wrong place?" Blaire felt as if the pastor were looking into her soul. "Maybe God has placed you in just the green pasture He wants you in, but you keep looking at Joe's or Mary's pasture and thinking that's where God wants you. Maybe it's time you considered that perhaps God has you right where He wants you."

Blaire's stomach clenched. She considered leaving the sanctuary, but she didn't want to make a scene. How could he say that? Why would God want her here in this barren wasteland? She knew He wouldn't do that to her.

Burke glared down at the open Bible in his lap. His thumb beat a silent tattoo on the edge of the pew. This sermon was precisely why he didn't come to church often. He'd only come the last few Sundays because he'd wanted to make Blaire feel at home in the community. Who did this pastor think he was? Why did he think he knew God's thoughts? Couldn't pastors be as wrong as anyone else?

As if in answer to Burke's unspoken questions, Pastor Walker said, "I don't want you to take my word on this. Check out the Scriptures, and see what pastures God placed some of His children in. Abraham had to leave his home and family and move to a strange land; the Israelites wandered in the desert for forty years; Jesus was born in a cave used to house animals." He walked down off the dais again. "Look at the prophets; look at Job—he lost all his wealth and most of his family. Look at the disciples and the hardships they endured. Are we any better, that we should expect to live in comfortable luxury, basking in the feel of a perfect pasture of our own making? No, I don't believe so. God has a purpose for each of us. He has a work for you to do, and He will place you in the right pasture so that you can accomplish His purpose."

The pastor lifted his hand, sweeping it across the crowd. "Don't try to escape the green pasture God has for you simply because the smell isn't quite what you expected or the view of the clouds isn't as clear. Ask God what His purpose is for you, then follow Him."

Burke's feet twitched with the desire to leave. It took every bit of control he possessed to stay in his seat. Why would a God who cared take away a little boy's mother, then his grandmother? That couldn't have been God's intention for his life. Granted, his grandmother had been older, and her death wasn't that odd, but what about his mother? She'd been young and vibrant, full of life. Would a loving God let a little boy grow up with only an authoritarian father who didn't have time for him? Although he and his father got along now, Burke remembered plenty of times when he'd wondered if his father would let him live to be an adult.

"In closing," the pastor said, "I want to remind you of God's love for you. He hasn't put you in a difficult pasture to punish you. He wants the best for you. He knows what's best. Trust Him."

Burke stood with the rest of the congregation. His fingers gripped the edge of the pew in front of him, and he didn't share the hymnal with Blaire for the final song. Instead, his feet were already easing toward the aisle, ready to leave this place as soon as possible.

With the taste of hot sauce from lunch still warming her tongue, Blaire snuggled into an overstuffed armchair and pulled out her cross-stitch. Manuel had gone home with a friend, and she could hear Isabel puttering around in the kitchen.

Burke lay in a recliner, and from the sound of his deep breathing, he was either asleep or nearly asleep. He should be tired. It had taken her several minutes to get outside after church. All the people who hadn't found out her complete history the previous Sundays were in line to get it this morning. She chuckled. They were a well-meaning group.

When she and Isabel stepped out into the warm sunshine, the first thing Blaire saw was Burke being chased by a crowd of youngsters. Girls and boys ran after him across the green churchyard. After a mad chase, Burke whirled, crouched down, and growled as he lifted one squealing child after another and swung them around like miniature airplanes. He pretended to be mad, but from their expressions, Blaire knew not one child was fooled. She shook her head. She couldn't imagine Richard ever doing something so impromptu or playful. His reserved manner would never allow such behavior.

"What are you making, *mija*?"

Blaire started as Isabel's soft voice sounded close beside her. Did everyone in this house sneak up on people? She sighed. At least she hadn't shrieked and thrown something.

"I'm working on a cross-stitch picture." She held it up for Isabel to see. "My mother knows I like giraffes and cross-stitch so she gave this kit to me for my birthday."

"It's beautiful." Isabel held the picture to the light, then peered at the pattern in Blaire's lap. "I don't think I've ever seen such an intricate pattern. Isn't it hard to keep the count right?"

Blaire shook her head. "I've had lots of practice. Counting is one thing I am good at. After all, I'm an accountant." She grinned. "And the only klutzy thing I can do with this is drop it on occasion or poke myself with the needle."

A chuckle drifted out of the recliner across the room. Blaire thought about sailing the hoop like a Frisbee right at Burke's head but decided that with her luck she would hit the lamp behind him instead. However, she did wrinkle her nose at him when his closed eyes would not see.

"You should have Isabel show you her quilts." Burke's sleep-laden voice held a hint of laughter. "I'll bet you've never seen anything like them."

"You make quilts?" Blaire couldn't keep the astonishment from her voice. "I thought that was mostly a Midwestern art form."

Isabel blushed. "My great-grandmother learned from a pioneer woman many years ago. She was fascinated by the woman's blankets, but my great-grandmother did them a little differently. Rather than make the patterns with small pieces of material, she wanted to make her blankets a picture of life as we know it. She handed down that tradition."

"Then you learned how to quilt from your mother?"

A flicker of sadness crossed Isabel's face. "No, *mija*. My mother died when

I was very young. I do remember her quilting, but I'm not sure if it is my own memory or the one planted there by my grandmother. Grandmother is the one who taught me to quilt. She also taught me to look at the world I live in and capture that picture on the cloth."

"May I see one?" Blaire began to put away her stitchery. "I can't imagine what you're talking about. The only quilts I've seen are ones where small pieces of material are stitched together to make a pattern or one big piece of material is sewn in such a way that a design is etched into it."

"Show her the one of Ike's ranch." Burke lifted his hands behind his head and scooted the recliner out another notch.

In a few moments, Isabel returned with a large cloth bundle wrapped in muslin. Blaire leaped to help her unwrap the quilt.

"I'm afraid this one is rather large." Isabel sounded almost apologetic. "If you take the bottom and move back that way, we can stretch it out and lay it on the floor for you to look at."

Blaire tugged the edge of the quilt and backed away. She gasped in wonder as the scene unfolded on the heavy blanket. Appliquéd on a cream background was a beautiful, vivid picture of the ranch house. Ostriches stretched their necks over the edge of the fence in the background, a hen with her chicks scratched at the ground searching for food, kittens tumbled over one another in abandoned play. The quilt was alive with everyday scenes.

"Isabel, this isn't a quilt—it's a work of art. You should have it hanging in a museum somewhere." Blaire took another step back. She pulled the heavy blanket open more. She leaned back and started to take another step away.

"Be careful, *mija!*"

Isabel's warning came too late. The back of Blaire's knee knocked against the corner of the recliner. She stumbled back. She tried to brace herself, but her foot slipped. With a cry she tumbled into the soft chair, landing atop Burke. The air whooshed out of him. She froze, her hand still gripping the edge of the quilt.

Burke's arms came down from behind his head. He tugged her to one side. "I'm glad you brought the blanket. I was getting a little cold."

Blaire thought her face would be permanently stained flame-red.

Chapter 6

Burke ignored the amused look on Isabel's face. For the moment he reveled in how right it felt to have Blaire next to him, his arms wrapped around her. He knew he should have cautioned her about getting too close to his chair, but he hadn't. Something deep inside wanted her to get closer. For the last hour he'd pretended to sleep while he watched her. He couldn't get enough of the expressions that chased one another across her delicate features. He loved the way she bit her lower lip in concentration as she counted a section of her needlework. He'd never seen such childlike joy as she'd shown when she first glimpsed Isabel's quilt. She was just like he'd always pictured her from Ike's descriptions.

His arms tightened. For a moment he almost thought he felt Blaire snuggle in a little closer to him. Then she pushed away and began to try to get out of the chair. It wasn't easy. How he wanted to pull her back, to keep her next to him. He wanted to run his fingers through her silky hair. The faint aroma of strawberry-scented shampoo tickled his nose.

Blaire swung her legs farther to the side, trying to get up. *She's leaving as soon as she can.* The thought jolted Burke. Why did he want to hold onto her when all she planned to do was leave this place as soon as she could? He slipped his hands behind her back to help her out of the chair, but his annoyance added strength to his push. Blaire flew out of the chair and landed with a thump on the carpet.

Swinging the chair into an upright position, Burke jumped up. "I'm sorry. I meant to help you out. I didn't mean to throw you halfway across the room."

"At least between the carpet and myself there was enough padding to keep it from hurting much." Blaire grinned. "I'm not sure you fared as well when I landed on you. Sorry about that."

Burke reached down to give her a hand up. "No problem." He patted his stomach. "All these well-honed muscles kept you from doing any damage."

Isabel snorted. Blaire and Burke burst into laughter.

"Let me help you with the quilt." Burke picked up the edge Blaire had dropped. "I have to agree with Blaire, Isabel. You should consider putting some of your quilts on display at the Center for the Arts up in Globe. Their purpose is to show local artists' work."

Isabel blushed. "I'm not an artist."

"You're an artist in the same sense as one who paints a picture or makes pottery." Blaire ran a hand over the fine-stitched quilt. "This is so beautiful, you should share it with others rather than keep it wrapped in muslin."

Isabel shook her head. "I'll think about it, but I can't see why anyone would want to look at these hanging on a wall. Now, why don't you help me fold this quilt? Then you two can go for a walk, and I'll start some supper."

Burke glanced at Blaire. Bright blue eyes gazed back at him. He lifted his eyebrows in a question. She smiled.

"That sounds like a good idea, Isabel. Maybe I can introduce Blaire to some of the plant life around here."

Early the next morning, Blaire stretched and wiggled down into the embracing softness of the bed as golden sunlight streamed through the slit in the blinds covering her bedroom window. She wanted to sleep longer. She felt like staying in bed all morning and doing nothing.

"Lord, I'm getting lazy. I can't remember when I've slept in so much on a work day. Help me to find a purpose here." Blaire closed her eyes. A picture of Burke, the edges of his eyes crinkled with laughter, flashed across her vision. "Lord, help me get away from this place before I don't want to leave. I need to get back to the city." She sighed and threw back the covers. "For now, just show me a purpose for my life, please."

A half hour later, freshly showered, Blaire headed for the kitchen. "Mmm, Isabel. I don't know how one person can make so many different delicious smells come from the same oven. You must spend all your time cooking."

"I would like that, *mija.*" Isabel set a steaming plate of food on the table. "Since your uncle Ike died, we have had many chores to do."

Blaire sat down and looked up into Isabel's dark eyes. "What do you do besides the cooking and housework? I thought Burke and Manuel did all the outside chores."

"They do all the heavy work—feeding the ostriches, moving them when it's needed, and taking care of the processing plant. But someone has to watch over the eggs and the new hatchlings. I also take care of the little garden we have. We all like fresh vegetables, especially those hot peppers you love."

Blaire grimaced, remembering the first time she'd eaten a fresh jalapeño pepper. Her eyes had watered. Her nose had run. Her throat had burned all the way down. She'd drunk what seemed like six gallons of water without cooling off the burning. Then she tried a second bite, determined it couldn't be as bad as the first. She'd been right. The second bite was worse.

"Maybe you can show me how to help. I'll do anything except sample the peppers to see if they're ready." Blaire fanned herself with a hand, and Isabel laughed.

"You don't have to help. We're used to our routine."

"No, I feel a little useless. Besides, just this morning I asked the Lord to show me His purpose for my life. Maybe until I get back to the city, my purpose is to help you out. I'll go crazy if I just sit around doing nothing all day."

"Finish your breakfast, then, and we'll head out to see how the babies are doing." Isabel began to rinse off dishes and load the dishwasher as Blaire savored the spicy ranch eggs she'd been served.

Stepping out into the early morning, Blaire drew in a deep breath. "You know, I thought I would hate it here. At first everything seemed so barren and empty."

"And now?" Isabel paused, giving her a questioning look.

"I don't know. I guess the desert grows on you. The mountains are different than skyscrapers, but they're God's handiwork. Sometimes when I sit on the porch swing, I can almost picture Him molding them, like a toddler molds clay. I picture the concentration on His face and the delight once He got them shaped just right." She felt her face warm. "I suppose that sounds silly."

Isabel shook her head. "Not at all. I love to look at this country and see how God worked. Most of the plants are prickly and seem unfriendly, but they had to be that way to survive. It was part of God's design. Did you know that the saguaro cactus roots don't go down into the ground like tree roots?" Isabel gestured at the tall cacti dotting the hills around them.

Blaire gazed up at a multi-armed cactus. "How does it get water without roots? Surely it can't live without water."

"Oh, saguaros need water, all right. They have roots, but the roots don't go down into the ground. There isn't any water up on the hills where the cactus grows. Instead, the saguaro's roots run in a large network parallel to the surface of the ground. Then, when we do get rain, the saguaro can take the most advantage of the small amount of moisture."

"I see." Blaire stared in wonder at the huge cactus. "God knew they needed roots going to the side or they would die."

Isabel smiled and led the way to the hatchery. "I think that's why God puts us all in different places. He knows we all have different needs. Like the pastor said the other day, God puts us in the right green pasture. We just have to accept that."

Blaire glanced up at the cacti on the hills. Burke had explained yesterday that saguaros only grew in a small area of the Southwest. They couldn't survive at higher elevations or in colder climates. *That is why I need to get back to the city. I could never survive out here, no matter how beautiful the country is.*

Mimicking Isabel, Blaire left her shoes at the door, donning sterile sandals and washing her hands with disinfectant soap. Burke or Manuel had already delivered the day's cache of eggs.

"Each day we have to put the new eggs in the incubator. You have to label them so we all know which eggs are which. If we get them mixed up, we'll never know who's supposed to hatch when. Burke insists on keeping good records." She gestured to a book on a table at the side of the room. "It's pretty self-explanatory. You can follow the previous entries and know what to do."

"Do you really trust a klutz like me to handle such big eggs?" Blaire chuckled. "You might end up with a floor covered in goo before I finish. The ranch could go broke."

Isabel grinned. "I suppose we've all dropped an egg on occasion. Don't worry. You'll be tossing the eggs around like a pro pretty soon."

Pulling open a door, Isabel gestured to the number at the top corner of the incubator. "We'll put today's eggs in number six. Then we have to check the other eggs and turn them."

They worked silently for several minutes. Blaire marveled at the pebbly feel of the giant eggs. As she helped turn the eggs, she wondered if she could actually feel movement inside or if her imagination was running wild.

Isabel watched as she recorded the information in the book.

"Doesn't Burke keep these records in the computer?"

"Burke and computers don't get along well. I'm not sure if he doesn't like the computer or if he hasn't had the time to familiarize himself with the program. If you would like to take over the computer work while you're here, I'm sure he would love it. I know Ike had good intentions, but that man didn't understand computers at all."

"I think I was raised by a computer." Blaire grinned at the mental picture. "I'll have a look at the books later today or tomorrow. Are we done out here?"

"Oh, no. This is only the beginning. Now I have to feed the babies." Isabel's dark eyes twinkled. "The new ones are the most fun. They require special assistance."

Blaire followed Isabel into the feed shed. Isabel scooped up a can of tiny, rough, green pebbles. "What kind of feed is this?" Blaire ran her hand through the coarse, granular mass.

"These are hay crumbles, made especially for the babies. The older birds get hay pellets, similar to rabbit pellets. They're made of compressed hay."

"I never thought about what they would eat. I guess I assumed they ate bugs or something like chickens do. If we had chickens, would the baby ostriches eat the chicken feed?"

"We don't keep chickens. We had them at first, but we found out the hard way that chickens and pigs contaminate the eggs of the ostriches. We had to get rid of the chickens. I don't think they eat the same feed, but I'm not sure. You can ask Burke. He would know."

Blaire followed Isabel's example and poured feed into a feeder. Then she sprinkled some of the pellets on the ground. Isabel's pen of young ones rushed right in and began to peck at the feed. Blaire's didn't seem to know what to do.

"What's wrong with these ostriches? They won't eat."

Isabel laughed. "They need you to teach them how. These are the new babies, and they haven't caught on yet."

"Teach them?" Blaire stared at Isabel.

"In the wild they would follow their parents' examples. Here, they don't have that example so you have to be their parent."

"How can I possibly do that? I don't even have a beak." Blaire suspected Isabel was jesting with her.

"Let me show you." Isabel eased down onto her knees in the dirt. She bent forward, her hand close to her face so that her fingers looked like a bird beak. Then she darted her face down toward the dirt as if pecking at the pellets. The baby ostriches tilted their heads to one side, watching the demonstration.

Blaire burst out laughing. "Do you really do this, or are you trying to trick the city girl into doing something silly?"

"I really do this. It's the only way to teach them that I know of." She chuckled. "But I try to do it when no one else is around."

"Okay, if you can, so can I." Blaire grabbed her hair with one hand, holding it back from her face. She folded the fingers of her other hand together, held them near her mouth, and poked at the ground. The little ostriches moved closer. Their bright eyes followed her jabbing motion. Their little heads tilted to the other side as they watched. "Come on, you guys, I'm trying to teach an important lesson here." Once more, Blaire pecked at the ground. One of the babies stretched its neck and pecked with her.

"He did it. Did you see that, Isabel?"

Isabel laughed. "You're a natural teacher, *mija*. Maybe you should give up accounting and teach babies to eat."

Blaire grinned and went back to working with the doe-eyed ostriches.

"Look here, Manuel. Those birds have been pulling at the fence again. I'll head up to the house and get the tools we need to fix it before they break out and run on us." Burke knew that once out and running, there would be no stopping the ostriches. They were too fast and too wild to catch easily.

"I'll wait here for you. While you're gone, I'll check the rest of the fence."

Burke strode down the lane, choosing to walk the short distance rather than taking the truck. For what seemed like the hundredth time that morning, he wondered what Blaire was doing. How had that girl gotten under his skin so fast? He could still see the sun dancing on the golden highlights of her hair when they went for that walk yesterday. For someone who didn't want to stay in Arizona, she sure displayed an avid interest in the plants and animals of the area. He loved her curiosity and challenging questions.

Lost in thought, Burke didn't notice Isabel and Blaire until he was nearly on top of them. He stopped and watched Blaire as she encouraged the young birds to eat. They stared at her with comical interest, dipping their heads down when she did, as if wondering what this funny-looking bird was up to. Burke bit his lip to keep from laughing and thought about slipping away without letting Blaire and Isabel know that he'd watched. Then he remembered the tools he needed. He had to go right by the pens. He couldn't avoid Blaire.

"That's a fine new ostrich we've got there, Isabel."

Chapter 7

Blaire's shoulders stiffened. A red flush drifted up her cheek. Burke could almost hear her wishing the ground would open up and swallow her. She released her hair, and the golden waves fell forward, a small curtain to hide behind. She pushed against the ground and straightened up, brushing the dirt from her knees. The baby ostriches' heads moved as one, following her upward movement.

"I suppose you think it's fun to laugh at me." Blaire ran her fingers back through her hair, pushing it away from her face.

Burke adjusted his hat on his head. He fought a valiant battle against the humor bubbling up inside of him. "I didn't come here on purpose to spy on you. I came to get some fencing materials out of the shed." He gestured toward the medium-sized barn behind the hatchery.

"You could have made a little more noise." Blaire leaned forward, her eyes flashing fire.

Burke rubbed his jaw. "I could have just burst out laughing. That would have let you know I was here." He tried to look contrite. "Look, I'm sorry I embarrassed you. I'll try not to do it anymore."

Burke started on toward the shed.

"Wait just a minute." Blaire charged out of the pen and up to him. "I'm tired of always doing something stupid and having you catch me."

Burke stopped walking and looked down at her. "Then the solution is simple. Stop doing something stupid." A thundercloud rippled across her face. Burke lifted his hands in mock surrender and backed toward the barn door. "Now wait a minute. I was only joking. You weren't doing anything stupid. All of us have had to teach the baby ostriches to eat at one time or another."

She crossed her arms, staring hard at him.

"It could have been worse," Burke said. Blaire looked doubtful. "I could have gone in the house and gotten the video camera. Just think of the ammunition that would have been." He chuckled, then began to laugh as he backed through the door and into the barn.

"This calls for war." Blaire followed him inside. "I believe I'll follow you around secretly and see if you don't do something stupid. Maybe I'll even bring along that trusty video camera."

"If it's war you want. . ." Burke reached over her head and pulled something off a shelf. "I'll give you war." Burke flourished a long feather duster, the ostrich feathers dancing with the sudden motion.

Blaire stared as if too surprised to move. Her mouth fell open. Her eyes widened. Burke chuckled. He took up what he hoped was a fencing stance. *"En garde,* mademoiselle." His feather duster nearly brushed her nose.

Jumping back, Blaire reached up on the shelf. She brought down a second feather duster. Her eyes took on a determined look. "This is a fight to the finish." Her twitching lips belied her solemn tone. "Surrender now, or say your prayers."

"I'll never surrender." Burke swept forward, aiming for her cheek. Blaire jumped back and parried his blow. She seemed to have a much better stance than he did. Maybe she was a swashbuckling movie fan.

Blaire twisted to the right and dusted his neck. The feathers' soft tickling made him jump. He fought hard, determined to get her back.

"You're wounded. Are you ready to surrender?" Blaire knocked aside his feather duster. Her blue eyes mocked him.

Burke barked a fake laugh. "Ha! Mademoiselle, I believe you were the one who set the rules. This is a fight to the death."

Blaire's feather duster whipped in with surprising speed. Burke felt his hat flying through the air.

"Now you're getting serious." He swivelled around to face her as she dodged and parried. "That was a mortal wound to my favorite hat. No one messes with my hat and lives."

"You don't seem to have the room to talk. So far you haven't landed a single blow." Blaire's flushed face and dancing eyes took the edge off her challenge.

"In a daring move, the illustrious swordsman leaps toward his opponent. He backs her against the wall and knocks her sword from her hand." Burke jumped forward, pinning Blaire against a stack of straw bales. He grabbed her feather duster, wrenched it from her hand, and tossed it behind them. With his other hand he held down her hands.

"Now the swordsman must decide. Is it death, or will he show mercy?" Burke tried to hold back his laughter. "He decides. No mercy."

The feather duster began a dance over Blaire's cheeks, arms, and neck. She giggled, trying to jerk away as the soft feathers tickled her. "Stop that. I surrender. I surrender."

"That won't work." Burke continued to tickle. "We agreed to fight to the death."

Blaire tried to step around him, but her foot slipped in the loose straw. Seeing her start to fall, Burke grabbed her, pulling her close to him. He looked down into those sky blue eyes. Time stood still. He held his breath. Blaire didn't move. The laughter stopped.

"The swordsman demands a penance. A kiss for her life." At Burke's soft whisper, Blaire's eyes widened. The kiss was sweet, drawing him in, making him long for more. The feather duster clattered to the ground. Burke released Blaire and stepped back. He knew for once his was the reddest face.

"I'm sorry. Manuel and I fence sometimes. I got carried away." He picked up his hat and shoved it back on his head.

"I'm hoping you require a different penance from Manuel when you beat him." Blaire's lips twitched, as if she wanted to smile but couldn't. Her voice had a slight quaver. She edged past him and almost ran toward the house.

Burke picked up the feather dusters and put them back on the shelf. What had come over him? Why did Blaire make him act this way? She was feisty and playful at the same time. Seeing her out there with her hands on her hips, staring him down, he'd wanted to grab her and kiss her. She challenged him. She was such a mixture of fun and serious, and he was never sure which one would show up next. Rather than confusing him, she was refreshing. Besides, he'd never met a woman so willing to laugh at herself.

Then when she'd followed him in here, he had no idea what had possessed him to start a fencing battle. Yet she played right along. He couldn't remember having such a good time with anyone else. Something changed, though. When he caught her in his arms, she felt like she belonged there. Their kiss felt right, too. He felt as if God placed her there just for him. He found himself wanting to get to know her. He wanted to get to know her in a way that would take a lifetime to complete. Burke rubbed the back of his neck. What was happening to him? Of all the women to be attracted to, he had to pick one who wouldn't be staying around long. He grabbed up the materials he needed and headed out of the barn. Maybe that was best. If Blaire left soon, then he could forget her. Because he sure couldn't seem to get her off his mind while she was here.

✑

Blaire rolled down the window as she drove toward town. The spring air felt good circling through the car. Maybe the breeze would chase away the turmoil of thoughts and images in her mind. Her lips still felt the kiss Burke had placed there moments before. This wasn't right. He worked for her. Hadn't she learned anything from her disastrous relationship with Richard? "You shouldn't date someone you work with. You shouldn't date someone you work with." Her hand pounded the rhythm of her words on the steering wheel as she spouted the litany.

When she'd run toward the house, she'd known she'd have to leave the ranch for awhile. Cleaning up, she'd grabbed some letters she'd written to her family and asked Isabel for directions to the nearest post office. The road wound through a canyon. On one side, steep cliffs rose perpendicular to the road. On the other side, the canyon dropped off to the floor where the Gila River followed its twisting path. Her uncle Ike's car, now hers, handled the highway's curves like a dream.

Above the cliffs in front of her, Blaire spotted the tall smokestack of the town's copper mine. A few minutes later she turned on the highway that ran through the center of town. The post office was two blocks into town, right where Isabel had said it would be. In a town this size, Blaire wondered how anyone could ever get lost.

"I'd like a book of stamps, please." Blaire smiled at the clerk. Her bluish white beehive hairdo made Blaire want to poke and prod to see what was hidden in those depths. How could anyone have that much hair?

"There's your change, dear." Spots of rouge brightened the woman's cheeks.

"Thank you." Blaire slipped the change in her purse and started to leave. She turned back. "Excuse me. Can you tell me if there's a real estate agent in town?"

The woman laughed. "Land sakes, no. We don't have much business here since one of the copper mines closed down. Too many people moved away. I believe there's a Realtor in Kearny, though."

"Is that very far?"

"I can tell you aren't from around here." The woman patted her impossibly high hair. "Kearny is about eleven miles that way." She pointed down the highway that ran through town. "You can't miss it. Are you looking for some property to buy?"

"No, I'm looking to sell." Blaire hesitated, knowing whatever she said would probably be around town before long. What did it matter? Maybe the news would reach some buyer before she even listed the ranch. "I inherited my uncle's ranch. It's north of town. Ike Mackenzie's place."

"Oh, yes." The woman's eyes sparkled. "I've heard about you coming to town, Miss Mackenzie. That Ike was quite a character." She nudged her hair and blushed. Lowering her voice, she leaned across the counter. "I think he might have been sweet on me. He sure was one for the flattery."

Blaire smiled at the revelation of a side of her uncle she'd never seen. He'd always had a way with words, but she couldn't imagine him being a flirt. As she walked toward her car, she wondered if sometimes women, and men too, read more into bantering than was meant. Had Burke thought she was flirting with him today? Was that why he'd kissed her?

She made the short drive to Kearny, nearly missing the small town nestled among the hills. Turning off the highway, she found the main street. After cruising up and down a few minutes, she stopped and asked for directions. In a few minutes she'd stopped outside Valley Realty. A scribbled sign taped to the door announced, "Be back in an hour." No time was given. Had the agent just left, or had they been gone for almost an hour? Blaire decided she didn't want to wait. She wasn't sure she wanted to list her property with someone that irresponsible.

The drive home took less than half an hour. The late afternoon sky turned an azure blue. Not a cloud darkened the horizon. For the first time, Blaire began to understand how such openness could give a person a sense of freedom. "Lord, I think I need to find a shopping mall. I'm in danger of singing a song about cows and open spaces. I need a couple of skyscrapers or at least a building with more than one story."

Back home, Blaire felt a restlessness she couldn't explain. She heard Isabel puttering in the kitchen. Not feeling like company, Blaire headed for her room. She picked up her cross-stitch and put it back down. She wandered around looking at her giraffes and the pictures of her family.

She plunked down on the edge of the bed. The waterbed moved gently, then stopped. Her Bible sat on the table by her bed. Blaire picked it up, rolled over onto her stomach, and stretched out across the bed to read. Thinking of the pastor's message from the previous Sunday, she turned to Psalm 23.

" 'The Lord is my Shepherd, I shall not want.' " She spoke the words softly, then stopped to think about them. "Yes, Lord, You are my shepherd. I gave You my life to do with as You see fit." She ran her hand over the smooth page. "So why do I feel like You're not in charge? Am I still trying to run my life? I thought I knew what You wanted for me. You brought me here, but I'm an accountant. I can't possibly do my job from here. I know nothing about running an ostrich ranch, so what do You want me to do? Can't You send me something in black and white? I'm willing to follow. I just don't know where to go. Lord, help me."

Tears blurred the fine print in front of her. Was she too concerned with her wants to see where the Lord was leading? "Lord, I don't know what I want. I only know I can't stand the thought of being hurt again. Protect me from Burke, Lord. I have to stay away from him. Help me sell this ranch so I can leave here before I find myself doing something I'll regret."

She thought of her relationship with Richard. Her feelings for him had never been love, but she'd been too blind to see. He was the boss's son. Every girl in the office wanted him to notice her. When he'd asked her out, Blaire had known that all the other girls were jealous. It had been a heady feeling. She could hear her mom once more saying, *Pride goeth before destruction.* Mom was right. She hadn't loved Richard. She'd used him as much as he'd used her.

"Thank You, Lord, for keeping me from making such a terrible mistake with my life." She and Richard had little in common. They'd never laughed together. They'd rarely talked of anything other than work or upcoming wedding plans.

Her thoughts turned to Burke. She could see his smile. He made her want to smile. He made her laugh. When she pulled a klutz move, as her family called it, Burke laughed with her rather than getting angry as Richard had done. Burke could be a wonderful friend. He was comfortable. They had so much in common. "Lord, I need to leave now. He's too dangerous. I don't want to lose my heart to him."

Chapter 8

The loud squeak of a chair wheel and the slam of a drawer woke Blaire early the next morning. She snuggled deeper into the covers and glanced at the clock. What awful hour was this anyway? She bolted upright in bed. Leaning closer to the night table, she gasped. Eight thirty! She'd slept until eight thirty in the morning? She wanted to slide down in the bed in embarrassment. She hadn't slept this late since she'd had the flu last winter.

She swung her legs over the side of the bed. "So much for country air being healthy. I thought I would rise at the crack of dawn, able to work long hours without tiring and eating like a horse without gaining weight. Now I find I can't even get to sleep at night."

The chair in the office creaked again. Blaire stopped her soliloquy. She had better be careful. If she could hear the chair, chances were good that the person in the other room could hear her talking. The sudden click of the door leading to the office answered her question. Whoever was in there must have realized she was awake.

"Please don't let it have been Burke." Even as she whispered her plea, she knew Burke was the only suspect. Isabel had already admitted that she didn't have anything to do with the computer, and Manuel mostly did the outside chores. Blaire recalled another time she'd heard the squeak of that chair. Burke must have heard her tell Isabel about Richard. In a way she felt relieved that he knew.

Burke had no way of knowing he was the reason she was so tired this morning. She'd tossed and turned all night thinking of his kiss, the need to sell the ranch, and wondering where God's green pasture for her could be located.

Blaire decided not to shower. She didn't feel comfortable with someone so close to her bathroom. This setup with the office sharing a bathroom with the master bedroom had been fine when her uncle was the one doing the office work and using the bedroom. As the situation stood now, however, she didn't appreciate someone else having such easy access to her room.

She slipped on a teal blue blouse, whose color was reflected in a scene-from-Africa skirt. Zebras and giraffes paraded in relief across a black background. Her sister and brother-in-law had sent the skirt to her for her last birthday. She missed her sister, Clarissa. They had been so close. She always wore something from Clarissa when she needed to talk to her sister. For some reason wearing something her sister had picked out for her helped ease the lonely ache.

The kitchen was empty when Blaire got there, and she assumed Isabel was out working in the hatchery. A bowl of fresh fruit stood in the middle of the dining table. A note from Isabel told her there were eggs in the refrigerator, cereal in the cupboards, and bagels in the bread drawer.

"So you finally decided to get up."

Blaire grabbed the counter to keep herself from jumping. She would not give Burke the satisfaction of knowing he'd startled her again. She turned. "I had a little trouble sleeping last night. I guess I decided to make up for it this morning." Blaire noticed that Burke's eyes looked a little drawn. Had he missed some sleep, too?

Burke nodded and leaned against the doorjamb. "I wondered if you could give me some help when you've had your breakfast."

"Me?"

"Sure. I need someone to wrestle a couple of those big male ostriches for me." Sea green eyes sparkled with mischief.

"Oops. I forgot to put on my wrestling clothes. Besides, I'm more the fencing type than the wrestling type." The reference to yesterday's mock swordplay slipped out. Blaire felt her face flame as she thought of the way the incident had ended. Her heart pounded. How could she still be so aware of Burke's closeness?

"Actually, I had hoped you might have your accountant clothes on. We had a big order in yesterday's mail. I'm still struggling with the way Ike set up the books."

Blaire pushed off from the counter. "You ordered an accountant?" She lifted her hand to her brow in a mock salute. "Here I am, front and center, sir."

"This branch of the service may be tough, but I will let you have some breakfast before you report for duty."

"One breakfast coming up." Blaire grabbed an apple from the bowl on the table. She tossed the piece of fruit up in the air. Burke cringed. With a snap, she caught the sweet missile in her right hand. "Ha! You didn't think me capable of doing anything remotely coordinated, did you?"

"You wound me, my lady." Burke staggered back, his hand covering his heart. "In my eyes you are the epitome of grace."

Blaire narrowed her eyes and waved her apple in his face. "You don't fool me. You're only saying that because you need help with the books."

Burke plucked the apple from her hand and took a big bite. "You're absolutely right. Get yourself another apple and follow me, Grace."

Laughter bubbled up inside her. Blaire chose a banana and trailed after Burke to the office. At his questioning look she said, "I wanted to be a fruit of a different color. Two of a kind might be too much."

❧

Burke pulled a second chair up to the computer. He considered kicking himself while he was at it. He'd spent a good portion of the night thinking about Blaire and how he needed to keep his distance. Then, the first time he saw her, he started in with the light-hearted banter. *Why do I do this?* Almost before he asked the question he knew the answer. Because she was so much fun to talk to and to tease. He couldn't ever remember feeling this way about another woman.

"I don't know how familiar you are with computers. Not long before he died, Ike had this one installed. He wanted to put all of the business records on the computer to keep better track of everything. I'm not sure he understood the machine, and I'm not good with these types of programs. I get lost every time I try to figure out what he was doing."

"What records did he want to keep track of?" Blaire leaned closer to the screen, scanning the various file names.

"Let's see." Burke leaned back in his chair and held up his hand, ticking the items off on his fingers. "There's egg production, the breeder program, egg sales, meat and leather sales, feather sales, and the sale and raising of our juveniles and early breeders." He frowned. Blaire was staring at him. "I think that's all."

"I had no idea so much was involved." She glanced at the screen, then back at him. "What do you want to try to look up first?"

"Let's try the juveniles and early breeders. The order form says this guy wants to buy twenty-four breeder hens, eight male breeders, and several juveniles."

"I thought you said this was a big order." Blaire's eyebrows drew together. She picked up a pencil and tapped it on the desk. "What do these ostriches cost, two to three hundred apiece? That doesn't seem like so much to me."

Burke tried to close his mouth. He knew he probably looked stupid with it hanging open. "Didn't the lawyers in Phoenix go over this with you?" He took a deep breath and tried to stop spluttering. "Do you mean you have no idea of the value of this ranch, your inheritance?"

Puzzled blue eyes met his. Blaire shrugged. "I don't think I gave the lawyers time to tell me much. They gave me a bunch of paperwork, but I haven't looked at it yet. Can you explain the value to me?"

Taking a last bite of apple, Burke stepped into the bathroom to wash the sticky juice from his hand. When she found out the real worth of this enterprise, would Blaire be even more eager to sell the ranch? He took a deep sigh and headed back into the office. He couldn't hide the truth.

"Your uncle Ike wanted to raise the best ostriches. He spent several years doing other things while he studied the markets and earned some starting money. He found out that the best birds are the South African black ostriches. He looked at different breeding stock until he found just the right line. That's what he bought. You have the best birds possible on this ranch. We don't just raise ostriches. We raise the cream of the crop, so to speak."

"I didn't even know there were different kinds of ostriches. What's so special about these black ones?"

"The African blacks have about 20 percent more feathers, and their hides are worth more than any other ostrich. Seventy percent of the value of the bird is in the skin and feathers."

"Poor things." Blaire swept her hair back from her face. "Is that all we raise them for?"

"They're like cows. You eat a hamburger and don't think about the cute little cow when you bite into that sandwich."

Blaire nodded. "I guess you're right. But I haven't just taught a baby cow to peck food in the dirt either."

Burke chuckled. "That's a good thing. A calf would look pretty stupid pecking in the dirt."

Blaire flipped the pencil at him. "So, how much does an ostrich cost?"

"That depends on the ostrich, its age, and whether the bird is for breeding or other purposes."

"Are you avoiding my question? I mean, how could a stupid bird be as valuable as a cow? There's something un-American about that."

Burke leaned back in the chair. "Now you sound like my dad and all the other cattle ranchers I know. They think ostriches are trying to steal their market away from them by appealing to health nuts."

Blaire twisted a hank of hair between her fingers. A frown wrinkled her brow. "Okay, I'll bite. What do health nuts have to do with ostriches?"

"Ostrich meat is lower in fat than even venison and higher in iron than beef. Beef and pork have more than nine grams of fat, and ostrich meat has less than three grams. For people looking to decrease their fat intake, this meat is a viable alternative." He grinned. "How's that for a commercial?"

"Okay, smartie, what about chicken or turkey? They're birds, and they're lower in fat than beef or pork." She leaned back and pointed her pencil at him. "And they're much easier to get in the oven."

"Too bad. You'll have to get a bigger oven. Skinned chicken has more than seven grams of fat, and turkey without the skin has five." He put his hand to his ear. "Hark, is that a group of health nuts at the door?"

They both laughed.

"I think we got off track." Burke pointed at the computer screen. "If you look in the breeder file, I'll show you a little of what ostriches are worth. I think that's the only file Ike had done much work on."

Blaire clicked on the filename and watched a column of figures pop up on the screen. She gasped and turned to Burke, her eyes wide. "These figures can't be right."

"Not all ostriches are worth this much. I told you Ike studied the market and picked his birds from the best. These are the birds we've set aside to sell as breeders. The younger ones sell for twenty-eight hundred dollars each, and the older ones sell for thirty-eight hundred each. We have between two hundred and two hundred and fifty of each age group set aside to sell this season. The buyer said in his e-mail this morning that he wants twenty of the younger breeders and twelve of the older ones."

Burke reached over and put his finger on Blaire's chin. He pushed up gently and chuckled. "You're going to catch flies that way." She didn't say anything, just stared at him. "You really didn't know how much this place is worth, did you?"

She shook her head, staring at him. A deep breath shuddered through her. "Do you realize those five hundred birds you're talking about will bring in more than a million dollars if they all sell? Just the one sale we're talking about will bring in more than a hundred thousand dollars. Where did Uncle Ike get the money to start the ranch? I had no idea he could afford something of this magnitude."

"He made some investments that paid off. Also, he put every penny he made back into building the stock. He worked hard to get this ranch going. You have inherited a business worth several million dollars. Ike talked a lot about how he wanted to have you come out here and help him with the ranch. He said your accounting skills would be put to good use."

"He invited me out here, but he didn't say anything about wanting me to work for him."

"I think he wanted you to see the place first. Ike thought you would be a natural here. He said you were always a good one to look for a new experience. Maybe that's why he liked you so much. You two had a lot in common."

Blaire leaned forward, studying the open file intently. Burke could almost see her mathematical training taking over. The columns of figures that were Greek to him obviously made sense to her. She clicked the file closed and opened another. There wasn't much to see in it. Ike had only begun to keep records on the computer, and the other files were mostly empty.

What would she do now? Would she be even more eager to sell the ranch? She could take the money and open her own accounting firm as she had mentioned. Or would she see what Ike wanted to do here and continue his dream? Burke hoped she would choose the latter, but she hadn't seemed eager to stay so far.

"Where did Ike keep his figures before he used the computer?" Blaire's blue gaze flicked to him before going back to the screen.

"In the books in this drawer." Burke opened a drawer at the side of the desk. "I think he kept pretty accurate records." He reached to pick up a book at the same time as Blaire. His hand closed over hers. Awareness of her made him pause. He looked up. Eyes wide, she had focused her full attention on him. Burke tried to think of something to say that would lighten the moment, but he could barely breathe, let alone think.

Chapter 9

The touch of the book's cool binding under Blaire's fingers contrasted sharply with the warm tingling sensation of Burke's hand on hers. Blaire looked into his green eyes. For once, he wasn't teasing. No laughter crinkled the corners of his eyes. Instead, a look of longing tugged at her heart. *I was right.* The words echoed inside her head. *He is dangerous. He's stealing my heart. I have to learn all there is about this ranch, then sell the place.*

Dragging her gaze from Burke's, Blaire pulled the book from the drawer. Burke let go, then sat back, releasing a long breath.

"I think I'll give you some time to look over the books. I'll stop back in later and discuss the buyer with you." He pushed back his chair and stood. She watched him slip his hat back on his head. "Do you have any other questions before I go? I think Ike left most everything in the desk somewhere."

Blaire glanced at the large oak desk. There were several account books in the open drawer. "I'll find what I need. You can go ahead with whatever you have to be doing." As he left, Blaire forced herself to ignore his retreating back. Instead, she immersed herself in the columns of figures, something that never failed to grab her complete attention. The world faded as she concentrated on the work in front of her.

A hand squeezed Blaire's shoulder. She jumped. The book on the desk slipped to the floor. The bang echoed in the small room. She whirled around. Burke grinned down at her.

"I've heard of people getting into their work, but you're amazing."

She felt her face flush. "The next time you might try calling my name."

"How many times?"

"What do you mean?"

"Well, let's see." He tilted his head back as if thinking and rubbed his jaw with his fingers. "I called through the window, I called from out in the living room where I stopped to talk to Isabel. Then I said your name twice in here before I touched you." He looked down at her again. "So, how often should I call you?"

Blaire pursed her lips. She could remember all the times she had been accused of being on another planet when her coworkers tried to get her attention. Flipping her hair back over her shoulders, she lifted her nose in the air and sniffed like a haughty snob. "When you reach the proper number of requests to merit my response, then I will answer, but only then."

Burke laughed, the corners of his eyes crinkling. Blaire joined him.

"I have to admit my coworkers would commiserate with you. My friend Susan used to keep a little squirt gun handy. She loved to come up behind me and squirt cold water on my neck."

Burke rubbed his jaw. "Hmm. I think I may have an old squirt gun I can resurrect."

"I wouldn't if I were you." Blaire narrowed her gaze. "I haven't told you what vile deeds I did to Susan to pay her back."

"What happened to vengeance belonging to the Lord?"

Blaire chuckled. "I thought He could use some help."

Burke lifted his hat and raked his fingers through his hair. "I give up. Now, in case you're wondering why I'm interrupting you, I have something to show you out in the barn. I just made a discovery. Since you are the owner, you need to take a look."

Curious, Blaire pushed back the chair and stood up. Stiff muscles protested. She rotated her shoulders, easing a kink out of her back. "I can't imagine what you need my advice on around here. I don't know anything yet." She smirked at him. "Unless you're asking for a fencing rematch." She groaned inside. Why did she keep bringing that up? "Let's go. I do need to stretch a little."

A gentle breeze stirred the leaves of the mesquite trees. The sun's rays, accompanied by a warm breeze, caused sweat to wash over Blaire on the short walk to the barn. She watched the male ostrich in the nearest pen. He stalked around the enclosure, fanning his dark feathers as if he were the one creating a draft. The hens pecked at the ground while scrutinizing their mate as he made the rounds.

Inside the barn, Blaire stopped to let her eyes adjust to the dim light. A variety of tools lined one wall. Everything from gardening implements to incubator parts had a place. Amazed at the orderliness, she wondered if Burke or Manuel kept the place so well organized.

"Over here." Burke beckoned to one corner where a few bales of straw lined the wall. "I was in here getting an extension cord when I heard them."

"Heard what?" Blaire stopped in midstride.

"These critters." Burke leaned down, peering behind one of the bales. He stuck one hand in, and Blaire could hear faint, high-pitched mewling sounds. She eased up next to him and leaned closer. Burke pulled out his hand, his fingers curled around a tiny spitfire.

"A kitten." Blaire held out her hands. "I don't think I've ever seen one so young." The little black-and-white kitten opened its small pink mouth and hissed, trying for all the world to act fierce. Little baby fur stood on end. Blaire giggled. "If he had some size to back him up, I think he'd eat me for dinner." She stroked a finger down the shaking back.

"Hold him next to your heart." Burke demonstrated, lifting a gray-and-white kitten up and cuddling it on his chest. "I think the heartbeat helps to calm them."

Blaire followed his example. She cupped her hand under the baby to support him. In moments the kitten curled up and went to sleep. "Look at these paws." She lifted one paw with her fingertip. Minuscule pink pads housed almost clear barbs that were so soft they couldn't possibly do much damage to anything.

She looked up to find Burke watching her. His large finger slowly stroked the back of his kitten as it slept. The tender look in his eyes caught and held her. She wanted to look away but found she couldn't. She wished he would touch her with the same tenderness. The kitten in her hand moved. Breaking eye contact with Burke, she watched the matchstick legs stretch out stiff and the little mouth open in a wide yawn.

"How old are they?"

"It's hard to say." Burke held his kitten up to eye level, as if trying to read the age. "They're probably close to two weeks, but not much older. Kittens open their eyes when they're about ten days old. These have their eyes open, but they still don't have a lot of coordination. That will come in the next week or two. Then they'll start wandering away from home."

"I didn't even know we had any cats." Blaire snuggled the kitten next to her cheek for a minute before handing it to Burke to put back.

"Ike tried to get rid of cats when they came around. He didn't like them around the ostriches."

"Why would cats make a difference?"

Burke straightened. "Have you ever been around cats during their mating season?"

"I've never had one. The neighbors did, though. I remember more than once having trouble sleeping because of the caterwauling going on in the alley behind our house. Is that what you're referring to?"

"Yep. That caterwauling, as you call it, will get the ostriches so upset they won't lay eggs. They hate unusual noises. Ostriches are bothered by strange animals such as coyotes howling or even cats walking by their pen. There are a lot of coyotes in the area. We can't keep them all away, but we try to discourage them from coming around the breeding pens."

Blaire glanced out the door at the huge birds. How could a little cat bother something so big? "Will we need to get rid of the mother?"

Rubbing the back of his neck, Burke grimaced. "I hate to do that. She's a good mouser. However, I think we should give the kittens away when they're old enough. We can always take them over to Dad's place."

"He's not afraid of ending up with too many?"

Burke's green eyes twinkled. "He has a hard time keeping cats around. They always get invited to lunch with the coyotes and don't know until too late that they're the main course."

Blaire gasped. "And you want to give these sweet little babies to him? Just so some ravenous beast can eat them? No way! We'll keep them ourselves first."

Her heart sped up as Burke leaned close.

"I hate to tell you this, but the coyotes don't care if the cats are here or at Dad's place. They'll eat them anywhere. Besides, here the cats have to contend with the ostriches, too."

"But we can protect them somehow, can't we?"

The tender look in Burke's eyes made her want to lean closer and back away at the same time. "I don't know how to do that unless you put them in a cage. I've never seen a caged cat that's happy. They're meant to be out hunting and wandering around." He lifted his hat and settled it on his head again. "You don't have to decide what to do with them right away. They still have to be with their mother for a few weeks. There is one thing you can do, though."

"What's that?"

"In order for them to make good pets, they need to get used to people. You can take time every day to come out here and hold them and pet them. Once they get used to you and me, they'll be willing to let anyone hold them."

Blaire tapped her finger against her lip and frowned. "I don't know. That sounds like a tough job to me." She grinned at Burke. "But I guess if you're willing to help out, I'll make the sacrifice."

Picking up a tiny calico, Blaire cradled the kitten close. Small spots of varied colors dotted her pure white fur. "This one looks like someone sprinkled her with color. I think I'll call her Sprinkles."

The shrill ring of a phone shattered the moment. Burke glanced up toward the house.

"Isabel must be outside. She's set the phone to ring where we can hear it. Shall we see who's calling?"

"There isn't an extension out here?" Blaire glanced around.

"No, but Isabel will have put the answering machine on. We can return the call if we need to."

They put the kittens back and headed toward the house at a leisurely pace. Burke stuck his hands in his pockets. "I hate to be pushy, but this could be the guy who wants to buy those breeders. How are the books coming?"

"Uncle Ike did leave things in a mess. Plus, I know nothing about running an ostrich ranch. I've never done this type of business before. At least, not from the ground up like this. I'm making some headway, but it's slow. Can you hold off on giving the guy a price for a couple of days?"

"That shouldn't be a problem." Burke looked down at her with what appeared to be amazement. "You mean you'll have the books straightened out that fast?"

She shrugged. "That's my job. Just because this is a new type of business doesn't make it much different than other businesses I've worked with. Mainly, I have to figure out Ike's chicken scratches in all the ledgers."

Burke laughed. "I used to tell him he should have been a doctor. He had the handwriting already figured out."

Isabel met them at the door. Her red-rimmed eyes were still wet with tears. She held a tissue to her nose.

"What's wrong?" Burke reached out to hug her. "Who called?"

"My friend Ophelia from church. Her son called." Isabel blew her nose and dabbed at her eyes. "She's been taken to the hospital. They think she's had a heart attack."

Burke pulled her into an embrace. Blaire reached over to rub Isabel's back. How had she come to care so much for this woman in such a short time? Seeing her hurting made Blaire's eyes sting with tears.

"Do you want me or Manuel to drive you to the hospital?" Burke leaned back to look at Isabel.

"No, *mijo.*" She sniffed. "I have too much to do here. We have to get the order of blown eggs ready to go to Tucson. Besides, if I leave, who will take care of the eggs and the cooking?"

"Manuel, Blaire, and I can take care of everything."

"But there's so much to do. I don't want to burden you with more."

Blaire patted Isabel's back. "You need to be with your friend, Isabel. I can do a lot more to help out. Burke will show me the things you do that I don't know how to do. I've watched you blow out the eggs. I'm sure I can to that."

Isabel dug another tissue from her apron pocket. "I do have the eggs separated and ready. But what about the meals? I could take the time to cook something before I go."

Burke turned her around and gently pushed her in the direction of her room. "Go get ready. I'll get Manuel to drive you. Don't worry about anything. Just remember how much we'll appreciate you when you get back. I'm sure Blaire and I can handle the cooking.

Blaire watched in silence as Isabel wiped her eyes and headed to her room to get ready to leave. Did Burke have any idea what he was suggesting? Did he know her cooking skills included peanut butter sandwiches and canned soup? In Chicago she'd never worried about meals. There were great delicatessens everywhere. Here, there wasn't a fast food place for miles.

Chapter 10

A cloud of dust rose in the air as Manuel drove down the driveway, taking his mother to the hospital to stay with Ophelia. The two women were like sisters. Isabel wanted to stay with Ophelia until her friend was discharged and could manage on her own.

Burke glanced at Blaire. Her blue eyes glistened with unshed tears. She had such a tender heart. He longed to pull her close, to cup her smooth cheek in his hand, to give her the comfort she needed. *I want to give her the love she deserves.* He shook himself mentally. Where had that come from? Sure he had an attraction to Ike's niece, but that's all it was. He clenched his jaw. *I'm not falling in love with any woman, no matter how much I admire her.* The problem was, deep down he knew it was too late. This woman had crept into his heart and made a place there. Now he would have to steel himself against the heartbreak that was sure to follow. He knew, without a doubt, that Blaire would leave one day. Facts were facts. Women weren't to be trusted.

"You probably want to get back to the books." Burke spoke more gruffly than he intended. He could see the question in Blaire's eyes and did his best to suppress the feelings of guilt that popped up. "I'll get busy on the outside chores. When Manuel gets back he'll help me."

"How long is the drive to the hospital?"

"Isabel said they took her to that new heart hospital in Tucson. That's about an hour-and-a-half drive from here. Manuel should be back in time for supper."

"Um, speaking of supper, what did you have in mind?"

"Isabel said she has some corn tortillas in the refrigerator. She put out some hamburger and suggested we make tacos. They're easy and pretty quick. I'll come in about five and help you."

Blaire looked relieved. "Thanks. I've never made tacos before. I'm pretty good at eating them, though."

"Is that a challenge?" Burke laughed. "You'd better consider carefully before you answer that one. I like tacos, but I'm nothing compared to Manuel. That boy doesn't eat tacos, he inhales them."

"Just how many tacos does he inhale?" Blaire's azure gaze took his breath away.

Burke cleared his throat and glanced down the driveway. "I've seen him eat a dozen tacos, then ask for dessert."

With her mouth opening and closing in rapid succession, Blaire looked like she was catching air. He laughed at her shocked expression. "This is just fair warning so you don't challenge him to a taco duel." He stepped off the porch. "I'll be back later."

The afternoon sped by. At five fifteen Burke managed to get to the house. He and Blaire had better get supper started before Manuel got home. As he opened the door he smelled hamburger frying. He wasn't prepared for the sight of Blaire in the kitchen. She had Isabel's apron on with the ties wrapped twice around her slender frame. She'd pulled her hair back into a ponytail, but the shorter strands curled around her face. She had her back to him, stirring the hamburger, then picking up a chunk of cheese to grate. The scene was so much like his dream of a wife and home of his own. He couldn't swallow past the lump in his throat.

"And you said you've never made tacos before." Burke grinned as Blaire jumped. Little strands of cheese now dotted the counter. One of the things he liked about her was her ability to focus on the job at hand. He didn't know which he liked more: her willingness to do the job, or the fact that he could scare her so easy.

She glared at him, then began scraping up the scattered cheese. "I know some things about tacos. What I don't know is how to make the taco shells. My mom always bought the preformed ones. The ones Isabel has are just flat."

He chuckled. "Those are corn tortillas, not taco shells. They can be used for a variety of Mexican dishes."

Burke rummaged in the cupboards until he found the skillet he wanted. With a crash of pans he pulled it free.

"No wonder Isabel doesn't let you help in the kitchen." Blaire had her hands clapped over her ears. "That sounded like you broke a cast-iron skillet."

"Nope." Burke held up the evidence. "They're too tough." He put the skillet on the stove. "I wanted this one because it's just the right size to cook a corn tortilla. You need plenty of oil, then you fry the tortilla on one side, flip it, and fold it. Let me demonstrate."

A loud buzz reverberated through the house. "That's the hatchery. I've got to go check and see what's happening. Go ahead and do the taco shells. They're pretty easy. Just don't cook them too long. Oh, and be sure to drain them good. The paper towels are over there." He pointed to the side of the sink.

Manuel pulled in the driveway as Burke left the house. The two of them headed to the hatchery and had the problem fixed before any of the eggs were in danger.

"I think I'm going to have to get some parts for the incubator soon." Burke held the door open for Manuel to enter the house. "I'll go to Globe tomorrow morning and see if they have them up there. If not, I'll have to go to Tucson the next day. I have to deliver the blown eggs anyway. I think Blaire plans to get them ready tomorrow afternoon."

Burke almost ran into Manuel's back as he stopped in the kitchen door. Peering over Manuel's shoulder, Burke could see what halted him. Blaire had her back to them and was removing what might have once been a corn tortilla from the skillet of oil. The oil-logged shell dripped grease on the stove as she swung it over to the paper towel. A long tear pulled it nearly in two. A pile of limp torn tortillas rested on the plate already.

Picking up the last of the corn tortillas, Blaire dropped it in the skillet. No sounds of popping or sizzling emanated from the frying pan. Disbelief filled him as he and Manuel moved across the kitchen. Blaire looked around. The look on her face stopped him from yelling about her ruining their supper.

"I don't think I did a very good job of making taco shells." She gestured at the plate of soggy mush.

"Why is the heat so low?"

She looked puzzled. "You said not to cook them too long. I didn't want to burn them so I turned the heat on low."

Burke resisted the urge to roll his eyes. "In order to cook them right you have to use a high heat. I should have told you that. But if you leave them in too long, they're so crispy you can't use them for taco shells."

Blaire looked like a whipped dog. "Is there any way to salvage these?"

"I think we're going to starve tonight," Manuel said. The poor boy probably thought he wouldn't live through the night without supper.

"Let's turn up the heat." Burke reached over and cranked the gas on high. "Then we'll recook the pieces of tortilla."

"But they won't make taco shells. They're all broken." Blaire lifted one with the tongs to demonstrate.

"Have you ever heard that when you have lemons you make lemonade?" Burke grinned. "Well, we'll make crisp pieces of tortilla and have taco salad instead of tacos."

Blaire and Manuel both brightened. Within fifteen minutes they were at the table eating and laughing as if taco salad had been the meal they'd planned all along.

Blaire worked into the night on the books. She hadn't intended to stay up so late, but once again she got lost in the figures. Entering the information onto the computer was a chore, but once done, they would save an immeasurable amount of time. And retrieving the information they needed would take a matter of seconds instead of minutes or hours.

The next morning, she groaned as she dragged herself out of bed. The smell of coffee and bacon filled the house. Slipping into a blouse and a pair of shorts, she headed to the kitchen to see if Isabel had come home during the night.

"Good morning, sleepyhead." Burke grinned at her.

She couldn't hold in the laugh. Burke stood at the stove, Isabel's apron tied loosely around him. Bacon and eggs sizzled. A plate of toast sat on the table with the plates.

"Is this your Suzy Homemaker outfit?"

Burke wiggled his eyebrows. "Just call me Sue for short. But remember, I don't do windows."

She laughed and grabbed the plates as he began to take up the eggs. "Where's Manuel?"

"Right here." Manuel walked through the door. His damp hair shone. "I checked the incubators, Burke. They're doing fine right now, but I think we need to find the parts for that one. If it goes down we'll lose several eggs."

"Sit down and eat." Burke carried the coffee to the table, then pulled out a chair for Blaire. "I'll run to Globe after breakfast and see what I can find. If they don't have the parts, I think I can rig it to work until I get to Tucson." He turned to Blaire. "Would you like to see the big city of Globe?"

She held her hand over her heart and pretended to be faint. "I'm not sure I can stand the excitement, but if you're there to protect me from those city slickers, then I'll try." She selected a piece of toast. "Is there a real estate office in Globe?"

A pained expression crossed Burke's face. His jaw tightened. "I'm sure there is. I've never needed one so I don't know where it is."

"Well, I'm getting to know the ranch well enough to list with a Realtor, I think." She tried to come up with something to ease the tension in the air. "Is Globe much bigger than Kearny?"

Manuel choked. He took a sip of coffee. "There's only a slight difference between about fifteen hundred and six or seven thousand."

Blaire blinked her eyes and tried on a dreamy expression. "Wow. Imagine that. Does this mean they have a supermarket? We could use a few groceries."

"Were you thinking of bread, peanut butter, and jelly so you can fix supper?" Burke's mouth twitched as if he were trying not to smile.

Lifting her nose in the air, Blaire gave him what she hoped was a freezing look. "I'll have you know I make the bestest peanut buster sandwiches in the whole world." She chuckled. "At least that's what my neighbor's daughter told me when I babysat for her."

"With a recommendation like that, we can't go wrong." Burke wiped his mouth, stood, and carried his dishes to the sink. "Do you think you can be ready to go in thirty minutes?"

"I'll meet you outside." Blaire watched Burke as he left. She could almost feel the hurt emanating from him. She didn't want to be the cause of that hurt, but she had to protect herself, too. She knew better than to become involved with someone she worked with. She'd learned that lesson well. *Why can't we just be friends? We get along so well. I love talking, laughing, and joking with him. Lord, help me to know what's right.*

Manuel cleared his throat. His tanned face mirrored concern. "I know this is none of my business." He stopped and tore a piece off his toast. "You know, Burke is upset that you're selling the ranch."

"I know that, but I don't understand why. I'll make sure all of you are taken care of by whoever buys the place. He knows how much I want to have my own accounting firm. How can I do that here?"

Manuel chewed his toast slowly. "I only know Burke watched your uncle Ike work hard to make this place what it is today. And Ike did that for you."

Blaire stared at the young man across from her. "What do you mean?"

"Ike used to tell everyone his ranch would be yours one day. He didn't have much family, and for some reason he felt connected to you." Manuel lifted his arm, swinging it in a circle. "All this was for you."

"But he forgot to consider my wants when he did this." Blaire took her plate to the sink. "I'd better get dressed for town."

The trip to Globe was cool despite the heat of the day. Burke barely spoke. Blaire stared out at the mountains they drove over. The hills she once thought bleak and barren were covered with cacti, trees, and shrubs. She particularly liked the red stems and thick green leaves of the manzanita Burke pointed out to her. The combination of colors was almost regal.

In Globe, the only real estate agency they found was closed for the day. "I can't believe this." Blaire felt like kicking the door. "Why is it that every time I find a Realtor they're closed?"

"Maybe God's trying to tell you something." Burke shrugged when she glared at him.

She sighed. "Well, I guess I can do the grocery shopping while you find the parts you need. Just be sure to tell me what kind of jelly you like on your sandwich."

Burke grinned and escorted her back to his truck. "What if I said I like bananas best?"

"On your peanut butter? I'd say you're a little strange."

He laughed. "I think we have jelly that Isabel made. Don't worry about buying any."

Burke insisted that they shop together. He seemed relieved that she hadn't been able to connect with the Realtor. He took a tour through the town, showing her several historic landmarks and buildings. They drove to the neighboring town of Miami, passing the tall mound of dirt Burke told her was waste from the copper mines. He took her to eat at an excellent Mexican restaurant. They sat in a small, semicircular booth. Their knees almost touched. Blaire couldn't remember ever being so aware of another person. She tried her best to remember her resolve to simply be Burke's friend.

"Hey, I think I need some ice cream for the drive home." Burke swung into the left turn lane across from a Dairy Queen. "Sound good?"

"I don't know. I'm eating all this delicious and fattening Mexican food. And now you want me to add ice cream on top of that?"

"You got it."

"Sounds good." She laughed. "I'll start my diet tomorrow, right?"

They contemplated the menu side by side. Blaire couldn't think with him standing so near. When Burke suggested a dip cone, she agreed. She had no idea what other selections were offered.

"Here, I'll carry this to the truck for you." Burke lifted the two cones.

"I can carry my own." Blaire stretched out her hand.

Burke raised his eyebrows. "You? I haven't seen you stumble and fall lately. I figure it's like an earthquake. You're due to slip any moment." He gave her a mocking grin. "I'll carry the cones."

Blaire made a face at him and opened the door. Burke was still grinning at her. He didn't see the family headed in their direction. An eager young girl plowed into him as he stepped through the door. Burke stumbled. One cone flew up and landed on Blaire's shoulder. He grabbed the girl to keep her from falling. The second cone smashed into his chest.

"Well, we're a matched set. I think you stood too close to the fault line, Mr. Earthquake." Blaire plucked the cone from her shoulder and used the napkins she'd picked up to attempt to wipe the ice cream off her blouse.

Burke took one look at her, his chuckle rumbling deep in his chest as he scooped melting ice cream off his shirt.

Chapter 11

Blaire heard a vehicle coming down the driveway as she stepped out of the shower. "Oh, please be Isabel. I don't want to have to try to cook again." She wrapped a small towel around her head and tugged on shorts and a T-shirt that featured a picture of a cute kitten circled by the words "Purrrrfectly Loveable."

As she ran a brush through her hair, a loud knock echoed through the house. She frowned. Isabel wouldn't knock. Burke would have used the kitchen door, and he wouldn't knock, either. Besides, like her, he was trying to wash off the remains of today's ice-cream bath.

She finished her hair and headed to the door. The banging began again, this time sounding as if the door would fall apart. "I'm coming." She trotted barefoot across the living room.

Through the glass she could see a giant bunch of roses atop two legs. The right foot lifted and headed for the door. She jerked it open before the foot connected.

"May I help you?"

"I'm looking for Blaire Mackenzie."

The high feminine voice startled Blaire. She'd assumed the jeans-clad legs belonged to a man.

"I'm Blaire."

The roses moved, and Blaire could see dark brown eyes peering at her through the flowers. The eyes appeared to be framed by hair dyed a vivid shade of royal blue.

"These are for you."

The huge bouquet moved in Blaire's direction. She groped through the foliage to grasp the large vase beneath the greenery.

"Flowers for me?" Blaire managed to find a handhold on the vase. "Thank you."

"No problem. Hope you enjoy them." The slender girl sauntered down the walkway to a blue minivan whose color clashed with her royal blue hair.

Blaire backed through the doorway, turning the flowers sideways. They still brushed the door frame, the fragrant blossoms swinging toward her as they cleared the opening. The clump of booted feet crossing the kitchen told her she wasn't alone anymore.

"What's this? Need some help?" She shivered as Burke's hands brushed across hers. He lifted the bouquet and took them to the coffee table. "You want them here?"

"I guess." Blaire swung the door closed and followed him. "I wonder who they're from."

"My guess is someone who has plenty of money." Burke straightened, tilted his hat back, and scratched his head. "There must be at least two dozen roses there, maybe more."

Blaire leaned over and inhaled the fragrance. She loved roses. "They're beautiful." She glanced at Burke from the corner of her eye. Had he sent them? Could he have gotten the wrong impression from her? "I can't imagine who could have sent them."

Burke rubbed his jaw. His eyes twinkled. "I don't suppose you want to open the card." He lifted the small florist card with one finger, then let it drop again.

"I didn't see that." Blaire snatched the envelope and pulled out the card. She resisted the urge to turn her back on Burke. Glancing down, she gasped. She felt as if someone had kicked her. The card fluttered to the floor.

"You okay? You're white as a sheet." Burke took hold of her arm.

"I'm fine." She stared at the white square on the carpet. "How could he?"

"How could he what?" Burke's hold tightened on her arm. "I think you need to sit down."

Blaire sank down on the couch. Her whole body trembled. She didn't know if the shaking was from anger, shock, or what. Her mind refused to grasp the words on the card.

"May I?" Burke reached for the note. She shrugged, unable to look at him. " 'Please forgive me. I love you. Richard.' "

Silence filled the room. "Isn't this the cad who dumped you?"

She nodded. Blaire reached for the vase. Her hands shook. She pulled them back, placing them between her legs.

"Would you like me to get rid of these for you?"

"Do you think the trash can is big enough?" She cleared her throat. Her attempt at levity fell flat. Blaire pressed her fingertips into the corners of her eyes. She wanted to scream and kick, but she didn't want Burke to see how badly she hurt.

"Manuel told me that Isabel called. Her friend Ophelia just got home from the hospital. Isabel is staying with her for a day or two. I could take the flowers over there for Ophelia. She and Isabel don't have to know where they came from."

The fragrance of roses, which Blaire normally loved, was causing her head to pound. She forced a smile that probably looked more like a grimace. "Kind of like giving flowers from a funeral to the residents of nursing homes, right?" She turned away from Burke. Right now she couldn't take the look of concern on his face. "That's a good idea. I'm sure Ophelia will love the flowers."

"I'll take them right away." Burke rested his hand lightly on her shoulder. "Will you be okay?"

She wanted to scream, "No, I'll never be okay again. My insides are ripped apart." Instead, she choked back a sob and nodded.

✒

Burke set the vase of flowers on the floor of the truck as far from the driver's side as possible. He opened the vent and cracked his window, hoping the cloying smell would be drawn out. He wanted to throw the flowers, vase and all, as far as he could, but he had already committed to giving them to Ophelia.

He didn't take long delivering the flowers. Ophelia, worn out from the trip home from the hospital, wasn't up to company. Burke left so Isabel could give her full attention to her friend. They both loved the flowers.

Within an hour Burke was bumping along a dirt track near the Gila River. Twisted mesquite trees draped shade near the water. He parked his truck and walked over to sit on the bank. A dribble of dirt cascaded down the embankment.

Burke's hand curled around a clump of grass, pulling it up by the roots. He tossed the missile into the midst of the flowing water. The heavy dirt on the roots made a splash. Ripples started to spread, then blended with the movement of the stream. He thought if he had Richard here he would throw him into the middle of the river. He'd never felt so protective and vulnerable as he had when he'd seen the wounded look on Blaire's face today.

He hadn't attended church with Isabel or Blaire since the Sunday when the pastor talked about green pastures, but he hadn't been able to get the message out of his mind, either. "God, I don't understand this. I don't understand You. Why is this happening to Blaire? If this is Your green pasture like the pastor said, then why does she want to leave, and why is she being hurt? I don't know if I even believe that Scripture is right."

Burke plucked another clump of grass from the bank and hurled it into the water. This was his place to come for quiet. He liked to sit and think. Sometimes he'd talked to God, but he hadn't done that in a long time. After his grandmother had died, this place had been a refuge for him. He'd never even brought a friend with him.

He picked a weed and began to pull the leaves from the stem. "Take the first part of that Psalm. The part that says You're my shepherd and I won't want. Well, that's not true. I remember praying with Mom when I was young. I asked You to be my Savior. But I still had wants. I wanted a mother to be there and raise me. I wanted a grandmother who didn't desert me. I wanted someone who really cared, and I don't think You ever did."

Burke wasn't sure how this conversation had changed from Blaire to himself. Tears burned in his eyes. A lump built in his throat. "Isn't the Bible saying You'll take care of our wants? Well, You never did that for me, God, and now it seems like You're not doing that for Blaire, either."

He put his hat on the ground beside him and covered his face with his hands. Pressing his thumbs into his eyes, he tried to stem his emotions. "I'm so confused, Lord. I don't want to love any woman. I know they can't be trusted. But I can't seem to help myself with Blaire. She's like the half of me that's been missing all along." He scrubbed at his face.

"Help me, Lord. I don't know why I feel so protective of Blaire. We've only known each other a few weeks, yet I feel as if I've known her forever. I think about her all the time. I want to run from her, but I can't." The water rippled and swirled below his feet.

Unwanted memories of Julie swam before him. His high school sweetheart. Beautiful, vivacious Julie, every guy's dream, but she'd belonged to him. They were engaged when he left for college. Only one more year and she would graduate. They'd planned to marry when he came home for the summer. "Lord, help me to know Blaire won't be like Julie. Help me know what to do."

No answers came. Burke didn't feel any peace. He wasn't even sure God had heard him or cared. The breeze dried the excess moisture from his eyes, and after a while he picked up his hat, climbed into the truck, and drove away feeling as confused as ever.

The ranch was quiet when he returned. Late afternoon shadows covered the house. He opened the front door and stuck his head in. "Hello?" The house echoed with an empty silence. Where had Blaire gone?

In the small house he shared with Manuel, Burke found a note saying he had gone to town to see some of his friends. Manuel had done most of the evening chores and had listed what was left to do.

Burke stalked to the barn. This still didn't explain where Blaire could be. Her car was parked out front so she had to be within walking distance. She wouldn't have gone with Manuel. *Why am I so worried about her? I don't want to watch out for her. I'd like it better if she just sold the ranch and left.* Deep down, Burke knew he was lying to himself. He couldn't stand the thought of her leaving.

Stopping inside the barn door, Burke waited for his eyes to adjust to the darkness. The late afternoon sun didn't light the interior. A sound near the back of the barn caught his attention. He smiled. The kittens. He'd forgotten about them.

Stepping carefully, he crept past the various implements cluttering the floor. His breath caught in his throat. Blaire was stretched out on her back in a pile of hay, her hair fanning out like a cloud around her head. The four kittens toddled across her stomach, trying to jump on one another. Each vied for her attention, their little tails stick-straight in the air. Blaire giggled as one tumbled down onto her neck.

Burke had never seen such an arresting sight. He leaned against a wall and watched them play. Blaire rolled over onto her side. As if suddenly aware of his presence, she looked up.

"Oh." She jumped up, kittens rolling off into the hay. She scooped them up. "I'm sorry." She held the little furballs next to her cheek, then flushed. "I didn't hear you come home." She pulled some pieces of hay from her hair and tried to brush off her shorts and top.

"I just got home." Burke crossed his arms over his chest, fighting the urge to wrap his arms around this alluring woman. "I stopped in to see my dad. He asked if we'd like to join him for supper."

Blaire's eyes narrowed. "What, and miss my famous peanut butter and jelly? I believe I'm offended." She stuck her nose in the air. The calico kitten pulled herself up on Blaire's shirt and nuzzled her neck. She giggled and tucked in her chin. "Sprinkles, stop that. I'm trying to be serious here."

"I didn't realize you'd gotten them so tamed." Burke walked over and picked up one of the kittens still on the ground. "You must have been spending a lot of time with them."

"I've never had a baby animal like this. I didn't realize they could be so cuddly." Blaire lifted the kitten up to her face. A tiny paw batted her nose.

"This is probably their cutest age." Burke squatted down and waved a piece of straw in front of the kittens. One pounced, then another. In a moment they were falling all over each other to catch the straw that kept eluding them. "I think they're ready to give away. Would you like to take them over to the ranch this evening?"

Blaire sank down into the hay. "I worry that they'll just end up being eaten by the coyotes. They're so little." She rubbed a kitten against her cheek.

"We can put them in my dad's barn. There's lots of hay there where they can hide. They'll be well fed. These kittens won't be in any more danger there than they're in here."

The kitten in Blaire's arms jumped to the ground, landing on one of the other kittens. They rolled over in a mock battle. She smiled, her azure eyes seeking out his. "I don't think they're in any danger here."

Standing up, she stretched. "Do we have chores to do before we leave for your dad's ranch? I'm already getting hungry."

Burke grabbed a can of feed and followed her out of the barn. He grabbed her arm. She stopped and looked at him.

"I don't understand." Burke stared into her peaceful eyes. No sign of hurt remained. "When I left, you were so upset. Now you act as if nothing has happened. Why?"

A smile washed over her. "I had a talk with Jesus. He heals wounds." She sauntered over to the ostrich pen where Burke was taking the food and leaned against a small tree outside the fence. Burke stopped beside her. The ostriches stalked across the enclosure toward them.

"When Richard left me, I thought my world would end. I blamed God at first. But the more I hurt, the more I realized my need to give my whole life to Jesus. I had prayed for Jesus to come into my heart as a child, but I'd never committed my life to Him as an adult. I was still running the show."

Blaire picked a leaf from the tree and twisted it in her fingers. "I can't explain the change when I put Jesus in charge of everything. In fact, I've been struggling with this issue still."

"How's that?"

"Well, I tend to think I know what God wants for me and then run with it. I forget that because I don't see the whole plan, there may be changes I don't know about."

Burke shook his head. "I don't think I understand."

Taking a deep breath, Blaire pursed her lips and let the air out slowly. "It's like the ranch. When I first heard about my inheritance, I was sure this was what God wanted for me. Then when I saw the ranch, I knew this couldn't be God's plan. Now, I'm not sure what to think. The more I'm here, the more I want to stay. This place has been a balm for me. I've never felt such peace." She brushed the hair back from her face. "On the other hand, I still feel I'm a city girl. I don't belong in a place like this."

Something grabbed Burke's pant leg and tugged. He looked down. One of the kittens was halfway up his shin, digging its tiny claws in to climb farther. "Hey, fella." He reached down and plucked the kitten off his leg. "Look who followed us out here." He held out the kitten to Blaire.

"You bad kitty." She took the baby from him and snuggled it to her face. "I'll put him back in the barn, while you feed the ostriches."

Burke started to head for the feed dishes when he noticed the ostriches acting funny. They circled a small pile of rocks about ten feet into the pen.

"Blaire, I think we've got trouble."

She turned. An ostrich neck snaked out toward the rocks. "Hssst!" A kitten jumped back from the ostrich. The fur spiked straight out from the kitten's back. A noise of half yowl, half growl, drifted through the fence.

Blaire grabbed his arm. "It's Sprinkles. You've got to save her."

Chapter 12

I don't know how I can help her." Burke started to circle to the gate. Maybe he could distract the ostriches long enough for the kitten to get to the fence. He heard another series of hisses as one of the ostriches tried to peck at the kitten. The poor kitten's tail looked like a pine tree with the branches perpendicular to the trunk.

"What are you doing?" Blaire hurried after him, clutching the other kitten.

He stopped with his hand on the gate, lifted his hat, then set it back on his head. "I want you to go to the part of the fence closest to the kitten. When you see the ostriches come my way, call her to you."

"But you could get hurt."

Burke gazed into Blaire's eyes and saw fear. Did she care about him? Was this concern different from the feelings she would have for someone else in this situation? Somehow, he wanted to hope this was special.

"I'll be fine. These ostriches know me. Besides, I'm good at rescuing damsels in distress, right?" He slipped the catch off the gate and let himself through. He waited until Blaire returned to the area closest to the kitten.

Gliding toward the feeding pans, Burke shook the can of feed in his hand. Usually, he slipped the feed in while on the other side of the fence. This time he hoped he could use the feed to distract the ostriches without angering the male. He shook the can a little harder. The feed rattled. The ostriches looked around.

The male ostrich lifted his head. He swung around. The females headed for the feeder. The male focused on Burke. He stalked across the pen like an avenging protector. Burke's heart pounded. He backed toward the fence. Maybe this wasn't the best idea.

Glancing to the side, he saw Blaire beckoning to the kitten. She called softly, but the male ostrich hesitated. He tilted his head and turned to look back at the rocks. Burke rattled the can.

In a flash of movement, the ostrich charged Burke. His wings stood out to the side. His neck stretched out, and his feet dug into the dirt. Breathing hard, Burke reached behind him. He felt the gate catch. He jerked the gate open and tumbled through, slamming the gate shut just before the enraged male reached him.

❧

Blaire paused in her attempts to get the terrified kitten to come to her. She couldn't believe how fast the male ostrich was running at Burke. She opened her mouth to scream, but there wasn't time. Burke nearly fell through the gate. The feed can dropped to the ground, spilling pellets in the dust.

"Mew."

She looked back to see the kitten slinking toward the fence and her. The ostrich must have heard the noise. He didn't slow as the gate slammed, instead circling around and racing across the pen. The terrified kitten flattened herself against the ground. She hissed. Her fur stood on end. The ostrich extended his neck, beak wide open.

"No!" Blaire waved her hand at him, trying to stop the charge. She wished for something to throw, but there was no time. The male grabbed the calico's tail. Raising his long neck, he flipped the kitten into the air. Yowling, the tiny cat flipped end over end through the air. Blaire held her breath. She'd never felt so helpless in all her life. Sprinkles flew over the fence and landed in the dirt with a thud.

Burke passed her as they both headed toward the small, inert form. He knelt down and touched the body. The kitten leaped up. On tiptoes she hissed and spit. Blaire covered her mouth, trying to hold in the laughter. Sprinkles looked like a caricature of a cat with its tail in an electrical outlet.

"Whoa there, sweetheart. I just want to see if you're okay." Burke held out his hand and continued to speak soft and low. Within minutes, the kitten had clambered into his lap, purring loudly enough to wake the neighbors if they had any.

"The knight in shining armor wins again." Blaire chuckled.

Burke grinned. "That wasn't exactly how I planned to get said damsel out of the pen. At least she's forgiven me."

"Well, I see you're right about the kittens. Now that they're weaned, we should take them to the ranch this evening. Somehow I can't picture cows running around with kittens dangling from their mouths." Even though Blaire knew the decision was right, she still would miss the kittens when they were gone.

⨀

June arrived. Blaire couldn't believe the heat in Arizona. She didn't remember the Midwest ever being this hot, even with the humidity factor. She had the books straightened out and all the ranch's business on the computer. Several of the breeders and young ostriches had been sold. She knew she had decisions to make that she'd been putting off. Did she want to sell the ranch or did she want to stay? She prayed every day for an answer, but nothing came. She knew she would probably be happier in the city. Hadn't she always loved her life there?

However, country life had grown on her. The majesty of the mountains around her home never failed to amaze her. The gorgeous sunrises and sunsets made her catch her breath in wonder. Most of all, the peace and time of refreshment with Jesus had been such a healing balm that she didn't want to leave. She'd even begun to enjoy all the attention she received at church.

Only two issues marred the horizon. Richard had continued to bother her. He sent her e-mails and had called several times. She never returned the calls or the e-mails, thinking he would take the hint. Since she hadn't heard from him in two weeks, she assumed her strategy had worked.

The other issue was Burke. Somehow, she'd fallen in love with him. She hadn't wanted to. She tried to stay away from him. She knew how dangerous it was to fall for someone she worked with. Despite all her protections against him, Burke had wormed his way into her heart. She didn't know what to do about him.

◈

"I need to talk to all of you." Blaire sat at the table with Isabel, Manuel, and Burke. They all looked at her. An expectant hush filled the air.

"What is it, *mija*?" Isabel stood and began to clear the supper dishes.

"No, Isabel, sit down." Blaire touched her friend's arm. "I want you to hear what I have to say."

Taking a deep breath, Blaire released a silent prayer for help. "I've enjoyed getting to know you. I can see why Uncle Ike loved you so much."

Burke's eyes narrowed. Manuel ran his finger over his unused spoon. Isabel folded her hands and lowered them to her lap.

"I can't decide what God wants me to do. I've prayed and have no clear answers. I've finished the books and know the value of the ranch." She wanted to close her eyes but didn't dare. "I know Burke is taking a delivery of blown eggs to Tucson tomorrow. I'm planning to ride along and visit a couple of real estate agents. I've already been in touch with them."

Burke's hands slapped down on the table. He pushed himself up.

"Wait." Blaire covered his hand with hers. She met his eyes, pleading silently with him. "Please, hear me out."

Burke sank back down. His fingers continued gripping the table.

"I know this is your life. I want to make sure you are taken care of, especially Isabel. If I do find a buyer, I'll see if they are compatible and will continue to keep you on here. If they don't want you to stay, then I will provide enough from the sale to get Isabel set up with a place of her own." She looked at Isabel. Misery gripped her heart as she saw the tears in the older woman's eyes.

"*Mija,* that is a wonderful gesture. You don't have to do this."

"I know, but I care so much for you, Isabel. You were all special to my uncle, and you've become special to me. I don't want to leave you without a job or a means of support."

"Whatever you do will be fine, *mija.*" Isabel patted Blaire's cheek and began to clear the table.

"Sounds good to me." Manuel tossed the spoon back on the table. "I'm heading for town."

Blaire focused on her hands. She didn't want to look at Burke. Would he be able to understand? He wanted so much for her to keep the ranch, but she wasn't sure she could stay around him much longer.

A large calloused hand brushed her cheek. She looked up. Burke leaned close. "Thank you. It means so much that you're thinking of Isabel." He stood and headed out the door without another word. Blaire escaped to her room before the lump in her throat turned into a bout of tears.

⁂

The day in Tucson flew past. Blaire loved visiting the woman who bought the eggs from them. She showed them her workshop. Decorated eggs lined the shelves on the walls. She showed them a lamp whose base was made from a hollow ostrich egg with a scene etched on it. When Blaire praised the artistry, the woman brought out some more lamps for her to look at. Blaire couldn't decide if she liked the one with the giraffes or the one picturing the resurrection best.

In the afternoon, Blaire and Burke visited the Realtors. Blaire decided which agent she wanted to work with and listed the ranch for three months to see what would happen. She thought if God wanted her to sell the ranch, He would provide a buyer in that short period. The Realtor, Janice Burns, was horrified. "You can't expect to sell such a large property in such a short time period. It just doesn't happen." Blaire had been adamant. Janice finally conceded and wrote up the contract.

By the time they left the real estate office, dark clouds were building in the distance. "Looks like we might get some rain today." Burke lifted his face to the wind. "I wonder if the monsoons are coming early."

"The air feels a little muggy." Blaire tugged at the collar of her blouse. "At least it's a little cooler."

Burke grinned at her, his eyes twinkling. "What do you say we do something special before we have supper and head home?"

"What did you have in mind?" Blaire couldn't help being suspicious. He was grinning like a Cheshire cat.

"Let's go to the zoo. We're not far from there." He looked like a little boy pleading with his mom. He leaned close as if whispering a secret in her ear. "They have giraffes."

"Why didn't you say so?" Blaire started walking to the truck. She laughed at the astonished look on his face. "You didn't expect me to give in this easily, did you? Now you know what happens when you say the magic word—giraffe."

It proved to be the perfect time to visit the zoo. Due to the clouds rolling in and the cooler temperature, many of the animals that normally slept through the hot afternoons were awake. Blaire decided that going to the zoo with Burke was better than having a young child along. From the moment they crossed through the gate onto the zoo grounds, he changed from a grown man to a little boy. He led Blaire from one exhibit to another. They watched the lions, the tigers, and the bears. He grabbed her hand and had her almost running when they heard the polar bears were swimming. First, they stood above, watching the huge bears cavort in the water with a bowling ball, acting as if it weighed no more than a beach ball. Then Burke led her underground to the windows looking out into the water. Bears turned somersaults and swam effortlessly in the deep water.

"They're so graceful."

Burke could hear the awe in Blaire's voice. She stood close, her shoulder brushing against his. He wanted to put his arm around her and pull her tight against him. What would it feel like to stand here with her head resting against his shoulder? He knew he had to be careful. She was his boss, and he didn't want to cross a line that would make her run.

"I think I hear the giraffes calling."

She turned and made a face at him. "Giraffes don't call. Besides, what would they say?"

He put his hand on her back, guiding her to the exhibit. A mother pushed a stroller down the ramp, and he moved closer to Blaire. "Be quiet. Let me listen." He tilted his head to the side. Blaire's mouth twitched as she watched him. "Ah, yes. They're saying something about seeing a beautiful young woman who has great taste in collectibles."

Burke held his breath. Had he gone too far? Would Blaire be offended with his flirting? He hadn't meant to; the words had slipped out.

Blaire's laugh set him at ease. She gazed across the fence at the stately giraffes. "I don't know why Uncle Ike didn't start a giraffe ranch. I would've loved raising them."

"But you would have a hard time eating them."

Blaire looked horrified. "I won't eat ostrich, either."

"Oops! Too late. I believe Isabel uses a lot of ground ostrich in her recipes." He leaned forward, studying Blaire's face. "Are you turning green?"

Thunder rumbled in the distance, cutting off Blaire's reply.

"We'd better finish up the zoo." Burke gestured at the sky. "Looks like if we don't get through soon, we'll get wet."

They stopped briefly to watch the monkeys chase one another through the tree limbs in their cage. The sky darkened, lightning flashed, and thunder rumbled louder and closer. Burke took her hand and led her through the maze of paths that wound past the various animals.

As they walked past the last row of cages housing the assorted members of the ape family, large drops of water began to splat on the sidewalk. Burke could see a deluge heading their way. Spotting a tarp set up over a nearby lawn, he pulled Blaire in that direction. They didn't have time to reach their car or even the covered eating area. Several other zoo visitors joined them in their temporary shelter.

"We'll wait here. The rain shouldn't last long," Burke said.

The skies opened and rain poured down. The air cooled. Burke pulled Blaire closer to the edge to allow two more people under the tarp. Lightning flashed, followed by a crack of thunder that shook the ground.

Blaire looked up at him and grinned. She said something. He shook his head, trying to tell her he hadn't heard. She turned and leaned close. Burke tried to concentrate on her words and not her closeness.

"How long will this last?"

Burke leaned close, his mouth beside her ear so she could hear. "It should let up in a few minutes. These downpours don't last too long."

An ear-splitting crack of thunder drowned Blaire's reply. Burke gestured for her to repeat what she'd said.

"And you call this a rain?" Everyone heard Blaire's words during a short lull in the storm. "In Chicago we get rain like this, and it lasts all day." Blaire's eyes sparkled with mirth. The wind picked up, blowing her hair across her face. She brushed the strands away from her eyes and stepped away from him.

Burke reached out to bring her back from the edge of the tarp, but he was too late. A sudden gust of wind lifted the center of the covering. Rainwater that had collected in a pocket cascaded down in a waterfall. Blaire's eyes widened. Water gushed over her face and down her back. Her mouth formed a perfect O. She looked as if someone had dumped a bucket of water on her head.

Burke couldn't resist. Biting back a laugh, he gestured at the storm. "Never mess with an Arizona monsoon."

Chapter 13

Blaire's hair and clothes were almost dry by the time they pulled up in front of the house. "Oh, I can't wait to get a shower." She held up her hand to stop Burke before he spoke. "I know I've already had one shower." She wrinkled her nose at him. "I was referring to a real washing with soap and shampoo."

"Was I going to say something?" Burke feigned an innocent expression. He chuckled. "Come on. I'll help carry in the groceries. I think we can get them all in one trip."

The night breeze carried the aroma of rain-washed ground. Crickets and cicadas sang their nightly chorus. Blaire tilted her head back to look at the sky. Remnants of clouds drifted across a star-sprinkled sky. A nearly full moon bathed the earth in a golden glow. She couldn't remember seeing anything this beautiful in the city. There, the tall buildings and bright lights blocked any view of the sky.

"You gonna stand out here all night? That ice cream you're carrying may not adjust to the heat."

Blaire hurried to where Burke held the door open for her. "Sorry. I just can't get over how much sky there is out here."

"If you want, we can sit in the swing for a while after we put away the groceries. This is the best time of year to sit outside."

Blaire looked up at Burke as she passed him. His hat and the darkness shadowed his eyes. Was this an innocent request? Could she sit beside him and ignore the attraction she had for him? Somehow it didn't seem to matter so much right now. They'd had such a wonderful day, she didn't want their time together to end.

"I think I'd like that." She smiled and headed for the kitchen.

Opening the freezer without turning on the light, Blaire began putting ice cream containers away. Burke flipped on the light as he entered the kitchen behind her.

"Hmm. This looks good."

Blaire shut the freezer and turned to see what he was talking about. "Are you thinking of eating again? What did Isabel leave out for you?"

She walked over to the table and peered around Burke. There on the table stood a large basket filled with greenery. Shooting up from the fake green plants

78

were a dozen heart-shaped cookies. Decorated in various pastel shades, each cookie said "I love you"in sparkling gold icing. A multi-hued pastel ribbon wound around the gold basket holding the arrangement. A small gold card nestled in the bottom of the basket. Blaire's name was inscribed on the card.

"Somehow I don't think Isabel made this."Burke fingered the colorful ribbon. "She's not usually this fancy."

A sense of dread descended on Blaire as she reached for the envelope. She slipped the card out.

"I can't believe he's doing this. I don't understand." Tears welled up in her eyes. "Listen to this." She couldn't keep the anger out of her voice. " 'My dearest Blaire. I can't get you off my mind. I'm coming to see you tomorrow. I love you more than ever. Your loving fiancé, Richard.'"

She threw the card at the basket of cookies. "How dare he consider himself to still be engaged to me? Who does he think he is? Here he takes off with the secretary, breaks our engagement, puts everyone out of a job, and he thinks I should forget all that."

Burke wrapped his arms around her, pulling her close.

"I'm ranting, aren't I?" Blaire could barely speak past the lump in her throat.

"You have every right to rant." The comforting rumble of Burke's voice made her relax against his chest. His hand rubbed her back. Tears slid down her cheeks.

"I'm so angry I could spit."

Burke hugged her closer. "Please save the spitting for tomorrow."

She slapped her hand against his chest. "Don't you make me laugh when I'm doing my best to throw a fit." A picture of her spitting on Richard in the expensive suit that he always wore flashed across her mind. Something between a sob and a giggle escaped her.

"You aren't laughing, are you?"

She tipped her head back. His green eyes caught and held hers. His mouth quirked up in a smile. Blaire pushed away from him. She wanted him to hold her too much. The temptation was too great. "Thanks for listening. I think I'm going to pass on the swing tonight. I need some time alone."

Burke gazed down at her. She couldn't look away. He reached up and cupped her cheek. She wanted to close her eyes and lean into the caress, but she couldn't. He nodded and stepped back.

"I'll see you in the morning."When he turned and left the kitchen, she felt as if some part of her was missing.

⁓

Early the next afternoon, a rented sports car pulled up in the drive. Blaire watched from the bedroom window as Richard climbed out from behind the wheel. He paused before closing the door, obviously surveying the ranch. With a flip of his wrist, he swung the door shut and sauntered toward the house.

"Thank You, Jesus. I can't believe the peace You've given me." Blaire hadn't been able to sleep the night before after Burke left. Instead, she'd spent a couple hours praying and studying her Bible. She'd come to realize that worrying about Richard wasn't what God wanted. She turned the matter over to God and spent the rest of the night sleeping peacefully. Now, she felt nothing. No anger, remorse, attraction. There seemed to be a shield between her and the world, as if God was protecting her.

"Blaire, you have a visitor." Isabel stood at the doorway, a look of concern on her face.

"Thank you, Isabel. I'll be right there." Blaire gave a final glance in the mirror before following Isabel to the living room. Richard stood with his back to her, his hands clasped together behind his back in what he always referred to as his board-of-director's stance. As he turned, she could see the frown on his face.

Richard caught sight of her, and his handsome features melted into the smile that won every heart at Bennett and Sons. He stretched out his hands. "Blaire, I've missed you so much." He waited, and she knew he expected her to come to him.

"How's Vanessa, Richard?"

The perfect smile showing his perfect teeth faltered. "Oh, that." He gave a slight laugh. "Surely you don't hold a little indiscretion against me, sweetheart. Every bridegroom gets a touch of cold feet and wants one last fling."

"I don't know any who have done that other than you, and I am not your sweetheart." An image of her spitting at Richard crossed her mind. She bit her lip to keep from smiling. Somehow that vision looked more and more tempting.

Richard managed to look wounded. "We're engaged, Blaire. I have the right to call my future wife by an endearment if I want, don't I?"

"In case you've forgotten, you broke our engagement, Richard. I have no idea why you're here, and I'd like for you to leave."

Striding across the room, Richard came within what she was sure would be spitting distance before he stopped. "Why, I came to see you and your new holdings. I know the wedding has to be delayed, but I'm sure we can arrange the ceremony by the end of summer."

Blaire's hands closed into fists. "Richard, understand this. I am not now, nor am I ever going to marry you. Our engagement was a major mistake on my part."

"Ah, Blaire." He reached out to touch her, and she backed up a step. "Always independent, weren't you? Come, let's go outside, and you can show me your inheritance."

She stared at him. "Is that what this is all about, Richard? Are you suddenly interested in me again because I've inherited Uncle Ike's ranch?"

"Of course not." The million-dollar grin spread over his face again. "I did read up on ostriches, though. They are fascinating creatures, aren't they? What kind of ostriches do you have here?"

"The kind with long necks and long legs." Blaire headed out the door, hoping she could walk him to his car and hasten his departure.

Richard chuckled. "No, dear. I found out that some ostriches are much more valuable than others. I wondered what type you have."

"We have South African blacks." She reached the sports car and turned. Richard was halfway to the first ostrich pens. *I'm gonna start spitting any minute, and he won't like it.* She stalked across the yard after him. From the corner of her eye, she saw Isabel walking toward the house with Burke and Manuel. She must have gone to tell them that Richard had arrived. Maybe they could all take turns spitting on him. *Lord, I have got to get my thoughts under control. Please help me not to be bitter over the way Richard treated me.*

Richard stood outside a pen of juvenile males, studying the ostriches, rubbing his chin. She remembered the gesture from all the times he would lean back in his chair in the office as if in deep thought about a client's accounts.

"So, Richard, have you reopened Bennett and Sons, or are all those people still out of work?"

His eyes widened in a totally innocent expression. "Why, Blaire, that was only a temporary layoff. All the workers who wanted to return are back to work."

"How many?" Blaire leaned forward, wondering if she would get a straight answer.

"Well, several of our former employees had already gotten other jobs by the time the layoff was over. Consequently, we didn't hire them back."

"How many are working now?"

He cleared his throat and turned back to the ostriches.

"What did you say, Richard? I don't think I heard you."

"Four." His composure slipped as he snapped at her. "We have four employees working right now."

She nodded, thinking of all her coworkers who'd been devastated last December when their place of employment had closed down. She hoped Richard was stating the truth when he said they had jobs. She studied his profile. What on earth had she ever seen in this pompous buffoon? Had she been so blinded by money, looks, and prestige that she'd overlooked his egotism? The thought was embarrassing.

"Richard, there is nothing here for you. If you came hoping to woo me into marrying you so you could have access to my money, it won't work. Now please leave."

Before she could step back, Richard's arm swept around her, hauling her close to him. "I always liked your feistiness, Blaire." He leaned close, his dark blue eyes holding none of the smile on his face. "I know you're just a little angry and hurt, but you'll come around. Now, why don't you show me this ranch I'm going to help you with when we're married?"

"I believe Miss Mackenzie asked you to leave."

Richard loosened his grip, and Blaire stumbled back. Burke caught her and pulled her to his side.

"Is this the hired help?" Richard gave Burke a condescending look.

"This is Burke Dunham, my ranch manager." Blaire turned to Isabel and Manuel, standing slightly behind Burke. "This is Isabel Ortega and her son, Manuel. They work here, too."

Richard clasped his hands behind his back and rocked on his heels. "I've heard that in border states like this, one can hire illegal aliens for much less pay. That's practicing good business, Blaire."

Anger raced through her. Isabel grabbed Manuel's arm. Burke stiffened beside her.

"Isabel and Manuel are U.S. citizens, Richard. I don't appreciate your insinuations. They are valuable to the running of this ranch."

"Would you like to leave on your own, or would you like for Manuel and me to escort you to your car?" Burke's jaw clenched as he finished speaking.

Blaire smiled at him, hoping to ease some of the tension. Burke glanced down at her, then placed a hand on her shoulder as if trying to reassure her everything would be all right.

"Oh, I see what's happening here." The sneer on Richard's face didn't add to his good looks. "You want me to leave because you've already replaced me. Is that your game, Blaire? Exactly what does this country bumpkin have?"

"I haven't replaced you with anyone, Richard. I didn't come out here looking for a man to marry. Burke is my manager and a friend. I couldn't run this ranch without him."

"So, you think I can't work with these stupid birds?" Richard's face reddened. "I'm telling you, I read up on them before I came out here. Watch this." He whirled around, opened the gate, and strode into the pen before they could stop him.

The young ostriches lifted their heads. They tilted them to one side. Richard continued to move toward them, although his stride had shortened.

"Richard, come out of there before you get hurt."

"I will not get hurt. I read that only the males who are mating are dangerous."

The dark-feathered ostriches spread out, circling and moving closer to the strange human. Blaire turned to Burke. He had his arms folded across his chest. He flashed a grin back at Manuel. They didn't say anything.

Suddenly, the ostriches began pulling at Richard's coat. Blaire remembered the ostriches doing the same thing with her skirt. Richard tried to back away, but more birds were behind him. He lost his balance and fell to one knee. The birds poked at him with their beaks. He fell on his face, covering his head with his arms. With expressions of glee, the youngsters entered into their new game. They began rolling Richard around the pen, pulling at him. Blaire heard a tear and saw a button pop off. She hated to think how much his suit cost. It wouldn't be worth anything now.

Richard yelled. The ostriches tilted their heads and stopped. Richard lunged upward, pivoting from left to right as if searching for the gate. He spotted Blaire and started to stumble toward her. The ostriches knocked him down.

"Will they hurt him?" She felt more than heard Burke chuckling behind her.

"Oh, I imagine he'll be a little sore, but they're just playing."

An ostrich plucked at a sleeve. It tore free. A foot stepped on a pant leg. Richard rolled closer to the gate, and the pant's leg tore. Within moments, Richard's fancy clothes were in tatters. He stumbled up and grabbed the catch. He swung the gate open and fell through. His jacket remained a pull toy in the pen. His shirt, minus the sleeves, only covered his shoulders. His pants, partially intact, were torn shorter than any shorts Blaire had ever seen. Only his tie remained unscathed, a ludicrous reminder of his once-perfect attire. Blaire looked away, trying hard to feel some sympathy.

Burke stepped forward and closed the pen before the ostriches escaped. Richard staggered to his feet. He tried to pull the ribbons of his pants together, but to no avail. With a look of pure hatred at the group watching him, he headed for his car in a limping stumble.

"I declare, Manuel, if that's the way they're dressing in the big city now, I believe I'll stay a country bumpkin." Burke's loud comment echoed across the grounds.

Richard jerked open his car door. He stepped behind the door and stopped. "You'll regret this, Blaire Mackenzie." Richard tightened his tie, climbed in the car, and spun out down the driveway.

Chapter 14

The whir of the newly installed fax machine woke Blaire the next morning. She climbed out of bed, stretched, then walked through to the office to see if a new order for ostriches had arrived. If so, she would have to let Burke know immediately. The fax machine had been her idea, and Burke loved the convenience. Prospective buyers could fax their orders rather than send them in the mail or via e-mail. This way Burke didn't even have to bother with the computer. Blaire quickly scanned the message:

> *Have found a prospective buyer for your ranch. Will be bringing the Wilsons to see the place this afternoon. Please try to be there to help show the place. I'm not familiar enough with your holdings to do a proper job. After this time I should be able to handle showings by myself.*
> *Janice Burns, Realtor*

A loud creak broke the silence as Blaire dropped into the office chair. A buyer? So soon? She hadn't expected that. What if they bought the ranch? She would have to leave. Would they want Isabel and Manuel to stay on? What would Burke do? Her heart ached. These people were her friends now. Startled, she realized she didn't want to lose them as friends. The loss would be too great.

"Wait a minute. What am I thinking?" Blaire got up and paced back into her room, the fax still clutched in her hand. "This could be the beginning of my dream. With the money from this sale, I'll start my own office. I don't have to go back to Chicago. Any big city will do."

For several minutes she continued to talk with herself about the advantages of the sale. She felt as if she were trying to convince herself of something that wasn't right to do. She sank down on the bed and picked up her Bible. Smoothing her hand over the leather binding, she chewed her lip. *Lord, I don't want to go against Your will for my life. I'm not so sure about You wanting me to be anywhere else.* She turned to the familiar passage in Psalm 23. "'He maketh me to lie down in green pastures.'" She ran a fingertip over the words as if that would help her understand better. "Lord, help me know for sure what You want. When these people are here today, make Your will clear. Thank You, Jesus."

She pulled on a pair of jeans and an old T-shirt. After freshening up, she headed for the kitchen. Manuel, just finished with his breakfast, stood and carried his dishes to the sink as she entered. Burke and Isabel sat across from each other. They all smiled at her. Blaire felt warmed. These people cared for her.

She tossed the crumpled fax on the table as she sat down. "I just got this fax. Janice Burns, the Realtor, is bringing a couple by to look at the place this afternoon." The warm atmosphere chilled. Burke's eyes darkened to a stormy aqua. His narrowed eyes and tightened jaw spoke volumes.

Blaire turned to Isabel. "I'll help you with chores and any cleaning that needs to be done, Isabel. They won't be here until afternoon."

Isabel patted her hand. A faltering smile began, then faded. "Thank you for the offer. I'll do my best to have the house ready for them."

Burke's chair scraped against the tile floor like chalk against a blackboard. He carried his dishes to the sink, then grabbed his hat from the hat rack and slammed it on his head. Manuel shot an accusatory look at Blaire as he followed Burke out the door.

Blaire stared down at her hands, folded in her lap. A lump filled her throat. Tears burned her eyes. She felt as if she'd lost a good friend. *Why do I care so much what he thinks? I'm not interested in him. He works for me.*

"Mija." Isabel's hand rested lightly on Blaire's shoulder. "I know you're confused about what you should do. I also can see how much you care for Burke. Trust Jesus, *mija.* He'll show you what to do."

Hot tears trickled down her cheeks as Blaire lifted her head. She tried to say something, but the words wouldn't come. Isabel wrapped her arms around Blaire. For several moments, Blaire leaned against the comforting warmth of the older woman. Isabel handed her a tissue and stepped away. Blaire wiped her eyes and blew her nose.

"Thank you. I do want to do what's right. I'm not trying to hurt anyone."

Isabel sat down in the chair next to her and clasped Blaire's hand in her own. "I understand that. I think Burke is hurting. He feels something for you, too."

"He does?"

"I've never seen him so interested in a woman. Maybe God brought you here to meet him." Isabel smiled, a far-off look in her eyes.

"That can't be, Isabel. I made the mistake of having a relationship with Richard when I worked for him. I won't make the same mistake again." Blaire stood and headed for the door. "I'll start in the hatchery. Let me know if there's anything special you want me to help with this morning." She closed the door firmly, forcing herself not to look at Isabel. She couldn't stand to see that she'd hurt her friend again.

✑⌒

The afternoon sun was falling toward the western mountains when Burke saw the white Cadillac easing down the driveway. Even at slow speed, the car created a cloud of dust in its wake. He could see Janice Burns's look of distaste as she pulled up in front of the house. A sprig of hope blossomed. Perhaps, if the Realtor disliked the place, the potential buyer would also be repulsed.

Janice stepped out and waved a hand at the settling dust. She adjusted her navy blazer, managing to look cool despite the heat. She walked around the front of the car, pausing to peer at the white paint as if to see how dirty her precious car had gotten on the drive out.

The passenger doors opened. A portly gentleman climbed out of the front, then turned to give his hand to the equally stout lady clambering out from the back. The pair reminded Burke of Tweedledee and Tweedledum from *Alice in Wonderland*. They wore identical white suits and matching royal blue shirts. Tall cowboy hats sat on white hair that curled out from beneath the brim. He blinked, wondering if he were seeing double. The main difference was the heavy turquoise necklace that clashed with the woman's shirt. Both had heavy turquoise bracelets and watches. Only the woman sported dangling turquoise-and-silver earrings.

Blaire stepped from the house. Burke couldn't take his eyes from her. The gauzy blue-flowered skirt and blouse she wore accented her trim form. He knew if he were close enough he would see the dazzling blue of her eyes made brighter by the outfit. She must have a curling iron, for her normally wavy hair curled lightly around her face. She didn't walk out to greet her company, she glided. He knew that she felt she was a klutz, but she had a grace few women ever attained.

"Good afternoon, Mrs. Burns. Did you have any trouble finding the house?" Blaire stretched out her hand to greet the Realtor.

Janice's smile looked a tad strained. "I don't think I realized quite how far away from town you are. I planned to get up here by myself, but the Wilsons were so enamored with your listing they insisted on coming out today." Janice made introductions, and Blaire shook hands with the rotund couple, Vern and Fran Wilson.

"This place is a mite off the beaten path to be asking so much." Vern Wilson waved a hand. The rings on his fingers sparkled in the sunlight. "I thought this was an ostrich ranch. I don't see many ostriches."

"Where is the main house?" Fran spoke like a bellows pumped her words out. "I'm surprised the employees' quarters are right here."

Blaire's back stiffened. "This is the main house." She gestured behind her. "This house is made of adobe and has been here for nearly one hundred years. My uncle redid the roof, replacing many of the rafters. If you would like to come in, I believe you'll be amazed by the western charm he achieved."

Fran leaned close to Vern as if to speak privately, but her words could have been heard in the next county. "I expected a mansion for the price. Where will our friends stay when they come to visit? I'll bet this house doesn't have the number of bedrooms we need when we entertain."

A red flush crept up Blaire's cheek. Her hands were clenched into fists. Burke leaned back against the trunk of the tamarisk tree where he'd been sitting in the shade doing some equipment repair. This couple didn't seem too sold on the place so far.

Vern stopped and leaned so far back Burke wondered if he would fall down. Of course, as round as he was, he might just bounce back up again. The comical thought made him bite his lip to keep from laughing.

"This tree has got to go." Vern pointed to the very tree Burke sat under. "First thing you know a tree like this will fall on the house. Someone could get killed." He shook his head and followed his wife through the door.

The urge to laugh had faded with the man's comment. Without this tree the house would be a furnace in the summer. Between the thick adobe walls and the shade of the huge tamarisk tree, Ike's home had always been a respite from the hot Arizona summers.

Leaning over his work, Burke tried to focus. For some reason all he could think about was Blaire. He'd been devastated this morning when she'd mentioned a buyer. For weeks, he'd pushed the possibility of her selling the place to the back of his mind. The longer he knew her, the more he wanted her to stay. Since the day they'd visited the zoo, he'd been struggling with his growing feelings for her. He knew women couldn't be trusted, but he'd also begun to pray. Now, he wanted to bridge the gap between himself and Jesus. He wasn't sure why that was important, but it was.

The door to the house opened. Blaire stalked out, then turned and waited. She held her right arm stiff against her side, fingers kneading the material of her skirt. Her curls were frizzed. He could almost picture her aggravated fingers combing through her hair. Noting the slight droop to her shoulders, the remnants of his anger faded. He wanted to hold her and let her know everything would be better soon.

Burke got up and sauntered toward the door. He knew without asking that Blaire would need his help for the next part of the tour. Her knowledge of the rest of the operation lay mainly in accounting. She hadn't had much experience at the plant.

"We could maybe keep this for a guest house." Vern thumped the wall as he walked out onto the porch. "It would take a lot of fixing up, but we could make this a real western treat. I think some of our guests would like the idea. Of course, it would take a total remodeling job. That means a lot of money."

"But, where would we live?" Fran breathed the words with a slow drawl.

"We'll just have to build ourselves a better house." Vern stepped away from the doorway, letting Fran out.

"What have we here?" Fran stared at Burke, standing a few feet behind Blaire. She lifted her hand and held it out to him like some medieval lady waiting to be kissed by a knight. Burke wasn't sure how she managed to lift her hand. Each finger held at least two huge rings. Her pinky couldn't possibly bend, being almost entirely encased in silver.

"This is my ranch manager, Burke Dunham." Blaire looked relieved to see him. She grasped his arm and pulled him forward.

"Ooh! Does he come with the ranch, too?" Fran batted her mascara-laden lashes at him.

Vern tilted back his head and guffawed. "Just because the place is backward doesn't mean you can still own slaves, my dear."

Burke shook hands with Vern, then Fran. Afterward, he resisted the urge to wipe his hand on his jeans. With a gallantry he didn't know he possessed, he offered to show them the rest of the ranch and explain the way everything worked.

For the next hour, Vern grilled Burke about the details of raising, selling, and processing ostriches. Although the man looked empty-headed, his questions revealed that he had an astute business sense. Surprised by the depth of knowledge they disclosed, Burke wondered just how much homework the man had been able to do in the short time he'd known about the ranch.

When they reached the house again, Blaire invited the Wilsons in for something to drink. Isabel had some lemonade for them. Manuel was working on the evening chores. Burke started to excuse himself, but the look of pure panic on Blaire's face convinced him to stay a little longer.

"We must be heading back to Tucson." Janice stood and straightened her jacket. "Thank you for showing us around. This is quite an operation."

Vern lifted his bulk from the couch, then turned to help Fran to her feet. He pursed his lips and gazed up at the ceiling before looking at Blaire. "I like this place. I'm looking for a tax write-off. A ranch like this should do the trick. By tomorrow I'll have an offer ready for you. I'm sure I can make it worth your while to sell to me."

"You really want to raise those birds?" Fran paled a little as she stared aghast at her husband.

"No." Vern shook his head. "I'm sure we'd get rid of the ostriches. Cattle would be easier to manage. At least it would be easier to find help for a cattle ranch."

"But Uncle Ike worked hard to build this ranch. He specialized in the best ostriches."

Vern grunted and tugged at his pants. "Can't help that, my dear. We'd be a laughing stock with our friends if we had giant chickens around. Now cattle, those make sense to have."

Blaire's shoulders sagged as she walked her prospective buyers to the car. Burke slipped out the back door. He wondered if he needed to begin planning his future. He loved working with the ostriches, but it looked as if his time at this ranch was about finished. He wouldn't stay and work for the Wilsons no matter how much they paid.

Chapter 15

The next evening Blaire wandered out to the porch. She hadn't slept well the night before. Burke had been gone most of the day. She wondered if he was avoiding her.

She trudged over to the porch and settled in the swing. Not having the strength to push, she sat still, contemplating the desert. A roadrunner darted down the hill, probably in search of his evening meal. She tried to picture him with a coyote chasing him down. Somehow, this small comical bird didn't match the long-legged fowl in the cartoon. The roadrunner paused, his head tilted to one side. He stretched out his neck and darted off into the brush.

The front door opened, and Burke stepped out. "Do you have dibs on the swing, or is there room for one more?"

She pulled her skirt closer and tucked it under her legs. "There's room."

The swing creaked as Burke lowered himself. He began to push, and Blaire found herself relaxing with the soothing motion.

"Isabel said supper will be ready soon."

"I think I'll pass. I'm not very hungry."

The quiet stretched between them. Blaire didn't have the energy to carry a conversation.

"What are you watching?" Burke lifted one arm and rested it on the back of the swing behind Blaire. She breathed deeply, trying to ignore the way her heart sped up at his nearness.

"There was a roadrunner over there on the hill. He ran in the brush, and I was wondering if he would come out."

Burke gazed at the brush for a moment. "He's probably after some critter that's come out for its evening meal."

Blaire glanced at him in surprise. He turned to look at her, and she couldn't look away. For once he didn't have his hat on. Short, straw-colored hair looked as if he'd run his fingers through it recently. Aqua eyes perused her with a seriousness she couldn't take right now. His broad shoulder looked like a perfect place to rest her head and try to forget the troublesome decisions she needed to make. She forced her gaze away from his.

"In the cartoon the roadrunner always ate grain. You mean they eat meat?"

Burke tilted his head back and laughed. "In the cartoon the coyote always fell off tall cliffs and lived. I don't think it was meant to be very accurate. Do you know another name they have for the roadrunner?"

She glanced at him and shook her head. "I don't know anything about them."

He leaned closer. Her breath caught in her throat. His eyes twinkled as if he were aware of her discomfort. "They're called snake killers."

Blaire's mouth dropped open. "That was certainly never in the cartoon."

Burke grinned. "Actually, they eat rather large rodents for such a small bird. They eat mice and insects, but they also eat gophers and snakes."

"How do they kill them? They seem like rather timid birds."

"Are you sure you want to know?" Burke's eyebrows lifted. She nodded. "I once saw one snap up a gopher. The gopher struggled, but the roadrunner raced to a nearby rock and killed it. Then the roadrunner swallowed the gopher whole."

"That's disgusting." Blaire pushed against the porch floor, sending the swing a little higher. "I realize I'm from Chicago and know nothing, but there are some things you can't fool me on."

His eyes widened. He put his hand over his heart and gasped. "You're suggesting I'm not telling the truth."

She leaned toward him. "Yes."

The door opened and Manuel stuck his head out. "Supper's ready."

"Say, Manuel." Burke's call stopped him from closing the door. "How do roadrunners kill gophers?"

Manuel glanced at Blaire, then shrugged. "They beat them to death on rocks." He closed the door.

"He probably knew to say that." Blaire crossed her arms, refusing to be fooled.

Burke stood and offered her his hand. "You can ask Isabel or look it up on the Net."

Her hand fit perfectly in his. He closed his fingers over hers and tugged. She came off the swing more quickly than she intended. Her left leg, curled beneath her all this time, had fallen asleep. She stumbled. Burke wrapped an arm around her. She fell against him.

"Here you are, falling for me again."

She could hear the overtones of laughter in his voice. The scent of aftershave mingled with hay swirled around her. For just a moment, she allowed herself to lean against him. His arm tightened. She thought she felt his cheek brush her hair. Her leg began to tingle. She pushed away.

"I guess we'd better go in." She forced a smile. "You made me talk so much I've worked up an appetite." Blaire realized spending time with Burke had rejuvenated her. She didn't feel the weight she had earlier. She still dreaded the decisions ahead, but somehow she knew she was closer to understanding the right one to make.

The phone rang as they walked into the kitchen. Isabel answered, and Blaire could hear a woman's excited voice from the table across the room. Isabel handed the phone to her.

"This is your Realtor. She says the couple who were here yesterday have made a good offer."

Blaire took the phone and turned her back on the table. She listened without comment, while Janice Burns gushed out the news of the generous offer. This was more money than she'd ever dreamed of having. Nothing would stand in the way of her dreams now. So why didn't she feel elated? Why was that sense of dread creeping back in?

"If you fax me all the information, I'll look it over and get back to you, Janice." She listened again. "Yes, I have your home phone. You wrote the number on the card you gave me. I may take the weekend to pray about this and call you on Monday morning." Janice wasn't happy with that decision. "I'm sorry. I'll let you know as soon as I can." Blaire hung up the phone. *God, You've got to help me with this. I'm so troubled. I want to live according to Your will, but the way just isn't clear. Help me.*

Breakfast was on the table when Burke finally entered the kitchen the next morning. He wasn't usually this late, but he'd tossed and turned most of the night. Thoughts of what Blaire would do with the offer from the Wilsons kept him awake far into the night. He kept remembering how she'd leaned against him when he'd helped her up from the swing. The scent of her hair and the feel of his arms around her haunted him long after he should have been sound asleep. A part of him wanted to trust her. Another part screamed that he couldn't do that. She would sell the ranch, take the money, and they'd never see her again. He'd even prayed, but he wasn't sure God had heard.

"Good morning, Burke." Isabel dished up a plate of food for him. She squeezed his shoulder. Somehow he knew she understood his dilemma.

"Would you like to go to church with us this morning?" Blaire's bright smile surprised him. She must be excited about the sale. "You haven't gone in a long time. All those admirers you have keep asking for you."

Burke grinned. He knew the younger kids at church loved to play with him. "I guess they know a kid when they see one. I'll see if I can get ready in time." He cut a bite of the hash browns. He felt better. Maybe church would help him find the answer he needed. Perhaps this time would be different.

The service was about to begin as Burke followed Isabel and Blaire to their pew. Blaire stopped to hug some of the women and greeted others as they walked down the aisle. He couldn't believe how relaxed and friendly she was with the people after her stiff, formal entry the first time they'd come.

They sat down, and Burke glanced around, acknowledging several greetings from people he'd grown up knowing. He clasped his hands together, waiting for the old uneasiness to start. Instead, a sense of impending excitement coursed through him. Did the feeling have to do with something that was about to happen or was his awareness of Blaire the cause?

By the time Pastor Walker stepped up to the pulpit, Burke could barely sit still. He gripped his Bible to keep from wringing his hands. Every song they sang during the service spoke of one's trust in or walk with the Lord. He couldn't break away from the feeling that God had a special message just for him today. He shifted, bumping against Blaire for the umpteenth time. Blaire glanced up at him, and he shrugged. How could he explain this restlessness when he didn't understand it himself?

Pastor Walker turned once again to Psalm 23. Burke was surprised to find that after all the time he'd been away, they were still studying the same short passage of Scripture.

"This morning we're going to finish up the last of Psalm twenty-three. In fact, those of you who have been here for the whole study know we're going to look at the latter part of verse six: 'And I will dwell in the house of the Lord for ever.' I'd like to start by clarifying some of the words in this passage." He pulled out a sheet of notes from beneath his Bible.

"Let's start with the word *dwell*. We all understand what it means to dwell in a house. I think most of us live in houses, so we assume the word *dwell* in this verse means to live in." He paused and looked at the congregation. "However, this word means more than to live in a house. This has a permanency as in the cleaving of marriage. It also carries a connotation of sitting in quiet, as in an ambush, or waiting. Then there's the word *house*. We all know what a house is. But this word *house* is to a building just like the word *church* is to a place. The church refers to a body of believers. Likewise, the word *house* in this verse is much more than a simple dwelling place.

"This passage is telling us to cleave to God. We can go to Him and sit quietly. We can trust Him with every aspect of our lives, not just with those parts we want to relinquish." The pastor leaned forward. His voice hushed. "God wants every part of you. He wants your hopes, your joys, your wants and needs, your expectations, and your fears."

Straightening, Pastor Walker stared down at his notes. "You know, this week I was reading again the story of Abraham and Sarah. Abraham is referred to as a man of faith, and he had a great faith. He followed God when no one else would. He left his homeland not knowing where he would go. He trusted God completely. . .for a time." Stepping out from behind the pulpit, Pastor Walker moved closer to the congregation. "What happened when famine came to the land? Abraham quit trusting God and went to Egypt."

The pastor stopped and rubbed the back of his neck. "This reminds me of our study of Psalm twenty-three, verse one. Remember the part that says, 'I shall not want'? God supplies all our needs according to His riches in glory as the Scripture says in Philippians chapter four, verse nineteen." He paused and gazed around at the congregation. "I looked this week and I couldn't find anywhere that says God will supply our wants. I wonder if Abraham had his needs met, but perhaps he had some wants that weren't being fulfilled." He grinned. "Maybe he wanted one of the new camels with the built-in TV/VCR." Everyone laughed.

"Whatever happened, Abraham decided to step out and take care of himself. He started trusting in himself rather than in God. When he got to Egypt, he lied about Sarah because he had misplaced his trust. He wasn't dwelling in God's house anymore."

The pastor's voice faded. Burke could feel the sweat beading under his shirt. Hadn't he accused God of not caring for his wants? Did he trust in God? From the time he was little he'd trusted in his mother, grandmother, and father. He'd thought he trusted God, but now he wondered. Was he expecting too much when he wanted to trust in Blaire? Was that an example of not trusting God?

Pastor Walker returned to the pulpit. "Let's look at the final words in this verse. . .'for ever.'" An expectant hush settled over the congregation. "Forever. All your life and into eternity. That's how long you're to dwell with God. That's how long you can trust Him with your life. He'll never leave you nor forsake you. He's always there. He wants what's right for you."

Closing his Bible, Pastor Walker carried it with him as he stepped down from the platform and stood in front of the people. "I want you to recall a time when you gave your whole life to God. I know you might be a Christian, but is there some part of your life you've withheld from God? Are you still trying to run things? Are you like Abraham, trying to head into Egypt rather than waiting on the Lord?"

Burke pulled himself up as the congregation stood and began to sing a hymn of invitation. He felt as if his fingers would make indentations in the pew in front of him. An urgency built inside him. He closed his eyes, trying to wait for the feeling to pass. Blaire began to sing, but he couldn't join her. As if from a distance, he released his grip on the pew and walked down the seemingly endless aisle to the pastor.

Isabel's gasp startled Blaire. She glanced over. Isabel had tears in her eyes. Blaire followed her gaze and saw Burke talking to the pastor. She'd been so caught up in the song and message, she hadn't noticed him leaving. Pastor Walker took Burke's hand, and the two of them knelt in prayer. The people continued to sing.

Pastor Walker stood and held up his hand. The song ended. "Most of you know Burke. He's been coming to church here for a long time. As a youngster he asked Jesus to be his Savior. Today he's come to admit that although he's a Christian, he's never completely surrendered his life to God until today. I wonder how many of us are the same way? We trust in our salvation experience, but we still want to control the reins. We want to call the shots."

He smiled at Burke and squeezed his shoulder. "I'm happy to say that we have a brother here whose faith is strong enough that he can admit that mistake. He's ready to trust only in Jesus. I'd like to close in prayer, then ask you to come give Burke your blessing."

Moisture burned in Blaire's eyes as she closed them for the prayer. She knew what it meant to learn this lesson. She'd had to be humiliated by Richard to come to the point where she'd surrendered her life to God. After her decision last night, she had the peace of knowing He was truly in charge of her life, too.

Chapter 16

The aroma of enchiladas made Blaire's stomach growl as she walked through the door after church. "I'll be out to help you in a minute, Isabel." She headed into the bedroom to put away her purse and slip off her shoes. She wiggled her toes in the thick carpet and sighed. Home. She wanted this to be her home. She longed to stay here, but what if she missed the city? What would she do if the isolation grew old? Uncertainty crowded around. She needed someone to talk to.

When she walked into the kitchen, Manuel was busy setting the table, and Burke was filling glasses with ice water. Isabel insisted they drink a lot of water. She said that, in the dry desert, water was the most important ingredient of one's diet. Blaire had to agree with her. Manuel complained on a regular basis. He would love to have a soda with every meal, including breakfast.

"Let me help cut the lettuce or the tomatoes." Blaire stepped up beside Isabel at the counter.

Isabel glanced at the oven and relinquished the knife. "Okay. I'll set the enchiladas on the table." She wiped her hands on her apron. "I don't know what to do with all this help. I think you are all very hungry."

"We must be desperate if you're allowing Blaire to use a knife. Aren't you afraid she'll toss it across the kitchen?" Burke made a face at Blaire when she turned around to glare at him.

She shook the paring knife at him. "Now listen, Buster." Her words were cut short as the knife slipped from her wet fingers. She gasped as the point dropped toward her bare toes. The blade clattered to the floor a half-inch from her big toe.

Large hands grasped her upper arms and lifted her, moving her to one side of the cutting board.

"I think I'll take over here before you can only count to nine on your toes." Burke's eyes twinkled as Blaire smirked at him.

"You probably think that was an accident." She put her hands on her hips and tilted her nose in the air. "Well, I'll have you know, I might have been doing that on purpose. Perhaps I'm an expert knife thrower and was only trying to fool you."

He leaned close. His nose nearly touched hers. "Well, are you?"

She couldn't think. "What?"

"An expert knife thrower."

He straightened, and she caught her breath. She wanted him to come close again. She wanted to touch him, to have him hold her. Instead she reached for the knife. He pulled it away from her.

"Before I give you this deadly weapon, I want to know we're all safe."

Manuel chuckled. Blaire could feel her cheeks begin to heat. "If you'll kindly step back against the wall over there, I'll demonstrate my ability." She grinned as Burke glanced at the wall.

"I think I'd rather just sit down and eat. Perhaps you can tell us about your circus days when you threw knives at poor unsuspecting souls." He picked up the bowl of lettuce. "By the way, are any of them still alive?"

Manuel guffawed. Isabel chuckled. Blaire followed Burke to the table. "I know you won't believe me, but there's Jack." She sat down. "Of course, now they call him One-Eared Jack."

When the laughter died down, they said the blessing, then began to serve the food. Before anyone took a bite, the phone rang.

"I'm closest. I'll get it." Blaire crossed to the phone and lifted the receiver. "Hello?"

Her face lit up. "Clarissa? Where are you?"

Burke looked at Isabel. "That must be her sister." Isabel nodded.

"You're going to be where?" Blaire was practically jumping up and down. "I can't believe this. Of course I'll be there. Call me when you get in, and I'll come down for the day. Can you come to the ranch?" She was quiet a moment. When she spoke again Burke could hear the disappointment. "I understand. It'll be great to see you. We have a lot to catch up on. Okay. Bye."

Blaire slipped back into her chair and picked up her fork. Her eyes were bright, and her eyelids fluttered several times before she looked up. "That was my sister, Clarissa. She and her husband are back in the States on deputation." Her voice grew thick, and she cleared her throat. "They timed this to coincide with my wedding." She shrugged as if to say the reminder didn't mean anything to her. "They'll be in Phoenix at a church Wednesday night. Clarissa wants me to spend Tuesday with her. I hope you don't mind."

Isabel reached over and squeezed Blaire's hand. "Not at all, *mija*. I'm sorry she won't be able to come out here, or at least that's what I gathered from your conversation."

"They have to be in northern California on Friday to speak at a missions conference. They'll have to leave early Thursday." She sighed and cut her enchiladas with her fork. "This is such a busy time for them. They need the support from the churches. I don't want to interfere with that."

Burke ate slowly, watching Blaire. He couldn't seem to take his eyes off her. A blond wave fell forward to partially cover her creamy cheek. Something had changed between them. Maybe the change was his, not hers. He shook his

97

head and took another bite without tasting any of the spicy food. What was different?

He thought back to his commitment that morning. *Am I that changed, Lord? Is trusting You giving me the ability to also trust Blaire?* With complete clarity he realized this wasn't an issue of trusting Blaire. He only had to trust Jesus. *"Blessed is the man that trusteth in the Lord, and whose hope the Lord is."* Burke looked down at his plate as his grandmother's favorite verse from Jeremiah came back to him. She used to talk to him about putting his trust in God and not in people or land. Now he understood. As long as he trusted God with his life, he could trust a friend or wife without worrying. Yes, they might hurt him sometimes, but God would be there to help him through the rough times.

For the first time, he could recall Julie and what she'd done without feeling agonizing pain. Blaire wasn't anything like Julie. Oh, he'd seen the signs that Julie wouldn't stay true to him before he'd left for college, but he'd chosen to ignore them. When he came home expecting to prepare for a wedding, he hadn't known the wedding would be between Julie and his worst enemy from high school days. That hurt enough, but the cruel words and taunts from Julie cut so deep he'd thought he'd never heal. The laughter as she'd draped herself across Bill's lap and said, "You didn't really think I'd be serious about a ranch boy like you? I want a man who's going places."

Only now, through the grace of God, could he see the lies she'd told him for what they were. He'd confided his hurt over his mother's and grandmother's deaths to her. She'd turned that confidence into lies. "I don't know any woman who wants you, including your mom and grandma." Her words and actions had left him with a complete distrust of women. He'd decided then to never again allow a woman into his heart. How could he have been so blind? A lump wedged tight in his throat as he thought of the healing God had done during church that morning.

Manuel scraped the last of the food from his plate. "I'm taking off for a while." He set his plate in the sink and headed out the door. Isabel sighed and shook her head. "You young people are always in a hurry to do things." She stood. "I'll clean up the kitchen, then go over to Ophelia's and check on her. I think she tries to do too much. Will you be okay?" She looked at Blaire, who nodded.

"I'll stay here and work on my cross-stitch or something equally exciting."

Burke cleared his throat. They both looked at him. His spoon slipped from his fingers and clattered to the floor. He felt like a nervous schoolboy.

"Been around me too long?" Blaire's eyes sparkled with laughter. Burke relaxed.

"Well, at least when I throw my spoon no one has to worry about losing an ear." He grinned and wished the table would disappear. Then she wouldn't be so far away. "I thought maybe you'd like to go down to the Gila River with me this afternoon. I know where some great blue herons are nesting." He held his breath.

Blaire smiled. "I've never seen a great blue heron or the Gila River up close. I'd love to go. Let me help Isabel with the dishes first."

"No, you two go on. I've got nothing better to do." Isabel flicked the dish towel at them. "It won't take long to get these cleaned up."

Burke pushed back from the table. "You might want to get on some different clothes. In some places the brush at the river is pretty thick."

"Aye, aye, sir." Blaire gave a mock salute. "I'll meet you topside in twenty minutes."

He felt like a love-struck schoolboy as he watched her sashay out of the kitchen.

Blaire tightened her grip on the hairbrush. Her shaking fingers couldn't seem to keep their hold. She'd already dropped the brush twice in two minutes. "This is crazy. You're acting like a teenage girl going on her first date. This isn't a date. Burke just wants to show you some more of the wildlife around here. He's still trying to convince you how wonderful this place is."

She paused. In all the excitement of Clarissa calling, she'd forgotten her need to talk to someone about staying or leaving the ranch. Clarissa would be perfect. She gave her hair a final brush, checked her lipstick, and headed for the door.

Burke was waiting in the swing, moving it in a gentle rhythm. He stood when she came out of the house. The swing jerked away, then came back and stopped against the back of his knees. He didn't seem to notice. He stared at her. Blaire glanced down, expecting to see something disgusting staining her shirt or jeans.

"I haven't eaten since I changed, so I know I didn't spill anything on me. Did I smear lipstick somewhere?"

Burke started. A red flush crept up his cheeks. "I'm sorry. The blue shirt—and your eyes. . ." He moved his hat back on his head. "You look nice." His green gaze caught and held hers. "Ready to go?"

Blaire followed him to the pickup. Already misgivings were starting to knot her stomach. What was she doing? Was she going with Burke to see these birds and the river or did she just want to spend time with him? Maybe she should back out now. Burke swung the truck door open and turned to offer her his hand. All thoughts of staying home fled. She placed her hand in his and climbed in the cab. A tingle of excitement flowed through her even after Burke released her hand and closed the door.

"How will we get down to the river? Every time I've been past on the highway, the drop seemed pretty steep. Are there roads?"

Shifting gears, Burke headed down the drive. "There are a few roads that lead down to public places on the river, but I don't usually go there. The river passes through my dad's ranch. I have a private place where I like to go."

Blaire tried not to stare at Burke as he drove. Although she managed to keep from turning her head, she still watched his strong hands on the steering wheel. She knew the work he accomplished with those hands, yet despite the strength in them, she'd seen how gentle he could be with the baby ostriches and the kittens. Burke was so complex. *I could spend a lifetime getting to know him.* The thought startled her. She forced her eyes and thoughts away from the man beside her.

The road down to the river turned out to be a dirt track. Gnarled limbs of mesquite trees swept out far enough from the trunks to provide shade. Burke stopped the truck under a tree not far from the river.

"Here we are." He shut off the engine and smiled at her. Tension crackled in the air.

Blaire opened the door and stepped out. She could hear the soothing ripple of the river nearby. The shade and the water cooled the temperature. She took a deep breath. The air held a fresh scent of wet sand and earth.

"This is so pretty, Burke. I'll bet you bring a lot of people to this place."

His smile was almost shy. "Actually, you're the first."

She stared. "Why is that?"

He shrugged, then took her hand and led her closer to the river. "When I was a boy, this was a special place I came to when I wanted to be alone."

She wanted to ask a million questions, but somehow she knew the time wasn't right. His short statement gave her plenty to think about. "Do you go swimming here? Is the river deep enough?"

They stopped close to the edge. Water rushed past, swirling around rocks and tree limbs.

"I don't like to swim in the Gila." Burke stepped close. "I've known too many people who drowned in this river. They didn't realize the danger with the tree limbs and brush below the surface along the edge. Either that or they fought the current rather than traveled with it."

Blaire was silent, staring into the suddenly deadly looking water. "I didn't think about desert rivers being so dangerous."

"Most places in Arizona have dry river beds rather than rivers like the Gila. Every year in the rainy season, people get caught in flash floods in the riverbeds. In fact, the Tucson rescue teams come up to Winkelman to train for flood rescues by using the Gila."

Burke squeezed her hand. "I didn't mean to talk about something so depressing. Come on." He lowered his voice to a whisper. "If we're quiet, we can see the herons." He led her downstream along a narrow trail that wound beside the river.

After about fifty yards he halted. Stepping to the edge of the bank, he pulled her forward.

"Do you see them?"

Blaire looked across the river. All she saw were weeds and water. The river flowed fast, cutting under the bank on the far side. Standing on the edge of the bank, leaning out, gave her the feeling of standing on the rushing water. Blaire shook her head to indicate she couldn't see the herons. She didn't want to scare the birds by talking.

Stepping closer, Burke put his arm around her and pulled her back against his chest. He put his cheek next to hers and with his hand on the other side of her face directed her gaze. Her heart pounded. She fought the feelings welling up inside. She wanted to ignore the birds and pretend she couldn't find them just so Burke would keep his hold on her. A flutter of movement on the opposite side of the river caught her attention. The weeds swayed. A tall blue-gray bird with a long slender beak and stick-like legs stood watching them. Blaire sucked in a breath. The bird tilted its head to one side as if deciding what they were doing. With a regal air, the bird stalked gracefully downstream through the flowing river.

She turned to look at Burke. He straightened. His arm stayed around her, pulling her close. She couldn't look away. The bird faded into the background. Burke leaned closer. Blaire closed her eyes. She felt his arms tighten around her. Her hands rested lightly against his shirt. She leaned forward.

His lips touched hers. The ground moved beneath her feet. She'd never felt a kiss like this. She felt like Alice falling down the rabbit hole. Burke gasped and tightened his hold. Their bodies splashed into the river.

Chapter 17

As the cold water wrapped around them, Blaire realized the earth really had moved under her feet! The Gila River's strong current pulled Burke and Blaire apart. She would have panicked, but Burke wrapped his strong fingers around her arm and wouldn't let go. He tugged on her, towing her to the surface.

"Put your feet down. You can stand up."

Blaire fought the current and discovered the water only came to her thighs. Like a young child demanding attention, the river dragged at her legs. Burke stared past her, a look of longing on his face. She turned and saw his hat bobbing in a wild dance on the surface of the water.

"Your hat." She tried to look remorseful. She couldn't do it. One glance at the freshly crumpled bank that had tossed them into the river brought home the hilarity of the situation. Blaire slapped a hand across her mouth, trying to hold back the laughter. She peeked at Burke. He watched her with a silly grin.

"That was some kiss, wasn't it?"

Blaire couldn't hold back the laughter. She leaned against Burke and laughed until tears mixed with the river water on her cheeks. She could feel the vibration of Burke's unrestrained mirth.

Burke pushed her away. She looked up at him. His hair, still mostly plastered to his head, was just starting to spring upright in comical little toothpicks pointing skyward. She lifted a hand to her head. She must look just as bad.

"Shall we stay here all day or are you done swimming?"

She looked down river, pretending to be in deep thought. "Since I forgot my raft, I believe I'll quit for the day."

Burke waded to the bank, placed his hands on the grass, and started to hoist himself out of the water. Another piece of the edge gave way. He tumbled into the water with the dirt and came up sputtering. Wiping away the water, he grinned at her. "I guess I wasn't clean enough. That'll teach me not to forget my weekly bath."

He headed for the bank again, this time examining the place he'd chosen to climb out before he placed his weight on it. Once on firm ground, he turned and reached a hand down to Blaire. His fingers were nearly as cold as hers, but their strength felt good. With one quick tug, she left the river behind and stood next to Burke, water streaming from her clothes into the grass. The warm sun felt good on her face.

Burke slipped an arm behind her back. His other hand cupped her cheek. His eyes, darkened with emotion, held hers in a powerful gaze. "I think there's something we didn't finish." His voice turned husky. He tightened his grip.

Everything in her ached for his embrace. Blaire tilted her head back. She leaned forward. A picture of Richard flashed through her mind. She closed her eyes. She could see the e-mail he'd sent, telling her the engagement was off. Pain ripped through her heart.

Burke's warm lips covered hers. She jerked her head back. Stiffening her arms, she pushed away from him. Ignoring the hurt in his eyes, she backed off. Burke let go of her.

"I think I need to go back home and change into dry clothes." She knew the excuse was lame. She wanted to fall back into his arms, but she couldn't do that. She refused to go back on her promise to herself. Never again would she fall for someone she worked with.

Burke stared at Blaire as she paused to squeeze water out of her blouse. *What did I do wrong? One minute she seemed to be enjoying my company, then this.* He ran a hand through his damp hair. A foreign feeling welled up inside. Remembering his vow at church that morning, he stared down at the ground. *Lord, I know I promised to give You complete control of my life. I meant that, but now I've taken matters into my own hands again. I'm sorry, Lord. I know I've fallen in love with Blaire. I'm not certain how she feels. Help me know what You want me to do. Thank You, Lord.*

He cast a longing gaze down the river where his hat had disappeared, sighed, and headed for the truck. His wet jeans weighed a ton. At least he had a spare hat at home.

⁂

"Who would have thought Phoenix traffic would be so bad?" Blaire slammed on the brakes as a red sedan darted in front of her. Gripping the wheel, she glanced in the rearview mirror and flipped on her turn signal. She needed to switch lanes to get on 101. A string of bumper-to-bumper vehicles refused to part. "Come on. I need to be in that lane." She tried to move over. The blare of a horn made her jerk back into her lane. She passed the exit for 101.

"I can't believe this." Blaire felt like pounding the steering wheel. She hadn't seen the sign for the exit because of her concentration on all the heavy traffic. Now she would have to get off and work her way back. She was following Burke's directions to get to northwest Phoenix, where her sister was staying. If there was an alternate route, she didn't know what it was.

A knot formed in her stomach. Keeping her turn signal on as traffic slowed to a near standstill, she tried to move over lane by lane. Getting off the freeway turned out to be tedious work. She was three miles past the turnoff for 101 and completely worn out before she reached an exit ramp.

By the time she pulled into the parking lot of the motel where Clarissa and her husband, Jim, were staying, Blaire felt weak from exhaustion and nerves. She climbed out and headed into the office to check in. Clarissa had arranged for them to have adjoining rooms.

"Blaire, it's so good to see you." Clarissa enveloped her in a hug. When she pulled back, Blaire could see the sheen of tears in her sister's eyes.

"It's been too long, Clarissa. Sometimes I wish Jim were pastoring a church in the States where we could see each other now and then. I miss you so much."

"Not half as much as I miss you." Clarissa pulled her inside the room and shut the door. "Jim has adjusted to missionary life better than I have. I still struggle with the language and customs. I always seem to say or do the wrong thing." She gestured at a table and two overstuffed chairs on wheels in the corner of the room. "Come on in and sit down. Do you want a soda or something?"

Blaire sank into a chair and tried to relax. "You can't imagine how awful the trip here was. I don't ever remember fighting traffic like that."

"What?" Clarissa pulled out the other chair and sat down. "Don't tell me the queen of the freeways managed to be intimidated by a few cars."

Blaire grimaced. "To think I used to live in Chicago where this traffic would be a joke. I didn't think anything of the delays. Now I feel like I've been run over by a truck, and I wouldn't have the energy to drive back home if the house was burning down." Her head dropped back against the chair, and she closed her eyes.

Cinnamon curls bounced as Clarissa shook her head. "Does this mean our shopping trip is out? I'm dying to get to the mall with you."

One eye cracked open. "Did you say mall?"

"Yep. The magic word." Clarissa smirked.

"Where's Jim?"

"He's spending the day with the pastor. They're doing door-to-door evangelism in the neighborhood around the church, hoping to get more people to come for the service." Clarissa leaned forward, a wicked grin crossing her face. "He won't be back before suppertime. We have all day for the mall."

Blaire raised her hands in surrender. "All right, I give. Bring on the shopping." She pushed up from the chair. "My car or yours?"

"Definitely yours." Clarissa grabbed her purse and the room key. "Jim has ours, and I don't want to walk."

Finding a parking place that was within walking distance of the stores proved to be a challenge. After cruising several aisles, Blaire spotted a car backing out. She wheeled into the space before anyone else could beat her to it.

Inside the mall, chaos ruled. "I haven't seen this many people in months." Blaire had to lean close to Clarissa to talk. The rumble of people conversing could have rivaled the sound of an approaching freight train.

"Where do you want to start?" Clarissa looped her arm through Blaire's. She pointed toward a trendy shop. "Oh, look, fake jewelry." She grinned. "And it's the cheap kind I can afford. Let's go."

For the next two hours they visited jewelry stores, bookstores, and clothing shops. At noon they edged through the crowds, looking for the food court. They stood in the middle of the open area in front of the various restaurants, perusing the variety of foods offered.

"What are you going to have?"

Clarissa brushed a stray curl from her forehead. "Something totally American. It has to be disgusting, too." She giggled. "I still crave cheeseburgers. I haven't gotten enough of them."

Blaire laughed. "Cheeseburgers it is then."

"With bacon."

"Whew, that is disgusting." Blaire raised her eyebrows in mock dismay. "Does it get worse than this?"

"Yes." Clarissa's eyes sparkled. "I want French fries and onion rings."

Blaire grabbed the back of a chair near them. "I think my heart is clogging." She wrapped her arm through Clarissa's and tugged. "I see the eatery of your dreams right down here."

A few minutes later they had worked their way back to the tables with a fully loaded tray. "I can't believe I let you talk me into milkshakes on top of all this other fat. I won't be able to eat anything but celery for a week." Blaire squeezed past a group of teenagers dressed in a style only they could appreciate. She set the tray down on an empty table.

The teens milled around, communicating more with shrugs and gestures than words before wandering off. Blaire glanced at Clarissa, whose troubled gaze followed the kids.

"I think every teen and preteen in Phoenix is here at the mall today." Blaire motioned to the milling throng passing through the food court.

"It's sad, Blaire. These kids get in so much trouble because they have no direction in life. Sometimes I think Jim and I are in the wrong country as missionaries. I wonder if we shouldn't come back here and try to minister to the youth in the cities. They sure need someone."

Blaire swallowed a sip of her milkshake. "You know, I used to think shopping at the mall was the only place to be."

"You don't anymore? When did this change?"

"I didn't realize I'd changed until I came down here to see you." Blaire stirred a fry in the ketchup. "I guess I used to think only of me. Shopping fulfilled something I needed. Today, there's no excitement like there used to be."

"I'm boring you? Is that what you're saying?" Clarissa's astonished expression was almost comical.

"No, I'm glad to be with you. I just don't enjoy the crowds and noise like I used to. The same thing happened on the freeway this morning."

"So, what is it you want?" Clarissa turned serious and leaned back in her chair.

"You know I wish you had time to come out to the ranch."

"Are you changing subjects on me?" Clarissa's eyebrows raised. "Why would I want to see this ranch? I thought you were going to sell out and move back to the city."

"I thought so, too." Blaire pushed her half-eaten sandwich away. "Something's changed. I'm thinking of keeping the ranch and living there."

Clarissa's mouth dropped open. "You, the all-time city girl, are going to live in the middle of nowhere with a bunch of birds? What brought this on?"

Blaire watched the milling crowds of teens and preteens as they wove in an intricate pattern along the mall walkway. She wanted to talk to Clarissa. They'd always had an easy rapport, but somehow she didn't know how to put her feelings into words. As always, Clarissa waited patiently.

"I know for years you've allowed God to lead you wherever He wanted you to go. Even when you married Jim and went to the mission field, you've always seemed to know exactly what God wanted you to do."

Clarissa's eyes widened. "Do you really believe that? You're talking like God wrote specific instructions for us and we've followed them to the letter."

"Well, you always seemed so confident. Have you ever doubted?" Blaire hesitated, stirring her straw in her milkshake. "Have you ever argued with God?"

A light, tinkling laugh drifted across the table. Clarissa's eyes sparkled with mirth. "You have no idea how I've argued with God. Which time would you like to hear about? The time we got to the village and found we were to live in a little hut with a dirt floor? Or when evening came and the hordes of bugs began eating us alive? What about the time I picked up a pot to cook in and found it occupied by a snake?" She shook her head. "I sometimes think all God hears from me are complaints. I keep telling Him how unsuited I am for the mission field, but then He shows me how I've made a difference in the lives of the women I've worked with. Maybe I haven't seen hundreds of people led to salvation, but I've taught cleanliness. There's less disease now than when we first came. The children don't have as many sores. Eating habits have improved. And they can all quote Scripture, and they want to hear Jim preach."

Blaire laughed. "Okay, okay, I think I get the picture."

"Now, tell me what you've been arguing about with God." Clarissa leaned forward, resting her elbows on the table.

A group of blue- and purple-haired teens strutted past. A young mother marched by towing a screaming toddler. Blaire sighed. She used to love the anonymity of the mall crowd. Today, the clamor and confusion irritated.

"Do you think we could continue this conversation back at the motel room? I'm getting a headache from all this racket."

Pushing back her chair, Clarissa began to clear the trash from the table. "I think that's a great idea. Maybe we should stop by an emergency medical center and have you checked out. I've never seen you leave a mall without buying something."

Blaire tossed her half-eaten sandwich in the trash bin and slid the tray on top. "Boy, you're tough on me today. Since you're insisting on junking out, I'll go buy us a couple of giant cookies to munch on this afternoon." She indicated the shop at the end of the row that sold cookies decorated with any message you wanted. "I'll get a regular size one and get you one of the platter-sized ones."

Clarissa grinned and patted her slender hips. "Sounds good to me. I'll take chocolate chip and a peanut butter too. Cookies have been in short supply lately."

"I heard a report that in Tucson some sort of group was experimenting with using worms in cooking. I guess they have lots of protein and are plentiful. They even had worm cookies. Maybe we could get the recipe, and you could teach Cookie 101 in your village. Sounds very healthy. Just think of the nutritional value." Blaire couldn't help laughing at her sister's horrified expression. "Come on, Clarissa." She looped her arm through her sister's and headed to the cookie shop. "I was only making a suggestion."

Chapter 18

The door to the motel room barely clicked shut before Clarissa tore open the sack of cookies. Their sweet, spicy scent filled the air. She pulled out a huge peanut butter cookie, broke off a piece, and popped it into her mouth. "Oh, this is heavenly." She paused in her chewing and glared at Blaire. "I think there is a conspiracy here. By the time we head back to the mission field, I'll have to have all new clothes."

She broke off another piece, then pushed the bag closer to Blaire. "Have one, sis. Save me."

"I don't think you have to worry." Blaire pulled out a chocolate chip cookie. "Mom said you'd lost weight, and I agree. You can put on several pounds and still look great."

Clarissa groaned. "This is a conspiracy. You should have seen the food Mom foisted off on me while we stayed with them. It's a good thing we're only on deputation for a few months." She brushed a cookie crumb from her blouse. "Now, tell me about your argument with God. The last I heard you were waiting for Him to show you what He wanted you to do. You talked about starting an accounting firm. What happened to that idea?"

Blaire spread out a napkin and began breaking her cookie apart in small pieces. "When I first heard about my inheritance, I thought the ranch was my answer to prayer. Then when I arrived, I found it was different from what I had pictured. I didn't want to keep the ranch. I wanted to sell out and move back to the city. I could take the profits and start my accounting firm."

"So what happened?"

"There were people involved. Uncle Ike had people working for him, and I couldn't disappoint them and just thrust them out in the cold, so to speak. I promised to stay for a while, learn the workings of the ranch, then sell."

"You've been here almost six months. Isn't that long enough to learn about the ranch?"

Popping a piece of cookie in her mouth, Blaire chewed slowly. "I don't know what happened. It's kind of a long story."

Clarissa shrugged. "We've got time."

Blaire began telling her sister about her arrival in Arizona and her introduction to the ostriches and the residents of the ranch. "I felt so bad for Isabel and Manuel that I couldn't sell the ranch right away. Then there was the pastor's message."

"Umm. The story builds. What message is this?"

"He spoke on Psalm twenty-three, verse two, and how God places us in green pastures, but we don't always see them that way. I keep thinking about that Scripture and wondering if this isn't the green pasture God has for me. If I leave, will I be giving up a blessing, or is this just the means to attain my blessing? I get so confused."

Clarissa leaned forward and placed her hand on Blaire's knee. "God isn't the author of confusion. I think He's making His will plain for you, but outside influences and perhaps you yourself are creating the confusion."

Blaire nodded as Clarissa sat back in her chair. Blaire set a chocolate chip on her tongue and sucked until it melted.

"What else?"

Why did her sister have to know her so well? Blaire struggled with her feelings a minute, then spoke in a soft voice. "There's Burke."

Clarissa's eyes lit up. She leaned forward again. "Burke? The ranch manager?"

Blaire nodded. Silence stretched between them.

"Do I have to sit on you and tickle you like you used to do to me so I'd tell you everything?"

Blaire laughed and made a face at her sister. "No. I'll talk even without your threats. I'm just not sure how to begin or what to say."

"Do you have feelings for Burke?"

Blaire nodded.

"Like you had for Richard?"

"No." Blaire was surprised at her emphatic answer. Clarissa leaned back in her chair and looked pleased.

"Good. We all knew Richard wasn't right for you, but there was no way to convince you of that. Now tell me about Burke. And don't you leave anything out. If you do, I'll know."

She was right. Clarissa had always known if Blaire was keeping secrets.

"The first time I met Burke there was a spark between us. I tried to ignore him. I even tried to dislike him." She sighed and wrapped her fingers together. "Nothing worked. He's wonderful. He works hard, he's fun and funny, he's sensitive and sweet."

"Whoa, is this a man or a saint?"

Blaire smirked. "Let me think for a while, and I'll tell you a fault." She tapped her finger against her chin. "Oh, yes. I know. He hates computers."

"What? You're interested in someone who doesn't like computers. Perish the thought." Clarissa placed her hand over her heart and collapsed back in her chair. Then she grinned and sat back up. "Okay, so he's Mr. Perfect. How is his walk with God?"

"He's been a Christian since he was a young boy, but just last Sunday he went forward at the end of the service and admitted he had never surrendered his life to Jesus. He's had a rough life, but in the last two days I've seen a change in his attitude. He's happier, more content, I guess."

"You're making this hard." Clarissa shook her head. "Mom's going to want a full report, and I won't be able to give it. I wish I had time to go to the ranch and meet this perfect specimen."

"There's a problem, though." Blaire stirred the cookie crumbs on her napkin.

Clarissa held up a hand. "Don't tell me. He's not interested in you, right?"

"No. I think he's interested. In fact, I'm sure he is."

"So what's the problem?"

Blaire hesitated. "I made a promise to myself that I would never date someone I worked with again. After Richard, I realized that only creates problems. This is a point of honor, I guess."

"You could fire him." Clarissa grinned. "I can see it now." She placed a hand dramatically on her brow. "Burke, honey, you're fired. Will you marry me?"

Blaire wadded up the empty cookie bag and threw it at Clarissa. "Cut it out. You would die if I asked some guy to marry me rather than waiting for him to ask. I remember your lectures on being a proper lady. What happened to that?"

"I guess I've been on the mission field so long, I've changed. You know, over there the women hit the men on the head and drag them off to get married."

Blaire's eyes widened. "Do they really?"

Clarissa crossed her arms over her stomach and doubled over with laughter. "Of course not. You're as gullible as you were when we were kids."

"Give me that bag back so I can throw it again." Blaire held out her hand. Clarissa grabbed the bag up and stuffed the missile behind her back.

"Seriously, Blaire. Do you think Burke is anything like Richard?"

"No, but I'm still scared of the commitment."

"Can you be content living without your accounting business?"

Blaire raked her fingers through her hair. "That's a funny thing about the ranch. This is such a big business that the books call for an accountant's skill. I've also thought about offering my services to other ranches in the area. For instance, Burke's dad has a big ranch, and maybe he could use an accountant. I would enjoy doing that."

Clarissa steepled her fingers under her chin and watched Blaire.

"You know, I almost feel like Uncle Ike knew me better than I know myself. It's like he planned all this, and all I had to do was take the time to realize how right Arizona and the ranch are for me."

"I don't know about Uncle Ike, but I know God knows you best. He's the one who's had all this planned out." Clarissa reached across the table and caught Blaire's hands in hers. "Blaire, trust Jesus with everything. Don't be afraid of making the same mistake you made with Richard. You're a different person, and from the sound of things, so is Burke. If God brought you together, perhaps you should listen to Him."

Blaire stared at her sister's fine-boned hands. Was Clarissa right? Was this another area where she was trying to maintain control rather than following God's path? *God, help me to follow You completely. I don't want to mess things up again. If Burke is the one You've chosen for me, please let me know. Let him know, too, God.* A surge of excitement and anticipation ran through her. Waiting one more day to get home felt like an eternity.

⟋⟍

Burke went to hang up the phone and missed. Shaking his head, he focused on where the headset should be placed and hung up.

"Who was that?" Isabel peeked in from the front room where she'd been dusting.

Burke tried to wipe what he knew must look like a silly grin from his face. "It was nothing." He rubbed his jaw, forcing the giddy feeling down. "Say, Isabel, I need to do some business. I'll be back after lunch sometime."

She frowned at him as if she suspected something was going on. "I'll let Manuel know."

"That's okay. I'll talk to him before I leave. I have some instructions for him."

"Burke, that real estate lady called again, asking for Blaire. She said the Wilsons are determined to buy the ranch, but Blaire says she doesn't want to sell now. They've made a better offer. Does this mean Blaire intends to stay?"

Burke frowned. "I don't know, Isabel. I hope she doesn't want to sell, but we can't make her stay. This has to be her choice."

Isabel smiled. "I'm glad you've gotten a peace about that, Burke. I believe Blaire wants to do what's right. She's not like Julie."

"I know." Burke sighed. "I guess for years I blamed God for everything bad that happened to me. I thought He was punishing me for something I did wrong or because He didn't like me. I know that's not true now, but when you're hurting, you can believe a lot of things." He ran his finger around the brim of his hat. "Then when Julie hurt me and blamed me for what happened to Mom and Grandma, it was too much. I can see I needed Jesus as the Lord of my life instead of putting my faith in people. I'm glad I've got peace about it now, too."

"What a lesson to learn." Isabel patted his shoulder. "In marriage, you need to trust Jesus first, then trust your wife."

Burke chuckled. "Good point, but who said anything about marriage?" Settling his hat on his head, Burke strode to the door. "See ya later." Blaire would be home later today, and based on that phone call, he had plenty to do before she got back.

⟋⟍

Blaire left late Wednesday morning for the trip back home. After making several shopping stops and grabbing a quick bite of lunch, she headed out of town. As the freeway turned once more into a divided highway, then finally a two-lane road, she breathed a sigh of relief. Tension drained from her back and shoulders. Her hands relaxed on the wheel. A wave of longing washed through her. She couldn't get home fast enough.

"Lord, what have You done to me? I'm even missing those crazy birds." Blaire thought of the stories she'd told Clarissa and Jim last night, keeping them all laughing for hours. They especially loved the story of Sprinkles flying over the fence. Jim, who didn't like cats much, said the ostriches must have good taste. She chuckled again thinking about it.

A picture of Burke popped into her mind. Of course, he hadn't been far from her thoughts since she'd come to Phoenix. She couldn't believe how much she'd missed him. Every time something happened, she found herself wanting to share the experience with him. "Lord, I love him so much. I thought I would never love anyone again. You were right to bring me here. I feel like I've found the other half of who I am. I know I hurt him last Sunday when we were at the river. Please, help me to make amends."

Warmth suffused her as she recalled Burke's kiss. She had never been kissed like that, or maybe she'd never felt that way about a kiss. "You know, Lord, what I'd like most is a husband who will pray with me about things. I've seen Dad and Mom pray together for years. I know Clarissa and Jim do, too. If a marriage is going to stay strong these days, the couple needs to be able to come before You together." She wondered about Burke. At first, he'd seemed so uncomfortable with the things of God. In the last two days, he'd changed. Would he be willing to pray with her? Would he put God first in a marriage? Somehow she knew he would.

The miles skimmed by. Blaire loved the mountains and cactus-covered hills as she drove between Superior and Kearny. Tired of sitting in the car, she almost stopped in Kearny for a soda, but the thought of home drew her like a magnet. She didn't stop until she pulled into the driveway and parked near the house.

I've been gone a day and a half, and I feel like it's been weeks. I must be going crazy. Blaire's heart pounded. She couldn't wait to talk to Burke. She needed to tell them all about her decision to keep the ranch and go on living here. She wanted to apologize; she wanted to take up on the idea in Clarissa's joke and drag Burke off by the hair. She giggled. He'd be furious if she bent his hat, even if the one he wore now wasn't his favorite.

"I'm home." Blaire listened to the echo in the house. No one answered. She carried her overnight bag in and plunked it on the bed. Planning to unpack later, she walked through the kitchen, wondering where everyone was.

A thud greeted her as she stepped out the kitchen door. She heard voices coming from the small house Burke and Manuel shared. Stepping around the tamarisk trees, she saw Burke in the back of his pickup accepting a box that

Manuel was handing him. She crossed the yard toward them.

"What's up?"

Manuel and Burke both jumped. Manuel greeted her, then trotted inside and shut the door. She thought she heard Isabel's voice from inside the house. Burke put his hand on the side of the truck and vaulted over the side.

"Hey, how was the trip to Phoenix? Did you have a good visit with your sister?"

She eyed the boxes and furniture in the bed of the truck. "I had a great time. What are you doing?"

"I'm moving out."

"What?"

"I'm going to stay with my dad for a while." Burke reached for her, and she stepped back. All the well-planned speeches flew away.

"Blaire, I've talked to Manuel. He knows the procedures of the ranch nearly as well as I do. He's going to take over for me if that's okay with you."

"Why would he need to take over for you?" Blaire felt like her mind wasn't working right. Dread crept up and wrapped around her heart.

"He needs to take over because I'm quitting." Burke didn't look at all remorseful over his announcement.

Chapter 19

B urke winced inside at the pained expression in Blaire's eyes. He wanted to kick himself. How could he have been so blunt? He'd planned his speech. The words were outlined in his head. He even knew the place where he would take her to explain why he was quitting and how he felt about her. Would she listen to him now? He didn't think so.

The glint of tears shone in Blaire's eyes. She whirled and stalked toward the house.

"Blaire, wait." Burke's mind raced. She halted but didn't turn around. "My dad is having a barbecue for some family and friends this weekend. He wanted me to make sure everyone here would come. Isabel and Manuel already know. Will you come?"

She half turned. Her blond hair lifted in the breeze. "I don't know." Her voice sounded hoarse, almost strangled. Blaire continued to the house, stepped inside, and shut the door with what sounded like measured care. Burke strode toward the house. He had to talk to Blaire and explain. He had to tell her the real reason he quit.

"Hey, Burke, we'd better get going. This is the last load. I have to get back in time to do the evening chores." Manuel came out of the house lugging a heavy box. "Mom said your dad called and wants you there right away to help him with something, too."

Pausing midway between the two houses, Burke felt a tug-of-war on his heart. He needed to keep his word to his dad and Manuel, but he needed to explain to Blaire, too.

"Ready?" Manuel called. The box he carried plunked onto the bed of the truck.

Swiveling back to the small house, Burke stuck his head in and called to Isabel. She answered from the room he'd used as a bedroom. He waved to Manuel to let him know he'd be right there, then stepped inside the house.

"Isabel." Burke pulled the hat off his head and ran his hands along its brim. "I didn't think Blaire would be home so soon."

"She's here already?" Isabel sounded as surprised as he'd felt.

He nodded. "She wanted to know what I was doing, and I told her I quit. She didn't give me a chance to explain why. I know I hurt her. Can you please talk to her? Try to get her to come to Dad's barbecue, please. I'll call and come by, but I'm not sure she wants to see me right now."

114

Isabel put down the rag she'd been using to dust the room. "I'll talk to her, *mijo*. You go see what your dad needs. Come back tomorrow and talk to Blaire. Okay?" She patted his hand and accompanied him to the door.

Settling the hat back on his head, Burke glanced at the silent house where Blaire had disappeared. He turned back to Isabel. "I'll call tonight if I can. If not, I'll be by tomorrow." He slammed the truck door behind him. The motor roared to life. Even the ostriches made him feel guilty. They stared at him as if he'd done something wrong.

Blaire sank to the floor by her bed. She pulled her knees up and rested her head on them. Tears that she'd been holding back from Burke's view began to soak her skirt. *Why, God? Why did this happen again?* The bed shook with the force of her sobs. *You brought me here to a supposedly green pasture. Is this it? If this is a green pasture of Your making, why am I hurting so much? Why did he leave?*

The pastor's voice seemed to echo through her mind. "The Lord makes us lie down in green pastures." Well, maybe this wasn't where God wanted her to be. Perhaps she'd been mistaken. Had God been mistaken?

A knock echoed through the room. Isabel called through the door. "Blaire, are you okay?"

Reaching for a tissue, Blaire blew her nose. "I'm fine, Isabel. I'm a little tired from the trip. I'll be out later."

Isabel was silent for a long minute. "We'll talk when you've rested. Don't miss supper."

Crawling up on the bed, Blaire stretched out. She pulled her worn, stuffed giraffe next to her and curled around it. Was there something wrong with her? At least Burke hadn't run off with a Vanessa. Or had he? As the speculations raced through her mind, exhaustion took over, and she drifted off to sleep.

The spicy scent of chili wafting under her nose woke Blaire. She stretched, slightly disoriented. Was Isabel fixing chili for breakfast? That would be strange. Loosening her hold on her giraffe, she opened her eyes and sat up. Her skirt, full of wrinkles, wrapped tightly around her legs. The late afternoon sun poked weary rays through her window. The earlier hurt came rushing back.

Climbing off the bed, Blaire determined to shower and get ready for supper. She'd prayed that God would show her why He'd allowed this to happen. She wanted to blame God, but deep down she knew He didn't want her to be hurt again. Perhaps Burke had a reason for quitting and running off like he did, but she wasn't ready to hear his excuse. She planned to stay far away from the handsome ranch manager who'd stolen her heart.

For the rest of the week, Blaire managed to avoid Burke. When he called, she told Isabel to tell him she was busy. She was usually working on the books or at some other job so she wasn't lying, but she could have stopped and talked to him. She didn't want to. Just when she'd come to terms with her feelings for Burke and had been ready to let him know she loved him, he'd done an about-face. Had he only pretended to care about her?

Early Saturday, Isabel began making mounds of potato salad and salsa to take to the barbecue at the Dunham ranch. Blaire helped cut vegetables, working quietly beside the chattering Isabel. She didn't want to go to the party, but she couldn't think of a reason to stay away that wouldn't offend Burke's dad. Scraping the peelings and vegetable waste together, Blaire headed for the door to dump them on the compost heap.

"You're awfully quiet, *mija.*"

Blaire jumped, scattering onion and potato peels across the kitchen. She set the pan on the floor and began to grab the stray parings. Keeping her back to Isabel, she hoped the subject would be dropped.

Isabel stooped and began to help clean the floor. "Are you okay?"

Blaire swiped at her eyes with the back of her wrist. "I'm fine. Sorry I spilled this on your clean floor."

"I'm not worried about my floor." Isabel picked up the refilled pan and set it on the table. "I'm worried about you. You haven't been the same since you came back from Phoenix. Is it because of Burke quitting?"

The lump in her throat kept Blaire from talking. She shrugged. Picking up the pan, she walked to the door. "I'll be right back." Her voice came out a hoarse whisper. She slipped out the door before Isabel could say anything.

The phone rang as Blaire returned to the kitchen. Afraid Burke was calling her again, she motioned to Isabel that she didn't want to talk and went to her room. Sinking down onto her bed, she picked up her Bible and ran her hand over the familiar cover. *Lord, thank You for the green pasture You've put me in. It hurts right now, but I've come to understand that You have a purpose in having me here. Help me to trust You completely with my heart, my life, everything.* She wiped a tear from her cheek.

Putting the Bible back on the nightstand, she stood and crossed the room to look at the pictures on the mantel. One was a picture of Uncle Ike holding her on his lap, taken years ago. She smiled. A feeling of contentment washed over her.

"Uncle Ike, you were right. This is the right place for me. These wide-open spaces have brought healing to my soul. I love the people here, the quiet." She laughed. "I even love those crazy ostriches. Thank you."

❧

The pickup truck bounced hard as Burke accelerated down the dirt track leading back to his dad's house. This was the most important day of his life, and he was late. All he'd had to do today was check the mineral licks set out for the cattle at various stations. That had gone well until early afternoon when he found the cow down with a broken leg. Not wanting to waste the meat, he'd field dressed her and climbed back in the truck. Then he'd hit a section of road that had been washed out in one of the summer rains. He'd taken more of his precious time rebuilding the road so he could pass the washout and continue on. Finally, when he thought he might not be too late, the truck had had a blowout. The spare had refused to come free. He was filthy, tired, and certain his dad's barbecue would be over before he arrived.

His fears were laid to rest when he eased down the steep hill across from the ranch house and jolted across the dry creek bed. More than twenty cars still packed the parking area near the house. Burke pulled around to the side away from the festivities. He backed up to the cooler where his dad always hung meat to cure. This time of year the cooler was off, but the big motor would get going quickly. He had to hang the cow's carcass before he could clean up.

The aroma of barbecued meat, rolls, and home-baked pies filled the air as Burke stepped from the house a bit later. He ran a hand through his damp hair and wished he'd worn his hat. Somehow he felt naked without it. His stomach growled, reminding him of how long he'd gone without food. Breakfast was a distant memory.

"Burke, where have you been?" Isabel waved at him from where she sat with her friend Ophelia.

He smiled and waved, his eyes continuing to scan the crowd. He couldn't see Blaire anywhere. Moving over to where Isabel and Ophelia were chatting, he greeted them, chafing at this need for small talk.

"Mmm. The food smells delicious. I'll bet you made half of it, Isabel. Is there any of that famous barbecue sauce of yours?"

"You know that's not really my barbecue sauce. It's your grandmother's recipe. Irene's Barbecue Sauce. Your father gave me the recipe years ago to make for these barbecues."

"And you make the best." Burke gave her a kiss on the cheek.

"Well, I had help today. Blaire helped with all the cooking."

"Isabel, where is Blaire?"

The two women glanced around at the crowd. "She was here talking with us not long ago." Isabel's brow furrowed. "You know she said something about wanting to walk. She also mentioned kittens."

"Thanks." Burke strode away toward his dad's barn.

"Wait, Burke, don't you want something to eat? Your dad said you've been gone all day with nothing to eat."

"I'll be back for some food." Burke couldn't stop the grin on his face. He felt like a kid headed for the cookie jar.

The musty scent of grain and hay greeted Burke as he stepped into the dim interior of the barn. Burke paused to let his eyes adjust. Soft laughter drifted out from behind a pile of loose hay. A sense of anticipation settled over him. At last, he would have the chance he needed to talk with Blaire.

"Oh, poor baby. I can still feel the little kink in the end of your tail. Do you have nightmares of giant birds tossing you up in the air?"

Burke crept closer and watched as Blaire lifted the half-grown calico cat and rubbed her cheek against Sprinkles's fur. From the way she pressed her ear close, he knew she could hear the motorboat purr as Sprinkles expressed appreciation for the attention.

"I sure hope these cows treat you better than the ostriches did," Blaire murmured as she stood, still holding the cat in her arms. "I'd better get back and see if Isabel is ready to go. I need to get back home."

Sprinkles climbed up and wrapped herself around Blaire's neck. Her tail draped under Blaire's nose like a giant mustache. Blaire reached up to rub the cat's head.

Burke chuckled. "What's your hurry?"

Blaire screeched. Sprinkles arched her back and hissed. Blaire whirled around. The cat jumped down and dashed off into the shadows. "I need to go." Blaire stepped to one side.

Burke moved to block her way. "We need to talk."

She folded her arms. "I think you made yourself quite clear when you quit without notice. Now if you'll excuse me. . ." She edged closer to the door.

Burke stepped to the side, bringing them almost nose to nose. "Blaire, I'm sorry. I know I hurt you, but I'd like a chance to explain. I've been trying to talk to you all week."

"I don't think we have anything to say to each other." She stepped away. She looked like a caged tigress ready to pounce.

"Please stay. I have so much I want to say."

The anger was beginning to fade from her eyes. "Such as. . ."

Trying not to breathe a sigh of relief, Burke took a deep breath. "Such as all I've been doing the last few days is praying about our relationship. Such as telling you how much I love you."

Her eyes widened. Her mouth dropped open.

"You know, I was only following the suggestion your sister made when I quit."

"My sister? You don't even know my sister. What does she have to do with this?"

"Clarissa called me after you left Phoenix. She said you would never consider marrying anyone you worked with. She told me how you want to do accounting for the ranchers around here. We had a long talk. I'm sorry I hurt you. It wasn't my intention. I was so surprised when you showed up early that I handled it poorly."

Blaire's eyes widened. She looked outside. Burke thought he saw a glimmer of understanding dawning in her eyes. "I didn't give you a chance to explain. I was so afraid you were leaving me that I rushed into the house. I should have listened to you."

Burke gave her his best repentant-little-boy look. "Will you forgive me?"

Sprinkles wound her way around Blaire's leg. Blaire tapped her finger against her lip. "Hmm. I'll forgive you on one condition." At Burke's questioning look she continued. "You have to forgive me, too. And," she added, tilting her head to one side, "I'd really like you to repeat what you said a minute ago."

"You mean the part about your sister?" Burke tried to remember what he'd said.

Blaire took a step closer. "No, I mean when you were saying the 'such as' part."

"Hmm. That wouldn't be the part where I said I love you, would it?"

She nodded.

He lifted his hand and cupped her cheek, marveling at the softness of her skin. He wanted to grin but was too nervous. "We have something else to talk about. I know we've both been hurt and may have trouble trusting each other. I'd like to pray together often. I know if we build a relationship on Jesus Christ, He will help us through any rough times we might have."

Fumbling a small box from his pocket, Burke dropped to one knee. Blaire looked down at him. Tears glistened in her eyes.

"Blaire, will you marry me?" He popped open the small ring box. Lifting her hand, he kissed the tips of her fingers. "I love you. I've prayed about this so much. Will you be my wife?" He held his breath and waited.

She nodded.

He slipped the ring on her finger. The stone sparkled even in the dimness of the barn.

"Yes." The rasp of her voice startled him. "Yes." She sounded stronger. She tugged on his hand, and he started to stand. "Yes, yes, yes." She leaped forward and threw her arms around his neck. The unexpected weight threw him off balance. He tumbled backward. Blaire fell with him.

The force of the impact knocked the breath from him.

"Burke, are you okay?" Blaire grasped his face in her hands. His arms came up to encircle her.

"I must say I do like your enthusiasm, my dear." He grinned and pulled her close for a kiss.

"Meow." Sprinkles poked her head between them. She climbed on Burke and lay down across his neck, purring like a runaway motorboat.

"Does this mean I need her permission, too?"

Blaire giggled. "You bet."

Epilogue

A trilling cacophony from the birds outside the window woke Blaire. Cool morning air wafted across her cheeks. She pulled the covers closer and snuggled in their warmth. Her eyes refused to open, but she sensed the source of the warmth close beside her and moved that way. She snuggled against the body next to her. The tangy scent of pine trees mingled with the spice of cologne.

Throwing her arm across the bare chest, Blaire nestled closer. Arms closed around her, holding her tight. She cracked one eye open and gazed up at Burke. His green eyes looked dark in the morning light. He lifted her chin and kissed her.

"Mmm. Nice." Blaire reached up to stroke his cheek.

"Good morning to you, Mrs. Dunham."

Blaire closed her eyes. "It's not morning yet. I'm still sleeping."

"Do you always talk in your sleep?"

"Mm-hmm. Ask Clarissa sometime. We used to share a room."

"Well, I think I should wake you up." Burke ran his fingers along her sensitive ribs.

She twisted and gasped. "Stop that. This is my honeymoon, and I'm sleeping in."

He chuckled. The tickling fingers attacked again. "This is my honeymoon, too, and I want to get up and do some of the hiking we planned."

"Burke, stop that." Blaire twisted away, giggling. She forced her eyes to stay closed. "You're not supposed to wake someone who's talking in their sleep."

"I've never heard that." Burke's laugh sounded sinister.

"This is like a sleepwalker. You aren't supposed to wake them, either. It could damage the psyche or something."

"Hmm. This is getting interesting. I've never seen a damaged psyche."

The bed dipped. Blaire opened her eyes to catch Burke in mid-leap. She squealed and tried to roll to the side. She was too slow. Burke caught her and began to tickle. Blaire did her best to move away, but her legs got tangled in the covers. Before she knew what happened, she was wrapped up in a cocoon. Still Burke tickled. She laughed so hard tears rolled down her cheeks.

"Stop that. I'm awake."

"Are you crying uncle?"

"Never."

Before Burke could start finding her ticklish spots again, she twisted to the side. Instantly, she realized her mistake. Only empty air stood between her and the floor. Blaire hit the ground with a thud that would have hurt except for the pad of blankets and sheets wrapped around her. She looked up. A pair of sea green eyes, round as saucers, stared down at her. She began to laugh all over again.

"Are you okay?" Burke poked the rest of his head over the edge of the bed.

"You looked so funny." Blaire gasped for air. "You reminded me of a little boy caught doing something he shouldn't."

Burke grinned. "Well, I don't think a husband is supposed to make his wife fall out of bed on their honeymoon." His eyes twinkled with mischief. "Now that you're awake, can we go hiking? These mountains are beautiful. We might even see some deer."

"I can't. I'm feeling all wrapped up."

Burke scratched his chin and looked thoughtful. "You know, if I pick up one corner of that blanket and give it a hard yank. . ."

"Don't you dare." Blaire tried hard to glare at him. "All right, help me out here, and we'll go hiking. But if you continue to tickle me, I'll feed you to the ostriches when we get home."

Burke slid off the bed until he was on the floor beside her. He kissed her softly. "An ostrich a day won't keep me away."

Blaire freed an arm and reached up to cup his cheek. "That's the best news I've heard all day."

Picture Imperfect

Dedication

Thanks to my husband, John, and all the Farrier clan who gave me such a love of camping in the White Mountains of Arizona. Also, thanks to Xena, the real-life squirrel, who fought so valiantly for those chocolate bars.

Chapter 1

J
ason, there are clouds lower than we are." Looking out the window, Jazmyn Rondell tried to drag her gaze from the steep drop-off on her side of her brother's SUV. Opening her mouth, she sucked in a deep draught of air, hoping to quell the nausea twisting her stomach.

"Don't you dare throw up in my new Explorer, sis," Jason said.

"If this stupid seat belt wasn't so tight, I could curl up with my head between my knees."

Jason chuckled. "I don't remember that helping when we were kids."

"At least I wouldn't have to watch when we drop into this bottomless pit." Jazmyn took another deep breath. "You tricked me into this, Jason."

"I didn't trick you. I told you the truth."

"Right. You said you needed to find a guide for your photography expedition. You didn't say we would have to drive up Mount Everest to find him. Couldn't you have picked someone easier to locate?"

"Thor Larson is the best. I wouldn't settle for less. The layout for this next book has to be spectacular."

"So why didn't you just call on the phone like a normal person would?"

"He doesn't have a phone."

Jazmyn swung around to face her brother. "What! No phone? He lives high enough to have jet pilots wave when they fly past, yet he has no way of communicating with anyone? What else should I know about him?"

Jason shrugged. "He's sort of a recluse. From what I've been told he keeps to himself except during hunting season when he guides hunters."

The SUV hit a deep rut, bouncing Jazmyn's head against the window. She forced herself to keep from checking to see how close they'd come to the edge of the precipice. She wouldn't admit it to Jason, but she would do just about anything for him, even climb Mount Everest.

"Jaz, I'm going to have a permanent record that you've ridden in my car."

"I'm doing my best not to throw up, Jason."

He laughed. "I'm talking about the fingers you're digging into the upholstery. They won't even have to use dust to see the prints."

"If we weren't trying to drive up this mountain goat track you insist is a road, I wouldn't have to hold on so tight."

"Lighten up, now; we're almost there. Besides, I know what's good for you."

"Yeah, right," Jazmyn muttered.

"I happen to be your twin," Jason reminded her. "Even if we didn't grow up in the same house, I know when you're miserable. Since Adam died you've shut yourself away from the world. You need some time out, and you promised to accompany me on my next photography shoot."

Pressing her lips tightly together, Jazmyn fought a wave of emotion. Adam, the only man other than Jason she'd ever trusted, had died in a fiery car crash twenty-one months and three days ago, one week before their wedding. From the age of eight, when her parents divorced and Jason left to live with their dad, Jazmyn had been virtually shut off from the world except for her mother. The year they turned nineteen, she and Jason got together again when he began to attend college in the city where she lived. Adam, Jason's friend, quickly became a major part of Jazmyn's life.

Jazmyn pushed away the memories. "Why couldn't this be like the last book where you took pictures of the kids playing at the park? Or better yet, shots of some tropical paradise?"

"Because that's not what the editor wants, and I shoot what he wants. Besides, you need some fresh mountain air. You're as pale as a ghost. The only sunlight you've seen lately is the kind filtered through the kitchen window. This will be an adventure for you."

"I don't need an adventure. I need to have my head examined for trusting you. We're exact opposites. How could you possibly know what's good for me? We may be twins, but I think they found you under a different cabbage plant."

The SUV tilted. Jazmyn felt the seat belt tighten, holding her in place. She pointedly looked away from the drop-off and up the hill on the driver's side of the gleaming black Explorer. "Jason, watch out!"

Jason hit the brakes, halting their already slow progress. "What?"

"He has a gun."

Jason leaned forward and peered up the hill. "Who?"

"A man. He had this huge gun. He was staring at me like he wanted to shoot." She reached out and clenched Jason's arm. "What if this was a warning?"

"Relax." Jason grinned. "Maybe he was a mirage."

"Jason, you don't have mirages in the mountains. I know he was real. He had these piercing eyes. He glared at me."

"Glared at you?" Jason leaned back and laughed. Jazmyn folded her arms across her chest, biting her lip to keep from yelling. Jason could laugh all he wanted, but she knew that man hadn't wanted them here. The way he stared at her, even for just an instant, sent a shiver down her spine.

Wrapping his hand around the gearshift, Jason put the SUV into first. "I know you get scared, but this is paranoid. You've got to start trusting God with your fears."

Gritting her teeth, Jazmyn forced her eyes back to the narrow track in front of them. "Stop." Her palm slapped the dashboard. "We can't go on. The road isn't there." She gasped as she looked closer at the deep cut washed out in the road. During a rainstorm this would be a waterfall shooting down into the valley below. Now dry, the bank rose up on Jason's side of the vehicle. The drop-off on Jazmyn's side split apart by more than two feet.

Jason revved the engine.

"What are you doing?"

He grinned as he put the SUV in gear. "Living dangerously."

"Jason!" Jazmyn yelped. She reached for the door handle and then felt the blood drain from her face as she realized the first step would be a long one.

Slowly the SUV edged close to the bank, the tires on the left side going up onto the hill. The Explorer tilted. Jazmyn squeezed her eyes shut. *God, why did I agree to come? My brother is crazy.* She waited for her life to flash before her eyes. Isn't that what people always claimed happened when they were close to death?

"Jaz, you can breathe again."

She squinted through one eye to see Jason grinning at her. Opening her eyes, she saw that the Explorer rested on all four tires, the washed-out road behind them. She gave a sigh of relief. "That was really foolish," she snapped. "What if we had gone over the edge?"

Jason chuckled. "At least I got some color in your cheeks."

Biting her lip to stop a smile, Jazmyn turned away. From the time they were toddlers until their parents' divorce, Jason had been dragging her into one adventure after another. Each time she had wanted to be furious but found she couldn't resist his impish grin. She couldn't stay mad at him.

Twenty minutes later, Jason rounded a sharp curve in the road and pulled to a stop. "We're here."

Jazmyn groaned. The cabin facing them looked like a slightly more modern version of an 1800s shack. A wooden porch stretched along the front, the weathered boards in desperate need of painting. Metal traps of various sizes hung from pegs along the walls, their sharp teeth grinning as if eager for a kill. A forest of pine and evergreen stood sentinel around the perimeter. In defiance of the building's aged look, a glossy dark green Ford truck rested under the trees to the left of the cabin.

"Jason." Jazmyn's whisper broke the silence. "What are we doing here?"

"Relax." He shut off the engine. Total silence rushed over them. "I can't wait to meet Thor. I hear he's a great hunter."

"I can just imagine. With a name like that he's probably some Norse god with a hammer in one hand and a lightning bolt in the other."

Jason laughed and opened his door. "I've heard some fantastic stories about him but never anything like that."

Stepping out into the cool mountain air, Jazmyn shivered.

"Cold?" Jason asked.

"Terrified would be more accurate. I didn't even notice the temperature." She wanted to throw something when Jason laughed at her comment. "Look, brother dear, I don't think anyone is home. Let's leave. Maybe you can find another editor to work for."

"Not a chance." Jason headed toward the cabin. "I've waited too long for an opportunity like this one."

They were nearing the porch when a pack of wild-eyed, sharp-toothed beasts rounded the corner and enveloped them. Jazmyn opened her mouth to scream. Nothing came out. She closed her eyes, certain they would be torn to pieces. Never had she seen such fierce animals.

"Loki, Odin!" The rough command echoed in the clearing.

Jason's hand squeezed her arm. She eased her eyes open enough to see that what she had assumed to be a dozen savage brutes were actually two dogs standing before her, their tongues lolling. No doubt they were savoring an image of her with an apple stuffed in her mouth.

Looking beyond the dogs, she gasped. *It's him,* she wanted to whisper to Jason. *He's the man I saw in the woods.* But the words stuck in her throat. She grabbed the back of Jason's shirt and leaned closer to him. The huge man at the corner of the cabin pierced her with an electric blue gaze. Hanks of white-gold hair stuck out at odd angles beneath the dark blue hunter's cap he wore. His mouth made a straight line over a clenched jaw. She tried to ignore the broad shoulders and muscular build. She didn't want to acknowledge the strange excitement that raced through her when he held her with his gaze. He looked like her idea of a Norse god. The sleeves of his flannel shirt were rolled back from his wrists to reveal muscular forearms. Time stood still when she lowered her gaze to his hands.

Jazmyn inched closer to Jason until her nose touched the fabric of his shirt. *He's just murdered someone.* Fear constricted her throat. She couldn't take her eyes from the long-bladed, bloody knife he held in his left hand.

"Thor Larson?" Jason's question startled her. He stepped toward the killer, holding out his hand, ignoring the growling dogs.

"Jason, stop." Her voice ended in a frightened squeak.

He ignored her. "I'm Jason Rondell. This is my sister, Jazmyn. I'm looking for a guide. I've been told you're the best."

Thor lifted his right hand toward Jason's outstretched palm. The carcasses of two rabbits dangled limply from his fingers. Bile burned in Jazmyn's throat. Black dots danced across her vision. *Oh, God, don't let me faint. Please get us out of here.*

In one deft movement, Thor transferred the murder victims to the hand with the knife. He shook Jason's hand, causing her brother to wince.

"I'm afraid you're mistaken, Mr. Rondell. I only guide during the hunting season. If you want to poach animals, you'll have to find someone else. Now, if you'll excuse me." Thor turned toward the cabin.

"Mr. Larson."

Thor turned back, one foot on the bottom porch step.

"I don't want to kill any animals. I'm a photographer. I need to do a layout for a book. It's an important shoot for me. I need a guide. I know you're the best, and I'm willing to pay well."

Jazmyn didn't understand how Jason could so calmly face a man who almost dwarfed him in size. Thor looked like he could wrestle a bear. For all she knew he did that as part of his daily routine. She breathed a sigh of relief that it wasn't her those brilliant blue eyes were boring into.

City slickers, Thor thought. *Why do they always come looking for me?* He raised his arm, rubbing his sleeve against his chin. The faint rasp of the stubble reminded him he hadn't shaved today. He studied Jason Rondell, wanting to say no, but something held him back. His gaze strayed to Jazmyn peeking out from behind her brother. Her wide eyes and tense stance reminded him of a deer caught in headlights moments before it bolted into the woods.

"Come on in." He gestured to the door. "I need to get these rabbits on to soak. Then we can talk."

Jason climbed the steps with Jazmyn doing her best to stay close to him. Thor fought back a grin as he watched her pale complexion turn white. She watched his hunting knife with a look of dread until she came abreast of him. Glancing up, she turned pink as she caught him watching her.

Thor strode through the door after the Rondells. "In there." He nodded toward the small sofa in the sitting area. "I'll only be a few minutes." Dangling the rabbits by their ears, he went onto the back porch where he had a sink installed for cleaning game.

Within five minutes Thor had the two rabbits skinned and soaking in salt water. He scrubbed his hands and took a minute to slick his hair into a semblance of order. He rubbed a hand over his stubbly chin, then shook his head. What did he care if he wasn't clean-shaven? He didn't want to impress anyone.

In his mind he could still see Jazmyn standing outside his cabin. She'd been terrified of his dogs, despite the fact they would rather lick people to death than bite them. The sun had glinted off the red-gold highlights in her hair, which hung in a mass of curls. Thor gave himself a mental shake, forcing the vision of her delicate features from his mind. He refused to be attracted to any woman. Never again would he allow a woman to get close to him. He knew he had to protect himself, and his secret, from all women. He would simply concentrate on playing the part of the backwoods hunting guide.

Thor stepped inside and strode into the sitting area. Jason stood at the far wall admiring the large elk head hanging there. Jazmyn huddled on the couch looking like a whipped puppy—utterly adorable.

"How can I help you, Mr. Rondell?"

"Please, call me Jason." The young man turned to face him, a personable smile lighting his handsome features. He ran a hand over his short-cropped reddish brown curls. "As I said, I'm a photographer. My editor wants me to do a layout for a book on wildlife in the White Mountains. I need someone who is familiar with the area and can get me the best shots."

"When?"

"As soon as possible. I'll need a couple of weeks' notice to get all my equipment ready."

Thor nodded and glanced over at Jazmyn. Leaning forward on the sofa, she held out her hand, trying to entice the old dog curled up in the corner to come to her. Her lips were pursed as she made soft kissing sounds. The dog slept on.

"It won't work." He could see he'd startled her. She looked up at him, frozen in place, her hand still outstretched.

"That's Frey," he said. "He was my first hunting dog. When he died I couldn't bear to part with him. Since I also do taxidermy, I stuffed him and kept him around."

A look of horror crossed Jazmyn's face.

Chapter 2

Y ou stuffed your dog?" Jazmyn's voice squeaked as she snatched her hand
back into her lap.

Thor gave a slow grin that reminded her of Jason's impish smiles.
"It's kind of like Roy Rogers and his horse Trigger. I wanted to keep Frey around
for the memories. He and I had a lot of good times together."

Jazmyn shuddered. What other dark secrets did this man have? What about
people he loved? If they died, did he stuff them so he could keep alive the fond
memories? And just what did he do with those who gave him bad memories?
Visions of the bloody knife he'd been holding earlier sent a shiver through her.
She pushed the vivid images away, unwilling to allow them.

"Would you like to see the rest of my collection?" Thor seemed amused at
her discomfort.

She shook her head. Why in the world did he think she wanted to see a
bunch of dead animals? She repressed a shudder and looked to Jason for help.
The goon that claimed to be her twin had his mouth open, probably planning
to say how he wanted to look at lifelike corpses. She glared at him. His eyes
crinkled with laughter, but he kept quiet for once.

"So, Mr. Larson, do you have any idea when you'll be available?" Jason gave
her a smirk that said she owed him.

"How long will this trip last?" Thor asked.

Jason frowned. "I'm hoping we can finish in two weeks, but it might be best
to plan for three just to be on the safe side. Will that be a problem?"

"Usually I only guide for a week at a time." Thor rubbed his chin. Jazmyn
could hear the rasp of his beard. Rather than being repulsed by his rough
appearance, she felt an almost overwhelming attraction. How could she get out
of this trip? She didn't want to spend two or three weeks in close contact with
this man. However, Jason would be a problem. Once he got an idea in his head,
he clung to it with the tenacity of a bulldog.

For the next hour Jazmyn listened as Jason and Thor finalized plans for
the trip. She tried to keep her eyes focused on her hands, but they kept stray-
ing as if they had a mind of their own. First she would find herself staring at
Thor. Then he would glance over and catch her with that brilliant blue gaze
of his. Embarrassed, she would look sideways only to find herself watching
the dead dog sleeping in the corner. Finally, she leaned back against the sofa

131

and closed her eyes.

"C'mon, sis." Jason gave her a swat on the knee, startling her out of her reverie.

"Are we going home now?" Jazmyn regretted the words as soon as they left her mouth. She didn't want them to know she had nearly drifted off, lulled by Thor's deep voice. Since Adam's death she hadn't slept well. At times like this the sleepless nights would catch up with her.

"Not yet." Jason grinned. "We're going with Thor a little farther up the mountain. He has a place he thinks I might be interested in photographing. Of course, if you want to wait here, you can sleep with the dog."

Jazmyn bolted off the couch. Her face burned when she looked at Jason's smirk and knew he'd been teasing her. Thor turned his back in an obvious attempt not to laugh. Still, she thought she could detect his shoulders shaking. Wasn't this nice, that he and Jason were such a chummy pair? She should have known. After all, they were like two peas in a pod; both loved adventure and tormenting helpless creatures—like her. Jazmyn stalked regally out the door.

A few minutes later she wished she'd stayed at the cabin to nap with the dead dog. Wedged in the front seat between Jason and Thor with nothing to hold on to, she found herself bouncing into one and then the other. The track they were taking up the mountain made the road to Thor's house look like a four-lane highway.

Potholes deep enough to count as swimming pools checkered the trail. Thor swung from one side to the other like a skier running a slalom course. Trees grew close, towering giants that threatened to tighten their ranks and not let the vehicle through. Pine-needled branches smacked against the side of the truck as if trying to discourage entry to this realm.

Jazmyn tried closing her eyes. A sudden swerve sent her careening against Thor's arm. Her eyes flew open. Thor grinned down at her. For a long moment Jazmyn couldn't look away. She felt as if he could see all the way into her soul.

"Rock." Jason's matter-of-fact statement made her jump.

Thor looked back out the windshield, grunted, and swung sharply to the right, his side-view mirror scraping against a tree. Jazmyn screamed and grabbed Jason's arm. She needed to pray, but her brain refused to function. Between her fear and this irrational attraction, all she could hope for was to be safe once more in her comfortable apartment. As beautiful as these mountains were, she wasn't sure she ever wanted to come back here.

The truck skidded back onto the faint track and straightened out. Jazmyn gripped the cloth so hard her fingers ached.

"If you want to drive, just ask. You don't have to push me out the door." Thor's statement only made her want to wipe the smug look off his face. How could she be so attracted to this man one minute and furious at him the next?

It didn't make sense.

She shook the hair from her eyes and tried to scowl. "I didn't realize you called this driving." If he could act like Jason, she could treat him the same.

Thor grinned, swerving around another mudhole, bringing her dangerously close to landing in his lap. Skidding to a stop, he shifted into park before he turned to her. "Your chariot ride is over, my lady. Now the walking begins."

"Walking? You said we would drive to the place." Jazmyn hoped they didn't hear the distress in her voice. Exercise was not high on her priority list. In fact, her idea of a workout was the same as her grandfather's had been—after a bath you drain the water and fight the current.

"We're only going a few hundred yards." Thor looked down at her and shrugged his shoulders. "Of course, you can wait here if you want."

Jazmyn breathed a sigh of relief. "Thanks, I'll stay here if you won't be too long."

"We shouldn't be more than an hour." He rubbed his chin, gazing up into the forest of pines. He opened the door and climbed out to join Jason, who looked like an eager puppy ready to bound off into the woods. Thor leaned casually against the door and studied her with his piercing blue eyes.

"If any bears come by, just ignore them." His deep voice boomed like a death knell. She pictured huge bears lumbering out of the woods in droves. "Be sure to keep the doors locked and you'll be safe. They rarely break out glass." His words sent her scrambling for the door at the same time Thor slammed it shut.

⁂

Thor swung the door shut and held his breath, stifling the laughter in his throat. He could hear his mother saying he should be ashamed of himself, but that look of abject terror in Jazmyn's eyes had been worth the teasing. Besides, for some unexplainable reason he wanted her to stay with them.

He wouldn't admit this to anyone, although he suspected Jason might have guessed the truth—he could have done a lot less swerving around potholes if he'd wanted. Instead, he found himself relishing the contact with Jazmyn. The scent of her lingered, along with the ripples of sensation created by her touch.

"Wait." Jazmyn swung the door open, bolted from the vehicle, and almost ran over them catching up. "I think I will go along." She walked close to Jason, but her eyes were swinging from one tree to the next as if watching for any wild animals that might want to have her for lunch.

The climb uphill wasn't too steep, but Thor knew that for someone unused to exercise it would be a strain. He kept the pace slow, stopping to point out various mosses and small wildlife to give Jazmyn a chance to catch her breath. He knew Jason understood why he kept stopping, but he had a hard time understanding his own motives. Normally, he would take a perverse pleasure in setting a grueling pace just to show city slickers how ill-prepared they were for the mountains.

Between the climbing and the thin air, they quickly became short of breath and begged for a break.

With Jazmyn he felt different. For some strange reason he wanted to help her to enjoy the experience. He shook his head and stopped to point out a squirrel scolding them from a branch above. When Jazmyn couldn't find it, he pulled her close, cheek to cheek, directing her until her eyes lit up with pleasure at seeing the squirrel. The closeness brought to life feelings he didn't want to explore. He released her and stepped away, stalking on toward the overlook. He was glad he wouldn't see her again after today. He'd sworn off women, their lies, and all the trouble they brought with them.

The faint rumble of the falls grew louder. The ground vibrated beneath their feet. Thor motioned, and Jason and Jazmyn followed his every move as they approached the cliff overlooking the forest pool. They didn't have to be quiet. The sound of the waterfall covered any noise they made. Wildlife frequently drank from the pool at the base of the falls. Thor hoped they wouldn't startle any deer or elk that happened to be there.

Within minutes he gestured for Jazmyn to sit with him on the rocks at the edge of the cliff. Jason dropped down on her other side. Her face paled a little as she peered over the edge of the steep drop-off. Hunkering down, she eased forward until she rested next to him. Her feet swung over empty space, while her fingers whitened from their grip on the rocks.

Jason and Jazmyn were speechless, staring at the beauty in the glade below. The waterfall plunged over rocks decorated with green moss into a mirror-like pool bordered by a carpet of jade-colored grass. A mixture of pine, scrub oak, and spruce trees circled the edge of the clearing. Various ferns grew on the hillside. A small stream bubbled and churned, wending its way down the mountain.

A doe stepped out from the trees, her long ears flicking back and forth as she stood like a statue checking for danger. At a silent signal she moved forward, and two fawns leaped from the forest to gambol across the grass toward the water. Their spotted backs twitched as they cavorted on their spindly legs.

Jazmyn gripped Thor's arm, apparently oblivious to her actions, and her mouth formed a silent O. She stared as if mesmerized by the scene below. Thor couldn't help studying her face. The climb had brought a rosy hue to her pale complexion. A strand of red-gold hair drifted across her cheek. He longed to brush the stray lock back into place.

As if sensing his perusal, she lifted her eyes and looked at him. He had the wild urge to kiss her. For that enchanted look in her green eyes, he, Thor the unapproachable, felt like he would do almost anything.

Chapter 3

Downshifting, Thor eased his truck into the crossing, the waters coming higher than in most years. The mountains had gotten a lot of rain in the last month, resulting in the rushing river.

"That's okay, boys." He grinned at his dogs' eager faces. They loved coming to the mountains with him. "This will keep any touristy types from invading our camp."

A dirt track led off into the trees. Thor pulled in and stopped the pickup. Rolling down the window and shutting off the engine, he reveled in the silence of the forest.

Loki scrambled across his lap to stick his head out the window. Tongue lolling, the dog appeared to be laughing in sheer delight at being at the camp again. Thor's cabin might be high by desert standards, but this place was another four thousand feet in elevation. He and his dogs always welcomed the change in temperature.

"Let's go." Thor flung the door open and the dogs leaped out. They rushed about, noses to the ground, checking to see who had been there in their absence. Overhead a squirrel scampered to a higher branch, stopping to scold the dogs for invading her territory.

Thor began to drag equipment from the bed of the truck. He and Jason had planned exactly what each would bring so they could set up camp. The more Thor talked with Jason the more he admired him. Jason knew his way around the woods and a camp. These two weeks could be relaxing and fun, a good break from the stress of running the company.

By the time Thor heard the rumble of Jason's SUV lumbering through the crossing, he had his tent erected and the camp's "kitchen" arranged.

"Hey, Thor," Jason called from his open window as he slowed to a stop beside Thor's truck. The dogs leaped in delighted anticipation. "Sorry we're running a little late."

Thor swung around, muttering under his breath. "Sorry *we're* late?" He stared in horror as a slender figure climbed out of the far side of the SUV. Jazmyn. Jazmyn of the enchanting eyes. Jazmyn, who had haunted his thoughts for the past two weeks. Jazmyn, whom he thought he'd never see again and would soon forget.

Jason bounded forward, grinning, hand outstretched. "I managed to convince

Jazmyn to come along and help with the photo shoots." He lowered his voice as he glanced over his shoulder at his sister. "She needs to get away and relax a little. She's strung tight enough to snap."

Acting on autopilot, Thor shook hands with Jason, but his gaze riveted on the woman standing beside the SUV. Her wide eyes drew him in as she stared at him. Thor wanted to argue with Jason about having Jazmyn here, but he could see from her pale, drawn look that she needed this. Nothing healed a worn spirit like time spent in the mountains. Fresh air, camp food, and exercise were sure to help her out.

"Jason, Jazmyn." He nodded in her direction. The thin air seemed to be making him light-headed, a problem he didn't often have. At least not when he was standing still, doing nothing. Maybe she would only stay a couple of days and then go back to the city for her job. For his peace of mind Thor hoped so.

"Jaz had all her accounts up-to-date, so she'll be able to stay for the whole two weeks." Jason flashed a smile at his sister, then lowered his voice. "Of course, she's never been camping before, so this could be quite an experience for her." He gestured at Jazmyn. "Come on over here and say hello."

Still wide-eyed, Jazmyn came over and offered Thor her hand. He had a wild urge to bow and kiss her fingers like some love-crazed knight but caught himself in time only to nod as he wrapped her hand in his.

"Accounts?" Thor asked, trying to make sense of what he'd heard. "Jason said you had your accounts up-to-date." Realizing he still held her hand, he let go. "What kind of accounts?"

"I run a small business from my home. Small-business web pages. I set them up and keep them current."

Thoughts of his own company flashed through Thor's mind. No way would she consider T.L. Enterprises to be small. No one would. Besides, he didn't want her to think of him in any other capacity than that of a backwoods hunting guide. Not with what he knew about the greedy nature of women. He didn't think he could take finding out this beauty was as manipulative as the other females who'd been in his life.

"Come on, Jaz. Let's get everything unloaded in case it starts to rain later," Jason called back over his shoulder. "I brought an extra tent so she could have her own."

Jazmyn stared after Jason's retreating back. "What are you talking about? I'm not sleeping in a tent. There are bears in these woods." She marched after Jason, her back rigid. "What do you mean a tent? You didn't mention this. In fact, you implied we would have access to a motor home. Remember?"

Jason's chuckle sounded forced as he tossed a sleeping bag at his sister. "I had to do something to get you to come. Besides, I never said we would use an RV. I only said that some people use them up here."

Clinging to the sleeping bag, Jazmyn stared, her mouth open. Thor leaned back against his truck and watched. He wasn't about to get in the middle of this.

"What about the bears?" she squeaked.

"Keep food out of your tent, and they won't bother you." The bag of tent poles clanked as Jason tossed them to the ground.

"What if they think I'm food?"

"With your sour disposition?" Jason laughed. "It'll never happen." He threw a second sleeping bag to Jazmyn, then picked up the tent and poles and went to pick out a spot to set up. The dogs lost interest and flopped down under a tree to watch. Thor didn't know whether to offer his help or stay out of the danger zone.

After he covered the kitchen area with a tarp to protect against rain, Thor pulled up a chair, settling in to watch Jason and Jazmyn. He could use a little break, anyway. At first he found them funny. Jason, knowledgeable about camping, barked orders, expecting Jazmyn to follow his rapid-fire instructions. The perpetual look of confusion on her face touched his heart, though. When he noticed the sheen of tears in her eyes, Thor had had enough.

"Why don't you take a break while I help Jason finish this?" he offered, taking the tent pole out of Jazmyn's hands and directing her to the vacated chair. "We'll have this up in no time." He squeezed her shoulder. "You'll be as safe as if you were home in your apartment, maybe safer. Some of the human animals in the city are much more dangerous than the animals in the wild."

Jazmyn blinked and turned away as if trying to hide the fact that she was about to cry. Thor fought the desire to put his arms around her. He'd never had such a strong attraction to a woman before, not even his ex-fiancées.

"It's okay. I came to help out, not to be a burden." Jazmyn's voice quavered.

The list of chores that needed to be done ran through Thor's mind. He wanted to come up with some job that would make her feel useful, not incompetent.

"On the way up here I stopped and cut enough wood for tonight and tomorrow morning. Why don't I help you up into the back of the truck? You can toss the logs out. Then if you still want something to do, you can stack them between those two trees over there." He pointed at a pair of trees near the fire pit he'd already dug, but not close enough to be a hazard.

⁂

After only ten minutes Jazmyn's arm muscles burned. Half the truck bed was piled with logs that Thor seemed to think were nothing more than sticks. She thought some of them weighed more than she did.

She hefted another one, preparing to toss it onto the growing pile beside the pickup. But when she heaved, the log slipped and crashed to the floor of the truck bed, coming to rest on her toe. She shrieked.

"Jaz, you okay?" Jason peered over the side of the truck.

Thor vaulted over the side, his blue eyes full of concern. "What happened?"

"That tree trunk landed on my toe," Jazmyn managed to say as waves of agony shot up her leg.

"Let's get this shoe off and see if the toe's broken." Thor shifted the log until it stood on end. "Here, have a seat." He patted the piece of wood. As soon as she was seated he un-laced her sneaker.

"You should have boots for up here in the mountains." Although he spoke to her, Jazmyn had the distinct impression that Thor's words were directed at Jason.

"Jason told me to bring boots, and I did bring them. I just didn't put them on yet." She gasped as he eased the shoe off. "I thought they were only for hiking."

She closed her eyes as Thor slipped her sock off. The sharp pain had passed, replaced by throbbing. She didn't want to look, but the sensation of Thor's touch seemed even more dangerous than having a broken toe.

"No blood, sis. You'll live." Jason sounded like he was holding back laughter. She opened her eyes and glared at him.

"Ouch!" She tried to jerk back from Thor's probing, but he had a firm grip on her foot.

"This might be sore for a few days." He smiled up at her, still holding her foot in his hands. Her pulse raced. Jazmyn tried to convince herself it was from the excitement of the moment and had nothing to do with Thor's touch, or the way she felt as he gazed at her.

"It doesn't look broken. I don't even think you'll lose the nail." Shaking out her sock, he eased it back over her toes carefully.

The image of Thor holding the bloody knife flashed through Jazmyn's mind again as it had a hundred times since the day she met him. In the past two weeks she'd convinced herself the man was a danger to society. She'd been terrified of coming up here with Jason but even more terrified to have Jason come alone. This man, treating her with such compassion, wasn't the same man who'd invaded her thoughts for the past few weeks. How could she ever have thought he would harm them?

"There you go." Thor held out a hand to help her to her feet. "I'd better get back to helping Jason. We still have a lot to do." He tossed the offending log from the truck as if it weighed nothing, then vaulted to the ground. Turning, he held out his hand. As she slipped over the side and landed on the ground, Jazmyn did her best not to wince. For some reason she wanted to show Thor she could be a good camper. She wanted him to like her.

Chapter 4

S taring into the crackling flames, Jazmyn didn't think life could get much worse. Every muscle in her body ached. Her toe throbbed. She'd been humiliated beyond what she ever thought possible. This may well have been the worst day of her life.

Jesus, You promised to come back for Your people. Now might be a real good time. She raised a questioning eyebrow at the night sky. Visions of being whisked up to heaven made her sigh. No more pain. No more humiliation. "How soon can I get there?" She glanced over her shoulder hoping no one had heard her. That's all she needed, for Thor to believe she was loony enough to talk to herself.

Jason and Thor were nowhere in sight. She didn't know what mischief they were up to now. All afternoon Jason had tormented her with one thing or another. To his credit, Thor hadn't actually done anything to her, but she'd seen him trying to hide a smile once or twice.

For years she hadn't been interested in men. Her mother had convinced her they all were bad. Then she met Adam and that opinion dissolved. When Adam died, Jazmyn wanted everything else to end, too. For the first time in two years, she'd met a man she might be interested in, and all she could do was make a fool of herself.

She sighed. This wasn't meant to be, anyway. Thor might make her react to him physically, but she had the feeling he wasn't on the same wavelength spiritually. She and Jason had had several longs talks about being unequally yoked, as the Bible called it. They had even attended a singles class at church on the perils of dating someone who didn't share your faith. She'd determined not to fall into that trap if she ever decided to date again.

Then why do I have to be attracted to a man who isn't a Christian? The question had plagued her for most of the afternoon.

The lantern Thor hung from a tree hissed into the night. Moths and other small insects hovered around the bright light, swooping and dipping in a graceful waltz.

The low rumble of male laughter drifted to her. She supposed Jason and Thor were still doing something to finish the camp setup. They'd both been fanatical about seeing that everything was in its place.

She'd felt nothing but helpless all afternoon. Every time she tried to step in and do something, they took over because she was doing it wrong. Even the way she stacked the wood was wrong, so Jason redid the whole pile. She wanted to scream.

Closing her eyes, she listened to the ripple of the river rushing past their camp. No cars. No sirens. No helicopters or planes. Absolute quiet could be unnerving. She almost wanted to jump up and yell, "Where is everybody?" How could anyone find this peaceful? Even Thor and Jason were quiet now.

From the corner of her eye she caught movement. Expecting her brother to be sneaking up on her, she stared into the fire. He wouldn't pull a fast one on her this time. She was prepared.

A slight dragging noise came from that side of the camp. Jason was being quiet, but she knew exactly where he was. She would wait till he was right behind her, then jump up and scare him. She grinned. That would serve him right, especially if Thor were there to witness her triumph instead of another defeat.

Her heart pounded. Sweat dampened her palms. A snuffling noise and another slight motion came from closer to her chair. She tensed, ready to leap to her feet.

Another burst of laughter rang out from across the camp. Jazmyn frowned. How could Jason be over there laughing and also sneaking up on her? What were they up to, anyway?

Something dark drifted into the ring of lantern light. Heart thudding, Jazmyn felt like the heroine in a horror movie, forwarding in slow motion, as she turned her head to look. A skunk, the size of a small dog, ambled toward her and the fire. The movement she'd spotted from the corner of her eye had to be the gentle motion of the black and white tail rising up and down. Her stomach knotted.

"Jason." Her constricted throat released the word as a squeaky whisper. The skunk paused a moment before continuing toward her.

Jazmyn wanted to leap off the chair and run for safety. How far did a skunk spray? Didn't a raised tail mean the beast was getting ready to douse everything with foul-smelling scent? She froze as the animal wandered nearer, too terrified even to draw her legs up onto the chair.

Two smaller versions of the approaching pest trotted into the light. Jazmyn sank tighter against the back of her seat, praying the fabric wouldn't tear and spill her to the ground. One of the babies scampered up on the rocks of the fire pit and began to sniff.

Earlier, after he'd gotten the fire going, Jason had burned all the trash from their meal. The baby skunk must have smelled the lingering aroma. Jazmyn clenched her fists as the small skunk leaned over and pawed at the coals. What would the mother skunk do if the baby caught on fire?

"Shoo." The baby didn't even look up. "Go away." Jazmyn knew these wild animals would never heed her quiet whisper, but that was all she could manage at the moment. She didn't know how this situation could get much worse.

Something brushed against Jazmyn's pant leg. She stared in horror as the mother skunk wound her way through her legs, the long fur of the skunk's tail waving in the slight breeze. If this were happening on television, Jazmyn might be able to appreciate how cute these animals were. As it was, only her terror glued her to her seat.

"Jaz, don't move," Jason said from somewhere behind her. She wanted to ask if he thought she was stupid. Was she going to jump up and down or something?

"We're going to make some noise. They'll leave the camp." Thor stepped into the shadows off to her left. She could see from the corner of her eye that he held a bucket and a stick.

"What are you doing?" She was already preparing for the onslaught of skunk scent.

"They don't like this sound. Don't jump. Stay still." Thor lifted the stick and beat on the bucket like a drummer from some band.

The baby skunk jumped down from the rocks. The mother scampered off toward the shadows, her babies close behind. Jazmyn's muscles cramped from being tensed so long.

"Relax, sis." Jason's heavy pat to her back reverberated through her. "You probably would have lost the scent by the time we got back to civilization." His laughter chased after the skunks.

⟡

"Once we get the camp set up, we'll start looking for the wildlife you want to shoot." Thor picked up the axe, hefting it to get the feel just right before he started splitting wood. Jason was finishing the tarps over the kitchen area. With the building clouds, having the tarps up was important.

"What will we be looking at first?" Jason asked.

Thor caught a glimpse of Jazmyn stepping from rock to rock down by the river. Ever since the episode with the skunks last night, she'd changed. Before she'd been uncertain about the mountains and the wildlife here. Now she appeared afraid of everything. Her gaze roved the hills around them, and she avoided areas of dense brush or high grass. Every new sound made her jump. The dark circles under her eyes told Thor she hadn't slept well last night.

"I thought we might try to find some elk. I've seen a large herd not far from here." Thor gestured toward Jazmyn with his chin. "Has she ever been in the mountains before?"

Jason shook his head. "Naw. She doesn't get out much. Stays shut up in her apartment and works on her computer. She's had some emotional setbacks. This trip may be hard, but I think it will be good for her."

"I'm thinking for her first time camping, the experience might have been better in a more controlled setting."

Jason shrugged. "You could be right. She's tough, though. I wanted something to shock her out of the depression she's been in."

"If you wanted shock, this should do it." Thor set up a log, stepped back, and prepared to swing the axe. Jason moved away to finish the tarps.

The pile of split logs grew as Thor swung the axe. After the first ten minutes, he removed his long-sleeved shirt. The cool air dried the sweat that had built up in the short time he'd been working. This was one of his favorite jobs in camp. Something about the rhythmic swing of the axe and the bite into the wood satisfied him.

From the corner of his eye he kept a watch on Jazmyn. The lack of sparkle in her eyes bothered him. He wanted to do something to help her adjust to the mountains. By the time he finished the splitting and stacking, he had an idea of what to do.

Curled up in a chair reading a book, Jazmyn looked pale and vulnerable when he approached her later. She glanced up, her luminous green eyes a little dull, from fatigue he guessed. Thor smiled.

"Jason says you haven't done much camping before."

She chewed her lower lip, an action he found fascinating. "This will probably be my only camping trip. I don't plan to let him trick me into doing it again." Moisture glistened in her eyes.

"I thought you might like to help out with the cooking." Thor hunkered down so he wouldn't appear to tower over her. "It's different from cooking at home, but the food always seems to taste better. I don't know if it's the air or just being outdoors, but eating in the mountains is a different experience."

"I can't imagine this being better than picking up a sandwich or soup at the corner deli."

"Then you haven't done enough work around camp." Thor grinned. "Are you game enough to help out?"

She nodded. He stood and held out his hand to help her from the chair. As he drew her up, he noticed a slight flush stain her cheeks. He wondered what thoughts were making her blush. Did she feel an attraction to him? Memories of another woman who acted coy and blushed, then broke his heart, sent a shaft of anger coursing through him. He let go of Jazmyn's hand and swung around to stalk off toward the kitchen area.

"I'm finished with the tarps. I'll get some water," Jason called as he set off toward the river swinging two buckets at his side. A breeze ruffled his hair.

"I want to show you how to work the stove first," Thor said as Jazmyn caught up to him. He unscrewed the pump on the gas tank. "Before you use one of these stoves, you have to pump the tank to build up pressure. Sometimes you have to pump a little during the cooking to keep the right pressure."

He demonstrated by pulling the knob out and plunging it back in. Holding the stove tight with one hand, Thor kept up the pumping action for a few seconds.

"Here, you try it." He stepped back to make room for Jazmyn. Her first try had the pump plunging in fast, but without doing any good. She looked at Thor in frustration.

"Here." He put his fingers over hers. "You need to cover this hole in order for the pressure to build." He tightened his hand and helped her to pump the stove.

"How do you know when you've done enough?"

Thor let go and Jazmyn continued to work the lever. "It depends on how full the tank is. Since I just filled it, you won't need to pump as long. You'll feel the pressure building and it will get harder to do."

She caught her lower lip between her teeth, concentration furrowing her brow. Thor admired her willingness to try this. Most of the women he'd known wouldn't go to the mountains unless it was winter and they were housed at a lodge for skiing.

"That's good." Thor showed her how to screw the pump shut. "Now you turn this lever up, light your match, and open the line for the gas to come out." He scraped a match along the stove and touched it to the burner. Flames shot up several inches. Jazmyn gasped and jumped back. Thor chuckled. "Don't worry. That's the way this stove lights."

He began to pump the lever again. "The flame will calm down in a minute. When that happens you turn this lever down, adjust the flame to the right heat, and you're ready to cook."

Thor plunked an iron skillet filled with hamburger meat on the grill over the burner. "We can make some sloppy joes for lunch. How are you at chopping onion?" He cocked an eyebrow, trying to ignore how much he enjoyed having Jazmyn here beside him. The picture of her helping him out around the camp was almost too appealing. Maybe encouraging her to cook wasn't the best idea.

"I'll have you know I'm an expert at chopping onions," she said. Thor gazed down into Jazmyn's eyes. A slight smile lit her features.

"Hey, Thor, we have company," Jason called out from near the river.

Jazmyn's eyes grew wide with horror as she stared past Thor. All color drained from her face. Thor swung around to see a black bear ambling down the hill toward them.

Chapter 5

That's the last of it." Jason backed out of the truck after stowing his photography equipment behind the seat.

A hush lay over the forest. Thor glanced again at Jazmyn's tent, wanting to know if she was okay, but knowing it wasn't his place to approach her until she came out. Jason had already given her a wake-up call. Last night Jason had spent quite awhile with Jazmyn, talking to her and reading to her from the Bible. Thor hadn't interfered. He only hoped what Jason said helped Jazmyn sleep. After the incident with the bear, she'd been too terrified to do much.

Bears sometimes wandered into camp in the mountains. If they were hungry and smelled food, they came to investigate. In a regular camping area, the forest service did their best to keep the sites free of bears, but out here nature took over. Fortunately, the bear hadn't stuck around. When Thor waved his arms and yelled, the creature changed its mind about being hungry. These small blacks weren't very aggressive.

But Jazmyn, having never camped in the mountains before, didn't understand this. She associated bears with attacks and mutilation. She'd been in a state of abject terror for most of the afternoon.

The sound of a zipper swung Thor's attention back to her tent. She stepped out, one hand still on the flap, as if she would jump back in if need be. Her nose wrinkled. Thor breathed deep, noting the pine scent of the forest and knowing that's what she was smelling, too. He wondered if she enjoyed breathing in this fresh air as much as he did.

"Good morning." He smiled at her.

"Morning? More like the middle of the night, you mean." At least she retained her sense of humor.

"C'mon, sis, you're slowing us down," Jason said. "Let's go."

"Without breakfast? No coffee?" Jazmyn's eyes widened. Thor recalled that she hadn't eaten enough to keep a bug alive yesterday. She had to be hungry this morning.

"I've already poured you a cup of coffee." Jason held up a travel cup. "Grab a granola bar and hop in. Your chariot awaits." He gave a courtly bow, one hand motioning toward the truck.

For the first time Thor noticed Jazmyn's attire. She wore jeans, hiking boots, and a T-shirt. Her jacket must still be inside. She stood there rubbing her arms, shivering.

"Where's your jacket?" he asked.

Her teeth chattered. "Do you realize where I come from the temperature is over a hundred degrees in the daytime? The nights aren't cold, either." She shrugged. "I wore my only long-sleeved shirt yesterday."

"You didn't bring a jacket?" Thor wanted to throttle Jason. Hadn't he realized Jazmyn wouldn't know what kind of clothes to bring to the mountains if she'd never been here before?

"Hey, I told her to bring something warm," Jason said.

"You told me sometimes it gets cool in the mountains. I brought the only flannel shirt I owned for the nights. I didn't expect the mornings to be so cold." She blinked several times.

Jason shook his head and ran a hand through his hair. "Sorry, Jaz. I didn't think about you not knowing what to bring. I've been going to the mountains so many years I just assumed everyone knew how to pack."

Thor reached Jazmyn in three strides. Her eyes grew round as she watched him stalking toward her. Tugging off his jacket, he wrapped it around her shoulders. He wanted to draw her into his arms and hold her until she stopped shivering, but he resisted the urge.

"I can't take your coat. You'll be cold."

He let his hands linger a moment on her shoulders. "I don't get too cold up here. I'm used to the cooler temperatures. Besides, I have a spare jacket in the truck. Ready to go?"

She nodded, shrugging into the jacket. She looked like a little girl playing dress-up in clothes several sizes too big. She was so adorable. He slipped his hand under her elbow and led her to the truck. Jason joined them with steaming cups of coffee, several granola bars protruding from his pockets.

"Why do we have to get up so early?" Jazmyn stifled a yawn as Thor fired up the truck. "Aren't the animals still sleeping?"

Jason laughed. "This is prime time for animal viewing. Early morning and dusk are the best times to find the elk and deer out feeding. The best light will be about the time we get there. Just because you sleep till noon doesn't mean the rest of the world does."

Jazmyn's cheeks pinkened. She lifted the coffee to her lips and took a tentative sip. Thor thought about telling Jason he had to treat his sister better or walk to the herd of elk. He blew out a breath. He liked Jason. For the most part he was a decent sort, but when it came to Jazmyn, he constantly baited her.

"What kind of animals are we going to see first?" she asked.

Before Thor could answer, Jason piped up. "We're going for the bears first." He peeled the wrapper from a granola bar. "I missed filming the one in camp yesterday afternoon, so we're going to find a few today."

Clenching his jaw, Thor fought back anger. Why did Jason do this to Jazmyn? "If you want to see bear, you'll have to hop out and hoof it. I'm taking you to the herd of elk like we planned earlier."

"Well, I guess I'll have to settle for them, then." Jason grinned and held out a packet to Jazmyn. "Granola bar?"

She took the proffered bar. Thor noted how she'd moved a little closer to him. He wanted to put his arm around her and tell her he wouldn't let anything bad happen, but he couldn't do that. Besides, he needed both hands to drive as he swung off the main road onto the track leading into the forest.

"Do all these places have to be so rough?" Jazmyn lifted her coffee cup, trying to keep the hot liquid from spilling as they thumped through a pothole.

"You don't find herds of wildlife along the interstate," Jason quipped. "They're out here because people don't come here often. They don't enjoy the malls or shopping."

"Once you get used to these roads, they aren't so bad," Thor said, ignoring Jason's comment. "Think of it in terms of people who refuse to use a computer because they don't understand them. Once they start using one they begin to enjoy what they can do."

"I'm not sure I see the comparison between computers and the middle-of-nowhere." Jazmyn's eyes twinkled.

Thor chuckled. "I'm just trying to say that a lot of people are afraid of the unknown, but when they get used to something, it can become enjoyable."

Jazmyn fell against him as he swung to miss a deep rut. "I can't imagine ever finding this enjoyable," she said. Thor looked away, not wanting her to read the disappointment in his eyes.

※

The engine strained as they crawled up a ridge. Jazmyn felt sure mountain goats would have trouble bounding up this track.

She tried to focus on the trees outside Thor's window so she wouldn't see the drop-off on Jason's side. If she looked out the windshield, the steep rise in front of them made her dizzy, too. Thor glanced down at her, his azure gaze making her as dizzy as the drop-off. She closed her eyes, certain there wasn't a safe place to look.

"Here we are." Thor's deep voice brought her out of her reverie.

Opening her eyes, Jazmyn gasped. Through the forest she could see a small open meadow ringed with trees. Bars of sunlight filtered between the branches, giving the scene a surreal quality. On the far side of the clearing, a few long-legged shapes moved through the remnants of the mist.

"This is spectacular." Jason's hushed whisper startled Jazmyn. "I need to get my equipment out and set up before the fog burns off." He eased the door open and clambered out.

Thor placed a hand on Jazmyn's arm as she started to follow Jason. She turned to find him staring down at her.

"I know you're not familiar with the wildlife here. These elk are as shy as any animal can be. We have to move quietly. No talking, either. If they see that we're here, they'll be gone just like that." He snapped his fingers and winked at her. Jazmyn thought she might agree to anything he said at that moment.

Outside the truck she pulled the jacket close against the chill air, savoring the man-scent on the coat. Thor strode around the front of the truck. "Need any help, Jason?"

"No." Jason dug through a bag, retrieving various lenses and film. "I'm not setting up a tripod or anything." He glanced at Jazmyn and then back at Thor. "If you want to help, you can make sure Jazmyn doesn't meet up with anything wild that makes her scream."

Jazmyn glared at him.

"I'm serious, Jaz. If you make any noise and scare these animals off, I'll feed you to the bears myself." He grinned to soften his words.

They watched as he slipped through the trees to the edge of the clearing. Jazmyn didn't know whether to be angry with her brother or not. He'd wanted her to come along, supposedly to help out. Now he didn't seem to want her here at all.

"Why don't we take a walk along the ridge?" Thor's hand grasped her elbow. Jazmyn couldn't remember when he'd taken her arm, but she enjoyed his touch. Wonder filled her at that knowledge. She hadn't wanted a man to touch her since Adam, or before Adam, either. What was it about Thor that was so different she found herself attracted to him?

"Will we scare off the elk?" she whispered.

"Not if we're careful." Thor began to walk, guiding her to a narrow trail. "We might even find a good vantage point where we can watch without endangering the filming."

Jazmyn almost laughed. "This sounds like a movie. Do you suppose the elk ladies are all made up and ready for their big day?"

Thor grinned. Her heart skipped a beat. "These ladies wear their finery every day."

As they continued along the ridge the sun burned off all the fog. This would be a bright beautiful morning. Thor had mentioned they should have rain by the afternoon, but right now there wasn't a cloud in the sky.

Staying away from the cliff edge kept Jazmyn's mind off Thor. She'd never thought she would be attracted to someone rough and rugged. Adam had been into computers. They had so much in common. They would talk for hours about their businesses, customers, and ways they would combine their enterprises once they were married. What would she and Thor ever have to talk about? Past pets? The various ways to chop an onion?

A high cry pierced the air. Jazmyn froze. Thor stepped up beside her. "Look." He pointed up at the sky. A gray-white bird soared overhead, graceful and free.

"What is it?" Jazmyn stared in awe at the beautiful sight.

"It's an osprey." Thor wasn't watching the bird anymore. He seemed to be looking up at the trees instead.

"Look, there." He pointed again, this time at a clump of pine trees. Jazmyn tried to figure out what he wanted her to see.

"See the dead tree, right in the middle?" Thor leaned close, helping her to sight on the right one. "Near the top of that tree."

She stared in the direction he indicated, found the pine, and let her gaze travel to the top. She drew in a sharp breath. "It's a nest."

"That's where the osprey has its young. Watch." The bird circled a few more times then glided down toward its babies.

"What's it carrying?"

"Breakfast," Thor said, smiling. "She's been out fishing and is carrying her catch back for the babies."

"Breakfast in bed? I don't think I would want stinky fish crumbs in there with me."

His low, throaty laugh warmed her. She couldn't help but join him.

"We'd better keep going if we want to see the elk." This time he led her off the path into the trees. "I think we've come far enough, but we'll have to be quiet from here on out."

They wound through the tall pines with Thor doing his best to keep them from making much noise. He often pointed out sticks to her, keeping her from stepping on them and making a loud snap.

As they approached the meadow Thor slowed. From behind him Jazmyn couldn't see much. She didn't want to look around him for fear of making too much commotion. She had no doubt Jason would feed her to the bears, or do some other horrible thing, if she ruined this opportunity.

Thor stopped. He motioned her to come up beside him. Jewel-green grass dotted with yellow flowers sparkled in the clearing. All the morning mist had departed, but dew clung in a heavy coat. They both crouched down, gazing in awe at the graceful elk.

Jazmyn didn't know how long they watched the herd or how long Thor had been holding her hand. The moment seemed magical. He pointed across the meadow. She could see Jason crouched at the edge shooting pictures.

Something thudded on her head and bounced off onto the ground. She looked at Thor from the corner of her eye. Had he done something to her? She looked around. There weren't any other animals around, and the elk hadn't thrown anything.

Thump. A second time something hit her head.

She tugged Thor's sleeve. "Did you—?"

He shushed her with a finger to his lips. Three of the elk closest to them swung their heads up, grass still sticking out from their mouths. They took a couple of nervous steps, then seemed to sense there wasn't any trouble and went back to eating.

Scrabbling sounded overhead. Jazmyn looked up just in time to see a brown blur before something hit her in the middle of her forehead.

Chapter 6

"O uch!" Jazmyn slapped her hand to her forehead. Her skin stung as if she'd been pricked by a hundred needles.

Thunder rumbled, although there wasn't a cloud in the sky. It took her a moment to realize the sound was that of the elk racing across the field. She'd done what Jason said not to do—make the herd stampede before he'd finished his pictures.

"I'm dead." Dread filled her even as she pulled her fingers away, noting a trace of red on them.

"What happened?" Thor asked.

"Something hit me." She pointed at her forehead, hoping there was at least some sign that she'd been wounded.

He pulled a handkerchief from his pocket and dabbed at her forehead. "What in the world hit you?"

"I don't know. I was just sitting here watching the elk and something hit my head twice." She hesitated, giving him a sheepish smile. "I thought you might be playing a joke on me. Then I looked up and, *wham*, this thing smacked into me."

A few drops of blood stained his handkerchief. He frowned and stared up into the trees. "There's your attacker." He pointed at an upper branch. A squirrel skittered along, hurrying to get to the trunk of the tree. "She must have been eating the seeds out of the pine cones and throwing the cones down when she finished. You happened to be right under her. These squirrels can get territorial, but they don't normally attack people."

He grinned. "We'd better get back and see how Jason fared. I'm hoping the elk didn't run over the top of him."

Jason wasn't as angry as she thought he'd be. In fact, he was excited. "You won't believe the pictures I got! I'd taken two rolls of film of the elk grazing and the calves playing. Then, when I was almost ready to quit, thinking I wouldn't get any other good pictures, they all started to run toward me. I can't wait to get that film developed." His voice rose as his hands acted out what happened. "I've never been that close or had an opportunity like that."

Thor's eyes twinkled with their secret as Jason wondered aloud what had spooked the herd. Jazmyn wasn't going to tell him. She didn't think Thor would, either.

By the time they returned to camp, it was almost noon. Jazmyn was starving.

"If that bear comes back today, he won't stand a chance. I'll eat him," she grumbled as she slid out of the cab of the truck. The granola bar had worn off long ago. Her whole body felt battered and sore. She couldn't remember the last time she'd walked so much. To top it off, all this walking was either uphill or downhill. By tomorrow morning she wouldn't be able to move.

After a quick lunch of sandwiches and chips, Jazmyn relaxed in a chair with her Bible. She hadn't done her study that morning because they left before it was light enough to read. Last night Jason had talked to her about her fears and how she needed to trust God more. He said she wasn't allowing God to lead in her life when everything made her afraid. Being a new Christian, she wasn't sure what to think, but she wanted to take the time to study some of the Scriptures he'd written down for her.

She'd only copied two Scriptures in her notebook when Thor pulled a chair close and sat down. "I thought you and Jason read the Bible last night. Wasn't that enough for the week?"

She started to laugh, then realized he was serious. "I like to study every day. In fact, I have to."

"Why is that? Does your church have some sort of rule about it?"

She smiled. "No. There's so much to learn. Every time I read the Bible I find something new that I didn't know before." Jazmyn paused, trying to decide how to explain the Bible's importance. "You know how new things come with instruction manuals so you can learn how to work them?" She waited for Thor to nod. "Well, the Bible is like an instruction manual for me. It's God's way of telling me how to live my life. In order to know, though, I have to take the time to read and study the manual."

Thor shifted. "I'm not much on reading manuals. I like to figure things out for myself."

Jazmyn didn't know what to say. She wished Jason were here to join the conversation. He always seemed to know the right thing to say about his beliefs. She was so new she didn't even know for sure what she believed. How could she ever convince a doubter like Thor?

"Hey, there are our friends." He gestured behind her.

She stiffened. "The skunks?"

He laughed. "No, they won't be out until after dark. These guys aren't nearly as stinky. Take a look."

First skunks, then bears. Now what was invading their camp? Swiveling in her chair, Jazmyn watched two chipmunks chase each other across the open area near the table. Their tiny tails shot straight up in the air like little masts.

The first one stopped. The second jumped on the first one. They rolled around, and then the chase began again. Jazmyn couldn't help laughing. She'd never seen anything so cute.

"I don't remember seeing them yesterday." She watched as one chipmunk raced into the trees while the other decided to explore the camp.

"They're sometimes a little shy the first day you're here. Then they come out to scavenge. The squirrels will be out, too. You have to be careful what you leave around, because they can get into almost anything."

"Do you ever leave food out for them?" Jazmyn gasped as the small chipmunk disappeared up the truck tire. "We have to get him out of there." She started to get up. Thor placed his hand on her shoulder, and she sank back.

"He's just being nosy. He won't stay there long." As if to prove Thor's point, the striped animal leaped back to the ground.

"As far as feeding them, I sometimes leave out little scraps in the morning. I don't want to entice bears into the camp. In the mornings the squirrels, chipmunks, and blue jays will fight over anything you leave out for them. They're very fond of pancakes."

"Then if you ever allow me to have breakfast, I want pancakes so I can feed them."

Thor chuckled. "I'll get up early tomorrow and make pancakes before we leave. Then, if you want to stay in camp, you can share your breakfast."

"Stay in camp by myself?"

"There's nothing to be afraid of. The bear won't come back. If it does, you only have to yell and wave your arms to scare it away. There aren't any grizzly bears around here. Most of the black bears are easily frightened off."

Like me. Jazmyn couldn't help the thought. Here she'd been studying the Scriptures Jason gave her about fear, and within a few minutes she'd forgotten them all. How could she ever grow as a Christian at this rate?

For the next two days Thor tried his best to ignore Jazmyn, but it proved impossible. From a fearful, timid city girl, she was changing to become accustomed to outdoor life faster than he would have dreamed possible. He watched her patiently coax the tiny chipmunks closer until one took a piece of bread from her hand.

When that happened her gaze met his, and a jolt of pure attraction seared through him. By the time he turned away he felt as if a smile were permanently etched on his face. He grabbed up the axe, splitting more wood in the hopes of taking his mind off the strawberry blonde in his camp.

Every day they were up before sunrise. Jazmyn refused to wait in camp, insisting she be allowed to accompany them on the photo sessions. Jason still baited her, but now Thor knew the reason for her brother's constant teasing.

When he'd pressured Jason about his treatment of Jazmyn, Jason had been hesitant to reply at first.

"You have to understand the situation Jazmyn grew up in." Jason stared at Thor for a long moment as if judging how much he could be trusted. "Our mother had emotional problems. When she and Dad divorced, the courts allowed her to take Jazmyn, while I stayed with Dad. Dad tried to visit and take Jazmyn places, but Mom blocked him at every turn."

"She didn't abuse her, did she?" Thor knew how hard divorce could be, but he couldn't imagine what Jason was leading up to.

"No, not in the physical sense." Jason frowned. "Mom was afraid of people. Later they discovered she had schizophrenia. She would be normal one minute and terrified of everyone the next. She kept Jazmyn cooped up in the house and taught her to fear everything."

He shook his head. "For years Dad and I lost track of them. Mom would move and not tell us where she'd gone. Dad was afraid of going through the courts. He worried about what would happen to Mom. Then later he felt that he'd failed Jazmyn. It was a terrible position to be in."

"I can see that." Thor could almost feel the man's hurt. What a tough decision to make.

"When I made contact with Jazmyn again, she was scared of her own shadow." Jason's lips thinned. "I found the only way to draw her out was to make her angry or make her laugh. I've been spending my time doing one or the other since then. She's come a long way."

The snippet of conversation faded. Thor found himself once again watching Jazmyn as she pursed her lips and made little kissing noises at the chipmunk. If he didn't get ahold of his feelings, she'd have him eating out of her hand by the end of this trip. He swung the axe over his head and buried it in the chunk of aspen. The two log halves flew in either direction from the force of the blow.

He chopped and restacked wood for the next hour, building up a sweat. The sight of Jazmyn, her hand outstretched, a smile lighting her face, refused to leave his mind no matter how hard he tried. If he kept this up, all their decent-sized logs would be kindling.

"What are we fixing for supper tonight?" Thor turned to find Jazmyn at his elbow. Her red-gold hair swung in a ponytail except for one wavy strand that had escaped and wove a sinuous pattern down her cheek.

Glancing up at the tilt of the sun in the sky, he fought to get his emotions under control. His chest felt as if a band of iron were tightening around him. He had to get out of here and away from this woman. He didn't know how, but she must have found out his secret and was using her wiles to trap him. Tomorrow he would escape.

"I'll throw some oak wood on the fire and cook pork chops." Thor leaned the axe against the tree trunk. "You can get some potatoes ready to bake in the coals. I'll show you where the potatoes and foil are."

He stalked away, doing his best to ignore the hurt in her eyes. The gruffness of his tone had startled even him. *That's okay. Maybe if she thinks I'm the ogre she first believed me to be, she won't turn on the charm so much.*

By the time Thor got the fire ready to cook, Jazmyn had the potatoes wrapped. Jason returned from his late-afternoon walk along the river for pictures. They ate in a companionable silence, each lost in his or her own thoughts.

Jason pushed back his plate and sighed. "It was nice to have a safe meal for a change." He flashed Jazmyn a grin. "I figured Jazmyn couldn't do much to food cooked over the coals."

"I'll have you know I fixed the potatoes." She lifted her nose as if putting on airs.

"Yeah, but there isn't much you can do to them." Jason chuckled. "They weren't burnt, because Thor watched over them."

Jazmyn leaned forward. Her eyes narrowed. "I marked which one was yours. Didn't you notice the small tear-and-repair job done to your foil?" She motioned to the wadded-up wrapper from his potato.

"So what kind of poison did you use, sis?" Jason lowered his voice as if he were in on some conspiracy.

"It wasn't poison." Jazmyn folded her arms over her chest. "You're my brother. I wouldn't do that." An impish look crossed her face. "You remember that plant Thor showed us yesterday? Poison ivy? You swore you could even eat it and you wouldn't have an allergic reaction. I rubbed that on your potato. We'll see if you were right."

Thor tipped his head back and roared. Jason gaped in astonishment.

"I think you've been had this time, Jason. She's getting better." Thor slapped Jason on the shoulder. "That must mean it's your turn for doing dishes."

Jason groaned. "Can't we just leave them out and let the bears lick them clean? That works for me."

"I don't think so." Jazmyn glared at her brother, her hands on her hips. "We're not leaving out any bear bait unless you're attached to it."

Chapter 7

The sky was still dark when Thor rolled out of his sleeping bag. Shivering in the predawn chill, he jerked on his clothes. His eyes felt gritty. Sleep had eluded him last night. Instead of the murmur of the river lulling him to sleep, visions of Jazmyn laughing, pensive, fearful filled his mind.

Stepping outside, he took a deep breath of the fresh mountain air. He'd always loved coming here for the solitude and peace, but this trip that contentment had been absent. He couldn't relax. His whole being seemed to be attuned to Jazmyn's presence. He didn't like that.

Faint grayness in the sky, seen through the tall pines, showed that dawn wasn't far off. Thor went about gathering what he needed, waiting for Jason to get up. Jason would try to talk him out of this, of course, but Thor was determined to carry through with what he had to do. He snapped his fingers. Loki and Odin leaped into the bed of the truck. They lay down waiting for him to lead them on a new adventure.

As he loaded the last of what he wanted to take into his pickup, Thor heard the hiss of a zipper. Jason stepped outside, closed his tent, then stood and stretched. His hair stuck up at all angles. He and Jazmyn bore a strong resemblance to one another. Thor wondered, even if Jazmyn hadn't come with Jason, if he still would have been reminded of her every day. After all, how many times had his thoughts strayed to her since that first meeting?

"Mornin'." Jason drew in a deep breath. He, too, appreciated the outdoors. Thor liked that about Jason. In fact, he liked a lot about Jason, although he was reluctant to admit it.

"Mornin'." Thor gestured at the fire. The coffeepot sat at the edge of the grill over the flames. "Coffee's just perking. Should be ready in a few minutes."

"That sounds good. I'll be back." Jason stalked off into the forest.

Thor dug out their cups. He added a couple of sticks to the fire. The pot was perking steadily now. He would give it a few more minutes, then pour himself a cup and be out of here.

"Mmm. That smells good," Jason said, holding his empty mug in one hand.

Crouching down, Thor plucked the pot from the heat. He filled Jason's cup, then his own.

"I'm leaving camp for a couple of days." Thor kept his eyes focused on the swirling black liquid in his cup. "We need some supplies, and I need to check on

155

some business." He glanced up.

Jason's brows drew together. "You didn't mention having to leave camp before. I still have lots of pictures to take."

"I figure you can use the next two days to get all the shots around here that you wanted. When I get back we'll spend most of every day out on the mountains. I'll take you over to Bear Mountain and see if we can find some bears. This time of year the raspberries are just starting to ripen. Bears love them." Thor clamped his teeth together to stop himself from chattering like a girl. Jason wasn't stupid. He might catch on to just why he was leaving.

For a few minutes they shared coffee and quiet. Jason seemed to be pondering the situation. As much as he talked about his faith and following God, he might even be praying. That idea really made Thor nervous. He recalled his mother praying for him before she died. Deep inside he always wondered if God told her things about him that no one else knew.

"I thought we brought enough supplies up for the whole two weeks." Jason sipped his coffee, watching Thor through the steam rising from his cup.

"I. . .uh. There are a couple of things I forgot." Thor shifted, rotating his shoulders. He had to leave *now*. He edged toward the truck.

"Whatever you think we need, I'm sure we can do fine without it. I'm used to roughing it." Jason paused. "Is this because of Jazmyn?"

"Jazmyn?" Thor stared at him. How had the man known? He groped for something to say, some way to deny the obvious attraction he felt toward her.

"Yeah. I didn't say for sure that I'd be bringing her. She doesn't need anything special. Before we came up here I told her the food wouldn't be like the corner deli." Jason flashed Thor a grin. "You don't have to treat her different."

Thor took a big gulp of coffee, trying to buy time. He couldn't tell if Jason didn't suspect a thing or was simply trying to give him an out. From the glint in Jason's eye Thor thought he was being teased.

"I didn't intend to get special food for Jazmyn." Thor tried to keep the defensiveness from his voice. "When I brought supplies I thought there would only be two of us. I'll pick up a few things, then check on some business matters with my sister."

Jason nodded, staring into the fire for a few minutes. The sky lightened. Across the river Thor could see a doe taking hesitant steps down to the water. She took a drink. Her head jerked up. Droplets of water scattered from her muzzle. She leaped back into the woods, disappearing into the undergrowth.

"That deer reminds me of Jazmyn."

Thor caught himself before he agreed with Jason. The grace and beauty of the animal took his breath away just as Jazmyn did, but he didn't want to share that information with her brother. "How so?"

"She's so delicate. I mean that in the emotional sense. She's been hurt. It's hard for her to build a relationship with anyone. She doesn't want to trust them; she wants to run away instead."

Thor wondered if Jason meant him instead of Jazmyn. Wasn't that why he was leaving this morning? Running away? His jaw muscles tightened. He wouldn't run from anything. He needed to go to town.

"She's starting to heal and come out of her shell," Jason continued. "I'd hate to see her hurt so bad she withdraws again." His green eyes, a shade darker than Jazmyn's, met Thor's.

"I'd hate to see her hurt, too." Thor cleared his throat. "I'm taking off. I'll be back day after tomorrow." He strode to the truck, patted the dogs before climbing in, and refused to glance in the rearview mirror as he eased across the river. On the off chance that Jazmyn was up early, he couldn't risk seeing her in tousled disarray. If the urge to protect her, to hold her, to love her rose up again, he didn't know how he could fight it. The best thing for him right now was to put as much distance between himself and that alluring beauty as possible.

On the four-hour drive to his cabin, he berated himself for being weak, for feeling an attraction to another woman after he'd seen how conniving women could be. *I will not fall for this woman. It's just because she's needy and I want to help her out. That's all.*

Although the argument with himself continued for most of the morning, Thor still wondered at his motives. No matter what he did, visions of Jazmyn popped unbidden into his head. All day he wondered what she was doing, wishing he was with her.

⁂

Warmth flooded the tent when Jazmyn woke up. Full sunlight filtered through the canvas, making her blink at the brightness. She yawned and stretched. It was late. Why hadn't Jason awakened her?

She could hear Jason humming as she unzipped the tent and stepped out. The smell of sausage made her stomach grumble. At home she would never dream of eating something as fatty as sausage for breakfast, but out here she couldn't wait to taste it. Jason and Thor were right. Something about the wilderness changed a person's taste in food.

"Mornin'." Jason smiled at her.

"To you, too." Jazmyn glanced around, wondering where Thor was.

"I thought you were going to sleep the whole day." Jason cracked an egg into the skillet.

"Why didn't you get me up? I thought we were going out early to get pictures again." She still didn't see Thor.

"Our guide left before daybreak." Jason avoided her gaze as he flipped the egg.

"He left? Why?" For the first time she noticed Thor's truck wasn't parked in the usual spot. The dogs weren't there to greet her, either.

Jason shrugged. "He said he needed some supplies and had some business to attend to."

"I thought you were his business right now." Jazmyn could feel anger worming up inside her. "He's supposed to be helping you get the photos you need."

"He'll be back day after tomorrow. We'll still have plenty of time for everything. You want breakfast first or a walk in the woods?"

Jazmyn blushed. She still hadn't become accustomed to going off into the woods to take care of her needs. Although she'd only used an outhouse once, and remembered the stench clearly, she would rather have that than just a tree between her and the rest of the world.

"I'll be right back." She headed off through the trees. Embarrassed or not, this was necessity.

By the time she returned, Jason was dishing up potatoes, sausage, and eggs for both of them. "I made you some hot chocolate today instead of coffee." He set the mug on the table. "I thought you might like the change."

Breathing in the spicy chocolate smell, Jazmyn almost purred. "Mmm. If I close my eyes, I can almost imagine there's a hint of cinnamon in here. Thanks." She wrinkled her nose at Jason, a trick they'd done to one another when they were kids. Their parents always got mad if they stuck their tongues out, so Jazmyn and Jason decided this gesture would mean the same to them, but no one else would know.

They prayed and both dug in. "I can't believe how hungry I am." Jazmyn popped a piece of sausage into her mouth. "At home I almost never eat more than a piece of toast for breakfast."

"I know." Jason raised one eyebrow. "You look it, too. I was hoping to fatten you up on this camping trip."

She wrinkled her nose at him again. "Well, if I stay here too long, I can audition for the part of Miss Piggy in the next Muppet movie."

"Nah. You'd never get it. Your hair is too red."

"If it didn't taste so good, I'd throw my breakfast at you," Jazmyn grumbled.

Jason finished his meal and took the dishes over to the dishpan. "I've heated water for dishes. I wondered if you could do them so I can walk downriver and try for some more photos today." He paused and looked at her. "Or would you like to go with me?"

"No way. I've had enough walking for a lifetime. I'll stay here and read or just relax. You go on."

"I think I'll pack a sandwich and some snacks in case I don't make it back by lunch. Don't worry about me, okay?"

"Will you be back in time for supper?" Jazmyn watched as Jason gathered the things he needed. She didn't want to let him know how much she dreaded being alone in camp all day. She'd go with him, but she knew she'd only be a hindrance.

Thirty minutes later she watched as Jason headed toward the river, his camera bag over his shoulder. Part of her wanted to run after him, but the bigger part wanted to stay. She needed time to sort out her feelings about Thor.

When Jason first said Thor had gone to town that morning, she'd been angry. Now she wondered if that wasn't just hurt over the fact that he'd left without saying good-bye. Several times since they'd arrived at camp she'd felt as if Thor were watching her. Had he sensed an attraction between them? She didn't know for sure. Her experience with men was minimal, but a few times she thought he might feel something toward her.

The rest of the morning passed quickly. After doing dishes Jazmyn settled down with her Bible. Studying proved difficult. The chipmunks had invited friends. Four of them now scampered around the camp, nosing into everything.

A big squirrel, her bushy tail waving, paused a few feet from the ground, her claws holding her fast to the trunk of a pine. She stared at Jazmyn with black beady eyes.

Getting a piece of bread, Jazmyn spent an hour throwing crumbs to the chipmunks. The squirrel got into the game, chasing away the smaller animals whenever she could. Jazmyn couldn't help but laugh at their antics. When she tried to interfere on behalf of the chipmunks, the squirrel raced up a tree to a branch overhead. From there she shrieked and chattered at Jazmyn for several minutes.

"I'm sure glad I don't speak squirrel language." Jazmyn gazed up at the disgruntled animal. "You're such a fighter, I think I'll call you Xena, the warrior squirrel." Xena didn't appear to appreciate her new name as she raced along the branch then stopped and screeched some more.

After lunch Jazmyn decided to take a walk. She'd told Jason she was tired of walking, but the truth was she needed time to think. She couldn't understand why Thor would leave so suddenly. Had she said something? Done something?

"Watch the camp, Xena." Jazmyn scribbled a quick note for Jason, picked up a long stick, and started up a faint trail. Maybe she could get to the top of this hill and see if there was a view.

Chapter 8

This is so stupid," Thor growled to the dogs, which were riding in the cab this time. "I can't stand to be there. I can't stand to be away. This is stupid." Loki leaned close and licked him on the chin. "Yeah, I know. I said that before."

He almost had to yell as the truck rattled down the dirt road leading back to camp. The late afternoon sun hung low in the sky. A herd of deer startled in the forest as he rounded a corner.

He hadn't been able to stay away a full day. He'd no sooner arrived at his cabin than he realized he had to go back. Guiding was his job and a serious responsibility, he told himself. How could he let a customer down like that? So he checked a couple of business matters, packed up the dogs, and left. After a quick stop at a store for a few special items, he began the long journey back to the mountain camp.

Clouds were building in the distance as Thor slowed for the river crossing. A faint rumble of thunder echoed from the distance. He could see Jason's SUV now. His pulse sped up. It was the knowledge that he was taking care of his responsibility, he told himself. This wasn't excitement at the thought of seeing Jazmyn again. Besides, he didn't need to align himself with another gold digger, and, as he well knew, most women were gold diggers, his mother and sister excepted.

A few minutes later he stepped out of the truck. The dogs piled out after him, racing from one end of the camp to the other. They were glad to be back.

"Hello," he called, expecting to see Jason or Jazmyn by the fire. There was no fire. It had gone out during the day, and no one had kept it up. A frisson of unease swept through him. Where were they?

Thor slammed the truck door shut and turned to study the river. Maybe they had gone for a walk before starting supper.

Loki and Odin trotted up, begging for attention. He rubbed their heads as his gaze wandered across the clearings and through the underbrush.

"Well, boys, I guess I should make myself useful. Let's get that fire going and get some supper started. They'll be hungry when they get back." Thor pushed back irritation at not seeing Jazmyn first thing when he arrived at camp. For all she and Jason knew he wouldn't be back for at least another day.

He had the fire blazing when Jason stumbled from the wooded path leading

160

to the river. The man looked scared and exhausted. When he spotted Thor he stopped and stared, but no smile lit his face.

"Jason, you okay?" Thor put the meat back in the cooler and walked over to where Jason stood zombie-like. "Where's Jazmyn?"

Jason shook his head. His mouth opened and shut like some marionette trying to speak. He took a deep breath and shuddered. "I can't find her."

"What?" Thor wanted to shake the man. "What do you mean you can't find her?"

Jason ran a hand through his hair. "I left this morning to walk the river downstream and get some pictures. When I got back this afternoon I found a note from Jazmyn saying she'd gone for a walk."

Thor relaxed. "She's probably on her way back then. She'll be getting hungry. . ."

"You don't understand. Jazmyn hates exercise. Remember how she complained about all the walking we were doing? If she went for a walk, she would have been back within a half-hour or so. I've been back for two hours, and she still hasn't returned."

Thor thought about the times he and Jason had taken Jazmyn out for the photo shoots. She had complained about the walking and her muscles aching. In fact, her hatred of exercise had gotten to be a joke between them.

"Look, I know she's not downstream. That's where I was." Jason gestured in the direction of the river. "I went upstream quite a ways looking for her and calling. I couldn't find any sign of her passing, either."

Thor's gaze strayed to the steep hillside behind him. He could almost hear what Jason was thinking. "If she's gone to find the top of the mountain, she could be anywhere by now." He felt heavy with dread. What he left unsaid, but knew Jason was also thinking, was the number of times people got lost this way. They thought it would be easy to walk to the top of the mountain, but the top was over a series of rises, not just straight up. After they went over a couple of small peaks, inexperienced hikers couldn't tell where they'd come up so they could return the same way.

"I'll head up and look for her," Thor said.

"I'm going, too."

"No." He stopped, noting the harshness of his voice and the effect it had on Jason. "You've been hiking all day. You're tired. Stay here. Get some supper cooking. She'll be hungry when I bring her back."

"Okay." Jason nodded. "You'll need some water."

"Get the jacket I loaned her. It might be in her tent." Thor glanced up at the sky. It was already cooling off. He didn't have much time. Grabbing a flashlight from behind the truck seat, he whistled to the dogs.

"I'll take Odin with me. He has the best nose." He grabbed the pack Jason handed him, knowing there would be water and food inside.

"I'll be praying." Jason's words followed Thor into the woods. Thor's mother always told him that, too.

Odin began to cast from side to side after sniffing at a shirt of Jazmyn's. Thor had noted where a small trail led up the hill. If he were an inexperienced person like Jazmyn, that's where he would head. He whistled. Odin trotted over. The dog sniffed the ground, the snuffling sound familiar and comforting to Thor. If any dog could find Jazmyn, it was Odin. He only hoped they found her before it was too late. So many things could happen to someone alone in the mountains.

A sharp bark caught his attention. Odin glanced up at him then trotted off up the mountain, his nose testing the air. Thor followed after him, wishing he knew how to pray like Jason and his mother. Fear for Jazmyn's safety threatened to consume him instead.

❧

Jazmyn's legs ached with the strain of climbing the hill. She paused to catch her breath. Far below she could still see the glint of the river through the mass of trees. Looking up she could see the crest of the rise not far away. "Who'd ever guess going uphill could be so tiring?"

An outcropping of white rocks covered with dry moss stood in her way. Skirting them would take too much time, so she found the best way up and scrambled over the rough surface. When she looked back down she'd lost sight of the river. That didn't worry her. All she had to do was head back down. Their camp lay straight below her.

Reaching the crest, she groaned aloud. This wasn't the top of the mountain but only a little dip leading to another part of the hill. She debated going back down, but a glance at her watch told her Jason wouldn't be back for a while. She didn't want to sit by herself in the camp for hours.

"May as well try to find the top while I'm this far." She started up again, walking more slowly than before. Halfway up the next section she came to another bunch of rocks. This time she went far enough to one side to avoid so much climbing. Her hands still hurt from the last rocks she went over.

Several times Jazmyn thought sure she would reach the peak, only to find another ridge to navigate. She had to work her way around fallen trees and huge boulders. When she finally reached what she thought had to be the top of the mountain, Jazmyn groaned. Another false lead. A low, flat rock stuck out like the outcropping in the *Lion King* movie. With the last of her strength she pulled herself up and lay down gasping for breath.

"Why am I killing myself like this?" Her whole body ached so badly she wanted to cry. She wouldn't be able to move for a week.

It was a moot question. She knew deep down she wanted the physical pain to override her emotional pain. Thor's leaving had hurt. Her mother's voice echoed in her head. "Men are all alike. They lie to you and then leave you." She pushed the thought away.

"I don't even want a relationship with him, Lord, so why am I hurting? He's not a Christian, and I'm committed to following You." Tears burned her eyes.

Last night as she lay in her sleeping bag, she determined not to have as much to do with Thor. She thought about how scared of him she'd been when she first met him and couldn't believe how mistaken she'd been. He wasn't some cruel killer. He had compassion and cared for people. How many times had Thor come to her defense when Jason teased her? She couldn't count them all.

This morning when she found out he was gone, her heart began to ache. She felt responsible, as if he wanted to be away from her. This afternoon she didn't know any more about why he'd gone, but she knew she missed him. Missed him more than she had a right to.

She must have dropped off to sleep on the warm rock. When she woke up, shadows were darkening under the trees. Sitting up, she rubbed her eyes. She'd better get back before Jason got worried about her.

Hopping off the rock, Jazmyn staggered. Her aching muscles had seized up as she rested. They were screaming at her now. She groaned as she stretched her legs out. At least going back would be all downhill. Going straight down shouldn't take long.

She was wrong. Straight down proved almost harder on her legs than walking uphill. Each step jarred her muscles. When she reached the bottom she stared around in amazement. Where was the river? She should be able to see it from here or at least hear the water. She couldn't hear a thing except the birds twittering overhead. She couldn't see much, either. The shadows had thickened among the trees.

Across a small ravine the hill rose up again. Jazmyn knew she hadn't come this way, yet to get back to camp she'd only had to go downhill. Hadn't she? She sank to the ground as she thought about all the times she'd gone around trees and rocks. At the time she was sure she wasn't changing course. Now she began to wonder.

She rested her forehead on her knees. "Okay, think, Jazmyn. There has to be a way out of this." She closed her eyes and pictured the mountains as she'd seen them from the lookout they stopped at yesterday on the way back to camp. The tree-covered hills seemed to roll on forever. No one lived near here. If she got lost, she might never be found.

Panic tightened her chest, threatening to cut off her breath. Rubbing her arms, she tried to ignore the chill racing through her. She didn't have a jacket or any food. She hadn't said in the note exactly where she'd be hiking. Jason would have no idea where to look for her. Thor wouldn't be back for two days, so he couldn't help. She hadn't even brought water.

She swiped at the tears trickling down her cheeks. She wouldn't survive the night. Before long some bear or mountain lion would be out hunting and smell her. How could she hope to fight a creature like that?

Fear washed over her. Sinking onto her side, she rolled into a tight ball. All the years with her mother came rushing back. She could hear her mother scolding her about the dangers of the outside world. "Stay away from men. They'll do nothing but lead you into trouble and then leave you to deal with it." Her mother's bitter voice rang in her ears.

"God, help me." The whisper startled her. She hadn't thought to pray. Why did prayer come so easy to Jason, while she always thought about it as a last resort?

Pushing against the ground, she sat back up. "God, I'm lost. You know where I am, though. You know how afraid I am. Please, Lord, help me to be strong. Help me to know what to do."

Keeping her eyes closed, Jazmyn assessed her options. She could go back up to the top of the mountain. However, if she tried that, she might end up on another mountaintop and be even more lost.

She could try to walk around this hill and see if she could find a road or the river. Another option was to wait right here. Maybe Jason would find her soon. A sob caught in her throat. How would he ever do that? Besides, if she tried walking in the dark, she might fall off some ridge.

Something crashed in the brush up the mountain. Jazmyn jumped. She scrambled to her feet, staring uphill. She squinted, trying to see through the shadowy dimness.

A rock skittered down. Taking a step back, she glanced from side to side, trying to find some sort of shelter. The trees were too tall to climb. Besides, a bear or cougar could climb up after her.

Brush rattled. Something big was coming down the hill—fast. She began to tremble. Should she shout? Her vocal cords refused to work. Should she run? Her legs wouldn't move. Paralyzing fear froze her to the spot as she waited for the end.

Before she could scream, something broke through the brush and hurtled into the air. She opened her mouth, but the breath was knocked out of her as the beast hit her in the chest, knocking her backward to the ground. This was the end. Any moment now her throat would be ripped out.

Chapter 9

S omething warm and wet slopped across her chin. Jazmyn waited for the fatal bite. She could feel warm breath on her face.

"Either eat her or let her up, Odin."

Her eyes flew open. Odin lay on her chest looking very pleased with himself. She turned her head to see Thor squatting beside her. The corners of his eyes crinkled with mirth. She burst into tears.

"Hey, you're supposed to be happy to see us." Thor shoved Odin off her and lifted Jazmyn to her feet as if she weighed nothing. He wrapped his arms around her. She clung to him, all her earlier resolve to keep her distance fading away.

The hike back to camp passed in a blur. Darkness settled in. Thor's flashlight was almost strong enough to power New York City. Odin leaped and cavorted around them for a few minutes then settled into the seriousness of leading them in the right direction.

Jason had supper on when they arrived. Jazmyn could see the relief in his eyes. She was too tired to talk and ended up in bed long before either of the men was ready to let her out of his sight. They'd become very protective. Her last thought before falling asleep was to wonder how Thor came to rescue her when he was supposed to be gone for two days.

Jazmyn almost cried when she tried to climb out of her sleeping bag the next morning. She recalled reading somewhere that the human body has over six hundred muscles. Every one of hers was making its presence known today.

"Mornin', Jaz." Jason grinned as she limped over to him. "Today I mixed the coffee and hot chocolate for you. Mocha java, I guess." He handed her a steaming mug. She almost kissed him.

Thor leaned against the table, studying her as he sipped his coffee. Morning light hadn't yet touched the sky. "Today we're going to a place that requires a lot of hiking. I'm not sure you should go with us. We'll be gone most of the day."

"I can wait in the truck while you're getting the pictures." Jazmyn could feel panic welling up. She didn't want to be left in camp again.

"Sis, just riding in the truck over rough roads will hurt. You've got to be sore. I watched you walk over here. You need to wait here."

"We'll be back by mid-afternoon, I hope. I've packed some sandwiches." Thor looked as if he wanted to say more but didn't. "Go back to bed. Get some more rest."

I will not be afraid. Jazmyn gritted her teeth and fought to swallow the lump in her throat.

"I have something for you." Jason set down his cup and went to the SUV. He rummaged around for a few minutes and came back carrying a large bag. "I brought this in case you had some time on your hands."

Taking the sack from him, Jazmyn waited for the joke. Jason picked up his cup and watched her. Thor looked curious. He did not know what was going on. Inside the bag were several drawing pencils and two artist's pads. She blinked to clear her eyes.

Jazmyn loved to draw. When she met Adam he encouraged her to do more than doodle on the edges of paper. During the years they dated she found a lot of comfort when she sat down to draw. Sketching came naturally to her, and Adam loved to watch her. When he died her desire to continue with her art died with him.

Her gaze met Jason's. She knew what he was saying. It was time to put Adam behind her. She had to move on with her life. Jason had tried to say this before, but she hadn't been ready to hear. For some reason, she thought she might be ready now.

In the flickering light of the lantern, she smiled at Jason. "Thanks. I think I might try this."

A look of profound relief crossed Jason's face. She thought of all the times he'd expressed concern over her continued pining for Adam. He'd wanted her to see a counselor. In fact, he'd set up an appointment with a counselor from his church, but she didn't want to talk to some stranger about her problems, especially when she didn't share that person's beliefs.

Her life had spiraled from there. Jason left town on a photo shoot for a new book. When he returned three months later, Jazmyn had almost become a recluse. Jason took her under his wing, saying he wouldn't leave her again until she was strong enough. Then he told her about Jesus and the strength and peace she would get from knowing Him.

Many times Jason had talked to her about God. Other times she'd laughed, but this time she was ready to listen. Her life turned upside down at that point but not for the worse. She was still learning to change, to accept.

She waved as Jason and Thor drove away. The last of her mocha coffee had cooled. She set the cup on the table and limped back to her tent. Thor's idea of getting a little more sleep sounded like a winner.

By the time she got up again, the sun was well overhead. She took a short walk along the river, careful not to lose sight of the camp. The movement seemed to relieve some of the soreness in her muscles.

⟲

Pulling a chair under the shade of the tarp, Jazmyn opened the bag Jason had given her, retrieving the pencils and drawing pad. After putting some bread crumbs on a rock, she waited for the squirrels and chipmunks to show up. The day passed in a blur as she lost herself in sketching. She'd forgotten how restful this could be.

Taking a break, Jazmyn rummaged in the supplies and found a chocolate bar. She settled back into her chair, broke off a chunk, and set the rest of the candy on the table beside her.

Her thoughts strayed to Thor. She couldn't deny the way her pulse sped up when she saw him this morning. The sight of him brought back the memory of him holding her last night. She'd felt so safe and comforted. When he carried her part of the way back to camp, she wanted to stay in his arms forever.

Lord, these feelings are so dangerous. I know that. Please show me what to do. Am I turning to him as a comfort when I should be turning to You? I don't want to do that.

Picking up her Bible, Jazmyn turned to the verse in 2 Timothy Jason had showed her. She read it again. "For God hath not given us the spirit of fear; but of power, and of love, and of a sound mind." *Lord, if these fears aren't from You, then show me how to get rid of them.*

Without looking, she reached for the rest of her candy bar on the table. Her hand met fur. She shrieked and jumped up. Her chair tumbled sideways. Xena the squirrel raced away with the candy bar in her mouth.

"Hey, come back here! That's mine." Jazmyn gave chase. Xena scampered up a tree, the wide bar held in her teeth. As Jazmyn raced over, Xena lost her hold on the candy. The chocolate fell to the ground. Xena leaped onto a limb several feet above Jazmyn and almost vibrated with anger. Jazmyn had to laugh as Xena screeched her outrage over losing the treat.

⁂

The sun was setting as Thor sped down the gravel road taking him and Jason back to camp. Dust spiraled up behind them. He knew that if a Forest Service ranger found him going this fast, his goose would be cooked, but he wanted to get back to camp. They were three hours later than they had planned to be. All he could think about was the panic that consumed him when Jazmyn was lost in the woods. He knew from the silence that Jason felt the same.

The hike had gone well. They'd found a flock of turkeys, an eagle, and an eagle's nest. Jazmyn would have enjoyed the wildlife, but the hiking was brutal. Besides, she would have fainted from fright watching him hold Jason's legs while Jason dangled over the cliff edge for pictures.

Rounding a curve, the tail of the pickup slid sideways. Thor swung the wheel in the direction of the slide, and the truck straightened out. Trees flashed past. Open meadows spread out on one side and then the other. Sparkling streams meandered through the woods. He ignored the beauty of the mountains he loved as his mind strayed to the previous night.

When he followed Odin into the forest after Jazmyn, fear held him captive. For the first time ever he wished he had the faith of his mother so he could pray and get help from somewhere. Would God even bother to answer a prayer like that? He wasn't sure. Thor always prided himself on his ability to care for himself and others. He didn't need any God.

Last night had come close to changing that opinion. What if he didn't find Jazmyn in time? She was always so afraid of everything. How could she cope in a darkening world when she didn't know what to do to protect herself? All those thoughts had raced through his mind as he let Odin lead him farther up the mountain.

When they found Jazmyn, he'd forgotten the need for God. He could take things from there. God surely had other things to tend to, didn't He? What was it Jason had said a couple of weeks ago when they met to discuss the trip? Something about God caring about every part of your life and wanting to be involved in every decision. That was a little too one-on-one for Thor. He would prefer a God who stepped up when needed, not one who meddled all the time.

"Looks like we'll have a late supper," Jason said as they neared the river crossing. "I can get the fire and lanterns going while you fix the meal."

"Deal." Thor's stomach churned. He didn't feel like food until he found out whether Jazmyn was okay. "Aren't you worried about your sister? You've been so quiet."

Jason gave him a tired smile. "I've been praying. That way I don't have to worry. I know God is handling everything."

"You mean you weren't worried last night?"

"No, I'm human," Jason admitted. "I was worried today, but I'm not now. Even when things don't go like I wanted them to, I know I can trust God's plan. If He's going to be my God, then I have to give Him all my life and let Him run everything. If I take something back by worrying or wanting control in some other way, I'm saying He's not good enough to be my God."

Jason's words struck Thor hard. Wasn't that the way he treated God? Like some tool he used only when he thought he needed Him. *Let me live my life the way I want, God, but be there in case I mess up and need You to bail me out.* That was his philosophy so far. Look how messed up his life had become.

Water sprayed up as Thor drove into the river faster than he should have. He switched on the wipers to clear the windshield. Flames were shooting up from a big fire in the fire pit at camp. Someone had either kept the fire going or gotten it started again tonight. Another concern sprang up to clench his stomach. Who had been in camp with Jazmyn while they were gone?

"I can't believe it," Jason said. "My sister kept the fire going."

"You sure?" Thor squinted, trying to see any other vehicles around the camp.

"There she is adding another log." Jason laughed. "If we don't stop her, she'll have a fire big enough to burn whole trees."

Jazmyn waved as they pulled to a stop in the usual spot. The dogs leaped to their feet and bounded over to the truck. Thor and Jason both hopped out.

The first thing Thor noticed was the smell. Someone had been cooking, and it smelled good.

"About time." Jazmyn stretched up and gave Jason a peck on the cheek. "I thought you were doing a night photo shoot."

"I came back here for that." Jason gave her a hug. "What smells so good?"

She smiled. "I thought you might be hungry, so I started some supper."

"I hope it's done. I'm hungry enough to eat one of these trees." Jason reached over and broke off a piece of bark, which he stuck in his mouth. He rolled his eyes and made sounds of delight. Thor couldn't help laughing.

"Stop that." Jazmyn plucked the piece of bark from Jason's mouth. "You don't know what animal may have been climbing that tree." She tried to give him a fierce look but ended up grinning.

"Let me put up my camera equipment and wash up. Then I'll be ready to eat."

Thor watched Jazmyn as she turned to look at him. She hesitated as if she wasn't sure she wanted to be around him. He understood. He didn't know how to act around her, either.

"So, what's on the menu?" he asked. "Anything I can help with?"

She shrugged. "I got the stove started like you showed me." She tried not to show her pride, but he could hear it in her voice. "I have some fried potatoes, pork chops, and peas ready to eat. I hope that's all right."

"That's my favorite meal." She was close enough to touch. He had to fight the urge. "I have to admit I'm amazed you did this, plus keep the fire going."

She glanced at the flames. "God is changing me. Last night He showed me I don't have to be afraid. I can depend on Him to help me out no matter what."

"I need to wash." Thor stalked away. Why did God keep coming up all the time?

Chapter 10

W hat are you doing?" Jazmyn stared at Jason as he stood near the fire. The morning sun cast its first feeble rays across the treetops.

"I'm having breakfast." Jason frowned at her, a look reminiscent of his childhood.

"You can't have that for breakfast." She put her hands on her hips and wondered if she sounded like their mother.

"Why not? Will the parent police come after me?"

"It's not healthy, you know."

"So what is around here?" Jason stuffed another marshmallow on a stick and held it over the flames. "Besides, this is our last day. I've used all my film, and I'm celebrating."

"But s'mores?" She gave a mock shudder.

Thor emerged as Jason pulled the perfect brown marshmallow from the fire. "Ah, you're fixing breakfast." He plucked the crispy treat from the end of the stick, stuck it between two graham crackers with chocolate, and bit off a huge bite.

Jason's mouth fell open. "Hey, that was mine."

Thor stuffed the rest in his mouth, his cheeks bulging. "Ou won it ack?" Jazmyn held her sides as she laughed at Jason's expression. Her brother wasn't used to anyone getting one over on him.

"All right, so I haven't done my share of the cooking." Jason grabbed two more marshmallows from the bag. "I'm fixing breakfast for us all."

Thor bowed to Jazmyn and gestured to a chair near the fire. "Have a seat, my lady. This knave will have your meal fixed in a few moments."

She spread her fingers in front of her face as if they were a fan. "My knight. Thank you."

Thor's mouth twitched. "Anything for my lady." He led her to the chair and held her arm as she sat down.

"All right, you two, enough of the theatrics. I'm thinking we should leave for home now. I may not be able to stand the two of you all day." Jason shoved a s'more at Jazmyn. "Breakfast is served."

"Watch out." Jazmyn pointed behind him.

Jason swung around as Xena skittered over to the box of chocolate. She bared her teeth and raised her tail.

"Be careful, Jason. She has this thing for chocolate." Jazmyn tried to smother a laugh.

Jason waved his hands at her. "Shoo. Get out of here."

Xena raised up on her hind legs and stared at him with her black beady eyes. She took a hop closer. Jason took a step. Xena leaped on the box and shrieked at Jason.

"Hey, she's vicious!" Jason called over his shoulder.

"You can tell she's a female by the way she's willing to fight for her chocolate." Thor grinned.

"Hey, I resent that." Jazmyn tried her best to stare daggers in Thor's direction. She and Thor looked at each other and started to laugh. Xena skittered up the tree, scolding them from a branch above.

The day sped by. Jazmyn watched as Thor and Jason took down any extra tarps they wouldn't need so there would be less to do tomorrow. She tried to ignore the heaviness that weighted her. When she'd first arrived at camp, she hadn't wanted to be here. She thought the two weeks would be interminable. Now that it was time to leave, she didn't want to return to the hot city and her nowhere job. The mountains had grown on her. She wanted to stay. Even the quiet had grown on her.

As evening drew near, a doe stepped out of the trees. Jazmyn reached for her pad and pencil. She had drawn plenty of chipmunks and squirrels, but this was the first time a deer had come close enough to sketch. She prayed the guys would stay quiet long enough for her to complete the sketch.

Her pencil flew over the paper. At the light scratching sound, the deer's ear twitched. Her large brown eyes stared at Jazmyn. She took a hesitant step and bolted into the trees, her white tail flicking up as she ran.

"You know, you're really good," Thor said as he looked over her shoulder. A shiver ran through her. She clutched the pencil and pad, wanting to hide her work but knowing it was too late.

"I didn't get finished before she left."

"Well, it looks perfect to me. What's wrong with it?"

"I didn't get her stance just right." Jazmyn tilted her head, studying the drawing. "Instead of a picture perfect, it's a picture imperfect."

"Ah. Kind of like life, huh?" Jason spoke up from her other side.

Jazmyn wrinkled her brow. "What?"

"You know. We all want the picture-perfect life. Perfect spouse. Perfect kids. Perfect job. Perfect house." Jason shrugged. "Then we find out that life isn't that way. We aren't perfect, and neither is this world."

Jazmyn nodded. "You're right."

Thor held out his hand. "Can I look at your other sketches?"

She took a deep breath. Sharing her pictures was like sharing a part of herself, and that was hard to do. Adam had encouraged her drawing but saw it as a hobby. She passed the pad of paper to Thor.

He pulled up a chair beside her and thumbed through the notebook. Jazmyn wanted to run away. The Scripture she'd read in Psalms yesterday flashed through her thoughts: "I sought the LORD, and He heard me, and delivered me from all my fears." Peace settled over her as she watched Thor turn the pages.

"These are really good." He glanced up at Jason. "Have you considered having her do some illustrations for the book you're working on? You know, these could emphasize the photos and make them stand out more." He was pointing to a sketch of the chipmunks playing on a rock.

Jason moved to Thor's side. "I hadn't thought of that, but you're right. I'll talk to my editor about using them. Do you mind, Jaz?"

"I don't know." She wasn't sure she was ready to have other people look at her drawings. What if they weren't that good?

"Jazmyn, these are very good." Thor spoke as if he'd been reading her thoughts. "I can almost see these creatures coming to life. What will it hurt to try?"

"Hey, you've been unhappy with your work situation for some time," Jason said. "Maybe this will provide an income and give you some variety, too."

Watching the emotions flit across Jazmyn's face, Thor found himself wanting to make the decision for her. He'd never seen such realistic renditions of the animals in the mountains. The chipmunks and squirrels she'd drawn looked as if they could leap off the page at a moment's notice. She had more artistic talent than most of the people employed in that department of his company.

He would have to consider his options here. He didn't want Jazmyn to know he was anything more than a backwoods hunting guide, yet he wanted her to have the opportunity to use her talents. Handing the pad back to her, he mumbled something about needing to start supper and walked away to think.

Supper was a silent affair. Thor detected a sadness in Jazmyn and wondered if she would miss the mountains. She'd changed so much in the past two weeks. She'd become more confident and less fearful. In short, she'd blossomed. He liked the change. He liked her. A lot.

Jason had the fire blazing by the time Thor and Jazmyn finished cleaning up the kitchen. The warmth proved welcome as the evening chill settled in. They all pulled up chairs around the fire.

"Do you think it's okay to have s'mores twice in one day?" Jason gave Jazmyn a puppy dog look that made her smile.

"Only if Xena is asleep." She looked over her shoulder at the tree where the squirrel lived.

"Squirrels don't usually come out this late," Thor said. "However, that one might make an exception if she smells chocolate."

"I'll make sure I'm well-armed first." Jason got up to get the needed supplies.

The gooey treats tasted even better than they had that morning. Jazmyn, who hadn't done well with roasting marshmallows, sacrificed four of them to the flames before she got one to stay on her stick. The white sticky masses bubbled at the edge of the coals.

Thor finished his dessert and got up to move the lanterns closer to them. Going over to the table, he found Jazmyn's pad and pencils. He brought them to her, making sure the light fell right so she'd be able to see to draw. She raised an eyebrow in question as he handed the drawing implements to her.

"I noticed our friends over there." He gestured toward the river where a white and black tail waved in the weeds. "I didn't see any sketches of skunks. If they come close, maybe you could do a couple of them for Jason's book."

"You don't give up, do you? My pitiful drawings would never be good enough for a book." She stared at the skunks wandering through the undergrowth. "You are right, though. I don't have any sketches of them."

Before long the mother skunk and her two babies made their way around the fire pit, snuffling in the dirt. The babies clambered up on the rocks close to the flames.

"Won't their feet get burned?" Jazmyn kept her voice to a whisper as if afraid to startle them.

"If they get hot, I assume they'll climb down." Thor flashed her a grin.

"Look." He nodded his head toward the fire.

One of the baby skunks was teetering on a rock, its tiny paw reaching for a mass of melted white goo. Its brother or sister scurried over to see what the first one was reaching for. Their noses twitched; their eyes shone in the firelight.

"You'd better get busy drawing, or you're gonna miss this one," Thor said.

"If I had a camera, I'd take a picture." Her eyes met his, melting his insides like one of her sacrificed marshmallows. "But I'd rather have one of your sketches to hang on my wall."

Jazmyn's pencil began to fly across the page. She didn't even seem to be aware that she'd started sketching. Thor quit watching the skunks and stared, fascinated, at the way the pair were coming to life on the paper. Who would have thought someone could do so much with just a pencil and paper? He couldn't even draw a stick figure.

Jazmyn drew in a sharp breath.

"Sis, you'd better stay still. Mama's here to see what's going on," Jason said.

Glancing down, Thor saw the mother skunk's tail partially wrapped around Jazmyn's leg as she paused to watch her babies. Jazmyn's face had paled. Her pencil stilled.

"Don't worry about her," he whispered. "She's not upset, just checking on her little ones."

Jazmyn flashed him a smile then turned back to her drawing. The mother waddled over to the fire pit and sniffed the warm rocks. Jazmyn flipped the page and started a new picture. Thor was entranced.

"You know, last spring I guided a group of men from a company called T. L. Enterprises. They were talking about how hard it is to find someone with an artistic bent to design computer pages for their products." Jazmyn and Jason both looked at him. Thor tried to keep his tone casual.

"You might try looking them up. With your experience on the computer and your drawing ability, they might hire you."

Jason nodded. "I've heard of them. They say the owner is a recluse and very eccentric."

"Could be." Thor tried to act nonchalant. "It's something to think about."

Later, as he lay in his sleeping bag, his hands behind his head, Thor couldn't get Jazmyn off his mind. Tomorrow she would disappear from his life. He didn't know how he could bear that. Despite his resolve never to get involved with another woman, this one had gotten under his skin and into his heart.

Chapter 11

Standing outside the huge building in the late summer heat, Jazmyn tried to convince herself that the warmth of the afternoon caused the trickle of sweat down her back. The truth was, she was terrified. All those Scriptures she'd memorized on fear and God's protective strength disappeared from her mind when she looked at this imposing façade.

T. L. Enterprises. A huge company. Much bigger than she'd thought, or she never would have agreed to apply for a job here. After Thor's recommendation of the place, Jason hadn't let up until she sent in her résumé. Within two weeks she'd been called for this interview. Her legs shook.

Air conditioning blasted her as she opened the door and walked into the lobby. After the intense heat outdoors, the building felt cold. Jazmyn wished she'd worn a jacket with her skirt and top.

She relaxed a little as the doors hissed shut, blocking the noise outside. She hadn't realized how loud the city sounds could be until she returned from the mountains. Many times she'd longed for that peace and quiet again.

Two security guards behind a circular desk in the lobby looked up when she came in. The younger one gave her a smile and a nod that told her she looked okay.

"Good morning. Can we help you?" His name badge said Mulligan.

"I have an appointment this morning." Jazmyn clutched her purse, trying not to look as nervous as she felt.

Mulligan stared at her as the older guard, Landers, pulled out a clipboard with a sheet of paper on it. "With whom?" He studied her as he waited.

"It's with a Kirsten. . ." Jazmyn fumbled in her purse. How could she have forgotten the woman's name? These men would think her an idiot. Tugging the paper free, she held it up. "Kirsten Barnes."

Both guards acted surprised. "Your name?" the older one asked.

"Jazmyn Rondell." She tried not to fidget as Landers picked up a phone and punched in some numbers.

"You'll need to wear this." Mulligan handed her a clip-on badge. He pointed toward a wall on the far side of the lobby. "Take the elevator to the tenth floor. Someone will meet you and take you to Mrs. Barnes's office. She's waiting for you."

Incapable of speech, Jazmyn nodded her thanks to the guards. Her shoes clacked so loudly on the tile floor they almost drowned out the pounding of her heart. As the elevator doors shut, she closed her eyes. "God has not given me a spirit of fear." She repeated the words until the elevator slid to a halt at the tenth floor.

The doors swished open. Jazmyn found herself face-to-face with a beautiful blonde. The woman's hair curved under her chin, the cut the envy of any model. Her bright blue eyes sparkled as she smiled. She had delicate pixie features.

"You must be Jazmyn. I'm Kirsten Barnes. Welcome to T. L. Enterprises." She took Jazmyn's hand in a firm grip.

Jazmyn was awed by the beauty of the lobby on this floor. A glass curtain wall looked out over the city, while the rest of the room was done in a gray-white that muted the brilliance of the sun. Enlarged photos of the outdoors made her long to be back in the mountains. Several vases and hand-woven baskets rested on pedestals around the room.

"My office is this way." Kirsten led her into a lavish office and gestured to a set of comfortable chairs. Jazmyn slid into one, expecting Kirsten to sit at the massive desk. Instead, the woman took the seat next to hers.

Another woman entered the office from a side door carrying a serving tray. She smiled at Jazmyn as she set the tray on the table in front of them.

"Jazmyn, this is my assistant, Madeline Henry. If you come to work here, you'll get to know her. Some people call her mad, but her friends call her Maddy."

Maddy winked at Jazmyn. "Kirsten is the one who spreads the rumor about me being mad. She thinks that way no one will steal me away from her." With a saucy shake of her head, the young woman left the room.

Kirsten shook her head and sighed. "She is right about one thing. I don't know what I'd do if someone stole her away from me. She's invaluable." She lifted a cup and gestured to the tray. "Would you like tea or coffee?"

Her mouth dry, Jazmyn tried to swallow. Kirsten seemed so nice, but Jazmyn had never been good at meeting people. "Coffee, please." She prayed she wouldn't rattle the cup with her shaking hands.

"I love coffee, too." Kirsten poured, placing the cup on the table in front of Jazmyn. "I see Maddy has provided some sweets. Would you like those now or after the interview?"

"I think later." Jazmyn cleared her throat, hoping Kirsten hadn't noticed the squeak in her voice.

Whatever she'd expected, this interview was like nothing she could have imagined. Kirsten treated her more like a friend, wanting to get to know her better. By degrees, Jazmyn managed to relax. By the time she finished her coffee, she and Kirsten were laughing about the camping trip and Xena the warrior squirrel.

"I haven't been camping in years," Kirsten said. "The last time I did any camping, my brothers dangled a snake from the awning over the tent. When I ducked out the next morning, I came face-to-face with the creepy thing. They said my scream scared off all the animals in the forest." She shuddered. "I still don't like tents. If I went camping again, I would have to sleep in a luxury camper with no awning and no brothers in sight."

Jazmyn laughed and waited for Kirsten to get down to the business of interviewing her. She was surprised when the woman said, "So, when can you start?"

Jazmyn almost choked. "You mean I have the job? I mean, I can start anytime."

"This is Friday," Kirsten said. "How about starting Monday? I can have your badge made up and all the paperwork done this afternoon." She smiled. "I did tell you Maddy is a miracle worker, didn't I?"

Jazmyn could only nod. She listened in silence as Kirsten explained the job description to her. Jazmyn would need to put in a certain amount of hours, but after the training period she could set her own schedule. This job was like a dream come true.

J·O

Thor drummed his fingers on his desk as he waited for his brother to answer the phone. Most people thought of his cabin in the mountains as an antiquated shack. They hadn't seen this back room. In fact, no one other than his brother had been in here.

This room was where he ran his business. He had all the modern conveniences here. He kept in constant touch with his sister, Kirsten, and his brother, Erik. The fact that they were his half-sister and half-brother had no meaning to him. They'd always considered themselves family growing up, and nothing had changed now. They would do anything for each other. Thor appreciated the way they conducted the hands-on running of his company so he could maintain his distance.

"You're hiding away," Kirsten would accuse him. "You can't stay up on that mountain all your life. You need to meet a decent woman and get married."

Since Kirsten had met her husband, Wes Barnes, she'd decided everyone should be married and happy like she was. Thor didn't believe that was possible. He'd had too many narrow misses with shallow women to want to try meeting any more of them. So why was he so interested in Jazmyn Rondell?

For the last few weeks since he returned from that camping trip, he'd been checking into her. He knew everything he could possibly learn about Jazmyn. He told his siblings he was doing a background check because he wanted to know if she would be a good future employee of T. L. Enterprises. That was a lie. He wanted to know her because she intrigued him. He couldn't get her out of his mind.

"Peterson."

"About time," Thor snapped at his brother. "I thought you were taking a nap."

Erik heaved an exaggerated sigh over the phone. "What is it this time, Thor? It's been five whole minutes since we last talked."

"Um. I wondered about. . ."

"I know. You want to know about the interview. Kirsten is still at work. When she gets home, I promise to have her call you."

"No." Thor could feel the sweat bead on his forehead. "I'm just interested in a new employee, that's all."

"Right." Erik snorted. "You've never bugged us before about a simple interview. Of course, you've never told Kirsten whom to hire for what before, either. Would you like me to pop out and get a ring? I could go right in and end the interview with a proposal from you. I'm sure that would be appropriate."

"Very funny, Erik."

"Listen, Thor. Kirsten has her work, and I'm trying to get some things done for my trip tomorrow. Why don't you come to town? Spend a few days at the house. You can see for yourself how Jazmyn is doing."

"I can't do that." Thor could hear a note of panic in his voice. "I. . .um. I have some work to do here." He could almost see Erik drumming his fingers on the desk waiting for the truth. "I can't let her know who I am."

Erik's tone softened. "You have to get over the past, Thor. If this woman is worth what you think, then your status won't matter."

"I know. I will tell her." He rubbed his forehead. "I'll tell her soon."

"Listen, I'll have Kirsten call you the minute the interview is over. Okay?"

"Okay. Thanks." Thor hung up the phone and ran his hands over his face. He had it bad. Here he was, a man who'd started a company from scratch and built it into a multimillion-dollar business, yet he was afraid of a relationship with a woman. What was his problem? He stopped that thought before it took him places he didn't want to go.

He could still feel the hurt from the three serious relationships he'd had with women. Every time he'd been sure this one was right. Twice Erik had warned him to be careful; the third time Kirsten had been the one to caution him. He hadn't listened that time until almost too late.

Loki padded across the room and rested his chin on Thor's leg. Thor stroked the dog's silky cheek. "I've been ignoring you two, haven't I?" Odin rose from the rug and ambled over to get his share of attention. "After Kirsten calls I'll take you out for a walk. Maybe we'll hunt some rabbits."

At the mention of hunting, the dogs' ears perked up. Loki trotted to the door and whined, looking back to see what was taking Thor so long.

"I have to wait for one more call." Thor clenched his fist to keep from picking up the phone and dialing again.

His hand had just wrapped around the phone when it rang. "Larson."

"Larson, who?" At Kirsten's lilting laugh Odin tilted his head to one side. "I thought this was a grizzly bear answering my brother's phone."

"Sorry." Thor knew he'd been gruff. "I'm a little testy right now."

"Testy? Try badger with its foot caught in a trap. No, I think the badger would be easier to take."

"I'm not that bad," Thor growled. "So how did the interview go?"

"She's right here. You want to ask her?"

Thor's heart plummeted. "You didn't tell her. She's not. . ."

In the background he could hear Erik joining Kirsten in laughing. "That was a rotten dirty trick. I think I'm going to give both of you a pay cut just to bring you down to size."

"You can't do that, brother dear. We're indispensable." He could imagine Kirsten waving her hand in an airy gesture.

"The interview," Thor reminded her.

"Oh, that." Kirsten finally turned serious. "You're right, Thor. She's wonderful. I loved her ideas. We spent quite a bit of time discussing her job description, and once she warmed up she had some great input. In fact, she had me wondering how we've managed without someone like her all this time."

"When is she starting?" Thor couldn't keep the eagerness from his voice.

"She's thinking it over," Kirsten said. "I think she's holding out for more money."

Before Thor could respond in horror he heard Erik in the background, "That was the meanest thing you've said in a long time, Kirsten."

"Sorry, Thor. Erik's right." Kirsten sounded humbled. "I just wanted you to know she's different from the others. She was more interested in the work than in how much she would make. I had to bring up the salary." She paused. "Monday. She starts Monday."

Relief flooded Thor. He had no idea why he felt this way. Staying away from Jazmyn had become a priority, so why did he want to know her schedule? Why did he care?

When Thor hung up the phone Loki danced in place in front of the door. The dog was too smart for his own good. Shoving back from his desk, Thor stood and arched his back to stretch his muscles. "I think instead of going hunting, we'll do a little fishing." Both dogs stared at him as if they were hanging on every word. "I could use a little time to relax. Now that I've gotten Jazmyn settled with a good job, I don't have to worry about her."

He followed the dogs out the door, trying to convince himself that he wouldn't think about her anymore.

Chapter 12

Settling back against the bank, Thor kept one hand on the fishing pole and an eye on the line leading down into the small lake. This was the life. Up early to catch a fish or two for breakfast. Several hours of business conducted in quiet from his place in the mountains. An afternoon hike ending with some more fishing, or hunting when it was in season, to get his supper.

What were the drawbacks? None. No power meetings filled with stress. No personnel problems to deal with. No women trying to cheat him out of everything he had worked for. No ties, except for a few with his family.

He could take on guide jobs if and when he wanted. This was what freedom was all about.

The dogs trotted out of the brush and flung themselves down on either side of him, panting from their run. Thor sighed. Even the dogs were contented.

Over a week had passed since Jazmyn went to work for T. L. Enterprises. Although he'd talked with Kirsten a few times to see how Jazmyn was doing, he'd managed to keep from going to town to check up on things. At that thought his stomach knotted. Staying away had taken every ounce of willpower he had. He didn't know how much longer he could do this.

A tug on his pole drew his attention. He reeled in the line, bringing up the smallest trout he'd ever caught. Loki cocked his head as if asking what his master had brought out of the lake. Thor chuckled.

"I think we'll give up on fishing for today." He unhooked the squirming fish and tossed it back into the water. "Let's go, boys."

Excitement coursed through him. He lengthened his stride, wanting to get home. The dogs trotted beside him, guarding him from every imagined threat in the forest. They were good dogs.

After washing his hands at the sink in back, he almost ran to the office. He didn't have any messages, so he clicked on the phone and speed-dialed Kirsten's number. She answered on the third ring.

"This is Kirsten." She sounded brusque. Thor frowned. She had to know it was he.

"Kirsten? This is Thor."

"Yes, sir. How can I help you?"

"Cut it out, Kirsty." Thor used the nickname he and Erik had taunted

Kirsten with when they were kids. She always hated it. "I'm calling to see how things are going."

"Could you hold a minute, sir?" Thor could still hear her muffled voice talking. "Can we finish going over these layouts tomorrow, Jazmyn? This call is important, and it's almost time to go."

His heart raced as he listened to the woman in the background. Even if Kirsten hadn't said her name, he would have known Jazmyn's voice. He heard it in his dreams. Sometimes he even heard her as he walked through the forest.

Kirsten came back on the line. "Are you so thick-headed you can't get a hint? I should have just told Jazmyn this was my lunkhead of a brother who checks up on her every day."

"I haven't called that often."

"Yes, you have. You've called every day, although I have to admit this time is different."

"How's that?" Thor almost didn't want to hear her answer.

"This is the first day you've called before quitting time."

Thor picked up his watch. He'd left it on the desk when he went fishing. Time had seemed to fly by. He'd assumed it was later in the day. He hadn't checked the hour before calling.

"Sorry, Kirsten." He rubbed his hand over his face. "I didn't notice how early it was. I haven't called you every day."

"Oh, that's true." Kirsten gave a dramatic sigh. "You didn't call me on Sunday. You did call on Saturday, however, to get an overview of the week. Thor, I'm thinking of getting my phone number changed just so I don't get any more calls from you."

"I'm concerned about a new employee because hers is a new position, that's all."

"Yeah, right. You may be deluding yourself, Thor, but no one else is fooled."

"No one?" Panic made him sit up straight. "Whom have you talked to about this?"

"Don't have a cow." Kirsten laughed. "Only Erik and I know. Of course, I may have mentioned it to Wes. We don't keep secrets, you know."

"Okay, so tell me how she's working out."

"The same as yesterday." He could picture Kirsten rolling her eyes. "Some of the designs and layouts she's come up with are incredible. I think sales are increasing, too, but it's a little early to tell. You'll have to give her more than ten days of work to know for sure."

"Does she seem to be enjoying the job?"

"Yes."

"What is it?" Thor gripped the phone hard. "What's wrong?"

"Oh, it's probably nothing. I need to go. Wes is coming to take me out to dinner tonight. I have to freshen up before he gets here."

"Kirsten. What is it? I know something's wrong."

"Look, Thor, it's probably nothing. Jazmyn just looks a little tired. Haunted maybe. Perhaps she isn't getting enough sleep or something is keeping her awake."

"Does she act afraid?" Thor wondered if Jazmyn's fears had returned.

"No, not afraid. I don't know. I have the feeling she has something on her mind, but we don't know each other well enough for her to share. Maybe her brother will be back soon and she can talk to him."

"Is he out of town?"

"He's helping some friend of his take pictures for a book. He'll be gone for several weeks, I think." Kirsten groaned. "Look at the time. Thor, I have to go. I'll be home later, but don't call me. If there's anything to tell, I'll call you. Don't worry about Jazmyn. She'll be fine."

Clicking off the phone, Thor began to pace. Loki and Odin watched him from their spots along the wall. Restless energy seemed to make sitting down impossible.

What was upsetting Jazmyn? Had she met some guy in the office? T. L. Enterprises was a big company. They had a lot of employees, including many single men. Had one of them approached Jazmyn? She didn't trust men. Maybe she wanted to keep her job but was afraid of the bozo who was after her. Anger burned in his chest.

"We'll see about this." Thor strode to his bedroom, pulled out a bag, and began to throw a few essentials in it. With Jason out of town and something upsetting Jazmyn, he intended to see what he could do to help.

He made the trip in record time. As he drove up the long driveway, a car turned in behind him. He climbed out of his truck as Kirsten opened the door of her car.

"I can't believe this." She was laughing as she ran to hug him. "Ugh. You didn't even take the time to shower. You smell like fish."

"I'm thinking someone from work is after her. Do you have any idea who?"

Kirsten glanced at her husband, who was sauntering toward them. "Thor, I don't think anything is wrong with Jazmyn. At least not anything that wouldn't be cured by seeing you again."

⌀

Jazmyn's footsteps echoed in the garage as she headed to the elevator that would take her to her office. She still couldn't believe she'd gotten this job. All these years she'd been afraid to go out and find something. Money wasn't an issue for her, so the income didn't matter. Her father had left a trust fund for her, and as long as she lived modestly, it would take care of her needs.

What she'd always wanted was to find a job that challenged her artistic skills. This position was perfect. She could incorporate her design ideas and the computer knowledge she had accumulated over the years.

At first Jazmyn was overwhelmed to be working so closely with a powerful woman like Kirsten Barnes. She'd expected her to be harsh and driven. Kirsten proved to be the opposite. Although she could get people to do the work, she was also funny and compassionate. Everyone in the company loved her.

In the elevator she leaned back against the wall and closed her eyes. Images of the mountains crossed her mind. She could almost hear the ripple of the river and see the chipmunks playing. How she missed being there.

She tried to push away thoughts of how much she missed seeing Thor. The rumble of his deep voice still came to her in her dreams. Sometimes she thought she saw him. This morning, on the way to work, she'd been sure he was following her in his truck. Then, two blocks from work, the truck turned off and sped away. It couldn't have been him.

"Lord, I want to see him so much I'm hallucinating." She shook her head. "What am I supposed to do?"

The elevator dinged and opened. Jazmyn stepped off, heading to her office. She'd come in before regular hours on purpose. Kirsten told her yesterday she could set her own schedule if she had something else to do. Today she had plans for the afternoon.

She'd been working for an hour when Kirsten stuck her head in the doorway. "You sure got here early. Big plans this afternoon?"

"Yeah." Jazmyn tried to sound casual. "I thought I'd go hiking somewhere."

"It's still pretty hot. Do you do much hiking?"

Jazmyn shrugged. "No. A few weeks ago I found out how out of shape I am. I thought I'd try to do something about it."

"Gotcha. You might try going to a gym. I can give you the name of the one I go to. It's not far from here. They'll give you advice on what exercises to do so you don't do too much at first. It can be fun."

"That might be a good idea." Jazmyn smiled. "That's probably smarter than going off hiking."

"Okay, I'll call you with the name and number. If you decide to join, we can work out together sometimes."

"That sounds good." Warmth flooded Jazmyn. She'd never been allowed to have girlfriends growing up.

"By the way, what are you doing for lunch today?" Kirsten asked.

"Probably the deli down the street." Jazmyn made a face. "I think I'm stuck on deli food."

Kirsten laughed. "See you later. I'd better earn my keep."

The morning raced by. When Jazmyn checked her watch she was startled to find that lunchtime was almost past. Grabbing her purse, she headed for the door.

Heat blasted her as she stepped outside. A light breeze ruffled her hair. Traffic noise and exhaust fumes made her long for the mountains once more. Maybe when Jason returned they could go back for a weekend.

The deli wasn't far. Most of the people were already leaving, their lunch hours almost up. Pushing open the door, Jazmyn breathed in the scent of fresh-baked bread. This place was the best find since coming to work down here. She loved the food.

The bell at the door jingled as she stepped up to the counter to order, and the person who entered got into line behind her. A frazzled clerk waited for her order.

"You know," Jazmyn said, craning her neck to see into the display case next to her, "I have this terrible craving for something chocolate. I think I'll have one of those brownies, too."

"Be careful. Some squirrel might steal it."

Jazmyn whirled around, her hand going to her throat. Thor. It was he. She wasn't imagining this time. He looked so good he took her breath away. "What are you doing here?"

He shrugged. "It's a public place, isn't it?"

Her face warmed. "You know what I mean. In town. I thought you hated the city."

"I do come into civilization every few months for supplies. Mind if I sit with you?" He leaned past her and gave the clerk his order. Jazmyn tried to still her pounding heart. How would she ever carry her food to the table when her hands were shaking so badly?

Niggling reminders that Thor wasn't a Christian pushed at the back of her mind. She ignored them. She wasn't pursuing a romantic interest but visiting with a friend she hadn't seen in a while. This couldn't be the same as the unequal yoking Jason talked about.

Thor stood so close they were almost touching. Jazmyn had to force herself not to lean against him. She couldn't help thinking about the way he'd held her the night she got lost. A shiver ran through her.

"Where would you like to sit?" His question startled her. He held a tray with both their food and drinks. "Lead the way."

She didn't realize until she reached the table that she'd picked one in a corner away from the other diners. She slipped into a chair. Thor sat across from her. His hand brushed hers as he handed her the sandwich she'd ordered. The contact was electric. Her eyes met his. He smiled, his gaze warm and enticing.

"So, how's the new job?"

She looked up. "How did you know?"

"I saw you coming out of the building." He shrugged. "I just put two and two together."

"It's fine." She unwrapped her sandwich and bit off a small piece. She didn't know if she'd be able to eat with Thor there. His presence did strange things to her. How had he known where she'd be? Did he ask one of the men he knew at T. L. Enterprises about her? She was pretty sure he didn't just happen to run into her.

Chapter 13

So, are you going to share that brownie with me, or do I have to be like Xena and fight for a bite?" Thor was already reaching for the huge brownie. Jazmyn wanted to shake her head to make sure she wasn't dreaming he was there.

"They have more brownies. You can buy your own." She tried for a saucy tone, rather than sounding as breathless as she felt.

"My mother always said you have to finish your meal before you can have dessert." Thor grinned. "You've stopped eating and still have half a sandwich left. That means I should get the whole brownie because I finished my meal."

"Then you're probably too full to eat any sweets. Those sandwiches are big enough to fill an elephant." Jazmyn reached for the brownie. Before she could pluck it up from the napkin where she'd placed it, Thor covered her hand with his. Her mouth went dry.

He leaned closer across the small table. "I think we should share this."

"On one condition." They were almost nose-to-nose. Jazmyn could smell the woodsy scent of his cologne.

"What condition is that?"

"I. . .um. I'm getting off early this afternoon. If you're not doing anything else, why don't you run some errands with me?" She couldn't believe she'd said that. Never in her life had she asked a man to do something with her. Her cheeks felt like they were on fire.

"Deal." Thor lifted her hand and retrieved the brownie. "See, I'll do anything for chocolate."

"And you accused Xena of being that way because she's a female." Jazmyn took her half and bit into the delicious sweet. "If I didn't know better, I'd accuse you of being a chauvinist." She winked at him and almost choked on her bite. Never in her life had she flirted with a man like this. Not even Adam. Theirs had been a steady, safe relationship. Around Thor her emotions seemed to be on a roller coaster.

The afternoon dragged by. Thor had agreed to meet her outside the building at three o'clock. She couldn't seem to concentrate on her work.

Maddy knocked and stuck her head through the door. "Jazmyn?"

"Come on in." Jazmyn smiled at the perky redhead. In the past week and a half, she had gotten to know Maddy pretty well.

"Kirsten had to leave early. She asked me to get these papers to you. This is a list of new products we're thinking of adding to our line. She wanted you to work up some display ideas and get them to her as soon as possible."

"Does she need this done today?"

"Nah." Maddy rested her hip against the side of the desk, a sure sign she planned to stay a few minutes. "Tomorrow, or even the next day, will be fine. You know what they say. No rest for the wicked."

Jazmyn lifted her eyebrow. "And you think I'm wicked?"

"I'm not answering that one. So, have you read the memo about the party?"

"Party?" Jazmyn frowned. "I didn't get any memo like that. Is someone retiring?"

"No. This is the big bash the boss puts on every year. The salaried personnel get invited to his mansion, where we stuff ourselves with food we could never afford. He usually has some sort of band or something to entertain everyone. There's a pool if you want to swim. It's great."

"Well, I must not be invited, because I haven't heard anything about it." Jazmyn felt relieved. Attending an event like that would only make her nervous. If they didn't invite her, she wouldn't feel obligated to go. "Maybe I'm too new to be included."

"I doubt that." Maddy crossed her arms. "I always go on the off chance I might get a glimpse of the mysterious big boss."

"Mysterious?"

"Yeah, the guy who started the company. He's some sort of a recluse. Doesn't like people."

"So how did he start a company that's so successful? I'd think you'd need to be a people person for that."

"Oh, no. He has others do that part for him. That's where Kirsten and her brother, Erik, come in. Rumor has it they're related to the big boss, but I don't know for sure. I haven't been here that long."

"It always amazes me how the rumor mill works everywhere you go," Jazmyn said. "I don't care what the man is like as long as I'm allowed to do my job."

"You will come, though, won't you?" Maddy began to rummage through Jazmyn's in-box. "I know you've got an invitation here somewhere. Aha!" She pulled out a white folded paper.

Jazmyn took the memo and read it. Tension tightened her muscles. She didn't want to have to attend some fancy party at a mansion. She wasn't interested in some mysterious boss. "I don't know that I'll be able to make it. This sounds pretty formal. I don't have anything to wear."

"You have four weeks to shop," Maddy countered. "If I have to, I'll take you to find something. You're going if I have to drag you there. It will be fun. Besides, how often do you get to go inside some swanky place? You won't believe how amazing this house is."

"You're impossible, Maddy." Jazmyn laughed. "Maybe Kirsten is right, and you're really mad after all."

"I'll be mad if you don't go with me." She wrinkled her nose at Jazmyn before she closed the door on her way out.

Jazmyn sighed and stared at the paper in her hand. She only wanted a job she enjoyed. She didn't want to see a fancy house or a reclusive boss. Four weeks. That gave her plenty of time to come up with an excuse. Maybe by then Jason would be back and they could make some plans. Right now she had to finish a few things and get ready to meet Thor. Her pulse sped up at the thought.

Standing across the street from the T. L. Enterprises office building, Thor tried to act casual. Inside he burned with impatience. Having lunch with Jazmyn only whetted his appetite for spending more time with her. Now that he was in town he didn't want to let her out of his sight. He tried to assure himself he was only checking up on a new employee's job satisfaction, but inside he knew better.

He still couldn't bring himself to tell Jazmyn he owned this company. Since he hadn't spent much time in the offices during the last few years, he didn't worry about anyone identifying him. Most of the employees were new enough that they didn't know Thor. Even Erik wasn't as visible as Kirsten. He supposed most of the workers thought Erik was the elusive boss.

The door across the street swung open. Jazmyn stepped out into the heat, fumbling with a pair of sunglasses to guard against the glaring sun. She didn't dress like a lot of businesswomen in power suits with padded shoulders. She wore an airy sort of dress with a floral print and a skirt that twirled in the light breeze. Her hair lay loose about her shoulders. Even from here Thor could see the highlights glinting in the sun.

He pushed off from the wall and strode across the street. The moment Jazmyn noticed him she lit up with a smile that brightened the day. His stomach did a flip-flop. Thor stuck his hands in his pockets to keep from pulling her into his arms and kissing her.

"Ready to go?" She tilted her head back to look up at him. He loved the fact that she didn't step away. When they first met she'd been terrified of him.

"I have to tell you, I'm not much of a shopper." He breathed deep, loving the fresh-washed scent of her.

"Neither is Jason. He doesn't seem to understand that when I go looking for a blouse to go with a skirt, the blouse not only has to be the right color, but the right style and material, too. Jason just wants to grab the first blouse he sees and leave the store."

"I knew I liked him for some reason." Thor grinned. "We shop the same way. Of course, buying flannel shirts to match my jeans isn't quite as difficult."

She laughed. He loved the sound of it and wanted to make her laugh some more.

"So which way are we headed? My truck is parked around the corner."

She hesitated. "My first stop is a little embarrassing, but I made the appointment this morning before I knew you'd be coming along."

"We can meet later if this is a problem." Thor tried to cover his disappointment.

"No. I. . .um, my boss, Kirsten, gave me the name of the gym where she works out. I have an appointment with a trainer there. She's going to show me around and talk about an exercise program for me."

He frowned. "I hope you're not doing this because you think you're fat. Women are always thinking they have to lose weight."

"I'm doing it because I couldn't walk ten feet up a mountain without having to stop and catch my breath. I want to get in better shape." She paused and glanced around. "You know, in case Jason and I go up to the mountains again."

A thrill shot through Thor. She liked the outdoors. He wasn't sure she'd ever want to go camping again, but she liked it. He thought he could float on air about now.

At the gym Thor waited in the lobby as Jazmyn followed a female bodybuilder into the inner sanctum. He waved them on, knowing he didn't want to chance going inside. This was the place where both Kirsten and Erik worked out. He might run into someone who had seen him with them before, and he didn't want to take the risk.

"Bored to pieces?" Jazmyn asked as she breezed into the lobby a half-hour later.

Thor tossed down the magazine he'd been leafing through and stood up. "Not a bit. Just gathering my strength for this marathon of shopping." As he pushed open the door for her, he put his hand on her back. He couldn't seem to resist touching her.

"I need to run by the mall."

"What, more exercise already? Your shoes don't look the type for running in."

"We'll take your truck, smarty. Bridget, my trainer, suggested getting my workout clothes at a store there. She says I can flash my membership card and get a discount." She gave him a wide smile as he opened the truck door for her. "I love discounts."

"The mall it is." Thor climbed into the truck, trying to hide his dismay. How had he gotten into this mess? He hated shopping, and most of all he hated malls. He made it a point never to go into one unless someone dragged him kicking and screaming. What was it about Jazmyn that had him eager to follow her anywhere? The thought of her in the mountains, out of her element, flashed through his mind. If she could do that, he could brave the mall.

School was out for the day, so the mall was teeming with teenagers.

"I haven't come here in a long time." Jazmyn leaned close to be heard above the din. She looked a little nervous.

Thor leaned down and spoke into her ear as he put his arm around her. "I remember when you were afraid of everything. You've changed so much I can't believe it."

A smile lit her eyes, those beautiful green eyes a man could get lost in. "Jason has been such a help, but I have to say all the credit goes to God and the peace He's given me. I have verses of Scripture memorized to battle my fears. At first I didn't think that would work, but I'm amazed at the courage God's given me."

Several times in the last few weeks Thor had found himself pondering the faith Jazmyn and Jason shared. They reminded him so much of his mother. He'd always thought only weak people needed God, but maybe this wasn't all about weakness and strength but something else entirely. When Jason got back, he wanted to find a time to talk to him about his faith.

"Here we are." Jazmyn led him into a store. The noise level dropped several decibels. Thor sighed with relief.

"I'll need shoes and some workout clothes." Jazmyn's mouth twisted as she perused the various racks and displays in the store.

"Here's what you need." He led her down an aisle to a rack of stretchy workout clothes. He started to pluck off a green set that would match her eyes, but the hanger caught on the rod.

He had pulled too hard. The display tipped. Thor grabbed for the rod and missed. The resulting crash brought store personnel running. He still held the green outfit, while the rest lay in a heap of color at his feet.

"This one would look good on you." He offered the outfit to Jazmyn as she covered her mouth to stifle the laughter.

Chapter 14

I think you owe me big time. That was a nightmare."

"Which part?" Jazmyn was obviously trying hard not to laugh again. Inside the store she'd laughed until she had tears in her eyes. He wouldn't tell her this, but he'd loved the sound of her laughter.

"What do you mean, which part?"

"Well, there was the part where you knocked over the exercise outfits. That, at least, was colorful."

"Go ahead. Laugh." He bit the inside of his lip to keep from joining her. It had been funny.

"Then there was the display of shoes you bumped into."

"They shouldn't have left all those boxes out in the middle where anyone could run into them." Thor could still see all the boxes skittering across the floor in every direction. He could also recall the look of horror on the faces of the staff.

"My personal favorite had to be when you got bored waiting for me and decided to try out the fishing equipment. I doubt if anyone had ever hooked, and tried to reel in, a security camera before." Tears shone in her eyes.

Thor laughed. "Okay, that's enough. Since you think I'm so amusing, I'm insisting you have dinner with me. After all this trauma, I can't face the thought of eating alone."

Jazmyn took a deep breath and wiped her eyes. "I don't know. I'm not sure if there's any safe food out there. I didn't bring bibs with me." They both laughed again.

Carrying her bags in one hand, Thor reached over and pulled Jazmyn close. Her green eyes sparkled as she looked up at him. Thor realized he'd stopped in the middle of the mall parking lot. His pulse raced. He wanted nothing more than to kiss this woman.

Lifting their two hands together, he traced his thumb along her lower lip. Her lips parted. He could see a smattering of freckles dusted across her nose. He leaned closer.

A car horn honked, spoiling the moment. They stepped to one side to let a teenager drive past, his stereo booming loud enough to shake the ground.

Somehow Thor had ended up with his arm around Jazmyn, holding her snug against his side. He loosened his hold. "So, I know this little Italian place.

They give out big bibs for messy eaters."

The tension of the moment faded. "That sounds like a plan," Jazmyn said.

As Thor headed them toward his truck, he ignored the warning lights flashing inside his head. The promise he'd made never to get involved with another woman seemed so distant now. He couldn't recall ever feeling this way before. Had he ever laughed like this with one of his fiancées? He didn't think so. Those relationships had all been about status and show.

Bruno's Restaurant was a quaint mix of Italian and Southwest. When they walked in, the hostess led them to a quiet table in the corner. The table was small enough so that their knees touched when they sat down. Thor tried to ignore how much he enjoyed this contact with Jazmyn.

He watched her from the corner of his eye. She was trying to decide what to order and couldn't seem to make up her mind. Perhaps she didn't like Italian food.

"I'm sorry, I didn't ask if you like Italian food," Thor said.

She smiled as she looked up. "This is my favorite kind of food. I haven't eaten out much, though. I didn't realize how expensive a place like this could be."

He hadn't expected her to be concerned over prices. He'd never been out with a woman who worried about how much he spent on her. In fact, he usually couldn't splurge enough.

"Order what you like. I wouldn't have brought you here if I couldn't afford it."

"I'm sorry. I didn't mean to imply anything." Jazmyn laid her menu down and smoothed the pages. "What are you ordering?"

"This place has the best ravioli I've ever eaten. They make it right here, even the sauce. It's an old family recipe. I knew the owners years ago. Anyway, I always order the ravioli, but everything's good. What's your favorite?"

Her gaze dropped to the menu. "Well, my absolute favorite has to be eggplant parmigiana."

"Then that's what you should have." Thor lifted his hand, motioning to the waitress that they were ready to order.

They sat for a long time talking after their meal. She was the first woman who seemed to enjoy hearing his stories of guiding hunters into the mountains. He couldn't remember the last time he'd talked so much about himself. Every time he tried to change the conversation to something about her, Jazmyn avoided his question and asked one of her own.

Only a few stars were out as Thor walked Jazmyn to the garage under the T. L. Enterprises building. How he wished this was the forest where stars were plentiful and the air was pure, not filled with exhaust fumes.

"Thank you for dinner." Jazmyn fished her keys from her purse, clicking the button to unlock her car. She smiled up at him. "Thanks, too, for the entertainment earlier."

"I aim to please. That's my motto," Thor said. He reached around her to open the car door. Before she could turn away, he cupped her cheek and drew her close. Her eyes drifted shut. The kiss he gave her was warm and sweet, full of promise. "Thanks for seeing me today." He stepped back, opening the door wide. "When you talk to him, tell Jason I'd like to see him when he gets back to town."

"I will." Her eyes glittered in the dim light. Was she crying? Thor frowned and started toward her, but she pulled the door shut. He watched as she left the garage. Had he done something to upset her?

For a long time Jazmyn lay awake thinking about the fun she'd had with Thor. She could still feel the sweetness of his kiss on her lips. Every time she thought about the mall and his clumsiness there, she had to laugh. Who would have thought? In the woods he seemed to be able to do anything, but in civilization he was out of his element.

Even so, Thor had tried hard to enjoy the places she wanted to go. The only time all evening that he'd been anything other than considerate was when she told him about the party T. L. Enterprises was having for the employees. When she mentioned the elusive owner and the rumors about him, Thor's eyes darkened. She changed the subject, not knowing what had upset him. Could it be he was jealous? That would be crazy, because she didn't care at all about the man who owned her company.

The alarm seemed to ring almost before she got to sleep. Her eyes were gritty. A morning shower and coffee revived her somewhat, but she wanted to go back to bed and sleep for another day at least. For what seemed the millionth time she wished Jason were home. She needed someone to talk to about her attraction to Thor. She didn't want it to become anything serious, yet she did enjoy his company.

"Morning, girl." Maddy smiled at Jazmyn as she dragged off the elevator. "You look like you had some night."

"Couldn't sleep." Jazmyn stifled a yawn. "If you hold my work, I could kick back in my office and catch some z's."

"I don't think that's going to happen. I've heard the big boss is in town, and he wants to see the designs for the new products. Maybe you'll get to meet him today when you're at your shiny best."

Jazmyn groaned. "That's all I need. Maybe I'll hide in the closet. You convince Kirsten I've been kidnapped and will only be released when the owner is gone again."

"I'll bring you a cup of my super-strength coffee. It's guaranteed to wake the dead."

"That sounds perfect." Jazmyn headed into her office.

Kirsten called to ask her if the new layouts were done. She didn't say anything about meeting with the boss, which filled Jazmyn with relief. Today was not the day for something like that.

"You're looking perkier." Maddy grinned at her from the open door. "Must be because it's almost quitting time."

"That's the best news I've had all day." Jazmyn brushed her hair back from her forehead. Maddy leaned against the doorframe and stared at her.

"Well, are you going to tell me or not?"

"Tell you what?"

"About your hot date last night." Maddy rolled her eyes. "The one that kept you up so late you almost didn't make it to work this morning."

"I wasn't even close to being late." Maddy was like a bulldog. Once she got ahold of an idea, she wouldn't let go until she worried it to death. "I did spend some time with a friend, but I didn't get home late."

"A friend?" Maddy's eyebrows rose. "As in a male sort of friend?"

"Yes." Jazmyn sighed. "He's only a friend, though. He knows my brother. It's nothing."

"Hmmm. I'll let you off this time. By the way, do you have a dress for the party yet?"

"I don't know if I'll go to the party, Maddy. It's not my thing."

"You're going." Maddy studied her. "I thought this weekend we could get together and shop for your dress. I think you need something that will knock the socks off all those eligible bachelors."

"Maddy, I'm not in the market for a husband. I don't want to knock their socks off. Then you have all those smelly bare feet."

Maddy laughed. "Girlfriend, we have to get you to that party. You don't know what you're missing. Tell you what. I heard they're having a sale at that little boutique in the mall, Lacy's. Why don't we run over there after work and just look around?" She gave Jazmyn a woeful look that made Jazmyn laugh.

"Okay. Let me finish up here, and I'll be ready to go. Maybe we can try out that new coffee shop and deli while we're there. I heard some of the girls talking about it the other day, saying it's really good."

"As long as you don't make me eat bean sprouts or something like that." Maddy patted her ample hips. "I have to keep up my image."

Jazmyn giggled and shook her head as Maddy closed the door. She'd never dreamed how much fun having a friend could be. She thought of last night when she and Thor had been together. She'd enjoyed the time they spent talking and laughing. Growing up, she'd missed out on friendships like those. Now she treasured the few she had.

The mall was teeming with people. Jazmyn stuck close to Maddy as they wended their way through the throngs.

"Here we go." Maddy looped her arm through Jazmyn's and slipped past a couple of women coming out of Lacy's laden with shopping bags. "I was in here last week. They have some really cute dresses back here."

Jazmyn followed Maddy through the maze of racks. She couldn't help but smile as she recalled Thor in the sports store last night. He would be a terror here where the clothes were so close together you had to squeeze to get past.

Maddy yanked a bright red dress from a rack and held it up to Jazmyn.

"I can't possibly wear this." Jazmyn took the hanger and put the wisp of cloth back.

"Why not? It's perfect."

"First of all, it's indecent. A front like that would show off my belly button." She chuckled at Maddy's look of outrage. "Well, maybe it wasn't that revealing, but it was too low-cut for me. Second, I don't like wearing red. It's too bright."

"It would be perfect with your hair and eyes, though." Maddy, not to be defeated, started rummaging through the clothes again.

A flash of green caught Jazmyn's eye. The color of the outfit Thor held up for her last night. The one he said would look perfect with her coloring. She reached for the dress. It was simple and beautiful. Deep down she knew it was fruitless to pick an outfit because of Thor. He wouldn't even be at the party.

She held the dress in front of her. "What about this one?"

Maddy turned. Her eyes widened. "You'll not only knock their socks off, they'll drop their teeth."

"Oh, great." Jazmyn grimaced. "Now I have a bunch of toothless guys with smelly feet."

Chapter 15

Pacing the floor, Thor felt like a tiger trapped in a cage. He'd been in town three days and already he was going nuts. Only the hope of seeing Jazmyn again kept him here.

"Sit down before you wear a hole in the carpet." Kirsten took a sip of her tea and leaned back in the plush chair. She had been going over some reports for the company. "Your pacing won't get Erik here any faster."

"Where is he?" Thor stopped near the window, gazing at the empty driveway. "Did you check to see if his plane came in late?"

"Thor, he only landed forty-five minutes ago. It takes that long to drive here from the airport. Plus, he still had to get his luggage and meet the driver. Be patient." She smiled. "Oh, I forgot who I'm talking to."

"I am patient," Thor growled, then realized how he sounded. "At least I'm patient with some things. Right now I'm having a little trouble." He sighed. "Is she—?"

"Yes, Thor, Jazmyn is working out just fine. How many times do I have to tell you this? She and Maddy have hit it off. Yesterday they even went shopping, as you know, since you were watching from the building across the street. Don't you feel guilty spying on the woman?"

"I wasn't spying." Thor shoved his hands in the pockets of his jeans. "I thought maybe I'd run into her again. I worry about her getting lonely with her brother out of town. She doesn't have any friends, you know."

"Well, that's changing. She has Maddy, and she has me." Kirsten flashed him a smile. "Since she joined my gym the other day, we made plans to work out together a couple times a week."

Panic raced through Thor. "You can't do that."

"Why not? I like her."

"What if you let something slip? I don't want her to know yet."

"Thor, she's not at all like Dana or Melissa or. . .what was the other one? Gloria." Kirsten sighed. "I know they hurt you, but you can't judge the world by greedy women like them. You were a different person then, too."

"I haven't changed." He moved closer to the window, putting his back to Kirsten.

"If I remember right, back then you were enamored with wealth and power, bro. Now you aren't. That makes you a different person to me." Kirsten's soft words struck deep in Thor. She was right. For a long time, when his company first became profitable in a big way, he'd been riding high on the excitement of fame and fortune. It had taken three times of being duped for him to come crashing back to reality.

"I still can't trust her. I have to be sure she isn't like them." His eyes stung. Yes, he'd been hurt, but that had been because of his own stupidity. He would not allow that to happen again. Ever.

Thoughts of his time spent with Jason popped into his mind. On one of their long walks Thor had mentioned his distrust of women. Jason had talked to Thor about Jesus. He said that Jesus had been betrayed by everyone He called a friend. They'd all run off and left Him to die. Even so, Jesus asked God to forgive all the wrongs done to Him.

Forgive. His mother had always talked about forgiving and not judging others by what one person had done. But three? He'd had three women do the same thing to him. Could it be that part of it was his fault? Was Kirsten right? If he hadn't been so greedy and power-hungry, would he have seen the shallowness of those women earlier?

A glint of light caught his eye. The long, dark car pulling into the drive would be Erik returning from his trip. He'd been out of the country doing business for the company. Erik was the liaison, making deals elsewhere for them, while Kirsten handled the local needs of the business. Few people in the company building where Kirsten worked had even met Erik. That's why Thor hoped his plan would work.

For the next thirty minutes chaos reigned as Erik's luggage was brought in and he changed into more comfortable clothes. Several of the hired help wanted to come by and greet him after his absence. Thor continued to pace the floor, waiting for his turn.

"So, bro, what brings you in from the wilds?" Erik sank onto the sofa, plunking his long legs on an ottoman.

"A woman," Kirsten said.

"What?" Erik's eyebrows shot up. "I thought you'd sworn off."

"It's not what you think." Thor glared at Kirsten, who crossed her eyes at him. "I came into town to ask you a favor and to check up on an employee."

"Would this employee happen to be female?" Erik's smug look made Thor want to start growling again. "Would her name happen to be Jazmyn? I haven't met her yet, but I can see that will have to change."

"She's a friend only. I'm concerned about her."

"I see." Erik nodded and put his hands behind his head. "So what's the favor you need? If it's anything more strenuous than rest and relaxation for today, I don't know if I'll comply."

"It's about the party next Saturday. I want you to pretend to be me."

Erik laughed. "Haven't I been doing that for years?" Thor hadn't been a visible part of the business in a long time.

"I want you to go a step further. I want you to meet her as if you're me."

"Thor, if you're planning what I think you're planning, this isn't a good idea." Kirsten frowned at him. "This could backfire on you."

Heaviness settled in Thor's chest. He knew the risk he was taking. Erik was the charming one. He had a charisma that attracted women to him, although he'd never returned the feeling with any one woman. What if Jazmyn fell for him? What if she became enamored with the status Erik represented? His shoulders slumped.

"I have to know, Kirsten. If she's like them, I want to know before this goes any further."

"What's going on?" Erik's brows drew together as he looked from Kirsten to Thor.

"Your brother is in love with this woman." Kirsten smirked as Thor started to protest. "I'm guessing he wants you to give her a test and see if she passes before he pursues the relationship. Am I right?"

"You don't understand, Kirsten. You're happy with Wes. You got a good man the first time." Thor turned to look back out the window before emotion clouded his speech.

A moment later Kirsten came up and hugged him. "Jazmyn is a wonderful person, Thor. You've changed. I think she'll be perfect for you."

✍〇

Stepping from the car, Jazmyn willed her knees not to shake as she stared up at the imposing house. She smoothed her dress, wishing she could return home and curl up in her bed with a good book. This was the last place in the world she wanted to be.

"Impressive, isn't it?" Maddy said. They'd ridden together in Maddy's car. Jazmyn had hesitated, knowing she would be dependent on Maddy to get home, but she knew she had to have someone go with her or she'd chicken out.

"If we leave right now, I'll take you someplace and buy you dinner, Maddy. We can talk girl-talk until all hours. Just please don't make me go in there." Jazmyn couldn't take her eyes from the well-lighted windows.

"No way, girlfriend. You've never seen a place like this one." Maddy looped her arm through Jazmyn's, dragging her toward the front door. "Come on. We're fashionably late. Let's get in there and see what's happening."

Jazmyn clenched her hands together, trying to get some warmth into her fingers. "I don't think I can do this." Her voice trembled.

"What have you been telling me ever since you started working at T. L.? Does that God of yours only give you courage at certain times and not others?"

Maddy was right. Jazmyn closed her eyes, praying for courage, for the fear to be taken from her. She was a child of God. There wasn't anything she couldn't do. She opened her eyes and took a deep breath. "Let's go."

"Maddy, Jazmyn. Welcome." Kirsten greeted them as the maid led them through the foyer. "Maddy, you know my brother, Erik. Jazmyn, this is Erik. Erik, Jazmyn."

The man standing beside Kirsten held out his hand to Maddy first. When he turned to Jazmyn he gave her a wink and folded her cold fingers inside his warm ones. Her hand seemed to disappear inside his. A picture of Thor and his huge frame flashed through Jazmyn's mind. For some reason Erik reminded her of him.

"Go on in and make yourselves at home. There's enough food and punch for an army." Kirsten waved her hand toward the groups of people gathered in the huge living room. "We'll join you as soon as the others have arrived."

Erik still held Jazmyn's hand. His eyes, a light, warm brown, gazed into hers. She tugged and he released her hand, giving her another wink as she turned away to follow Maddy.

Maddy leaned close as they moved away from Kirsten and Erik. "Well, girlfriend, you sure made an impression."

"Is that the elusive boss you spoke of?"

"Some people say so because he isn't around very much, but I've heard rumors that even Erik isn't the big guy. I don't think he started T. L."

"Will the founder be here tonight?" Jazmyn gazed around the room. She saw a few of the people she'd met in the last few weeks. Most of them, though, she'd never seen before because they worked in different departments from hers.

"He's never been here before. For all I know, Erik could be the founder. The other is just a rumor." Maddy grabbed her by the arm. "Come on. I see some people you have to meet."

Time passed in a swirl of faces and names that Jazmyn couldn't hope to remember later. She didn't know how Maddy knew so many people. The woman bubbled as she worked her way around the room, dragging Jazmyn behind her.

When they reached the doors that opened onto a lighted patio, Jazmyn excused herself and stepped outside. She had to get some fresh air, some quiet. A band had begun playing inside, and that, combined with the buzz of conversation, made Jazmyn want to get away.

A light breeze ruffled the loose strands of hair on her neck and around her face. The grass and trees around the house reminded her of the mountains. She could almost hear the rippling sound of the river that went past their camp.

"I see someone else needed to escape."

She swung around, startled to see Erik standing a few feet behind her. She hadn't heard him come outside.

"I'm sorry. Maybe I shouldn't be out here."

"No, you're fine. I wanted some fresh air, too. Kirsten is the people person. I do this once a year. The rest of the time she's the one who interacts with the employees."

"I see." Jazmyn wanted to go back inside, but she didn't want to be rude. She didn't feel comfortable with this stranger, even if he was Kirsten's brother.

"I hear you're our newest employee. Working in layout and design on computers. Am I right?" He gave her a warm smile.

She nodded. "I've only been with T. L. a few weeks. I guess that's why I've never met you at the office."

"Oh, I'm not there much. In fact, I just returned this past week from a business trip overseas. That's the part of the company Kirsten wants no part of. She wants to be home for Wes, and she hates to fly. Do you like the outdoors?" He gestured at the expansive grounds. A path wandered through them lighted by old-fashioned lampposts.

"I went to the mountains recently with my brother and a friend. Until then, I hadn't known how much I liked being outdoors. The smell is so fresh and clean." Jazmyn clamped her mouth shut, wishing she hadn't said so much.

Erik stepped forward and offered her his arm. "Take a walk with me." He smiled as she glanced back at the house. "Don't worry. They won't miss the two of us. We won't be long."

They strolled through the grounds. Erik stopped from time to time to point out a particular plant or tree to her. He talked about his trip overseas and his work with the company. Jazmyn began to relax. Something about Erik warmed her. She liked the man, mostly because he reminded her of someone else.

When they arrived back at the patio, Erik patted her hand before she let go of his arm. "I seem to have spent the whole time talking about myself. Typical male, I suppose." They both laughed.

He leaned close to her. "Would you like to go to dinner sometime? Then you could tell me all about you. I can afford to take you anyplace you want, you know."

She stepped back. "Thank you for the offer, Erik." Jazmyn looked out at the lawn. "I. . .um. There's someone." She hesitated. "I just can't." She fled through the doors into the bright, noisy room without looking back.

Chapter 16

The door clicked shut behind Jazmyn as she slipped into Maddy's office. She leaned against the wall, her heart pounding.

"What are you doing, girl?" Maddy stared at her from across the room. "Is the bogeyman after you?"

"Shhh." Jazmyn held her finger to her lips. A low murmur of voices came through the door then faded.

"You want to tell me what this is all about?" Maddy said.

"I didn't want him to see me."

"Who? Is one of those low-lifes bothering you?"

"It's. . .it's Erik. Kirsten's brother. He's been around a lot since the party. He keeps asking me to go out with him."

Maddy's mouth fell open. "You mean the hunk? You're hiding from him?" She shook her head. "Girl, I'd better call 911 and get you some help. That man could have his choice of a hundred girls just by snapping his fingers." She let out a low whistle.

"Then let him have those hundred girls. I don't want to be one of them." Jazmyn crossed to a chair and slumped down into it. "I didn't tell you about the night of the party and how he asked me out. He even hinted that he had enough money should I want to go out with him. As if money makes the difference."

"Well, to some of us it would." Maddy's eyes turned dreamy. "When you think about that incredible build and handsome face, I'd say money just adds the final touch to the picture." She gave an exaggerated sigh.

Jazmyn laughed. "Maddy, you're impossible. What happened to the doctor you were talking about last week?"

"I found out the hours he works. And I found out about the cute little nurse who helps him more than she should."

"Yeah, well, I don't want to go out with anyone right now." Jazmyn pushed up from the chair. "I guess I'd better see if the coast is clear and get back to my office. It's time to go home, anyway, since I came in early." She grinned at Maddy. "Next time, I'll tell Erik to ask you."

"Girlfriend, you're the best." Maddy fanned her face. "You know, if I didn't think Kirsten would kill me, I'd apply to be Erik's personal secretary and fly all over the world with him. What a tough job."

Jazmyn smiled all the way to her office. Having a friend was wonderful.

Maddy gave her plenty of opportunity to witness, and Jazmyn believed one of these days her new friend would become a Christian, too.

At home she kicked off her shoes and sank onto the couch with a sigh of relief. The last two weeks of work had been more stressful than before. Erik's pursuit had been subtle, but there. Although she found him attractive and nice, she had no romantic interest in him at all. He seemed to think she should.

She didn't want to admit that for some reason Erik reminded her of Thor. When he came around she couldn't keep her mind on her work, not because of an attraction to Erik, but because of his similarity to a backwoods guide. *Girl, you've got it bad.* She could hear Maddy's voice echoing in her head.

The phone trilled. She leaped up, hoping Jason had made it home. He'd called a few days ago to say he'd be in sometime today but probably late.

"Hello?"

"Jazmyn." Her heart lurched at the sound of Thor's low voice over the phone. "I called to see if Jason had gotten home."

Her heart plummeted. *That's okay,* she told herself, *you don't want to be around him, anyway. Remember the unequally yoked thing.*

"He's supposed to be home sometime today. I haven't heard from him, though."

"Okay. I'll call him tomorrow." He paused. "I'm in town for a few days again."

"We could meet for lunch tomorrow." Here she was asking him out again! What was the matter with her?

"That would be great. Is one o'clock okay?"

"That's fine. I'll go in early and get the rest of the afternoon off." Jazmyn's hands were shaking as she hung up the phone. What had she been thinking? One minute she was determined not to have anything to do with the guy, and the next she was asking him to go out with her.

Mid-morning the next day, Jazmyn called the deli down the street. They had a special deal on picnic lunches they packed in boxes. Thor might appreciate going somewhere out of the way for a lunch instead of eating inside with a lot of other people. There was a park not far from here that might do. She'd worn slacks to work for this reason.

"Mornin', Jazmyn." She started as Erik came up behind her.

"Good morning." She stepped away from him. Erik always seemed to come right up beside her.

"How about going to lunch with me today?" Erik placed one of his big hands on the wall behind Jazmyn.

She sidled away. "I'm sorry, I already have plans."

"Too bad." He smiled, his handsome face close to hers. "When are you going to stop avoiding me and agree to go somewhere together? I know you're interested in someone else, but he can't give you what I can, can he?"

Jazmyn bristled with anger. "I don't find a man attractive for the size of his wallet. Now please leave me alone." She stalked down the hallway to her office, praying no one had heard that exchange. She also hoped it didn't cost her this job. Despite Erik, she enjoyed working here. She would even like Erik if he would quit asking her out and just be her boss.

"That was an interesting bit of interplay," Maddy said as she slipped into Jazmyn's office and closed the door. "I can't believe that man. He's never acted that way with anyone else."

"I don't know what it is." Jazmyn sank into her chair. "I don't know how to stop him, either. He's Kirsten's brother, so I don't want to complain to her."

"Maybe I can be discreet and say something."

Jazmyn gave her a pointed look.

"Okay, so maybe I'm not the most discreet person in the world. At least it's better than me practicing my martial arts on the guy." She posed in a mock karate stance.

Jazmyn couldn't help laughing. "Maddy, you don't know any martial arts."

"That's true." Maddy straightened her blouse. "But I learned from my mother how to swing a mean rolling pin. Maybe I'll bring one to work with me." She turned to the door and then grinned over her shoulder at Jazmyn. "If I use the rolling pin to knock him out, can I play the nurse and kiss him to make him feel better?"

"You're hopeless." Jazmyn waved her friend out the door. She glanced at the clock and saw it was time to meet Thor. Striding down the hall to the elevator, she tried to slow her pulse. Anticipation made her want to race down the stairs.

Relaxing in the shade across from the T. L. Enterprises building, Thor wanted to shout up at Jazmyn to hurry. He wanted to see her. He wanted to know if her face would light up with a smile when she saw him. He wanted to know if she cared about him as much as he cared about her.

Last week at the party Kirsten and Erik hosted for the employees, he'd watched Jazmyn from a place where no one could see him. She'd been stunning in a green dress that he knew almost matched the deep green of her eyes. How he'd longed to be close to her, to touch her, to kiss her again.

The door swung open. Jazmyn stepped out, and Thor crossed the street. She smiled when she saw him.

"Ready to go?" He almost couldn't think.

"Yep." She touched his arm. "First stop is the deli. I've ordered us a picnic lunch that we can take to the park."

A thrill shot through him. She wanted to be alone with him. She'd thought about what he would like and planned this just for him.

"Instead of the park, why don't we go to a pretty spot I know about." He glanced at his watch. "I know it's a little late, but we could be there in half an hour. Can you wait that long?"

"I'm fine." She gave him a mischievous smile. "I ordered some brownies. We could share one on the way to stave off hunger."

"That sounds like a plan to me." Thor had to fight the urge to pull her close and kiss her.

When they arrived at the little canyon, he couldn't help feeling pleased at Jazmyn's exclamations of delight. She was like a little child on an outing for the first time. He wanted to sit back and enjoy her excitement.

"Oh, a waterfall!" Jazmyn covered her mouth with her hands. Her eyes shone as she turned to Thor. "It's not as big as the one near your cabin, but it's beautiful. Can we eat over there on the rocks next to the water?"

"You read my mind, lady." Thor swung the basket from the truck and took Jazmyn's hand in his. "Be careful where you step."

They spread the lunch out on a boulder and sat on a flat rock across from it. Jazmyn had ordered sandwiches, potato salad, lemonade, and brownies. She'd even remembered what Thor ordered the last time so she could get what he wanted.

Thor's stomach rumbled. "I guess that's my signal to start eating." He paused. "Do you want to pray first?"

Jazmyn seemed surprised but pleased. When they'd been camping, he hadn't thought about prayer. He hadn't prayed at mealtimes since his mother passed away. She'd been the one who insisted they all attend church and who read stories to them from the Bible.

The food disappeared fast. Thor was glad to see Jazmyn eating. Sometimes at camp he'd thought the squirrels and chipmunks ate more than she did.

"How's the job?" He tried to act casual.

"It's okay."

"Problems?"

She leaned back against the rock next to him, staring at the waterfall. "There's this guy at work."

"Is he bothering you, or do you want to tell me to get lost because of him?" Thor was almost afraid to hear the answer. She hadn't encouraged Erik, but that could be because she wanted to say good-bye to Thor first.

"No. I mean, I don't want him to bother me. That's the trouble. He keeps asking me out."

"Can't you tell him you're not interested?"

"Believe me, I've tried." She sighed and plucked a blade of grass. "He doesn't seem to take the hint, and I've been pretty up-front about it."

"Why don't you talk to your boss about him?"

"That's part of the problem." Jazmyn frowned. "This guy is the boss. He's been out of the country for a while. Maybe he'll leave again soon."

She jerked the blade of grass in half. "He even had the nerve to suggest I might want to go out with him because of his money. A couple of times he's tried to give me little gifts, but I wouldn't take them."

Thor wanted to duck away in shame. Hearing Jazmyn, he wondered how he could have doubted her. She had a whole different set of values from the women he'd been involved with before. He had to stop this charade soon. The problem was, if he told her now, what would she do?

"You know, I even liked this guy the first time I met him. He seemed so nice. I guess you don't see a person's true colors right away." She looked up at him and smiled. "Look at you. I thought you were a murderer the first time I saw you. I wouldn't have guessed what a decent person you are."

Thor cleared his throat. "You never know why a person does things sometimes. Give this guy another chance. Maybe he'll turn out to be decent after all."

Jazmyn looked so dejected he couldn't resist putting his arm around her. She leaned her head against his shoulder. Contentment flowed over him. He stayed quiet, thinking he could sit like this with her forever.

This morning he'd called Jason and set up an appointment to see him tonight. He had to find out more about these beliefs Jason and Jazmyn shared with his mother. Then he could talk to Jason about the dilemma he'd gotten himself into. He'd deceived Jazmyn for so long he wasn't sure she would understand when he told her the truth about everything.

They sat so still that a few blue jays flew down to peck at the leftover crumbs from their lunch. The birds fought and chased one another until he and Jazmyn laughed aloud, scaring them away.

"I'd better get back to town." Thor stood up and helped Jazmyn to her feet. "I have an appointment tonight." With his arms still around her he couldn't resist one sweet kiss that left him longing for more.

Chapter 17

S tanding outside the small house, Thor rubbed his palms on his pant legs. When he'd arranged this meeting with Jason, he'd been so sure he wanted to talk about this. Now he wanted to be anywhere but here. Some force urged him to run far and fast.

He clenched his jaw and rang the bell. The sound echoed in the house. He heard footsteps approaching. Too late. The door swung open.

"Thor, glad to see you." Jason held open the door, gesturing for him to come inside. "Please excuse the mess. I only got back two days ago, and I haven't finished unpacking." He led the way through a maze of gear and photography equipment to a small kitchen.

"Coffee?" Thor nodded, and Jason grabbed two mugs from a cabinet. He filled them and carried them to the table. "I can't believe how time gets mixed up when you travel around like this."

For the first time, Thor noticed Jason's rumpled appearance. His hair had grown out quite a bit in the last few weeks.

"I've heard of teens paying good money for a hairdo like that." Thor couldn't help grinning.

Jason ran a hand over his mop. "Yeah, I guess you're right. Where I was they didn't have any barbershops. I didn't trust the men wielding knives that close to my throat." He grimaced. "I'll have to get it cut tomorrow before Jazmyn sees me. She'll think I'm turning into a sixties hippie or something."

"So where did you go for this photo shoot?" Thor knew he was grasping at anything to postpone the conversation he'd come here for.

"All over. I've been to so many places in the last month, I wasn't sure I'd know home when I got here." He took a swig from his mug and sighed. "We were mostly in Africa. There are more countries there than I can name. Did you know that?"

Thor chuckled. "I looked at a map once."

"Well, I am glad to be home. I think I could sleep for a week, though."

"I've heard jet lag is pretty tiring." Thor took a sip of coffee and tried not to grimace.

"Sorry about the brew." Jason lifted his mug. "I got home and didn't have any of the good stuff, so I'm using some Jazmyn left here. I've been too tired and too busy to get out to the store. Did you know Jazmyn got a job at the place you recommended? She loves it."

"I've been in town a couple of times since you left. I ran into Jazmyn, and we had lunch together. She did seem happy."

"I doubt you just stopped by to chat, Thor. What's up?" Jason's intense stare made Thor uncomfortable. He didn't know how to bring up the subject of religion now that he was here. All those burning questions had flown out of his head.

Shoving his chair back from the table, he crossed to the back door and stared out at the small yard. The grass was long and full of weeds. Everything had a look of neglect, which reflected Jason's having been gone for so long.

"I'm having trouble sleeping, living." He rubbed the back of his neck. "I don't know how to say why I came here. I needed to talk about something, but now I can't seem to remember why."

"This wouldn't have to do with some of the talks we had in the mountains, would it?" Jason asked.

"Yeah, I guess it does." Thor leaned against the door facing Jason. "My mother believed like you do. She prayed all the time, took us to church. Her last words to me were that she had prayed for years that I would give my life to Jesus. She was dying with the hope that someday I would do what I needed to do."

Jason stayed quiet.

"All those times you talked, I tried to ignore you. I kept hearing my mother's voice echoing what you said. It won't let me go. I don't know what to do. I feel like someone's following me around whispering things in my ear that I can't quite make out. I think I'm going crazy. I've been living a lie. I can't do it anymore."

Jason shook his head. "You do have Someone whispering in your ear, you know. You're not crazy." Thor stared at him. Jason grinned. "The Spirit of God convicts us of our need for Jesus. You have a lot of people praying for you."

"So what am I supposed to do?" Thor crossed back to the chair, sank down, and rested his head on his hands.

"Have you considered giving your life to Jesus, Thor?"

"Yes. I keep hearing my mother's words, but I don't know how to do this. I'm sure she told me, but it's been so long." He swallowed hard against the lump clogging his throat.

Thor listened as Jason began to talk about sin and Jesus paying a debt on the cross. As Jason talked, Thor could recall his mother saying some of these same things to him long ago, but he hadn't been ready to listen then. Now he wanted to take the next step beyond listening. He had a weight inside that wouldn't be relieved any other way. He didn't know how he knew this, but it was true.

As they prayed together tears streamed down Thor's cheeks. He couldn't remember the last time he'd cried, but he wasn't embarrassed. The weight lifted. Something indescribable washed over him.

Jason's eyes glistened when Thor looked up after the prayer. They both smiled, but Thor couldn't think of anything to say for a moment. His heart was too full. Jason seemed to understand. He refilled their cups and they drank in silence.

"Before I go I need to ask your advice." Thor shifted, uncomfortable again. "I've been sort of lying to you and Jazmyn."

"Lying how?"

Thor told him all of it. That he owned T. L. Enterprises. That he only worked as a hunting guide to stay away from the city. That he'd been duped by three women after his money and power. That he'd fallen in love with Jazmyn but didn't know how to tell her who he really was.

"Sounds to me like you've been running away for a long time." Jason traced a pattern in some coffee drips on the table. "You need to make things right. Talk to Jazmyn. Tell her who you are and why you deceived her."

"What if she hates me?" Thor wanted to take back the childish-sounding words.

"She may be hurt, but give her some time. Part of the reason you did this was because you didn't trust Jazmyn. That will hurt her. She'll need time. Be ready to give it to her."

Jason followed Thor to the door, slapping him on the back. "You're my brother in Christ. I'll stick up for you and put in a good word."

"Hey, girlfriend." Maddy waved at Jazmyn as she crossed the garage to the elevator. The door whooshed open and Maddy held it, waiting for Jazmyn to catch up.

"Thanks, Maddy."

"You're running late this morning."

"I went to the gym early and lost track of time." Jazmyn was still trying to catch her breath.

"Why would you want to go before work?"

"There's been someone coming in the afternoons." Jazmyn wished the elevator would move faster. "I wanted to avoid them."

"Them, or him?" Maddy smirked. "I think I smell a good story here."

"What? Are you getting a job as a reporter?" Jazmyn put one hand on her hip and tried to imitate Maddy. They both laughed as the elevator doors slid open.

"If this is as juicy as I suspect, I may start an in-house newspaper," Maddy said, grinning. "Come on, let's continue this in your office. I don't want anyone else to scoop me."

"I won't say a word until I have some coffee. I didn't have time to stop anywhere on the way from the gym."

"You drive a hard bargain." Maddy shook her head. "Get prepared to talk. I'll stow my purse, get the coffee going, and be right back. I'll even see if I can scrape up something to eat since you probably didn't stop for any of that, either."

Jazmyn couldn't help smiling. "Maddy, you're a gem."

Flicking on her computer, Jazmyn ran through the messages on her desk, putting them in order of importance. This would be a busy day, but she liked it that way. Working hard would keep her mind off her troubles.

"Here we go." Maddy came in carrying a tray with two coffees and a couple of muffins. "I swiped these muffins from Kirsten's box. You'd better enjoy them. She isn't in yet, so I've got a few minutes."

Taking a sip of hot coffee, Jazmyn closed her eyes and leaned back in the chair. "I don't know how you do it, Maddy. You seem to know what I want before I do."

"I'm into bribes, girl." She plopped down across from Jazmyn. "So give."

"I don't know." Jazmyn hesitated, uncomfortable.

"Does this have anything to do with Kirsten's hunky brother who's been following you around like an infatuated puppy dog?"

"Has he been that obvious?"

"Girlfriend, the whole office is buzzing about it. Makes all us single girls want to try on your shoes for a while."

"I would gladly give you my shoes. I'm not interested, but he doesn't seem to get the picture."

Maddy tilted her head. "I think I hear the boss. I'd better go. We'll talk about this later."

The morning passed quickly. Jazmyn had given up on getting any lunch when Maddy poked her head in the door. "Kirsten says we're ordering from the deli and having it delivered. Do you want your usual?"

"Sounds good. Make mine with a layer of caffeine or something that will give me an energy boost. Otherwise I may not make it through the afternoon."

"That'll teach you to work out early." Maddy clicked her tongue as she shut the door.

⤳◦

Lunch hadn't had time to settle when Maddy swung into the office, slammed the door, and placed her hand over her heart.

"Maddy, what's wrong?" Jazmyn stared at the drama unfolding in front of her.

"I'm dying. You won't believe what just happened."

"I think you'd better sit down before you faint." Jazmyn pointed her pencil at the chair. "Take note that I'm way too busy to call the paramedics for you."

"He's here." Maddy gasped. She slid into a chair, her eyes wide.

209

"Who?"

"The missing owner I told you about. You won't believe this one. He's beyond hunk status."

"So who is he? Why's he finally here?" Jazmyn shuffled through her papers trying to find a certain drawing. She'd stopped paying much attention to Maddy's theatrics. She had work to finish up.

"I thought Erik was cute, but I found out this is another brother of Kirsten's. He's even bigger than Erik and looks like some Norse god or something. Jazmyn, you have to see him. You won't believe it. I think I'm in love."

"Maddy, you're in love with someone new every two days." Jazmyn couldn't help smiling. "I keep telling you that love isn't based on looks."

"Well, if it was, this is the one I'd want to look at for the rest of my life." Maddy eased the door open and peeked out. "Quick." She motioned with her hand, her voice an exaggerated whisper. "Girlfriend, you have to see this."

Jazmyn sighed. There was no heading her off. The only thing that would satisfy Maddy would be for her to come and look at the latest hunk. At this point she was even willing to drool a little just so Maddy would leave her alone. She stepped to the door and started to pull it open.

"No," Maddy hissed, pulling Jazmyn to the other side. "Don't let him see you. I've heard he's as spooky as a wild animal."

A rumble of voices could be heard in the hall. One in particular struck a chord in Jazmyn. She knew that voice. She leaned her head next to Maddy's and peered out, feeling like a teenage girl spying on boys.

Kirsten and Erik stood in the hallway talking to another man whose back was to Jazmyn's office. He reminded her of someone she knew.

"Just wait until he turns around," Maddy whispered in her ear.

As if he'd heard, the man turned to glance at her office. Maddy eased the door closed, but not before Jazmyn got a good look at his face. The man talking to Kirsten and Erik was Thor. Her Thor.

"Maddy, that's not the owner of this company. He's the friend of my brother's that I had lunch with."

Maddy's eyes widened. "I'm telling you he is the head of this place. Kirsten introduced me to him just before I came in here."

The air in the room congealed around Jazmyn. She had trouble breathing. Thor was not the owner. He was a simple hunting guide. He wouldn't have lied to her.

The door to her office swung open. Thor faced her with Kirsten and Erik at his back.

Chapter 18

Jazmyn, I need to talk to you." Thor stood in the door to her office, flanked by his brother and sister. Kirsten's assistant, as she'd been introduced, stood near Jazmyn, her eyes wide as saucers. Thor ignored her. His whole attention trained on Jazmyn, whose white face and glittering eyes made him wonder if she were about to faint.

"You lied to me. You're a fraud." It wasn't Jazmyn's words but the tone of despair that cut Thor.

"You really do know him?" Maddy was staring at Jazmyn now. "I thought you were joking."

"I thought I knew him." Jazmyn took a step back. "But I guess I was wrong." She lifted her chin, her green eyes darkened and cloudy like a storm-tossed sea. "Would you please leave my office? I have work to do."

"Not until we talk," Thor growled as he took a step toward her.

"No." She held up one hand. He stopped. "I don't want to talk to you."

"Jazmyn, I talked to Jason. He understands."

"I sincerely doubt that. Jason hates lying as much as I do." She rounded the desk, opened a drawer, and grabbed her purse. "If you won't leave, I will."

She edged around the other side of Maddy as if she were afraid Thor would leap forward and attack her.

"Jazmyn." Kirsten blocked the door.

"I'm sorry, Kirsten. I know we have a lot to do today. I promise I'll come in early and make it up to you." A tear escaped. Jazmyn swiped at her cheek. "Excuse me. I need to leave."

She tried to dart out the door, but Erik caught her and pulled her to him. "Jazmyn, please, give him a chance."

"Let me go, Erik." A small sob racked her. "I can see you were part of this deception, too. You must have had a great time laughing at me. All of you." She shot Kirsten an accusing look over her shoulder.

Kirsten raised her hand, opening her mouth to protest, but Jazmyn was gone. Thor listened in stunned silence as the elevator door dinged. This hadn't gone at all as he'd planned. If Kirsten and Erik hadn't waylaid him and introduced him around, he would have been in Jazmyn's office before anyone could alert her that he was here.

"I'm sorry, Thor." Kirsten placed her hand on his arm. "Give her some time.

She's just hurt right now."

Heaviness filled Thor. He wasn't angry; he was afraid. For the first time he'd found a woman he could trust, and he'd betrayed that trust. How could this ever be resolved? How could he make Jazmyn understand why he'd done what he had done?

"I need to go. I'll try to find her." Thor hadn't the vaguest idea where to look for Jazmyn. He had the feeling she wouldn't go home, but where would she go?

As if she could read his mind, Kirsten whirled to face her secretary. "Maddy, do you know where Jazmyn would go?"

"I'm not sure. You could check the gym, but she already went there once today." She shrugged. "She likes coffee. Maybe she went somewhere close by to grab a cup."

"Thanks." Thor squeezed Kirsten's shoulders and headed for the door.

"Thor." He turned back to see what Kirsten wanted. "If I see her, I'll try to talk to her. Do I have your permission to say anything about why you did this?"

He hesitated. In order for her to understand, Jazmyn would have to be told, but he hated that thought. He gave a short nod. "Tell her."

"Do you want me to go with you?" Erik took a step as if to follow him. "I know she doesn't think highly of me right now, but I could at least help look."

"No. Thanks." Thor strode down the hall to the elevator, wondering what he should do now. This afternoon certainly hadn't gone as he'd planned.

Outside the sky had clouded over, matching his mood. He wanted to go off into the woods and walk for hours. If he had Loki or Odin here with him, maybe they could track Jazmyn down. He'd left them at the house and didn't want to take the time to get them. Where would she go?

The gym wasn't far. He decided to walk, stopping by the coffee shops on the way to see if she might be in one of them. She wasn't in any of those places, and she wasn't at the gym. On the way back to the T. L. building, he thought of checking the garage. Quickening the pace, he hurried past the rows of cars until he reached the space designated for Jazmyn. Her car was gone. He felt like kicking something. Hard. Why hadn't he thought to check here before going off on a wild goose chase down the street?

Hurrying to his truck, Thor revved the engine and sped from the garage, ignoring the glare from the guard. Where would she go? Home? To the mall? He didn't think Jazmyn was the type of woman to drown her sorrows in a shopping spree. He turned away from the mall toward her apartment building.

Thor pounded so hard on Jazmyn's door that he was surprised it didn't crash open. He hadn't seen her car in the parking lot, but he hoped she might have parked elsewhere to fool him. She wasn't home. He slumped against the wall beside her door. He was running out of places to look.

Jason. Once again Thor wanted to kick himself. Of course she would go to her brother when she'd been hurt like this. They were so close. Jason would be able to pray with her.

Prayer. Why hadn't he thought to pray? Wasn't that what Christians were supposed to do? Pray about everything? Thor shook his head. Maybe he wasn't a real Christian after all. He sure hadn't thought about talking to God over this situation. He hadn't even prayed this afternoon before he went to see Jazmyn. What kind of Christian would make a mistake like that?

Relief flooded him when he saw Jazmyn's car parked in Jason's driveway. She was here. He'd found her. He realized a small part of him had been concerned that she'd done something reckless. Knowing she was safe brought great peace of mind.

The frown on Jason's face as he opened the door told Thor he might not be welcome right now. He opened his mouth to speak, but Jason held up his hand to stop him.

"Yes, she's here, Thor. No, you can't see her."

"I have to talk to her, Jason. She's got to understand."

"She won't understand a thing right now. She's been hurt too bad." Jason's look and his tone softened. "Thor, you lied to her. All her life, our mother told her all men lie. She'd started to believe Mom was wrong before you did this. Go back home, Thor. Give her some time."

Thor stared at the door as Jason closed it. He wanted to force it open. He had to see Jazmyn. Instead, he turned and trudged down the walkway to his truck.

~

Stepping off the elevator, Jazmyn felt her heart pounding. She half expected Thor to be waiting to pounce on her. She hadn't been to work in two days. She wanted to quit, but Jason convinced her not to. When Kirsten called and begged her to come back, Jazmyn relented. Kirsten promised Thor wouldn't bother her at work, but Jazmyn hadn't been sure that would stand. After all, he was the owner.

"Hey, girlfriend. Good to see you." Maddy came flying out of her office and enveloped Jazmyn in a hug.

Maddy stepped back, her hands still holding Jazmyn's shoulders, her gaze penetrating. "You okay? I'd say you haven't been sleeping. Those circles under your eyes get any darker, people will mistake you for a raccoon."

"I'm fine." Jazmyn almost choked on the words.

"Come on. I'll get some coffee and go over the pile on your desk with you. Kirsten's gone for the day, but she's given you enough work to keep you busy for forty-eight hours straight. She must be from the school of thought that hard work is good for the lovesick."

"I'm not lovesick." Jazmyn couldn't help feeling a little better around Maddy. The woman could talk a person to death, but she was a sweetheart. Jazmyn hadn't realized how much she missed her.

The day sped by. Jazmyn had expected to have trouble at work, but she was so busy she didn't have time to consider her woes. Although she hadn't realized it before, work was exactly what she needed to take her mind off Thor.

A week passed before the workload slowed down. Thor called her twice, but she was out of the office both times. He said he'd gone back to his cabin in the mountains so she could have some time. He didn't want to push. He wanted her to know how sorry he was for what he'd done.

Jazmyn refused to talk to anyone about what had happened. She didn't try to contact Thor. When Jason said he had something important to tell her concerning Thor, she brushed him off, refusing to listen.

Sleep eluded her. She lost weight. Every time she looked at food she recalled the lunches she'd shared with Thor and the way love had slipped into their relationship. At least on her part. Maybe what happened was God's way of separating them since Thor wasn't a believer. She told herself that often, hoping to be convinced it was the truth.

"Jazmyn, it's lunchtime." Kirsten smiled from the doorway. "Would you go with me? I have something I need to discuss with you, and my afternoon schedule is filled."

"Sure. Let me get my purse and my notebook." Jazmyn pushed back from her desk and stood, stretching the kinks out before she grabbed her things.

"I have no idea how we managed before you came to work here." Kirsten led the way to the elevator. "You've taken such a load off of me."

Kirsten had reservations at a little bistro where the hostess led them to a private table. Jazmyn slipped into her chair and tried not to stare around her. She'd never been in such a fancy restaurant.

Kirsten kept the conversation light as they nibbled at bread and ate their salads. When Jazmyn couldn't eat another bite, she pulled out her notebook.

"You won't need that." Kirsten pushed her plate away. "I wanted to talk to you about my brother."

Dread sent a chill through Jazmyn. "I'd rather not." She could feel the lump growing in her throat. "I enjoyed the lunch, but we'd better get back." She started to get up.

"Sit down, Jazmyn." Kirsten gave her a sad smile. "I don't usually assert my authority as boss, but this time I must. I've watched you this last week. You've worked like a maniac, and you look terrible. This can't go on."

Jazmyn blinked and stared down at her plate. Part of her wanted to storm out of the restaurant. The other part wanted to stay, to hear what Kirsten had to say.

"Will you listen? Please?" Kirsten's fingers closed over Jazmyn's and she gave a light squeeze. Jazmyn nodded, not trusting her voice to work.

Kirsten sighed. "I've thought about this. I wasn't even sure where to begin. Thor was such a bright child. He succeeded in school and in every business venture he tried from the time he was six and had a lemonade stand. He had every parent on our street stopping to get a drink. In college he could do no wrong. That was where he got the idea for T. L." She gave Jazmyn a sad smile. "By the way, that stands for Thor Larson."

Jazmyn's eyes widened. It had been there all the time if she'd only put it together. After all, Thor was the one who recommended she try for a job there.

"Thor's business succeeded beyond his wildest expectations. He suddenly had more money and power than any young man his age should have. I'm afraid it went to his head, although he, of course, didn't realize it.

"He began to date a young woman who fawned over him. Erik and I could see that she was a gold digger, but Thor was blinded. To make a long story short, she almost had him at the altar before he discovered her true colors."

Jazmyn blinked back tears again, this time for what had happened to Thor. She started to speak, but Kirsten held up her hand.

"He didn't learn easily. The same thing happened to him twice more before he gave up on being in control. He turned the outward running of the company over to Erik and me. He went off to the mountains and became a hermit. He swore he would have nothing to do with another woman." She blew out a breath as she watched Jazmyn. "He kept that vow until he met you. He didn't tell you who he was because he was afraid."

Jazmyn wanted to say something, but the words wouldn't come. All this time she'd thought he was playing her for the fool, but he was afraid of what she'd do to him.

"Give yourself some time to heal, Jazmyn. I'm sure you need that." Kirsten gathered her things and stood. "I don't like to interfere, but I hate seeing you and my brother hurting like this when I care about both of you so much."

Chapter 19

Insistent banging. Jazmyn cracked one eye open. Seven in the morning. Saturday morning. Her day to sleep in.

"This better be good." She searched near the bed for her slippers as she pulled on her robe. "This better be a matter of grave importance." She glanced in the hallway mirror and groaned.

Jason waited outside her door, bouncing with impatience. As she opened the door, she gave him a scathing look, designed to intimidate an army general. Jason grinned.

"Whoa. Where's my camera when I need it?" He snorted a laugh. "Of course, right now you'd probably break the lens."

"Nice to see you. Come back later." Jazmyn started to close the door, but she wasn't quick enough.

"Wait a minute, sis." He stuck his briefcase in the door, then pushed his way into her apartment. "You're going to be glad I came over here."

"I can't imagine that happening this early." Jazmyn yawned.

"Tell you what." Jason turned her in the direction of her bedroom. "Why don't you go wake up and get dressed. I'll fix coffee and see what I can drum up for breakfast."

She trudged back down the hall feeling a little better. At least if someone had to wake her up, it was nice to have him fix breakfast.

Her hair still damp from the shower, Jazmyn wandered to the kitchen, following the delicious smells. Jason must have heard her coming, because he had a cup of coffee waiting for her on the table. Two places were set, and a plate of toast stood between them. She leaned over, breathing in the fragrant aroma of cinnamon hazelnut.

"Well, you do clean up nice." Jason carried plates with omelets to the table. "There for a minute I thought you were on your deathbed. I almost dialed 911."

"You know better than to come over here this early on a Saturday." Jazmyn snagged a piece of toast for her plate, then took her first bite of omelet. "I didn't even know I had these ingredients in the refrigerator. How did you do it?"

"That would be my secret." Jason winked. "A guy can't give up all his secrets, you know."

Jason inhaled his breakfast. While she chewed and savored, he cleared his place and retrieved his briefcase. When he opened it on the table, a receipt fluttered out, coming to rest beside Jazmyn's plate.

"Secret, huh?" She gave him a disgusted look as she read the omelet ingredients on the grocery receipt dated this morning.

He looked sheepish. "Well, I wasn't sure what you'd have available. You don't cook much. I figured you'd at least have eggs, so the rest was easy."

"You must be sweetening me up for something. What is it?"

He laughed. "Actually, I have some rather good news, and I wanted to make sure you were awake and ready before I sprang it on you."

"Good news?"

Like a little boy eager to bring out his best show-and-tell, Jason reached into the briefcase and drew out some papers. "Look at this." He handed them to her.

Jazmyn's brow furrowed as she studied the form he'd given her. "What is this?"

"It's a contract." If he smiled any wider, his face would split. "I sent a few of the drawings you made at camp to my editor. He wants to include them in my book. You'll get some advance and a small percentage of the royalties. It isn't much, but I thought you'd like it."

She stared at the contract. Her drawings? In a book? "How did you? They really liked them?" She couldn't seem to make a coherent thought. Thor had suggested this, but she hadn't taken him seriously. She hadn't thought Jason would, either.

"I took a few from the drawing book. I didn't think you'd miss them." Jason looked anxious. "He wants to see more of the sketches. If you want, that is."

Grabbing the papers away from her, Jason thumbed through them until he came to a page of photographs and sketches. "See, this is what they plan to do. Your drawings will be sort of whimsical additions to my photographs." He was right. This picture of an elk racing across a field also had a sketch of Xena on a pine branch, scolding whoever had offended her.

Tears sprang to her eyes. "This is wonderful, Jason. Thank you." She jumped up from her chair and gave him a bear hug.

"Now that I've gotten you all softened up, are you ready for what else I have to tell you?"

She stepped back, suspicious. "Out with it."

"I have to go back for a few more photos. You need to come and do some more sketches, too. My editor would like some of your work on almost every page." He fiddled with the papers still in his briefcase. "I'll call Thor and arrange for another week. Can you get off work?"

"No." She backed away until she came up against the counter. "I don't want to go up there again."

"Is it because of Thor, or because you don't want to camp?"

"I. . .I loved the camping. I just can't be around him, Jason. You don't understand." She crossed her arms over her stomach, digging her fingers into her sides. "I can't be around him."

"Jaz, why?" Jason crossed to stand near her. "Do you dislike him so much? Are you still mad?"

"No." Her brain fumbled for a way to explain without saying too much. "I talked to Kirsten, his sister. Or rather she talked to me. Thor has a reason from his past that made him do what he did. I can understand, and I forgave him."

"Then what is it? I thought you liked him."

"I. . .I can't be around him." She couldn't think of anything more to say.

Jason chuckled. "I get it. You like him. In fact, I would guess you think you like him too much. Is that right?"

Her face warmed. "He's not a Christian, Jason. I have to stay away from him."

"Ahhh." Jason's eyes twinkled. "I guess he didn't get the chance to tell you about his visit with me. That's why he came to see you at the office that day, to tell you who he really is."

"What visit? What are you talking about?"

"The night before you saw Thor at T. L. Enterprises, he came to my house and asked me how to become a Christian. We talked, and he prayed to receive Christ. He's a Christian now, Jazmyn. Does that make a difference?"

"A Christian?" She couldn't breathe. Thor was a Christian. She could tell him she forgave him. There would be no barriers between them. Tears of joy moistened her eyes.

"So will you go with me again?" Jason asked.

Jazmyn thought of the smell of the pines, the ripple of the river, Xena the squirrel, and Thor. They seemed to fit together in the outdoors, and she realized she loved them all. "I'll ask Kirsten if I can get the week off. I don't know if she'll let me since I haven't worked there that long."

"My guess is that if she knows you're going to mend bridges with her brother, she'll let you go." Jason gave her a quick hug. "This time, be sure to pack heavy clothes. The weather will be even cooler in the mountains now."

Jazmyn smiled as she thought of snuggling up to Thor and letting him help her stay warm. She couldn't wait.

⁊◯

"For the life of me I don't understand why you're back in town, Thor." Kirsten sounded exasperated as she leaned against her husband, Wes, on the couch. They were trying to watch a movie, but Thor knew he was distracting them. His constant pacing and prowling around the room had to be annoying.

"She's right. You're acting like a tiger in a cage." Erik tossed a piece of popcorn into his mouth. "What brought you back to town, anyway?"

"Nothing." Thor stalked to the back door and stared out at the dark yard.

How could he explain that he hoped to see Jazmyn and talk to her again? He wanted to tell her he was sorry. Maybe he'd dreamed of her forgiving him and falling into his arms.

He turned back into the room and flopped down in an overstuffed chair. How many times had he been up and down this evening? He was acting like a lovesick animal.

He paused in his thoughts. That was the problem, wasn't it? He loved Jazmyn, but she hated him for what he'd done to her. Her mother had told her all men were worthless liars. Is that what she thought of him?

Thor wanted to pace the floor again. He started to get up, but one dagger glare from Kirsten froze him in place. What could he do? Jazmyn didn't want to see him. Kirsten advised him to give her more time before he approached her. How long did a man have to wait?

"I'm going out." He ignored his jacket on the way to the door. Up in the mountains he needed a coat by nightfall. Here in the valley the temperature was still mild.

He wound through side streets, taking his time to think, to plan what he would say. He recognized his need for someone to help him, but asking would be hard. By the time he pulled up in front of the small house and cut the engine, he thought he knew exactly how he would approach this.

When Jason opened the door every argument Thor had planned flew out of his head. This was Jazmyn's brother. He was probably angry with him, too.

Instead of slamming the door in Thor's face, Jason swung it wide, a welcoming smile on his face. "Thor. I tried to call that number you gave me, but your phone was off. I was going to drive up to see you tomorrow."

"Me?" Thor stepped inside, dread making him want to run. Had Jason wanted to chew him out?

"Yeah, it's about my book." Jason led the way to the kitchen. "Coffee? Soda?"

Thor couldn't imagine Jason offering him something to drink if he planned to yell at him. He began to relax. "A cola would be nice."

Jason filled a glass with ice, popped the tab on a cola can, and set them in front of Thor.

"I need to go back to the mountains for some more pictures to round out my book. The editor gave me some specifics. He wants me to have them ready within three weeks. I wondered if you would be able to guide for me again."

"You shouldn't go up there right now." Thor stared at Jason. Didn't he realize what time of year this was?

"Why not?"

"This is hunting season. Do you know how many irresponsible hunters there are in the mountains where we were?"

Jason looked perplexed. "But you guide them. You should be familiar enough with the favorite areas to keep us safe."

"I don't like it." Thor frowned. "You have to stay still for too long. Besides, the animals are much harder to find. They're spooked right now. It doesn't take long after the season opens to have them running at the sound of a pin dropping."

"Then we'll have to be quiet. My editor gave me this deadline. I'll go do the photos with or without you. With you would be much easier."

"It's just too dangerous. I can't take you." Thor knew he was being unreasonable, but he couldn't seem to help himself.

Jason tilted his head as he studied Thor. "You're not making any sense. What's the real reason you don't want to take me?"

Thor began to pace. He could see the light from the street lamps illuminating part of the yard while the rest was swathed in shadow. "I don't know. I feel like my life is a mess. I don't know what to do."

"Come sit down." Jason's tone softened. Thor could hear the caring. He crossed back to the kitchen chair and sank down.

"You know, quite often when a person first becomes a Christian, they face trials right away. That might be why you're so confused. Let's pray first, then we'll talk."

When Jason finished praying he squeezed Thor's arm. "Now tell me why you feel like your life is falling apart."

"Because I was living a lie. Now I have to pay the consequences. I thought I'd lost your friendship. I know I lost what I had with your sister."

"That's the real problem, isn't it?" Jason asked.

"Yeah. I'm crazy about her, Jason. I love her, but now she won't see me or even talk to me. Kirsten said to give her time, but that doesn't seem to be working, either." Thor hated the desperation in his voice, but he couldn't seem to stop. He felt as if a dam had broken inside.

"How much time have you given her, Thor? Some hurts go very deep." He sat back, running his hand through his hair. "I told you before that our mother soured Jazmyn on men for years. She did tell her that all men lied. She also told Jaz that all men leave eventually. When her fiancé, Adam, died, that's what Jazmyn thought—that he'd left her. A lot of people get angry at those who die for that very reason." He paused. "Anyway, when you lied to her it was like proving that the two main things Mom taught her were true. That will take time to get over."

He squeezed Thor's arm again. "I'm not saying she'll ever be more than friends with you, but you can pray about it. God can mend hurts and heal hearts."

Chapter 20

Thor arrived at the camp early. Loki and Odin exploded from the truck when he opened the door. He drew in a deep breath, savoring the clean pine scent. He loved this place.

Last week he let Jason convince him to be the guide for this second photo shoot. There shouldn't be too much danger. They both knew enough to wear bright clothing. This spot was so isolated that few hunters came here. Being around Jason might bring Jazmyn to mind more often, but he thought about her all the time, anyway.

Pushing those thoughts aside, he began to unload and set up camp. By the middle of the afternoon he had the camp looking pretty good. He and the dogs had just returned from cutting wood when he heard a vehicle approaching. He tossed a log from the truck bed and hopped down to wait. This would be Jason coming.

He waved as Jason drove his SUV into the river crossing. Loki and Odin bounded forward, eager to greet the newcomer. Jason ground to a stop on the far side of camp. The dogs fell all over each other trying to get there first.

Thor strode across the camp to greet his friend and help him unpack. For the first time he noticed that a second person rode in the SUV. It was Jazmyn. Tousled and beautiful, she caught Thor's gaze. She stared at him. He could see something in her eyes. Was it hatred? Disgust? Jason hadn't said he would be bringing his sister this time, too.

Thor shook hands with Jason. He nodded at Jazmyn. "Need some help unloading and setting up?"

"I think we can manage if you have other stuff you're doing." Jason shrugged into a warm coat. "Brrr. I haven't been up here this time of year in a long time. I'd forgotten how chilly the air can be."

Thor grinned. "Not chilly, invigorating. Look at the dogs. They act like young pups when I bring them up this time of year."

Jason laughed. Bending over, he gave both dogs a good ear rubbing. "Any place in particular you want me to set up the tents?"

"Anywhere's fine. I'm going to finish with the wood so we can have a fire. That will be important tonight."

He stalked back to his truck, wondering how he would be able to manage a whole week around Jazmyn. After he and Jason had talked, Thor believed

Jazmyn would never be able to love him as he loved her. He'd accepted that, but he didn't know how he could manage to be in her presence without letting her know how much he still loved her. Would always love her.

He'd been doing a lot of Bible study and prayer this past week, hoping to heal his bruised heart. For the first time he'd found a woman with values he admired. Now that he wasn't consumed with himself, he understood how shallow he'd been in his former relationships. As long as he stayed away from her, he might be able to love Jazmyn from afar. Being close wasn't going to work.

He threw the rest of the wood off the truck, then stacked the smaller pieces. Grabbing up the axe, he split the bigger logs, reveling in the feel of the strenuous labor. As he concentrated on chopping wood he tried to ignore Jazmyn as she helped Jason set up their tents.

From time to time she cast strange looks at him. Thor thought she might be as uncomfortable around him as he was around her. The solution to this problem had to be keeping busy. He would take Jason out from dawn to dusk. He only hoped Jazmyn wouldn't want to tag along. Having her in the truck next to him would be unbearable.

"Let me help you get this stacked." Jason wandered over as Thor finished splitting the wood. "Jazmyn is arranging her tent. Are you upset that I brought her?"

"You can bring anyone you want."

"I didn't tell you that she's doing some drawings for my book. My editor really liked her work."

Thor couldn't suppress his surprise. "You mean the sketches she did when we were up here before?"

"Yeah. I sent some in without her knowing it." Jason shrugged. "I thought it was worth a try."

"I still have the one she gave me. The picture of the baby skunk trying to fish marshmallows from the fire." Thor didn't tell Jason the sketch was framed, hanging on his workroom wall. Every time he saw it, he thought of Jazmyn and their time in the mountains. "She's so good at capturing the action of the animals. I'm glad they're using them."

"She plans to stay in camp while we go out for the pictures. That will give her plenty of time to draw." Jason picked up an armload of logs. "I wasn't sure if she'd be able to get off work, but your sister let her go. That was nice of her."

"Where do you want to start shooting?" Thor wanted to get off the subject of Jazmyn. "We could start over in the canyon we hiked and see if we can find the eagles. There might be some bear there this time of year."

"That sounds good." Jason paused as if thinking. Behind them, Thor heard the tent zipper. He braced himself. Jazmyn must be finished setting up her things. Would she want to join them?

"Ahhh!" she cried out. Something clanked loudly.

Jason and Thor both whirled around. Jazmyn's arms windmilled as she fell back against the tent. The poles collapsed. The canvas gave, then sank to the ground. Jazmyn's feet flew up in the air before hitting the ground with a loud thud.

"Jazmyn!" Jason started to run. Thor passed him. He hadn't heard a shot, but they'd been talking. What if some hunter had sent a wild bullet their way?

A fold of the tent covered Jazmyn's face. She was shaking like a leaf. It must be from pain. Thor dropped to the ground on one side as Jason knelt across from him. Jason lifted the tent flap covering her features.

Tears ran down her cheeks.

"Jaz, where are you hurt?" Jason leaned closer.

"I'm not." She gasped out the words, her body still shaking. Jason looked at Thor as if they'd both realized in the same instant that Jazmyn wasn't hurt. She was laughing, not crying. She'd been clumsy, managed to knock down the tent, and thought it was hilarious. Thor couldn't help smiling as he climbed to his feet, leaving Jason to help his sister up.

Xena scampered out on a branch not far over Jazmyn's head. She knew the squirrel was eyeing the chocolate bar she'd placed on the arm of her chair. She wanted to tempt the squirrel so she would come out and go through her antics.

"Come on, sweetie. I need you to pose." Jazmyn sat with pencil poised as Xena's tail jerked upward.

Chattering noisily, Xena leaped for the trunk of the tree. She hopped a few steps, paused, cocked her head, and looked at Jazmyn as if to say, "Get away from my chocolate."

The pencil flew as Jazmyn tried to capture the spirit of the defiant squirrel. Xena had such personality. Within moments she'd finished. On the paper a very perturbed Xena stared up at her. Jazmyn wondered if the people who bought this book would understand that Xena wanted chocolate. She was almost willing to fight for it.

"Tell me, girl." Jazmyn set the pad down and picked up the candy bar. "Have you ever had any guy troubles?"

Xena skittered a few steps up the trunk and paused to watch as Jazmyn peeled away the wrapper. Her beady black eyes followed every movement, her body tensed, ready to grab and run.

"I would give you some of this, Xena, but you wouldn't believe the problems that can come from eating chocolate. What if you ended up fat because you ate too many candy bars?" Jazmyn broke off a bite. "You might not be able to fit into that little hole where you sleep in the winter. That would be a shame."

She stuck the bite in her mouth, savoring the sweetness. Xena skittered back down a couple of steps as if wondering where hers was.

"Think of this as my doing you a favor." Jazmyn wrapped the bar back up and stuck it in her pocket. Xena did not seem to appreciate the favor. She raced up to the branch. Her chattering and scolding startled a couple of birds.

Jazmyn laughed. "I think I'd like to learn that phrase to repeat to a certain man I know. He did something really mean to me. I'd be willing to talk about it and, after making him sweat, even forgive him." She sighed as Xena scampered farther up the tree. "Okay, I won't make him sweat. I'll forgive him, but he has to be willing to talk. So far we've been here four days, and he hasn't said anything to me that wasn't necessary."

She slammed her sketchpad shut and stared up the tree. "I could be a face-less robot and he wouldn't care." She clamped her lips together. This had to be the worst she'd ever been. Here she was, talking to an animal.

"Lord, You know what I'm trying to say. I listened to what Kirsten told me about Thor. I didn't want to forgive him, but then I understood he hadn't meant to hurt me. He was protecting himself."

She stood and stretched. "I'd like to talk to him about it, but maybe I read his interest wrong. He doesn't seem to want to have anything to do with me. Unless I'm way off, I think he is sorry I came up here with Jason."

Placing her drawing book in the SUV, Jazmyn wandered down to the river. The steady ripple of the water soothed her. She'd love to have a house right here where she could listen to this sound every night as she was falling asleep. It would be better than counting sheep.

"Lord, I know I hurt him by being unreasonable, by not listening. Help me make that up to him somehow. Show me how." Jazmyn thought about Queen Esther in the Old Testament. Esther had waited patiently until the time was just right to speak to the king. She hadn't rushed in and started throwing out wild accusations. She'd demonstrated great wisdom and trust in the Lord to the point of putting her own life in jeopardy.

"Keep me from rushing in, Lord. I want to grab him and shake him. I know that's not Your plan." She bent down to retrieve a handful of pebbles. "Lord, these represent the things I want. I'm giving them all to You, relying on You to provide for my needs and to help me forget my wants." One at a time Jazmyn threw the pebbles into the river. Each time she thought of a selfish want that she'd been holding on to. When she finished she felt better. She would wait and see how the Lord worked.

She almost had supper finished when the guys returned. Jason began to sort and store his film. He would take the next half-hour to get his cameras put to bed, as he put it.

Loki and Odin rose and stretched, their tails wagging as they watched Thor striding toward them.

Shadows were growing long already as the sun fell behind the trees. The fire had almost died out. Jazmyn had tried to build a new fire on the old coals, but it was more smoke than flames.

"I hope you don't mind that I started supper. I remembered your recipe for sloppy joes. At least, I think I got it right." Jazmyn bit her lip to stop from chattering. Thor looked grim and tired. He wouldn't want to be bothered with what she had to say.

He nodded at her. "Smells good. I'll work on the fire." As he moved away, Jazmyn couldn't keep from watching him. She loved the graceful way he walked, as if he were aware of everything around him and prepared for anything. She imagined the Apaches who used to live here moved the same way.

During supper Jason kept up a running commentary on everything they'd seen that day. He told Jazmyn about the wild turkeys. She couldn't help but laugh as he described the way their heads kept popping up out of the grass they were hiding in.

"You'll never guess what else we saw today." Jason looked like a little boy about to burst at the seams with his news.

"Um. A deer." Jazmyn laughed as Jason rolled his eyes.

"We saw the wolves." He leaned forward, excitement shining in his eyes. He'd already told her about the program to reintroduce wolves in this area. Only a few had survived, so the chances of finding one were slim.

"Jason, that's wonderful." Jazmyn jumped up to give him a hug. She knew what this would mean to his editor.

"Tomorrow we're going to look for elk, but the next day we want to try to find the wolves again," Jason said. "If you have all your sketches done, maybe you can go along with us."

Thor pushed up from his chair. "If you'll excuse me, I'm going to bed. Dawn comes early." Was he angry that Jason asked her to go with them? Did he dislike her so much that he couldn't stand the thought of being in the same vehicle with her?

Jazmyn sank back down. She stared at the crackling flames. *God, help me to be like Esther.*

Chapter 21

Jazmyn's breath puffed out in a white cloud as she stuck her head out of the sleeping bag. Jason scratched on the side of the tent. He called to her for the second time.

"I'm awake." She shivered, drawing the bag tight around her shoulders. "This isn't funny, Jason. Even Santa Claus and his elves don't like it this cold."

"Just be glad we don't have six feet of snow to go with it." Jason slapped the tent. "Up and at 'em. Time to get moving. Thor's got coffee on. He's fixing some breakfast."

She groaned. It must be three hundred degrees below zero. "I shouldn't have been working out so much. It would have been smarter to put on blubber like a whale."

"Are you talking to yourself in there, sis?"

"I'd never do such a thing." Jazmyn gritted her teeth, reaching for her clothes. The jeans and sweatshirt were so cold she almost couldn't bear to touch them, let alone put them on. The other mornings hadn't been this cold.

"I hope you kept your clothes in the sleeping bag last night so they're warm this morning." She could hear Jason walking away.

"Fine time to tell me," Jazmyn muttered under her breath. She snuggled back into the sleeping bag, hoping the clothes would warm up fast. At least she had her socks on, but her shoes were probably like blocks of ice.

A few minutes later she unzipped the tent and made a beeline for the fire. She stood close, feeling like a chicken on a spit as she rotated to warm her whole body.

Jason came over carrying a plate of hash browns and eggs. The thought of warm food set her stomach growling.

"Here, have a seat." He snagged a chair and pulled it close to the fire. Jazmyn sank into it. She accepted the plate from him. "Thor and I will be right over with ours."

Jazmyn waited until the men joined her. From the corner of her eye she watched Thor. She couldn't help it. Being close to him this week, without the rapport they'd shared before, had been sheer torture.

She'd also spent the week watching Thor to see if he'd changed at all. Did he become a Christian in name only as so many people did? She didn't think so. He was a strong person, a decision maker, but from what she'd learned he hadn't always thought about how his decisions affected others. Although he still had the assertive traits, they now appeared to be tempered by consideration for others.

She wondered if that was why he stayed away from her. Maybe he thought she didn't want anything to do with him, so he was intent on not pushing her. Today she had to find a way to change that. She'd come to the realization that she loved him and didn't want to live without him.

"About done, Jaz?" Jason tossed his paper plate into the fire. "Good breakfast, Thor. Hit the spot."

Jazmyn stared at the bit of egg and mound of potatoes still on her plate. She didn't want to be rude, but if they were going over some of the rough roads they usually traveled looking for wildlife, she didn't want to eat too much.

"Don't worry about finishing." She looked up to find Thor standing beside her. "Done?" At her nod, he reached for her plate. "I'll leave the potatoes for our little friends."

He strode away from camp. Jazmyn couldn't stop watching him. Every time he spoke to her, her pulse sped up. She hoped this time he would warm up to her.

"If you drizzle chocolate over the potatoes, Xena will be yours forever." She almost clapped her hand over her mouth. Had she said that? Jason was laughing behind her.

Thor flashed her a smile, the first all week. "That's just what I need. A neurotic, chocolate-addicted female."

Warmth flooded through Jazmyn. Maybe they could get past the hurts. Maybe today Thor would open up to her. She needed to be patient, though. With the pushy women he'd been involved with before, he didn't need her to be pushy, too.

"Where are we going first?" Jazmyn asked as she climbed into the truck.

"I thought we'd head up to Hannigan's meadow area. We might find some bighorn sheep there. Then we'll circle back to Kettleholes. That's where we saw the wolves yesterday. Jason wanted to try to get a few more shots of them." Thor moved the truck to the side of the road to let a vehicle piled with hunters go past.

Jazmyn tried not to lean against Thor at all. The moment they'd shared in camp hadn't lasted. When she climbed in the truck next to him, she sensed he didn't want her to be there. She tried to ignore the hurt, but she kept wondering what had happened. He hadn't even given her the chance to apologize for the way she'd behaved when she learned his true identity. Perhaps she should have forced the issue, should have faced him down.

As they topped out at Hannigan's meadow, Thor slowed to turn onto a side road that was little more than a track. Nothing moved in the wide grassy area.

Back in the trees he pulled the truck off to the side and parked. "Okay, we walk from here."

The hike in the thin mountain air wasn't easy, but Jazmyn could tell her workouts at the gym were helping. She didn't feel like she would pass out at any moment as she had the last time.

Thor hunkered down. He motioned Jazmyn and Jason to come closer. As if he weren't thinking, he reached back, grasped Jazmyn's hand, and tugged her down beside him. Over the top of the brush she could see the mountain sheep. Two mothers were grazing about thirty yards away. As she watched, three babies bounded into view. Her breath caught at the beauty and grace of the animals. The young ones were almost too cute.

Beside Jazmyn, Jason brought up his camera. From the corner of her eye she could see him studying the angles, looking for the best shots. He motioned to Thor that he was moving around to a better spot. Jazmyn held her breath, hoping the sheep wouldn't see them and flee before Jason got the pictures he needed.

The babies looked as if they were playing tag, bounding uphill and down chasing one another. Jazmyn was reminded of cartoons she'd watched as a child when the sheep would leap stiff-legged from one place to another. She wanted to laugh out loud but couldn't.

She glanced down to find her fingers still entwined with Thor's. Looking up, she saw him gazing at her. He turned away, his hand releasing hers, but not before she saw the longing in his eyes. He did still love her. She was sure of it. Now she had to wait for the right time to act.

✧

Kneeling down, studying the wolf tracks, Thor knew they weren't far away. He knew the den would be close. By this time of year they would be teaching the young to hunt in the pack, preparing them for life on their own.

"This way." He spoke low, not in a whisper, because that might carry too far. Jazmyn and Jason caught up to him. They needed to hurry. They'd taken too long with the sheep, and now dusk was too close. Besides, they'd heard a gunshot not too far off. Thor didn't trust any hunter's accuracy in this light.

He tried to ignore the way he felt about Jazmyn. All week he'd had to avoid her in order to deal with her presence. "Give her time." Both Kirsten and Jason told him that. Well, how much time did he need to give her? How would he know she was ready?

Kirsten had told him about her lunch with Jazmyn. She said Jazmyn felt awful for being so angry with him, but she sure hadn't apologized. Maybe she thought she was justified. Then again, maybe she didn't want to encourage him, didn't feel for him what he felt for her.

After her teasing comment this morning he'd hoped they might at least become friends. Then he realized he didn't want to be just friends with her; he wanted to marry her and be with her the rest of his life.

In the truck he noticed how she tried her best not to touch him, even on the rough roads. It hurt to think she disliked him that much. Although he tried not to show it, he'd looked forward to her touch, even an impersonal one.

He crouched down again and motioned to Jason and Jazmyn. "Go over to that group of trees and wait. I'm going down over this ridge. It's a steep drop-off, but there's a cave down there that might be a good spot for a den. If they're there, I'll come and get you. Watch your step, though, it's almost straight down."

He waited until they were settled, then approached the ravine, keeping low. As he neared the edge, something flashed on the far side of the chasm. He eased out over the edge. A deer leaped up, racing full tilt out of the gorge, her breathing labored, blood running down her flank. Thor scrambled up, trying to get away. Something hit him hard in the side. Pain shot through him.

He must have blacked out. When he came to, he was lying at an odd angle, his side throbbing. He touched his shirt. Something sticky covered his fingers. Blood. He closed his eyes, letting darkness wash over him.

"Thor. O God, please let him be alive." Soft fingers touched his face. Thor didn't want to open his eyes. He was afraid he was hallucinating, thinking Jazmyn cared enough to be here to help him. She would never climb down such a steep slope.

The fingers brushed his hair back, flicked pieces of debris from his face. He forced his eyes to crack open. The dream Jazmyn looked very real. Tears made her eyes a bright, glittery green. She leaned over and kissed him on the forehead. Her lips were warm and soft like real lips. This was a dream he didn't want to end. He closed his eyes.

"Thor, you have to look at me." Jazmyn's breath warmed his cheek.

His eyes opened again. She was still there, still as beautiful as ever, and crying over him. If he could move, he would pull her to him and give her a long kiss.

"That would be wonderful." Jazmyn smiled at him. Thor realized he must have spoken the thought out loud. "I don't think you're up to the grabbing, but I can help out in the kissing department."

He almost forgot the pain in his body as she covered his mouth with hers. It was the sweetest kiss he could ever remember, and the most meaningful.

"Now we need to get down to business." Jazmyn lifted his first-aid kit. She must have brought it from the truck. "Jason took off to get help. I get to play doctor."

Her fingers trembled as she opened his shirt. "We saw what happened. Some hunters must have been after that deer. They shot at her, but you were in the way. They got you instead."

"I'm not sure I'll taste as good." Thor winced as she tugged the shirt away from his side.

"I'm sorry." Tears pooled in her eyes. "I'm trying to be gentle."

"You're the best doctor I've ever had." He forced a smile. He managed to take her hand and lift it to his lips. His kiss brought a flush of color to her cheeks. "I love you, Jazmyn. I always will." A single tear tracked down her cheek. "I know I hurt you, but I didn't mean to. You don't have to return my love; I just had to tell you."

He closed his eyes and let her hand drop. He heard her start to sob. Something soft touched his cheek, again and again. She was kissing him. He opened his eyes.

Her green gaze caught his. "I love you so much, Thor Larson. If you think I'm going to let you say you love me and then watch you die, you're crazy. You will live through this. Understand?" Her white face had a determined look.

"As you wish, my lady."

"I know this will hurt, but I need to check your wound. I'm thinking you might have broken some bones in the fall, too, so I don't want to move you."

He gritted his teeth and held his breath as she worked the material free of the wound. Darkness closed in, but he heard her voice. He clung to the sound. "This doesn't look at all bad. I'm going to try to cover this with some gauze and tape it down. I'm hoping that will stop the bleeding."

Time passed in a haze. A shout sounded from above. The steady beat of helicopter rotors drew near. Someone other than Jazmyn was now leaning over him, examining him.

"Thor, can you hear me?"

He opened his eyes. Jazmyn leaned close. He wanted to tell her how beautiful she was, but his mouth didn't work.

"The rescue team is here. They're going to put you in a basket and get you to the helicopter. You've lost a lot of blood. They think you have some broken ribs, a broken leg, and a concussion. I'll see you at the hospital. Jason will bring me."

She leaned over. Her kiss was so sweet. "I love you, Thor. Now and always."

He couldn't quit smiling as they loaded him onto the stretcher and hoisted him into the air.

Epilogue

Thor watched Jazmyn as he ended his phone conversation. The windows were wide open, letting in a fresh fall breeze. She stood on a platform he'd built for her. In one hand she held a sponge, in the other a palette of paint. She was putting the finishing touches on a woodland scene along one wall of the nursery.

"Was that Wes?" Jazmyn didn't look away from her work. She must have heard him set down the phone.

"Yep. The new father. Kirsten and Wes have a new baby boy."

Jazmyn turned to him, her face shining. "How soon can we go see him?"

"Whoa, there." He reached her in three long strides. "Be careful. Just because the scaffold is safe doesn't mean you can't fall off." He swung her down.

Taking the painting equipment from her hands, he pulled her into his arms for a long kiss. When he stopped, she was as breathless as he was.

All around him the walls were covered with scenes of the forest. "Do you know what happens when you're surrounded by forest? You run the risk of being attacked by a wild animal."

Jazmyn laughed. "The problem is my wild animal has turned into a tame husband." Her arms snaked up to wrap around his neck. "Maybe I'm the one becoming wild."

"Only when I bring out the chocolate. Then I can see traces of Xena in you." Thor gave his wife another kiss.

"That's because I'm craving it and can't have it," she pouted.

He nibbled at her lower lip. "I'm trying to help you out. I've been eating plenty of chocolate for you."

"You're awful." She gave him another kiss. "I should get out of here and let the paint dry. Let's see if Erik's heard about the baby."

Thor closed the windows. Taking her hand, he paused to look around the room. Jazmyn had done a remarkable job of making the nursery feel like the outdoors.

"Kirsten and Wes may have had their baby before us, but ours will have the best bedroom."

"Are you sure you don't mind living in town now?" Jazmyn gazed up at him, concern evident in her green eyes.

He took a deep breath. "No. Kirsten will need me to step in while she's with

231

the baby. As long as we can get away once in a while to the cabin, I don't mind at all. How about you?"

"I can be content anywhere you are, Thor. You know that, don't you?"

Pulling her close, Thor rested his chin on her head. The lump in his throat kept him quiet. A year had passed since he'd been hurt in the mountains. Jazmyn had been with him every step of the way while he healed. Six months ago, they'd married and moved up to his cabin in the mountains. She hadn't complained once, until the day he told her they would have to move back to town for a while.

If he had any doubts about the sincerity of her love, he could look at the changes in her. She was the one who insisted their child would live in the forest no matter where they were. She'd taken him on a shopping spree when they got to town. Stuffed toys placed around the baby's room represented all the wild animals from the mountains.

They continued down the stairs. Thor didn't think he could be more content than he was now. They may have rough times ahead, but he knew their faith and love would see them through.

Picture This

Dedication

Many thanks to my editors for their hard work. Without them, this book wouldn't be in your hands. Thanks to my family for their love and acceptance of my quirks. Also, thanks to God for the beauty of the Sonoran Desert. Those early morning walks with Him and the encounters with the javelina provided material for this story.

Prologue

The sound of laughter startled Madeline Henry from her reverie. She smiled at Jazmyn Rondell's teary expression as she gazed up at her new husband. Looking elated, Thor Larsen released Jazmyn from their first kiss as man and wife. Maddy realized she'd missed part of the vows and the pastor's message. Her mind kept wandering to last night and what was to come today during the wedding and reception. Once again she would be in close contact with Jason Rondell, Jazmyn's twin brother. The evening stretched before her with no relief in sight.

As the recessional started, Maddy glanced over to find Jason watching her, that quirky grin of his lighting up his handsome features. She sighed. He must have been a terror when he was young. With that impish look, he could have gotten anything he wanted. She would have a very real fight on her hands to hold on to her heart tonight, since she was required to spend a good portion of the evening next to Jason, the groomsman who would escort Maddy.

The matron of honor and the best man, Thor's sister and brother, smiled at one another as they began their walk down the aisle out of the church. Maddy's mouth went dry as Jason stepped forward and waited for her. *All you have to do is take his arm,* she told herself. *Pretend he's not someone who makes the world tilt.* She gritted her teeth in a smile that must have looked as fake as it felt. The minute her fingers touched the jacket covering Jason's arm, Maddy knew this wasn't going to work. The electricity was so strong she wondered if she should check the ceiling for a lightning strike.

In the receiving line, Jason stood so close his arm brushed hers every time she reached out to shake a hand or give someone a hug. Maddy racked her brain trying to think of an excuse to bow out, but her brain seemed to have gone on vacation.

The sweet torture continued when Jazmyn asked the photographer to take several pictures of Jason and Maddy together, saying she loved the way they blended—whatever that meant. Maddy didn't want to consider. She wanted to shake Jaz and say, "Don't you know I can't have a thing to do with your brother? Don't you realize who I am and what I've done?"

The reception was like a fairy tale come true. Held outdoors in the garden area of the Larson mansion, the whole place sparkled with the tiny twinkling lights strung through the trees. Chinese lanterns swung in the slight breeze. The heavy, sweet scent of flowers combined with the ethereal music of a duo playing the harp and flute added to the enchanted feel of the night.

"I didn't get the chance last night to welcome you." Jason's forest green eyes shone dark in the lantern light.

"Welcome me?" Maddy's breath caught as Jason leaned closer to her.

"As a sister." One side of Jason's mouth tilted up as he stifled a grin. "You know, a sister in Christ. Jaz told me you became a Christian. She was very excited."

Maddy stared. What was he saying? Did he just want to congratulate her? Always before when a man looked at her this way, she knew what it meant. But Jason wasn't at all like the men she'd known before. She knew all about him from Jazmyn. Jason was such a strong Christian—he reminded her of Paul in the Bible after he encountered Jesus. Why would he want to know her or be interested in someone like her? He wouldn't. That had to be the answer. She had no clue how to interpret anything a Christian man said or did.

Her eyes began to burn, a sure sign that soon her face would be as red as a sunset and blotchy enough to look like she had the measles. "Excuse me." Maddy scooted her chair back so fast it fell over. "I need to go. . .um, somewhere." Before Jason could even stand up, she rushed toward the house, hoping she could find somewhere to hide before she fell apart.

Chapter 1

W ill you look at that boy?" Maddy dropped the last of the papers on the conference table as Jazmyn and Thor Larson entered the boardroom of T. L. Enterprises. She couldn't believe it had only been fourteen months since the wedding, and already Jazmyn cradled a baby in her arms. Maddy hurried over to them. "Never mind about what I just said. That is not a boy. He must be an alien. A human boy wouldn't have grown so fast. Just couldn't happen." She winked at Jaz as she reached out to stroke the pale gold strands of hair on the baby's head.

"I think the doctor said something similar." Jazmyn chuckled as she unwound a strand of her strawberry blond hair from the baby's fist. "He thinks I'll need a pack mule to cart Caleb around before he's much older. By the time I'm thirty-one in a couple of months, I'll be all stooped over." Maddy chuckled, and Jazmyn shot her a look. "Hey, don't you laugh. Your thirtieth is coming pretty soon."

Thor, owner of T. L. Enterprises, winked at Maddy before he crossed to the coffeepot and helped himself to a cup. The man's huge frame made the room shrink. Maddy couldn't believe how much he'd changed since he'd married Jazmyn. Even though he owned T. L., he'd never come to the offices, choosing instead to let Kirsten and Erik, his half sister and half brother, be the visible ones.

Thor had built the company from the ground up. His high-end import business catered to the wealthy, while another area of his enterprise dealt with those who wanted more reasonably priced imports. He sold everything from art to furniture that was brought over from Europe, Asia, and sometimes more exotic locales. "Is everything set up, Maddy?"

"It sure is." Maddy lifted the baby from Jaz's arms. She cuddled Caleb close, giving Jazmyn a sweet look as she batted her eyelashes at her. "I just knew you wanted to fix your own coffee. It's much too hard to do while you're holding a baby."

"Oh, I'm used to juggling by now. After a few weeks of having a baby around, you learn to do everything one-handed." Jaz reached out for Caleb.

Maddy turned her back to thwart her best friend's grab. "That's okay. I can tell how much you need a break. Besides, with six younger sisters and brothers, I know a thing or two about babies. And I know enough to hold them while they smell sweet."

"Are you suggesting my son may not be sweet all the time?" Thor glowered at Maddy, but she knew him too well to believe he was angry.

"Hey, with you for a dad, I'm surprised this boy doesn't smell like he's been in the woods wrestling bears and cleaning fish."

Thor threw back his head and laughed. "As soon as Jazmyn lets me take him, we're off to do just that." At Maddy's glare, he said, "Well, at least I can teach him to camp and fish. We'll save wrestling bears until he's two. I hear when they're that age they can do anything."

Maddy chuckled softly as she dipped her head to kiss Caleb's soft cheek. His little mouth made sucking motions. One tiny fist waved in the air for a moment before he relaxed into deep slumber. She hadn't seen the baby since he was two weeks old. Thor had taken his family to their cabin in the mountains and left Kirsten in charge for a time. She'd missed visiting with Jazmyn.

"Isn't he due for a checkup?" Maddy asked.

"He already had it yesterday morning." Jazmyn poured a cup of coffee, added her favorite creamer, and sighed as she took her first sip. "I wanted to call you, but he was so fussy after getting his shots that I knew we wouldn't be able to visit. He's had a little fever, but the baby medication keeps that down. Maybe by tomorrow we can get together."

"I hear they have some awesome sales at the mall." Maddy gave Jaz a wicked grin. "Plus, they opened a new coffee shop there that has a mint cream iced coffee that's pure heaven."

"Mmm. I can't wait." Jazmyn smiled up at her husband. Thor looked like he'd swallowed a whole lemon sideways.

"I think I have something else to do whenever you're going to the mall." He leaned over to kiss Jazmyn on the cheek. "I know Martha, Kirsten's nanny, will be happy to watch Caleb while you go out. If not, she might recommend someone."

"Oh no you don't." Maddy spoke up before Jazmyn could say anything. "You're not gonna deprive me of time with this boy. Besides, I plan to start early teaching him the right way to shop and dress. Otherwise you'll have him wearing animal skins and boots."

Thor grimaced as he reached out to caress Caleb's head. "Nothing pink or ruffly or I'll have to cancel his mall privileges."

"Hey, did you start without us?"

Maddy swiveled around to see Kirsten Barnes, her immediate boss and Thor's half sister, enter the room followed by Thor's half brother, Erik Peterson. Kirsten pushed a stroller holding her eight-month-old son, Peder.

"Sorry we're running a little late." Erik, a younger, slightly smaller version of Thor, carried Peder's diaper bag. "When I stopped to pick up Kirsten, Peder decided he didn't like the outfit Kirsten put on him. He's a boy who wants to be wearing the right clothes for the day."

"No problem. We just got here, too." Thor gave his brother a hug before giving Kirsten the same, plus a peck on the cheek. He squatted down beside the stroller to give Peder some attention. Peder chortled and waved his arms at Thor.

Erik gave Maddy a quick hug as he took Caleb's tiny fist in his. Still asleep, Caleb wrapped his fingers around one of his uncle's. Maddy laughed in delight at the wonder on Erik's face. When Kirsten had gone on maternity leave, Erik had taken over her duties. He and Maddy had become such good friends that she considered him a brother.

Kirsten brushed her straight blond hair behind her ear as she began to push Peder to the connecting door. "Before we get started, Jaz and I can take the babies into my office. Martha came with us, so she can watch them." Jazmyn plucked Caleb from Maddy's arms and followed her sister-in-law. Within a couple of minutes they returned to the boardroom.

"I have all the papers we need on the table." Maddy hurried to get Kirsten a cup of coffee. "There's coffee, tea, and water for whoever would like some."

"What? Nothing to sustain us through this dreary meeting?" Jazmyn gasped with mock horror.

"Just what kind of a girl Friday do you think I am?" Maddy tried to look offended. It felt so good to have Kirsten and Jazmyn back here. She leaned over to open a cabinet door and whisked out a tray of pastries from Jazmyn and Kirsten's favorite French bakery.

"Mmm. I'm drooling worse than Caleb and Peder put together." Jazmyn snatched up a napkin before picking out a blueberry-filled pastry. "After all this time in the mountains, I've been dying for one of these. It's all I thought of on the way to town yesterday."

"Sweetheart, why don't you and Kirsten sit together?" Thor gave Jazmyn a hug as he guided her to the table. "We'll put the tray of goodies between the two of you."

"Hey, I'm not sure that's fair." Erik stretched across the table to snatch the filled croissant Kirsten was about to take. He grinned at Maddy. "I'm just saving my sister from having to exercise off all those extra pounds."

Maddy laughed. She turned to Thor. "You said to get enough of the papers for six. There are only five of us. Are you expecting someone else?"

"Yes, he should be here any minute." Thor glanced at his watch. "I guess he's running a little later than the rest of us. Go ahead and close the door. We can start the business part. He'll come in when he gets here."

"So, who's coming?" Maddy watched Thor over her shoulder as she reached out to close the door. She heard hurried footsteps a moment before someone rushed inside and collided with her. Maddy fumbled to gain a grip on the doorknob so she wouldn't tumble backward. A strong arm caught her around the waist and hauled her against a very masculine chest. Her heart raced. She knew who it was before she even looked up into those incredible green eyes.

"Jason's here," Thor said.

✌

"Nice hair." Jason fought to keep from tightening his hold on Maddy. "Did you think about brushing it this morning?" He smirked at the spark of defiance in her brown eyes, which had the intriguing quality of reflecting the red of her hair.

Her eyes narrowed. "My hair is fine. Now please let me go."

With reluctance Jason eased Maddy back and released her. He hadn't gotten close to her since Jazmyn and Thor's wedding more than a year ago. Every time he came within range, she took off faster than a gazelle with a lion on its tail.

"I thought you must have gone through a major gale on the way to work this morning."

"Jason, lay off." Jazmyn crossed to give him a kiss on the cheek. "Maddy looks wonderful in that windblown style, and you know it."

She did look incredible, but Jason knew he wouldn't admit that or Jaz and her cronies would have a field day with the information. Maddy's hair, a little too bright to be called auburn, had been streaked with blond highlights that shone in the lighting of the room. Her wide brown eyes appeared to take on the color of her hair. Her full mouth could make a man lose his train of thought. Jason didn't want to admit, even to himself, how much he'd wanted to see Maddy again.

"Now that you're finished knocking the secretary over, how about we all get down to business?" Thor clapped Jason on the shoulder before leading him over to a spot beside Maddy's chair at the table. "Maddy, would you bring Jason a cup of coffee, please?"

Looking as if she'd rather be anywhere in the world except in a room with him, Maddy brought Jason a steaming mug. Some of the brew sloshed over the side when she placed the cup in front of him.

"I'm sorry." Maddy grabbed a couple of napkins from beside the pastry tray to mop up the spill. Her knuckles bumped the cup and more coffee dribbled down the side. Her cheeks darkened until they were almost the shade of her hair.

"Maybe you should let me do it." Jason covered her hand with his. He could see everyone at the table watching them and knew Maddy was embarrassed. He'd heard often enough how efficient she was. As he sipped his drink he realized how right his sister had been about her friend.

"You remembered." Jason leaned close as Maddy sat down next to him. Her fading blush returned.

"What?" she asked.

"How I like my coffee. I can't believe you remember, since you only fixed it once or twice more than a year ago." He watched in amusement as she picked up her papers, tried to straighten them, and flipped half the pages on the floor. Jason bent to retrieve them at the same time Maddy did. They were nose to nose, both holding the dropped information, when Maddy met his gaze with those incredible red-brown eyes. His thought processes blipped. Jason couldn't remember what he'd been trying to do.

"Maddy." Thor's deep voice had them both straightening like a couple of school kids caught passing notes. "You've done a great job outlining the agenda here. I'm thinking since we're starting so late and I can hear at least one of the upcoming board members protesting our absence. . ." He paused, and they all heard the lusty cry from Kirsten's office. "I suggest we cut the meeting short. We can come back in for anything that needs to be discussed this afternoon or tomorrow. Jazmyn and I will be staying in town most of the time for the next few months."

Everyone nodded. Maddy jotted a few notes to herself on the top page. A second cry joined the first in the room beyond. Jazmyn and Kirsten looked uncomfortable, each ready to run to her baby's rescue.

"I have one item that has to be discussed, however." Thor picked up a pencil and tapped it on the table. "Maddy, I don't have this one outlined."

The crying in the other room abated. A sigh of relief drifted around the room. Jason almost laughed at the various reactions.

"I want to do something special for the employees of T. L. Enterprises. Jazmyn and I have discussed several options in addition to the normal Christmas bonus and party that we'll be giving. We wanted something that would last, something they could have to remember everyone and their time here. We have several employees who will be retiring soon. Our idea will give them something to take with them."

Thor paused and smiled down at Jazmyn. Jason's heart caught as he saw the love in Thor's eyes. He'd given up ever being able to look at a woman that way. With his job, the most he could ever hope for was an innocent bit of flirtation. Too many times his heart had been broken by women who promised to be faithful and wait for him to return from an assignment, only to find they didn't honor their word.

"Jazmyn came up with the idea of doing a photo album or book for each employee. I agree with her. We can put in pictures and maybe some of their comments. We could even do a longer bit about those who will be leaving us soon."

"That's great." Erik leaned forward, enthusiasm lighting his face. "We could include a bit about how you started in business and what the company goals are."

Kirsten nodded. "Is that why you asked Jason to be here?"

"It is." Thor's bright blue gaze locked on Jason. "Do you have the time to do a photo shoot for us?"

Jason nodded. "I guess that depends on what you're wanting. I don't have any pressing assignments right now." He could feel Maddy shift next to him. The thought of spending more time around her had an appeal.

"We don't want formal pictures," Thor said.

"Maybe one, don't you think?" Jazmyn smiled up at her husband. "We could get everyone together for one picture and have it spread out on two pages."

"That's good." Thor looked back at Jason. "Mostly, we want candid shots of the people at work or interacting with one another."

"When do you want these done?" Jason asked.

"As soon as possible. I'm afraid we're getting a late start. We'll have Maddy help you with the photos, but we'll have to figure out how to get the books done in time to give them out before the end of the year. At least that's the goal. That only gives us a couple of months."

"If Maddy can help me, I think we can do it together. Of course, she'll have to commit most of her time to the project." Jason could almost feel Maddy's astonishment and knew it rivaled his own. He'd wanted to spend some time with her, but how would he manage to be in her company so much and remain objective when visions of her wide, saucy smile had interrupted his work for more than a year? In close contact, he might not be able to keep from doing more than just thinking about kissing her.

Chapter 2

"Maddy, can you come in here?"

Kirsten's call over the intercom had Maddy blowing out a hasty breath. She stood, straightening her blouse, smoothing her skirt, and checking her hair a final time before she picked up her notepad and pencil. *I should have called in sick. It wouldn't really have been a lie. My stomach feels like a hamster is using it for an exercise ball.* This was going to be a long morning. She knew Jason was in the office with Kirsten and Jazmyn.

Swinging the door open, Maddy tried for a nonchalant air as she entered. "I'm here." Her usual upbeat tone sounded tinny and flat this morning.

Kirsten cocked her head to one side and studied Maddy as if she were a bug in an exhibit. Jazmyn sat to one side, her fingers covering her lips as she tried not to smile but failed. Maddy didn't look at Jason, but she could feel his gaze. Why was it when she walked into a room with Jason in it, a connection clicked into place and she could tell exactly where he was? This was crazy.

"Maddy, I'd like to know what this is." Kirsten moved her coffee mug a couple of inches across the desk.

Puzzled, Maddy frowned. "Your coffee." What was Kirsten talking about?

"Take a look, Maddy." Kirsten gave the cup another push.

Crossing to the desk, Maddy gazed down into the liquid in question. The scent wafted up to her. Her eyes widened in horror. She gasped and glanced up to Kirsten. "You didn't drink any, did you? Do I need to call 911? I'm so sorry. I don't know what I was thinking."

"Calm down, Maddy." Kirsten held up her hand. "I can still smell almonds and know enough not to ingest any. I would like to know how Jazmyn's almond creamer got in my coffee. Trying to poison me?" Kirsten was referring to her serious allergy to the nuts. The last time she'd ingested something with almonds, she'd ended up in the hospital for two days.

Jazmyn's tinkling laugh made Maddy's face flame. She wished the floor would open up and swallow her whole.

"I. . .I don't know. I thought I got your cinnamon creamer. The bottles are similar colors. I was thinking about this morning's project. . . ." Maddy bit her lip to halt her words before she said something even more embarrassing. For instance, how she couldn't think of anything other than she would be working with Jason for the next few days. She'd tried hard to put him out of her mind, but he consumed her thoughts. The way his vivid green eyes sparkled when he teased her. The little dimple on his left cheek that only showed up when he laughed. He was at least six inches taller than her five-foot-four, and with his slender build and strong arms, she wanted to snuggle next to him in the worst way. Her fingers twitched with the desire to brush through the pale brown-gold waves of his hair. She gave herself a mental shake to halt those images.

"It's okay, Maddy. You have a lot on your plate right now." Kirsten's smile let Maddy know her boss wasn't upset. "However, it would be nice to have some coffee that I can drink and still live."

Maddy dropped her notebook and pencil on the edge of the desk. "I'll wash out your cup and be right back. I'm so sorry."

As she headed for the small kitchen off Kirsten's office, Maddy avoided Jason's gaze. The center of her back burned. She knew he was watching her leave. The pull to look at him almost overpowered her.

Within minutes she returned with a steaming mug of coffee for Kirsten. Her face warmed as she placed the fragrant beverage on the desk. She gave Kirsten a saucy smile. "Here you go. This time I only added a touch of almond so you won't be able to smell it."

Jason and Jazmyn burst into laughter. Kirsten joined them as she picked up the mug and took a sip. "Okay, Maddy, I don't want to know who put out the contract on me. Let's get down to business before I expire." She narrowed her eyes at Maddy. "Remember, if anything happens to me, you have to change all Peder's dirty diapers."

Maddy gasped. "Oh please, anything but that!" This time she joined in the laughter.

"Okay, Maddy, Jason. Thor wants a lot of candid shots." Kirsten pulled out a page of notes. "Maddy, make sure everyone is in at least two pictures. We don't want to slight anyone."

"Did you already arrange for the group photo?" Jason leaned forward, his elbows resting on his knees. His question was directed at Kirsten, but his gaze locked on Maddy when she glanced his way.

Maddy cleared her throat, hoping no one noticed the slight tremor in her hands. "Everyone is supposed to be here at three o'clock this afternoon. We can spend the morning doing candid shots."

"That sounds good to me." Jason stood and stretched. Maddy couldn't help sneaking a peek at his lean form. She knew he spent a lot of time outdoors, but she'd forgotten how well toned he kept himself. She averted her gaze, mentally chastising herself for not watching her thoughts.

Picking up her notebook with the list of employees from Kirsten's desk, Maddy headed for the door with Jason following behind, glad to get out of this office but having mixed feelings about working with Jason. Because her pulse sped up every time she got close to him, she knew being with him for too long might endanger her heart. No way could she allow herself to become enamored with him.

"Um, Jason."

Maddy paused, her hand on the door handle, to see what Jazmyn wanted with her brother. Jason had turned back, too.

"You might want to take your camera along." Jazmyn's smirk mirrored the one on Kirsten's face.

"Just testing to see if you noticed." Jason sauntered back to his chair where he reached underneath to retrieve his camera bag. The back of his neck had turned an interesting shade of pink.

"Maybe Maddy needs to walk beside you so you don't get distracted." Kirsten snickered. "Remember, we want pictures of all the employees, not just the executive secretary."

Jerking open the door, Maddy strode through without looking back at Jason. What were Kirsten and Jazmyn up to? They'd become close in the last year. Maddy hoped they weren't planning to do a little matchmaking. She hoped they understood why she wouldn't be a good match for Jason. If not, she would have to find a way to tell them.

⁂

"As far as I know, none of the employees have heard that we're doing this book or taking pictures." Maddy pressed the elevator button for the fourth floor. Jason breathed deeply, drawing in the fresh scent of soap and shampoo. Citrus, perhaps.

Today the blond highlights had been replaced with pale red-gold streaks in her hair. She still looked tousled, with her chin-length hair cut in a layered look and blown dry to create a hairstyle with pieces of hair pointing in all different directions. Her hair constantly looked wispy and windblown, but the style suited her well. From where he stood, Jason could see the curve of her cheek and the full pout of her mouth. He shifted, forcing his gaze elsewhere. "They all know to be here this afternoon, though, right?"

"Yes, we even have a couple of employees who were willing to come in on their day off to be in the picture. Thor announced that a blowup would be made to hang on one of the walls." She flashed him a smile, causing Jason's heart to stutter. "He didn't say more than that because he was afraid of giving away the surprise. So far, the only ones who know about the book were at the meeting last week."

"So, how are we supposed to explain me taking pictures?" Jason asked.

The elevator dinged, announcing their floor. Maddy turned to him as the door glided open. "That may be a bit tricky. We thought you could take photos of some of the merchandise for a company brochure. I think Thor talked to you about that, too. Thor had several items put in each area where we would be working. We're hoping no one notices your aim might be a bit off."

The sparkle in her eyes made Jason smile. It seemed nothing could dim Maddy's spirit for long. Jazmyn had praised her for being such an encouragement in the workplace. Just the few glimpses he'd had let Jason know how right his sister had been.

He fumbled with the clasp on his camera bag as he followed Maddy from the elevator down the hall. The room they entered was large and airy with an excellent view of Tucson. Today happened to be a clear day with little smog, which was unusual. However, the brilliant sunshine outside wasn't an anomaly for southern Arizona, not even at the beginning of winter.

"Hey, Maddy, looking good." A young man straightened up from bending over a desk where he'd been speaking with a middle-aged woman. "Still going for the finger-in-the-light-socket look, I see." His grin sent a twinge of emotion spiraling through Jason.

"Gerald, I'll be happy to help you get this look anytime you want. We have plenty of convenient sockets around." The whole room exploded in hilarity at Maddy's saucy reply. The young man, Gerald, whose shaved head gleamed in the sunlight, joined them.

"Let me run out and get a wig first." Gerald's gaze was a bit more interested than Jason thought was necessary. He stepped up beside Maddy, coming closer to her than he normally would have.

"Where do you want to start?" Jason directed the question at Maddy, but his eyes never left Gerald's.

Maddy turned to him, her mouth open to ask something. Her eyes widened as she noted how close he stood. She drew in a deep breath and just stared at him for a long moment. The others in the room faded as Jason looked into her warm brown eyes.

Maddy expelled a breath and took a small step back. Her tone was so low he had to lean forward to hear her. From the corner of his eye, Jason saw Gerald frown.

"Do you need a certain light in this room?" Maddy asked.

"Just show me what you want photographed, the T. L. items. You can talk with the employees and distract them some while I move around shooting the pictures." Jason fought the urge to move closer. Maddy nodded, gestured to the various pieces displayed around the room, then moved away.

For the next two hours, they worked this way—Maddy talking and joking with her coworkers, Jason working a pattern to shoot discreet candid photos. He did try not to get Maddy in all of them but knew that when he developed the film, her pretty face would be in more than he'd want to show Thor and Jazmyn.

PICTURE THIS

He tried to reconcile the way he was drawn to her—to explain to himself that she was a friend of Jaz's, thus a friend of his. He refused to become involved again with a woman. After the last time, he knew his heart couldn't take another blow like that. Even Jazmyn didn't know how much he'd been hurt by Denise.

When he'd found out about her treachery, he'd left the country, telling Jazmyn he'd gotten another assignment. While it hadn't been a complete lie, his publisher had given him some minor work that any photographer could do when Jason had begged for something to get him away from Arizona.

"Whew, I wouldn't have guessed making small talk would be so tiring." Maddy leaned back against the elevator wall as they headed down to the ground floor. She wanted him to take some pictures of the lobby and the guards for the book.

"I'm about ready for a break." Jason checked his watch. "It's way past lunchtime. You want to go across the street and grab a sandwich after this?"

Thirty minutes later, they were seated at a table. Jason grimaced as his stomach growled. The smell of fresh bread made his mouth water. Jason said a quick prayer and bit off a chunk of sandwich. His satisfied hunger combined with the good flavors had him almost humming with contentment.

"I didn't realize I'd starved you." Maddy took a sip of her coffee.

"It was getting hard to lift the camera." Jason flexed his hand and winked at her. Maddy blushed. Jason dug a chip from the bag he'd gotten with his sandwich. A seed of hope touched his heart. Could this time with this woman be different than the past?

The café door swung open. Erik Peterson leaned inside and waved to Maddy. He beckoned her toward him, and Jason watched as Maddy excused herself and stepped outside with Erik. Thor's brother put his arm around Maddy's shoulders, engaging her in some earnest conversation that looked to have nothing to do with business. The old stereotype of the boss and the secretary crept into Jason's mind. He'd heard rumors about Erik's party lifestyle as a bachelor. He wasn't about to stay around and get hurt again. He gathered up his trash, trying to ignore Maddy's confused look as she came back to the table.

"I need to take off for a bit and do some things," he said. "I'll meet you back at T. L. in time to set up for the group shot this afternoon." Jason grabbed his tray and his camera bag and headed for the door. He forced himself not to look back. He knew if he saw the hurt on Maddy's face he wouldn't be able to maintain his resolve to stay away from her. At all costs he had to protect his heart.

Chapter 3

I wish you could hear the rumors flying around here." Thor clapped Jason on his back hard enough to almost spill the cup of coffee in Jason's hand.

"Rumors? How would I hear them? I haven't been here since I finished the candid shots." Jason grinned at his brother-in-law. "I've been slaving away getting photos downloaded and aligned on pages."

"Some work." Thor rolled his eyes.

"Hey, you should see the editing I had to do on your photos to keep you from looking like a wild man." Jason stepped into the elevator after Thor. He watched as the numbers began rising as they climbed. With each floor his heart rate increased. He could almost feel himself getting closer to seeing Maddy again. He'd been determined to ignore the way she attracted him, yet the past two weeks had dragged by. He'd had trouble keeping his mind on his work and off the executive secretary of T. L. Enterprises.

"I'll bet mine are the only pictures you didn't have to touch up at all." Thor grinned. "Well, Jazmyn's, too."

"Uh-huh." Jason took a sip of coffee. "I'm holding that one over your head. Wait until she hears you thought her photos needed work."

"In that case, I won't clue you into the rumors." Thor crossed his arms over his expansive chest. "Just remember they included you."

Jason almost choked. "Me? Why would rumors at T. L. include me?"

Thor stared at the ceiling as the bell dinged announcing their arrival at the floor of the executive offices. Jason knew his brother-in-law well enough to know he wouldn't say a word if he didn't want to.

"Okay, give." Jason gave an exaggerated sigh. "I'll keep all your dirty secrets."

"As if I have any." Thor grinned. He reached out to hold down the button to keep the door closed. "Rumor has it that you and Maddy are a secret item. It seems several of the employees caught you taking pictures of them while Maddy was talking to them. Since you were supposed to be taking pictures of the wares, rumors say you have a major crush on our sassy secretary." Thor reached out and snagged Jason's coffee cup before it hit the floor.

Snatching the cup back, Jason tried to think of a plausible reply when his brain refused to respond. He gaped at Thor. "What?"

"You heard me." Thor's grin widened. "I just wanted to let you know why all the ladies will be whispering behind their hands. You might even get a few comments from my dear sister and yours." Thor released the door button.

Still struggling to catch his breath after the bombshell Thor threw, Jason bit back a groan as the elevator opened. Maddy stood there, a cup in one hand, a sheaf of papers in the other. Her bright smile for Thor widened into a strained caricature as her eyes met Jason's.

His hand holding the briefcase filled with photos began to sweat. What would she say if she knew about all the extra shots he'd taken—ones he knew he didn't need, but couldn't seem to keep from taking? What would any of them say if they could see the extraordinary shot he'd printed out and framed? He'd considered using her as a background on his computer screen but feared Jazmyn might see it sometime when she was visiting.

"Good morning." Maddy stepped to one side so they could exit the elevator. "I was just off to deliver some paperwork. I'll be back as soon as I can."

Her pink cheeks told Jason she must be thinking about all the rumors flying. Had she known he was coming in this morning and been planning an escape before he arrived?

"We'll need you in the executive boardroom." Thor glanced at his watch. "Say in half an hour? Will that give you enough time?"

"You need me there?" Maddy's gaze darted to Jason and back to Thor. "Um, I'll try to be finished and back by then."

"We'll wait." Thor's tone and his grin told Jason the boss knew exactly why his secretary was leaving.

The elevator doors clicked shut. Jason heard the hum as it began to descend. He wished he could have climbed back in that car even if he'd had to ride to the first floor with Maddy. He didn't want to be here—to face everyone who thought Jason's dreams were coming true when that wasn't about to happen.

"Shall we?" Thor headed down the hallway toward his office. Jason walked beside him, doing his best to ignore the pointed glances and amused looks directed his way. If Thor hadn't said anything, Jason would have wondered. He certainly would have noticed, because these employees weren't being subtle.

Inside Thor's office with the door closed, he turned to Jason. "I've called Kirsten, Erik, and Jazmyn. They'll be here, along with Maddy, and we can look over what you've got. Then we'll get the book to the printer. I think we've just got time to get it all finished so we can hand them out at the Christmas party."

"Sounds good." Jason put his briefcase on a table and flipped it open. "I've printed out six copies. They aren't that professional, but you'll get the idea of how it will look. Jazmyn helped a lot with the design and setup." He shot Thor a grin. "I'm the photographer, not the layout person. She had some great ideas I think you'll like."

Taking the folder with the booklets from the briefcase, Jason tried to hand them to Thor. He held up his hands. "Save that until everyone arrives. We can all look at them together and have a discussion. Want some more coffee?"

"No thanks." Jason placed the folder on the table. "I thought I'd leave these with you. You can take your time with them and let me know what needs done. Just remember I have to have them to the printer by Thursday to get them back in time."

"No way." Thor grinned back over his shoulder as he filled his cup with steaming coffee. "I know what you're doing. You don't want to be here when Maddy gets back." He turned around and leaned back against the counter. "Is it because you don't want to make Maddy uncomfortable, or are you the one being put on the spot?"

His low chuckle made Jason feel as if the man had seen the photo he kept on his nightstand.

"I'm thinking maybe she's gotten to you."

"Oh, look at this picture of Rose." Kirsten's delighted exclamation had Maddy glancing over to see what page she'd turned to. "This looks just like her. If I didn't know better, Jason, I'd say she could climb right off this page and start lecturing about work ethics and their importance."

Erik groaned. "If she spent more time practicing her work ethics and less time lecturing, it would help."

"Now, Erik." Kirsten frowned at him. "She's in charge of making the new hires productive. That's a tough position."

"Yeah, but she loves that speech that she gives so much, everyone here could quote her verbatim." Erik's imitation had them all laughing.

"Maybe so, but at least they listen to her. She does get people to try." Kirsten turned the page. Maddy tried to find where they were in the booklet. She'd lost track when Jason brought them all bottles of water from the refrigerator and then sat down beside her. This was why she'd tried so hard not to be here today. The past couple of weeks had been torture. She didn't want to be around him because she couldn't think, but when she wasn't around him, he was all she thought about anyway. How had this happened?

"What do you think, Maddy? Anything you'd like to add or change?" Thor asked.

"No." She shook her head, trying to keep her focus on the pictures, not on Jason's hand resting on the table close to her arm. "I love the little captions Jazmyn added. How did you pick what to put for each person?"

"That was a bit tricky." Jazmyn's face reddened. "I had to eavesdrop a bit. Thor and I have been talking about this for some time, so I've been making notes at various functions. I'd overhear someone comment about a pet and jot that in my notebook. When the time came to add in little pictures, I knew what most of the people liked."

"What a marvelous idea. They are going to love this." Kirsten's obvious delight made Jazmyn's cheeks turn a darker red.

A faint wail came through the closed doors. Maddy bit back a grin when Kirsten and Jazmyn went on instant alert. Even Thor's gaze focused on the door leading to the room where Martha was watching Caleb and Peder.

"Sounds like we're done here for the moment." At Thor's dry comment, both mothers excused themselves and headed for their babies. "Jason, you can work on the changes we've discussed. If we have any more to add before the Wednesday deadline, we'll have Maddy get in touch with you. So far, this all looks great. Thanks so much."

He stood up. "Will you be coming to the Christmas party, Jason? I told Jazmyn to invite you."

"I don't think I'll be able to make it." Jason clicked his briefcase shut as he stood. "I have a short assignment to do. I'll be leaving town and won't be back until a couple of days before Christmas."

"Where are you off to this time?" Maddy had to ask. She couldn't help her fascination with Jason's job. He flew off to exotic locations all the time, places she'd only dreamed about visiting.

"I wanted to get the job on a beach somewhere in Hawaii." The teasing in Jason's eyes made her smile. "Instead, I'm going to some hunting lodge in Canada."

"A hunting lodge?"

"Yeah, I'm supposed to shoot some pictures for their new brochure. I'm just hoping the bad weather holds off until I get back, but they're probably ordering it so I can get some shots of snow falling."

Maddy pushed back from the table and stood. When she turned, Jason still hadn't moved. They were almost eye to eye. The comment she'd been about to make wouldn't form. He had the most intense green eyes she'd ever seen. She wanted to stand there forever, close to him.

"If you two want us to leave, we will." Thor's amused tone had Erik laughing.

Maddy's face couldn't have grown any hotter.

Chapter 4

Hey, Maddy girl." Erik Peterson's call halted Maddy as she reached the elevator. She'd been trying to escape after hearing Jazmyn say her brother was on his way to see her. Maddy had managed to avoid Jason since before Christmas when they'd finished up the employee photo books. The rumors had finally died down, and she didn't want to resurrect any of them.

"Hi, Erik. I heard you were back, but I didn't know you were coming in today." Maddy gave her boss's brother a hug.

"I talked to Kirsten and Jazmyn. They both agreed I can take you for coffee across the street." Erik's eyes widened into his imitation of a little boy trying to get what he wanted. Maddy was very familiar with this expression.

Putting her free hand on her hip, Maddy tilted her head to one side. "What is it you want this time?"

"Maaad-dy." Erik drew out her name. "You're wounding me. I haven't seen you since I left before New Year's on this trip."

"Erik, it's only been two weeks since I've seen you."

He grinned. "Yeah, but something's happened. I have to talk to you."

"Me, not Thor?" Maddy looked up at Erik, noting that something seemed a little different about him.

"Definitely not Thor. I have to talk to you." Erik reached around her to push the elevator button. "Jazmyn says we can have forty-five minutes and not a second longer." His imitation of her boss had Maddy laughing.

"Then let's go. I can drop this stuff off at the front desk and pick it up on my way back in." Maddy stepped into the elevator when the door slid open.

The coffee shop wasn't crowded at this time of the morning. Erik led her to a table by the window, away from any other people. Maddy breathed in the scent of her hot raspberry latte before taking a sip.

"So, what do you need to talk about?" Maddy lifted one eyebrow. "Need some advice on your love life?" She made a face at him. There was a time when she thought maybe she and Erik could become more than friends, but after getting to know him, she knew that wouldn't happen. She and Erik both agreed they were more like siblings than anything else.

"As a matter of fact." Erik shifted and glanced around the small shop.

Maddy leaned closer over the table, excitement stirring inside her. "You have a girlfriend? Really? Do Kirsten and Thor know? Of course they don't." At Erik's look of exasperation, Maddy paused. "Okay, give."

"Promise to keep it a secret?" Erik's scrutiny made her want to squirm. He knew how close she was to Kirsten and Jazmyn.

"I promise." Her heavy sigh had him grinning. "Just don't keep me in suspense."

"You know how Kirsten used to always do these buying trips with me? Well, we always had Zuria Olivier help us. She's from our division in France."

Maddy nodded. "I've met her before. Petite. Beautiful. Dark hair. Big eyes."

Erik's expression turned wistful. "Yeah. That's her."

Snapping her fingers in front of his face, Maddy said, "Wake up, Prince Charming. I need to hear more."

Red stained Erik's cheeks. He glanced around before leaning over the table until their noses were almost touching. "I always thought she was so perfect, but with Kirsten along everything was just business. This time Zuria and I spent so much time together. We ended up eating our meals out. I found out that she's always been attracted to me, too, but tried to keep her distance because she works for the company. She didn't want to jeopardize her job."

"So you told her she works for Thor, not you, right?" Maddy grinned at his dumbfounded look. "Trust me, I know you well enough to see that one coming. What did she say?"

"We are both considering how to proceed." Erik glanced out the window. "I didn't want to come home. I've talked with her at least once every day since I've been back."

"Erik, you've only been home two days." Maddy bit her lip to keep from laughing.

"Maddy, have you ever felt this for anyone? You know, you can't get them out of your mind? All you want to do is think about them, be with them, talk about them? It's like an obsession."

Silence stretched between them as Maddy thought about Jason. She couldn't allow her mind to go there, but he was to her what Zuria was to Erik.

"Maddy, you do have someone, don't you?" Surprise laced Erik's tone. "Who is it?"

"No one." Maddy felt her face warm. That wasn't a lie, was it? She and Jason weren't seeing each other or anything.

"Give." Erik reached over to touch her chin, lifting until she met his gaze.

"Erik, you know about my past. I can't see anyone."

"Why not?" Erik's eyebrows shot up. "I thought you were a new person in Christ. Doesn't that wash you clean?"

Maddy shifted in her seat. "Maybe. Yeah, I guess it does, but I still have consequences for my lifestyle choices before I became a Christian. Besides, I have a weakness in that area. I can't risk a relationship."

"You think God isn't strong enough to overcome your weakness?" Erik grasped her hand. "Maddy, if you choose a Christian to date, you can trust that he will also want to keep your relationship pure. Perhaps you're selling Jason short."

Maddy gasped, and her eyes widened. "How did you know?"

Erik chuckled. "I think it's been pretty obvious to all of us working on the photo book. I'm amazed Kirsten and Jazmyn haven't tried their hands at any matchmaking between you two."

Pulling her fingers from his, Maddy took a drink from her latte. Could she trust Jason? He was such a jokester, which attracted her to him. Would his lack of seriousness lead to situations that would be emotionally dangerous for her?

Standing in the shadows of the T. L. Enterprises building across from the coffee shop, Jason watched Erik and Maddy through the window. When Erik lifted Maddy's chin with his finger, Jason thought he was going to kiss her. A bolt of pure jealousy shot through him. He hadn't known he was capable of feeling such strong emotion about a woman.

After weeks of not seeing Maddy, he thought surely he'd recovered from the brief infatuation he'd had with her. Now he knew the truth. He still cared for her. He wanted to be around her, to get to know her. Couldn't she see Erik wasn't the right man for her? For a brief moment, he thought about crossing the street and interrupting the two of them. When Erik took Maddy's hand, Jason turned his back and walked to the doors of T. L. knowing he couldn't go in and drag her away from Erik like he wanted to.

By the time he reached Jazmyn's office, Jason had all unwanted emotion tamped down tight. No way would he let this ruin his time with his sister. He hadn't seen her much lately, and now he was off on another photo shoot, although this one was closer to home.

"Hey, Jason." Jazmyn's welcoming smile made him glad he'd stopped to see her. She held Caleb to her shoulder, patting his back. "I just finished a feeding session with the linebacker here." She grinned as she held up her son.

"I think he's gained twenty pounds since I last saw him." Jason took his nephew, lifting him over his head. "I have to do this while I still can. I'm not into weight lifting."

"Be careful, he just ate." Jazmyn's bemused expression told Jason he was toying with danger.

Cradling a smiling Caleb in one arm, Jason pulled Jaz close for a hug. He couldn't believe the change in her since she'd met Thor. Health and contentment radiated from her. "Good to see you, sis. Are you treating Thor right?"

Jazmyn arched one eyebrow. "Aren't you supposed to ask it the other way around?"

He chuckled. "I know Thor's too besotted to treat you any other way. I'm worried you'll get too spoiled and I won't be able to stand your company."

Jazmyn snorted her disbelief. "Like living in the mountains most of the time is going to spoil me." She grinned. Jason knew Thor made her stay at their remote cabin as much as possible. He also knew Jazmyn had grown to love their home there as much as she used to love shopping at the mall.

"So, what are you up to?" Jazmyn asked. "Ready to stay home for a while?"

"Me, the travelaholic?" Jason jiggled Caleb as he sat down beside Jazmyn on the couch. "I'm leaving next week for a new assignment."

"Again?" Jazmyn rolled her eyes. "What foreign port are you off to this time? Let me guess." She held up one hand. "In December you went to Canada, so this must be some warm weather place. Tahiti? Cayman Islands?"

"Not even close." Jason grinned. "This place is so remote and unheard of, you'll never guess where. I'll even give you a hint. It's in Arizona."

"Hmm." Jazmyn tapped her finger on her lower lip. Her narrowed eyes studied Jason as if she were trying to decide what he was up to. "It must be some unusual town in Arizona. How about Strawberry? Or Why? Maybe Surprise?"

"Nope, none of those towns." Jason glanced down as Caleb bit down on his finger. "Ouch, he's got teeth now."

"Yep, he's got two. The better to bite you with." Jazmyn laughed. "Okay, let me think of other remote towns in Arizona."

"You'll have to do better. Those are well-known, out-of-the-way places. I'm talking about a place in Arizona no one has heard of."

"Then you have to be talking about Dudleyville." Maddy's saucy voice made Jason jump. Caleb's face crumpled as he startled, too. The baby began to cry.

"I'm sorry." Maddy hurried over. "There are some people who cry when they hear about the town where I grew up, but most of them don't think it's that bad."

Jazmyn laughed. "I'd forgotten about Dudleyville, Maddy. Is that it, Jason?"

"I can't believe I actually know someone from that place." Jason couldn't keep the shock from his tone.

"I didn't mean to interrupt you." Maddy reached down to lift Caleb up. At her touch the crying stopped. Caleb cooed as he stretched up his chubby arms to grab at her dangling earrings. "I just got back and was seeing if you had anything pressing. The office door was open."

"No problem, Maddy. I do have a couple of things for you. Jason was just trying to let me guess where his next job is taking him."

"Well, Maddy guessed it." Jason watched Maddy protect her ears from Caleb.

"Dudleyville?" Jazmyn and Maddy spoke at the same time. They looked at each other and began laughing. Jason didn't know if they were amused at the idea of him taking pictures in Maddy's hometown or that they both spoke together.

"Yep. I'm heading up there for two or three weeks. The Arizona-Sonora Desert Museum has a lot of the animals and plant life I'll be looking for, but I prefer to shoot it in the wild. If I can't find what I need, I'll arrange to do the photos there when I get back."

"You do know Dudleyville doesn't have a motel, don't you?" Maddy's raised eyebrows told him she thought he was crazy to go there.

"So I found out. I can stay in Mammoth or Kearny. They're about the same distance."

"I'm thinking you'd be better off driving from Tucson every day." Maddy rolled her eyes. "It would only take you a little over an hour to get there."

"Yeah, but I'd want to be there before dawn. I've heard the animals I need to shoot are early risers. I don't want to have to leave home at three or four in the morning."

"Hey, I know what you could do." Jazmyn clapped her hands, her eyes glowing. Jason had a feeling he wasn't going to like this at all. When he could see the wheels turning in his sister's head, it usually meant she was trying to mess with his life in some way he didn't want.

"Maddy, I remember you mentioning some good friends of yours who lived close to Dudleyville. Maybe Jason could rent a room from them."

"The Dunhams." Maddy nodded. "Burke and Blaire. I can call them."

"You know what would be even better." Jazmyn leaped up to grab Caleb and twirl him around. "Maddy could take some time off and go with you. That would give her a chance to visit her friends, and she could show you around. She grew up there, so she should know the best spots to get the photos you need."

Jason could feel the color draining from his face as fast as it was from Maddy's.

Chapter 5

As he parked his car in front of the house Madeline shared with her aunt Amelia, Jason put his head against the steering wheel. "Okay, Lord. I'm not quite sure how this happened, but You know. Help me maintain my distance from Maddy as we work together. I know it's a great idea to have her help me, but I don't know how I'll manage to work with her without losing my heart. Give me wisdom here, Lord."

Hearing the slam of a door, Jason looked up to see Maddy lugging a huge suitcase down the walkway. He climbed from the car and hurried to help her. "Hey, you packed enough for both of us. I'm not sure why I brought anything at all."

"It's the forty pairs of shoes." Maddy waved back at the house where her aunt peered out the window. "A girl has to be prepared."

"Forty pairs?" Jason could feel his jaw drop. "How many feet do you have?"

Maddy rolled her eyes as she opened the car door. "I knew you wouldn't understand the necessity." She heaved an exaggerated sigh and plunked down on the seat.

Jason climbed in and fastened his seat belt. He tried to ignore how fresh and breezy Maddy looked with the blond tips on her spiked red hair and the gauzy red scarf around her neck. Her brown eyes with their hint of red sparkled like fire, maybe a reflection of the girl within. He tamped down the longing to find out. They were working together, nothing more.

"Ready to go?" Jason took a deep breath. A light lemony scent filled the car. He almost groaned aloud. How would he manage to be close to her for two weeks? "Want some coffee on the way?"

"That sounds wonderful. The trip will take about ninety minutes. I have to have something to keep me awake so I can tell you how to drive."

"Does that mean you want to ride in the back so you can be a backseat driver?"

"Nope, this will be fine. From up here I can give you hand signals if my mouth is full of coffee." Maddy's smile didn't seem as genuine today. Jason remembered the times he'd been charmed and amused by her wit and humor. This subdued version of her told Jason she wasn't comfortable with their arrangement, either.

He drove in silence to a drive-up window to get their coffee. As they left town, traffic became sparse. Buildings gave way to desert vegetation. Tall saguaros, rotund barrel cacti, prickly pear, yucca, and his least favorite, the cholla cacti, spread across the landscape. With the mountains rising stark and beautiful in the background, Jason had to admit this was one of his favorite spots in the world.

"I thought I heard Jazmyn say you'd lived with your aunt Amelia for a long time. Did she used to live in Dudleyville?" Jason had to do something to break the silence and try to put Maddy at ease. Her grip on her coffee cup threatened to squash the container.

"Yes. I had an unusual home life. I have six younger brothers and sisters." Maddy took a sip of coffee. "After my sophomore year of high school, the rest of my family moved back East. Dad got a better job, so they left. My aunt Amelia took me in. We lived in Dudleyville until three years ago when we moved to Tucson. That's when I got the job at T. L. Enterprises."

"Jazmyn mentioned your friends own a ranch. Not in Dudleyville, but close to there." Jason could see Maddy's shoulders relaxing as she rested against the seat.

"Their ranch isn't a normal one." She shot him a quirky grin.

"How's that?" Jason lifted his coffee to take a sip.

"They raise ostriches." Maddy laughed as Jason sputtered, almost choking on his drink.

"You're kidding, right?"

"Nope." Maddy's earrings swung wildly as she shook her head. "Blaire's uncle left her his ranch in his will. She thought he'd left a cattle ranch and almost died of shock when she found out she'd inherited a bunch of overgrown chickens. That's the way she puts it." Maddy laughed, and Jason wanted to hear her do it more.

"So how did you and Blaire meet? Were they neighbors of yours?"

"No, I was dating Manuel Ortega. He works for Burke and Blaire. When I'd go out to see Manuel, Blaire would come out and talk or invite me in the house. She was from the big city, where I'd always wanted to live. She was still adjusting to country life. We just hit it off."

Jason swallowed hard. Did Maddy still have a thing for this Manuel? Did he work at the ranch now? He wasn't sure how to ask without sounding jealous. He didn't want to give Maddy the wrong idea.

"What does one do on an ostrich ranch?" He shook his head. "I guess I'm wondering what you'd do with ostriches. I get this mental picture of cowboys on horses lassoing tall, skinny-necked birds while the branding iron is getting red-hot in the fire."

Maddy tilted her head back and laughed. "I guess a lot of people might get that picture, but it isn't quite that way. You'll see when we get there." She glanced over at him, her big brown eyes wide. "Did you know a lot of ostriches are raised in Arizona? In fact, Chandler has a special Ostrich Festival every March."

"You're kidding." Jason glanced over, wondering if he could believe her.

"It's true. Look it up on the Net." Maddy held up one hand as if swearing to tell the truth. "They have a marketplace, booths, and everyone's favorite—the ostrich races."

"Ostrich races?" Jason felt like a parrot, but he couldn't hide his disbelief.

"Yep. Burke and Manuel enter every year. I used to go, but I haven't for the last two years because I've been so busy with work." She began to chuckle. "You have to go sometime. The races are hysterical. The ostriches are not horses. They don't want to go where their riders direct them."

"People ride these birds?"

"In a manner of speaking." Maddy laughed again. "They do their best to stay on and guide their ostrich, but they usually end up falling off and have to chase their mount. The races are more for fun than anything."

Jason shook his head. "I don't know whether to believe you or not. This sounds so fantastical that you have to be pulling my leg."

Maddy finished the last of her coffee and placed the cup in the holder. She held both hands up. "See, I'm not touching your leg. This is the absolute truth. If you don't believe me, ask Burke or look it up."

⁓

Parking in the shade of a huge tamarisk tree, Jason and Maddy climbed out of his car. She watched Jason bend back to stretch after the long ride. She studied him as he viewed the ranch for the first time. On one side of the trees, in the middle of a small patch of green lawn, stood a low, rambling adobe ranch house. On the other side were several large pens, each one having various numbers of ostriches of all sizes.

The door of the house burst open. Two young boys raced out followed by a little girl whose chubby legs churned as she tried to keep up. A young woman, her blond hair almost as short as Maddy's, waved as she hurried to keep up with the children.

"Maddy!" Ike and Jed Dunham, Burke and Blaire's twins, reached her first, both leaping at her at the same time. Maddy was propelled backward against the car where the threesome ended up in a giggling wedge of arms and legs.

"'Addy!" Caitlin, the little sprite, her blond curls bouncing as she ran, clapped her hands but didn't throw herself forward.

"I can't believe you're here." Blaire engulfed Maddy and the boys in a huge hug. "It's been so long." They rocked back and forth. Maddy's throat tightened. It had been several months since she'd seen Blaire. She hoped they had time to catch up. Maddy needed to talk, and Blaire had always been a good listener.

Blaire pushed away and turned to Jason. "How rude of me. Maddy, is this your friend, the photographer?" She walked around the car and held out her hand. "I'm Blaire Dunham. Welcome."

Jason smiled and took her hand. "Thank you for having me. You have a beautiful place here."

"Maddy, Maddy, guess what we have." The boys had backed away but pulled at Maddy's hands, urging her toward the house. "We have a kitten."

"No way." Maddy narrowed her eyes, planting her feet and halting their progress. "I know you're trying to fool me."

"No, we do. Daddy built a pen that goes out a window where the ostriches can't see the cat. We even got her tutored so she won't have any babies."

"That's *him* and *neutered*." Blaire snickered. Maddy bit her cheek to keep from doubling up in laughter.

"You really have a cat?" Maddy asked. She looked at Jason, seeing the question in his eyes. "Cats and ostriches don't get along, so they've never been able to have one before."

"Come see." The boys pulled hard on Maddy's arms.

"I'm coming. Let me introduce my friend, and he can come, too." Maddy straightened as the boys eased their grip. "Blaire, you and Jason already met. Jason, these are her two monsters, er, boys, Ike and Jed."

"We're twins." Jed pointed to himself and his brother.

"This is their sister, Caitlin." Maddy gestured at the little waif with her chin. "Caitlin is three, and the twins are two."

"No we're not. We're five." Jed emphasized his point by pulling on Maddy's finger. She grinned.

"Really? Five? No way. You can't be that old."

"We are." Ike nodded as if to prove he was right. "We even got to have a party at the pizza place in Kearny. They had balloons."

"Whoa, it must be so then." Maddy chuckled. "So, show me this kitten; then we'll show Jason the ostriches."

The boys set off at a run, dragging Maddy behind them. She glanced back over her shoulder to see Caitlin look up at Jason, her blue-green eyes wide as she lifted her arms. "Wanna see," she begged.

Jason swung her up and walked beside Blaire toward the house where Maddy and the twins were already disappearing through the door. Maddy could see the surprise on Blaire's face. Caitlin didn't take well to strangers. That she allowed Jason to pick her up would win him points in the friend category.

"See, here's the window." The boys released her hand and raced across the room to an open window. They stood on tiptoe and peered over the casement.

"There she is." Jed pointed outside.

"He." Blaire spoke from behind them.

Maddy flashed her a smile. "What did you name your kitty?"

"Mister." Ike's solemn expression had Maddy biting her lip. "Mister, because she wanted to be a girl, but after the tutoring she can't have babies, so she's like a boy."

From behind her, Maddy heard Blaire groan. Jason drew in a long breath. "That's, um. . .very logical." She could hear the repressed humor in his tone.

"See, Mister can come in through the window, but she can go out and play in the tree and on the ground outside. The wire keeps her from getting around the ostriches. Here, Mister." Jed called out the window to the kitten sprawled in the shade of the tree. He twitched an ear but made no move to come inside.

"Why don't we go out and look at the ostriches?" Maddy straightened. "Maybe when we come back inside, Mister will be ready to come in and meet us."

"Okay. Race you." Jed dropped her hand and took off running. Ike was only a split second behind his brother. Caitlin wiggled in Jason's grasp until he set her on the ground. She followed the twins.

"They look like a handful." Jason's comment had Blaire snorting laughter.

"You have no idea. Why don't you two go on? I've got to check with Isabel and let her know you're here. I'll be right out."

As they stepped outside, Maddy could see the three kids waiting for them at the first pen. Jason headed for the car. "I'm going to grab a camera. I know the ostriches aren't what I came to take pictures of, but I want some anyway."

Maddy waited for him, and they crossed the packed dirt drive together. The wind teased the red scarf she'd put on this morning. She probably should have left it in the car so it wouldn't catch on one of the pens and get torn.

"Hey, you gonna take my picture?" Jed stood tall and posed as they approached. Beside her, Jason chuckled.

"I just might," Jason said. "I wanted to take some pictures of your chickens first. I've never seen such big ones."

Ike and Jed fell to the ground laughing. Caitlin copied them.

"These aren't chickens." Jed jumped to his feet.

"They're birds, aren't they?" Jason asked.

"Yes." Jed nodded.

"They have feathers, two legs, and they lay eggs, don't they?" At the boys' nod, Jason said, "Then they must be chickens."

"No, they're ostriches." Ike rolled his eyes. Jed giggled. "They're like chickens, but they're bigger and bigger."

"I see." Jason winked at Maddy and grinned. She felt a little flutter of attraction, something she'd been trying to avoid.

Two ostriches stalked close to them, peering over the top of the enclosure. Jed and Ike began jumping, trying to reach up and touch the birds.

"Why don't all of you stand together and I'll take your picture with those giant chickens behind you?" Jason backed a few steps away.

Maddy stood close to the pen and picked up Caitlin. The twins stood at her side. Jason lifted his camera and made adjustments. Something tugged on Maddy's scarf. The bit of cloth jerked tight, cutting off her air. She could feel her eyes bulging but couldn't say a word. Between holding Caitlin in one arm and Jed hanging on her other arm, she couldn't move. Jason peered through his camera.

She could be dead before he took the picture.

Chapter 6

Peering at the images through his camera, Jason wanted to laugh at the fake grins on the twins' faces. Those boys were as mischievous as the day was long. Caitlin was gazing over Maddy's shoulder instead of at the camera. Maddy's eyes were huge, her cheeks turning a dark red. Jason frowned. The day was cool. He was glad for his long-sleeved shirt, but he didn't need a jacket. Why would Maddy be so flushed?

He glanced up. White showed around Maddy's brown eyes, giving her a wild look. Caitlin swatted at something over Maddy's shoulder. Maddy's arm jerked where Jed hung onto her. Jason realized Maddy was trying to release her arm. Something was wrong.

As he hurried forward, he could see her scarf tight against her neck. Too tight. Jason raced closer. The boys released Maddy's arm. She reached up to scrabble with her scarf.

"Hey, the ostriches have her." Jed pointed behind Maddy. He stretched up to swat at something. A tall neck popped up. The bird let go of the bit of red and jumped back. Maddy tugged the scarf. She gasped in a deep breath and stumbled forward.

Jason caught her before she fell. He eased Caitlin to the ground then pulled Maddy into his arms. Her color began to improve with each breath she took. Between her shaking and the unshed tears in her eyes, Jason couldn't resist the urge to hold her tight. He loosened the scarf even more, checking for any damage to her neck.

"You okay?" He brushed his hand over her cheek, marveling at how good it felt to hold her like this. Maybe they could shut out the world and stay like this forever. She tilted her head forward, leaning her forehead against his chest. Jason couldn't resist kissing the top of her head. He breathed deeply and knew he'd never forget the feel or the scent of this woman.

"Is she choked to death?" Jed's blunt question brought reality crashing back. Maddy pushed away, her cheeks red again, but this time with a faint blush that made her more beautiful.

"I'm. . ." Maddy cleared her throat. "I'm fine."

"You sound scratchy." Ike stared up at her.

Maddy smiled. "My throat feels a bit scratchy. Maybe we can try this again, but I'll have my scarf around front where the ostriches can't reach it. How's that sound?" Her eyes met Jason's. He could see how important this was to her and knew she didn't want the kids to know she'd been scared.

"Okay, everyone line up again." Jason backed away. He kept a close eye on the huge birds peering over the fence. Their comical faces didn't give a hint of malice, but he wasn't planning to trust them again.

"Hey, Mad Girl."

Jason lowered the camera, glad he'd finished getting the shots he wanted. Maddy's face lit up. She set Caitlin on the ground and raced off, her arms spread wide. "Manuel!" Her cry cut off as the young man in work clothes and boots swept her up and swung her around.

Maddy's delighted laugh sent an arc of jealousy spiraling through Jason. He'd never felt anything like it before. On the way up she'd mentioned being Manuel's girlfriend at one time. He'd hoped that was over. Now he wasn't so sure. Stuffing down emotions he didn't want to feel, Jason tried to convince himself he wasn't interested in her anyway.

"How are Cassie and Sarah?" Maddy took a step back as Manuel set her on the ground, but she didn't pull her hand free of his.

"They're wonderful. You'll have to stop by as soon as you get the chance. Cassie doesn't like to take the baby out in the cold." Manuel shot a glance over his shoulder at a tall, blond man approaching. "I have to tell you Sarah is the prettiest baby ever."

"I think not." The bigger man shoved Manuel aside and pulled Maddy into an embrace. "How's my girl?" He kissed her on the cheek. Jason's jaw began to ache before he realized how tight he'd clenched his teeth.

"Burke." Maddy kissed him, too. "It's been too long. These kids of yours have grown like weeds."

"It's the ostrich feed." Burke grinned. "We were hoping for longer necks on them, but instead I think we're getting longer legs."

"I'll tell Blaire you said that." Maddy laughed and punched him on the arm. "Oh, let me introduce you to Jason."

As the three children surrounded Burke and Manuel, Maddy took Jason's hand and drew him forward. She made introductions, and they all headed for the house.

"What kind of pictures do you want to take, Jason?" Burke carried Caitlin on his shoulders as the boys raced ahead.

"I'm looking for native wildlife. My publisher gave specific instructions for javelina, great blue herons, and, if possible, some of the cat family."

"We have cat." Caitlin gazed down at Jason, her expression solemn.

"Then I'll have to get a picture of your cat." Jason smiled. He didn't want to consider why he was feeling so relieved since finding out neither of these men was interested in Maddy.

"Oh, you'll be turning right where the streetlight is." Maddy gestured at the lamp glowing in the dark. "Are you sure we needed to be out this early? Everyone's asleep. It's too dark to take pictures." She bit her lip to stop the grumbling.

"Not an early riser, I see." Jason's bright grin did nothing to improve her mood. "Now I know why you and Jazmyn are such good friends. You share something in common."

"Smart girl." Maddy took a sip of coffee. "Do you realize how cold it is this morning? Where we're going, down by the river, our breath will come out in icicles."

Jason—the lout!—laughed. "That I have to see. The thermometer at Burke's read thirty degrees this morning. He said it would only be in the low twenties down here. That's not so bad."

Maddy groaned. Their ideas of not bad were polar opposites.

"How deep is the water?" Jason stopped the car at the edge of the river.

"Right now, only a few inches at the deepest." Maddy leaned forward. "The only time you have to worry is when it's been raining a lot. The river can come up pretty fast, and the bottom is just sand, so you can sink. I've known people to lose their car at this crossing."

"Well, that's comforting." Jason shot her a look. Maddy just grinned, figuring it was overdue payback.

"Oh." Maddy gasped as she climbed from the car. Her breath whooshed out in a white cloud. "This is too cold."

"Brisk." Jason winked at her. She drew in a sharp breath and regretted it when her lungs ached from the chilled air. "This is brisk. Canada in December was cold."

"You win." Maddy shook her head. "We're going across the road and down this little back road. Almost no one comes this way, so it should be quiet."

"Where does this lead?" Jason asked.

"To Mammoth." Maddy huffed as she tried to keep up with him. "Most people don't know about this unless they've lived here a long time. When the river is up, you can take this road to get to the bridge at Mammoth. Sometimes it's the only way to cross the San Pedro River."

"When we get back to the car, we can walk down to the crossing. Most mornings you can see herons there. They probably heard your car and disappeared." Maddy wanted to bite her tongue. She couldn't seem to keep quiet around Jason. Ever since he'd caught her in his arms yesterday, she'd been able to think of nothing else. She'd felt the light kiss he'd planted on her head.

Maddy tried to ignore how close she'd come to lifting her face and kissing him. Every part of her longed for that connection. In fact, she longed for more than was decent. That was the problem. After the lifestyle she'd lived before becoming a Christian, she couldn't trust herself to have a relationship again. The hard truth was that she liked being close to a man. Kissing. Touching. She wasn't at all sure she would be able to control those ungodly urges inside her since she'd been so used to doing what she wanted before.

To halt the thinking process, she began to tell Jason about Dudleyville. "There's a cross on the hill right above us." Maddy pointed to the peak on their right. Rocks and cacti were visible in the dim light. "The cross is silver, and when the sun hits it in the early morning, you can see it from a long ways. Sometimes vandals damage the cross, but someone always comes along to fix it up. This is one of the things a lot of people like about Dudleyville. They say it's a reminder that Jesus is always there watching over them. I never understood that until this trip."

She slowed her prattling to glance up. The sun wouldn't be up yet, and from this angle they wouldn't be able to see the cross anyway. "Maybe when we're done I can take you up there. You can see for miles. It's a beautiful view."

"Maddy. Maddy." Jason's touch on her arm caught her attention. She realized he'd been saying her name, and she hadn't paid attention.

"Sorry. What?"

"You'll scare off all the animals." Jason took a step closer. "To photograph shy animals, you have to be quiet. Burke said the javelina could be anywhere along this road. We need to listen for them. Okay?"

"Maybe I don't really want to see any javelina." Maddy glanced around. Dawn was close, so the darkness had given way to dim light. "They chase dogs and will kill them, you know. They have these tusks. You've heard stories about wild pigs."

"First of all, javelina aren't closely related to pigs, although most people think they are." Jason gave her arm a squeeze before releasing her. "They can't see well at all. If you stand still, they won't be able to tell you from a tree."

"Gee, that's comforting." Maddy rolled her eyes.

Jason's low laugh slid inside to warm her. "Don't worry. They aren't very dangerous. I talked with Burke about them. He said on occasion he's gotten pretty close to them. They stomp the ground and snort a lot, but they aren't very aggressive."

"Stomping and snorting would make me run." Maddy fell in step with Jason as they walked down the deserted dirt road. The crisp air had become invigorating. She didn't realize she would enjoy this so much.

The day brightened. The soft crunch of sand under their feet was the only sound in the early morning. Maddy was beginning to wonder if they would see any animals today. Rustling in the brush off the road had Jason holding up his hand for her to stop. She waited to see what would happen.

Jason leaned close, his green eyes holding her gaze. "We'll keep going on the road a little more." His words were so quiet she could barely catch them. "We may have to go through the brush if we don't find anything soon."

Maddy looked at the impenetrable tangle of trees lining the roadway. She did not want to try that. Who knew what was in there?

A long, straight stretch of dirt lined out before them. At the end the road twisted up and around a hill. Maddy bit her lip to keep from talking. This was going against her nature. When she was nervous, she talked. Being this close to Jason made her want to converse.

The short hill was steep. Her leg muscles could feel the pull. She wasn't used to this much hiking. Maddy was just thinking about talking to Jazmyn about her gym when a loud, low bark made her shriek. Chaos erupted. Animals raced in all directions. A huge dark javelina with long tusks stood a few feet from Maddy.

She turned to run. Strong arms grabbed her. Jason jerked her close. His mouth was next to her ear. He whispered something that didn't register. She buried her face in his coat, already imagining the feel of those fierce tusks digging into her legs.

Chapter 7

Hold still." Jason's breath warmed Maddy's temple when he spoke. She fought the desire to nestle closer to him. The feel of his arms around her drove away the fear of attack.

The rustling of underbrush and grunting of startled animals abated. Maddy's heart slowed. She lifted her face from the front of Jason's coat. At the side of the road a huge javelina stared at them, his black beady eyes and wicked-looking tusks frightening yet fascinating. Maddy may have grown up here and seen javelina at a distance, but never this close.

"Maddy, I need you to move." Jason's whisper tickled her ear, reminding her how close they were. She glanced up at him, and her breath caught at the intensity of his green eyes. "I have to take some pictures while he's posing." Jason winked.

"Sorry." Maddy started to take a big step back, glanced at the javelina, and thought better of the move. She eased to the side of Jason farthest from the stationary animal.

Keeping his movements slow and easy, Jason lifted his camera. The peccary snorted and stomped. His whole body tensed as if he was ready to charge. Maddy couldn't help admiring the resolute attitude of this male who was so determined to protect his family who'd disappeared into the undergrowth.

The faint click of the camera had the javelina stomping and snorting again. He still didn't approach, but Maddy couldn't help wondering if he would. She recalled what Jason said about their eyesight being poor and made sure she didn't move. There were worse things than to be thought of as a tree.

"Let's try going on up the hill."

"Wait." Maddy grabbed Jason's arm before he could move. "What if he charges us?"

"I don't think he will as long as we don't threaten him. His herd has disappeared, so they're safe. He's just keeping an eye on us." Jason still held his camera but gave her arm a reassuring squeeze with his free hand. "I want to see if he'll rejoin his family group. Then maybe we can follow and get pictures of them."

"Follow quietly in all this undergrowth?" Maddy's eyebrows shot up as she gave Jason a skeptical look. "I don't know how that's possible."

"Maybe their hearing is as bad as their eyesight." Jason's grin set her heart racing again. "Maybe they'll think we sound like trees as well as look like them."

PICTURE THIS

"I think this is the first time I've ever been compared to a tree." Maddy gave an exaggerated sigh. "At least I hope I don't look like some huge old redwood."

"Don't worry." Jason's eyes twinkled. "Only someone with the very poorest eyesight would mistake you for timber of any sort."

Heat burned Maddy's cheeks. Part of her wanted to explore Jason's comment, but the wiser part knew better. For once she managed to hold her tongue.

Jason was right. The javelina swiveled in place to watch them as they moved in slow, nonthreatening steps up the hill. As they passed close to him, Maddy noted the dark, bristly hairs that covered his body. Around his throat were bands of lighter colored bristles. She remembered something about them being called collared peccary. This must be the trait that gave them the name.

"Do you see skunks?" Jason asked. He glanced around.

"It's the javelina," Maddy said. "They have this gland and give off an odor similar to skunks. I've heard their scent is stronger when they are afraid."

"Ah, I seem to recall thinking I smelled a skunk just before this fellow barked at us. Amazing how much he sounded like a dog."

"I've never startled one before." Maddy kept her tight hold on Jason's arm as they moved away from the staring animal. "He did sound just like a big dog giving a warning."

They circled the hill, going out of sight of the peccary. Jason halted in the shade and lifted his camera. "Hold on. I want to check the pictures and see how they turned out."

Maddy peered over his shoulder. He'd taken some full body shots and some close-ups of the big male. "He didn't smile." She felt rather than heard Jason's chuckle at her comment. Maddy backed up a step. She hadn't realized how close she'd been standing.

"Some of these are really good. I wonder if we can convince him to gather the family so I can get a group photo."

"Maybe if you offer a special group rate with an enlargement they can hang on a tree somewhere."

Jason grinned. "Nah. I'll just offer them a signed copy of the book. They can carry it with them and show everyone they're celebrities."

Maddy laughed. "That should do it."

"Let's go back down now. If he's gone, we'll try to find a spot to head into the brush and follow him." Jason grasped her hand as they turned. He glanced down. "Hey, your hands are like ice."

"That's what happens when you're out in below zero weather without gloves." Maddy couldn't help her dry tone or the exaggeration.

"It is not below zero. This is southern Arizona."

Maddy sniffed, trying for a haughty demeanor. "That depends on whether you're looking at a Fahrenheit or Celsius thermometer."

Jason's head tilted back as he laughed. "You've got me there. Come on, Miss Dying-of-the-Cold. Let's follow some beasties and warm up."

When they rounded the corner, Jason noted the male javelina had disappeared into the underbrush. He hesitated over taking Maddy with him through the dense vegetation. He'd done it himself hundreds of times to get the photos he needed, but dragging a female along reminded him too much of the first time he'd taken Jazmyn to the mountains.

"Look, if you want, you can wait here on the road or head back to the car. I can follow the peccary herd and see if I can get what I need."

"No way are you leaving me." Maddy's eyes narrowed as she stared at him. "It's barely daylight. I don't intend to walk down this deserted road by myself. Who knows what other animals might be here."

"Maybe I should take you back to Blaire's." Jason did not want to do that but had to offer.

"No." Maddy put her hands on her hips. Her chin jutted forward. "You would miss this chance to find the javelina. Jason, I grew up here. I can take wading through some brush."

He studied her for a moment before nodding. "Okay, let's look for the best place to follow them. We'll have to be quiet."

Leading the way to the spot where the male had been standing, Jason noted the prickly pear cactus with its chewed pads. The animals must have been eating breakfast. He almost shuddered at the thought of chewing on something with so many stickers. They must have tough mouths to be able to do that.

"Let's go down here." Jason indicated a faint trail. Dried leaves made it impossible for them to walk without making noise. Jason could picture the herd laughing as they kept well ahead of the people.

"This isn't working." Jason huffed out a long breath. "We'll never find them at this rate. Why don't we head back to the road? We can find some place to sit down and have those breakfast burritos and some of the coffee Blaire sent."

Maddy's stomach rumbled. She grimaced. "Uh, sounds like a plan to me. I could eat one of those javelina right about now."

Jason laughed. "You would eat something that smells like skunk?"

Maddy flashed him a grin. "You do know that hunting season for javelina starts in a few weeks, don't you? A lot of people around here like to hunt them and eat them."

"Really?" Jason held some branches aside so Maddy could step back onto the road. He led the way to a few boulders and shrugged out of the backpack to get to the food. "Doesn't the meat taste funny with such a strong scent gland?"

"I've heard it's all in how they're dressed and cooked. Some friends of mine used to have javelina barbecues every year. The meat is pretty good."

"You have amazing friends. Some eat ostriches. Some eat peccary. What's next? Lizard and cactus stew?" Jason took a bite of his burrito.

"Hmm. I'll have to suggest that to Blaire for supper tonight. After all, the boys caught that lizard yesterday." She grinned as Jason made a face.

"Why don't we head back toward the car?" Jason balled up the wrapper from his burrito and drained the last of his coffee. "I'd like to walk down to the river and see if we can find some great blue herons. Maybe they'll be doing a bit of early morning fishing."

"Sounds good." Maddy stood up and brushed off her pants. "You know, the next time I'd like chairs that have been warmed first. These rocks know how to hold in the cold." She shivered.

"I'll remember that." Jason thought about taking her hand again. He'd enjoyed the closeness they shared this morning, but he didn't want to encourage anything further. It would be too easy to desire a relationship with Maddy. With his job and the amount of traveling he did, he couldn't afford to become serious about any woman. Perhaps someday he'd settle for a photography job that didn't require his being gone for months, but not yet.

As they rounded the next curve and started down the hill, Jason grabbed Maddy's arm, pulling her to a halt. When she glanced up at him, he nodded at the road in front of them. The big javelina stood in the middle of the track with two of the others close to him.

Jason crouched down, tugging Maddy down with him. He leaned close. "I think I can get some good shots from right here." He spoke softly but could see that she heard him. "I don't want to spook them and lose this opportunity."

He sighted in with the zoom feature and began to take pictures. The peccaries glanced back over their shoulders into the brush behind them. The undergrowth rustled and two juvenile javelinas stepped out. They trotted across the open area, and Jason got a few shots of them, knowing the brownish-gray bristly animals would show up better against the lighter dirt road than in the brush.

The peccaries had all moved to the far side of the road. Jason couldn't see them well enough to get any more pictures. He adjusted the camera so he could see what he'd gotten when he heard Maddy's sharply indrawn breath. He glanced over at her. Her lips were parted. Her eyes were shining as she gazed at the road. When he turned to see the cause of her entranced look, he saw a mother peccary who had just stepped onto the roadway. Two tiny javelinas hovered at her side. Their bristles were a dull orange-red, not the gray or brown of the older peccaries. Jason figured he could cup one of them in the palm of his hand.

"Pictures." Maddy's reminder brought him out of his trance. He whipped up his camera, adjusted the settings, and began shooting. These were pictures worthy of a book cover. His legs began to ache from the crouched stance before the mama and her babies disappeared from sight. He breathed out, not realizing until then that he'd been holding his breath most of the time.

"I've never seen anything like that." Maddy's whisper held a note of awe. "They were adorable." She joined him in standing erect.

Jason turned to make a comment. Maddy's luminous eyes were huge. He couldn't seem to look away. They shared a moment that would connect them forever, something they wouldn't share with anyone else. He could feel more than that. This was the connection that had been between them from the moment they met.

Her eyelids drifted half shut as he leaned close. Jason knew he shouldn't do this, but he couldn't seem to stop. He cupped her cheek. His lips brushed hers, and their sighs intermingled. He kissed her again, his thumb caressing the curve of her jaw.

Maddy leaned into him. Her arms wrapped around his neck. He felt the camera between them. Maddy must have felt it, too. She jerked back, pushing at him with her palms.

"Jason, stop." She jumped away. Her wide eyes spoke of panic. "We can't do this. We have to talk."

Chapter 8

Maddy took off running toward the car. Startled javelinas scattered into the brush. "Maddy, don't run!" Jason saw the lead boar stamp his foot. Maddy skidded to a halt. The javelina took a few stiff steps toward her, huffing his displeasure. Maddy stood frozen as Jason stopped beside her.

"You're okay." He kept his voice low, hoping to pacify both Maddy and the angered peccary. "Let's start walking. As we move away, he'll calm down." Jason started to take Maddy's arm when he remembered her reaction to his touch a moment ago. He didn't know what had gone wrong, but he didn't want to upset her further.

Within a few steps, Jason glanced back to see the boar disappearing over the hill like the rest of his herd. "They're gone. Are you okay?"

Maddy sniffed. She nodded her head but didn't look at him.

"Hey, I'm sorry. I didn't know my kisses were so objectionable." Jason leaned forward to try to see Maddy's face as she sniffed again.

She stopped and faced him. Her eyes were reddened. She swiped a tear from her cheek. "Look, Jason. This isn't going to work. I'm sorry." Maddy looked away, as if seeing his confusion was more than she could bear.

"What isn't going to work?"

"Us. Me." Maddy swung her arm in a wide arc. "All of this. I can't show you around anymore." She met his gaze again, hers full of so much misery he wanted to pull her into an embrace and never let her go.

"I didn't mean to upset you, Maddy. I won't do it again." Jason fought from turning his uncertainty into anger. "I thought you wanted the kiss as much as I did."

"I did. I don't." Maddy's full lower lip trembled. "I have my reasons, okay. I can't talk about it right now, but I just can't have any sort of a relationship. It won't work."

Jason shoved his hands in his pockets. He counted to ten. "Okay, you're right. I like you a lot, Maddy. I enjoy being with you, but I can't afford to have any sort of relationship, either. Since we agree on that, maybe we can still work together. We'll just keep our distance, so to speak. Will that work?" He could see the indecision in her eyes. Jason grinned and winked. "We can be like a lot of the schools and have an inch rule."

"Inch rule?" Maddy's eyebrows shot up.

"You know, you can't get within so many inches of someone of the opposite sex."

Laughter bubbled out of Maddy. She hiccuped. Her hand flew up to cover her mouth. Her cheeks reddened. Jason couldn't stop a laugh.

"Okay." Maddy started walking toward the car again. "But I think we should have a two-foot rule. We can't get within two feet of each other. Agreed?"

"Sounds fine to me." Jason waited a beat. "I can have Burke measure off a stick two feet long. We can take it everywhere we go so we aren't tempted to get too close."

"I'll carry it. That way if you get too near, I can use the stick on you." Maddy gave him a wary look.

Jason chuckled. "Only if you tell me why we have to do this."

The flush on Maddy's cheeks paled. She faced forward and her gait sped up. She didn't say any more on the way to the car.

The next two days were spent at home with Blaire and the kids. Burke told them this winter was wetter than any they'd had in some time, but Jason wanted to grumble at the overcast skies and rain that kept them inside. They did have a lot of laughs with the twins playing games. Those boys could find more ways to win. More than once he'd had to refrain from joining in a tickle session with the kids and Maddy. He'd ached to have a reason to touch her, but he kept his distance. He could feel the magnetic pull toward Maddy growing stronger. He just hoped he had the strength to stay away.

⁂

"Hey, sleepy, time's wasting." Jason's grin made Maddy want to turn right around and go back to bed. She knew her disheveled appearance must be amusing, but right now she didn't feel like laughing about anything.

"Why did you wake me up? I thought maybe we were in the middle of some disaster when you banged on my door."

"It will be a disaster if you don't get ready to go. The sky is clear. We have to get going to get some good shots. We're behind schedule." Jason's perkiness wrenched a groan from her.

"If the weather cleared last night, it will be colder than usual. I have to have coffee before we go." She rubbed her hands over her face trying to wake up. She hadn't slept well the past few nights.

On the drive to the back road, Jason inhaled deeply. "I love the smell of the Sonoran Desert after a rain. There isn't anyplace else that smells as good as this."

"You would know. From what Jazmyn says, you've been everywhere in the world." Maddy could feel her brain waking up. "You should do a book—*Where in the World Is Jason?* It might be a best seller."

"Hey, I'll put the idea to my publisher." Jason's grin faded as he stopped at the river. "Are we okay to go across?"

"Burke said we should be fine if the river isn't too high. If it comes up more while we're over there, we'll just go around to the bridge at Mammoth to get home."

"Sounds good." Jason eased forward.

The water was deeper than usual but not too high. "Besides, it's not raining north of us."

"That doesn't matter." Maddy gestured toward the south. "The San Pedro is one of the rivers in the United States that flows north. The water here comes from Mexico. The San Pedro flows north to Winkelman, where it converges with the Gila River. From there the river travels mostly west to Florence." She knew they could both note the dark clouds toward Tucson that might mean the river would rise even more.

The early hour combined with the end of the rain brought out more animals than Jason or Maddy expected. He got some shots of a coyote just as the light was getting strong enough. They saw the herd of javelinas again, plus some deer.

"What's that?" Maddy started to reach for Jason's arm before she pulled back, remembering their new rule. The loud squeal in the dense undergrowth between them and the river had her heart pounding.

"Some animal is in distress." Jason continued walking. "We'll be fine. Whatever it is, I'm sure it doesn't want to bother us. Why don't we walk down to the river and see if the herons are there?"

Maddy trudged beside him, her hands safe inside her jacket pockets. She didn't want to let Jason know how much this self-imposed restriction of hers was costing. Every day she could recall the feel of his larger hand wrapped around hers. He comforted her, and she longed for that feeling again.

O God, please help this to be over quickly. You know I can't allow any man to get close to me.

Last night she'd stayed up talking with Blaire after everyone else had gone to bed. For the first time, she'd confided in someone about her doubts and fears. Blaire had tried to assure Maddy that she had no reason to fear a relationship, but Maddy knew better. None of her friends knew the complete reason she avoided men now. She didn't intend to tell them, either.

By the time they reached the car, a light mist had started. "Will you still be able to take pictures if it's raining?" Maddy asked.

"As long as it doesn't come down too hard. This isn't bad." Jason started down the hill leading to the crossing. Maddy fell in step beside him. She didn't mind the moisture. In southern Arizona rain came so seldom she'd always enjoyed walking in the rain.

The river wasn't the usual quiet murmur. As they drew closer, they could hear the muted roar of the water. Rounding the bend, Maddy halted in amazement. Since they'd crossed this morning, the river had risen several inches. The water rushing past them was muddy and filled with sticks and debris.

"Looks like you're right about the rain to the south." Jason's brow knit in a frown. "Good thing I've got an SUV. The higher clearance should get us across."

"You're not thinking of trying to ford here, are you?" Maddy stared at him in amazement.

"Why not?" Jason's grin didn't quite reach his eyes. "I've gone through mountain streams this fast."

"But they have rocks underneath. This is sand. It will wash out from under you." Maddy could feel her anger and dismay growing. Jazmyn often talked about the chances Jason liked to take. "We can take the back road to Mammoth and cross there. It's a little rougher and longer, but better than losing your car in the river."

"You're as bad as my sister." Jason turned around and headed toward the car. "Living dangerously is what makes life fun."

"I am not driving across there with you." Maddy wanted to stamp her foot.

"How far is it to Mammoth from here?" Jason asked.

"Probably about fifteen miles on the back road." Maddy opened her door and climbed inside the car out of the increasing rain.

Jason clambered in and slammed his door. "That will be a long walk if you don't go with me then. You might get a little wet."

"You wouldn't." Maddy's mouth fell open. She couldn't believe his audacity. "Jason, do you realize the number of people who drown every year in Arizona because they try to cross rivers or washes that aren't safe? I don't know about you but I don't want to become a statistic."

"Maddy, I've spent a lot of time in the wild. I know what I'm doing." Jason steered the vehicle toward the crossing. He stopped to study the rushing water in front of them. Maddy started to breathe a sigh of relief. He would see the stupidity of trying this and turn around.

The engine revved. Jason put the vehicle in gear and eased forward. "Jason no." Maddy could hear the note of hysteria and panic in her voice. Jason didn't even glance at her. His full concentration was on the river in front of him.

Maddy held her breath, too frightened to pray. She could imagine the tires losing their grip as the sand washed out from beneath them. They eased into the mainstream. The water pounded against the car. The carpet on the floor turned dark as moisture seeped in under the door. Maddy heard a thunk and glanced through the window to see a large branch working its way around the SUV to continue on downstream.

"See, we're going to be fine." Jason wiggled his eyebrows at her. The ca jerked. Jason fought the steering wheel. The water rose higher on the vehicle. The back end eased around to the side, and they swept off the road into the river.

"Jason." Maddy stared at him, terrified. They were going to drown. She knew it.

"Maddy." Jason took her chin in his fingers. "We'll be fine. Why don't you call Burke and have him bring that big truck of his to pull us out. I'll climb out the window and see how bad it is and if we can get to the bank."

Maddy's fingers shook so badly she had trouble hitting the right buttons. God must have heard the prayers she hadn't been able to voice. Burke answered on the first ring. He and Manuel would be there in a few minutes.

Jason eased out the window. Maddy watched with mounting horror as he inched along the side of the vehicle. The water was over the bumper now. She shook at the thought that he might lose his footing and be swept away. Moving over behind the steering wheel, Maddy leaned out to tell him to come back inside until Burke and Manuel arrived.

Before she could say a word, her worst fears happened. Jason's boot slipped. He grappled for a hold. His fingers couldn't grasp the slippery surface, and he shot down the side of the vehicle. The river caught his legs with greedy hands.

Maddy cried out. She lunged and grabbed. One of Jason's arms wrapped around hers. She pulled. The river pulled, too. Bracing her feet against the door, Maddy closed her eyes and fought for Jason's life. His other hand came up to clutch the edge of the window.

With an unexpected lunge, he was inside. Maddy fell back. Jason toppled onto her. His hair was plastered to his head. His clothes were soaked and getting her wet. She'd never felt so good.

He grinned, his eyes sparkling. "I think we may be breaking your two-foot rule."

Chapter 9

"You are incorrigible." Maddy wanted to toss Jason back into the river and hug him at the same time.

"I'll bet Jazmyn told you that." Jason wedged his hand on the steering wheel and began to lift himself off her. "You can't believe everything a sister tells you about her brother. I can't possibly be that bad."

"That's for sure." Maddy glared at him, wanting him to believe she was mad. "Although I'm beginning to think Jazmyn was more right than wrong."

Jason chuckled as he gazed down at her. He started to release his hold on the steering wheel and ease back down. "In that case, maybe I'll have to do something to live up to my horrible reputation." His gaze lowered to her mouth as he drew closer.

"Don't you dare." Maddy pushed at his chest. "Get off me now. We have to get out of here."

Laughing, Jason levered himself up. Maddy wiggled out from under him, pinching her leg against the steering wheel, and managed to get back on the passenger side.

"Jason, we have to get out of here. The river is even higher."

"I know." Jason reached over into the backseat. He grabbed his camera bag. "Here, put my camera in this. I don't want it ruined from the water." He handed her a waterproof pouch. "Then put the bag across your back and shoulder. I'd carry it, but I'll need my hands free when Burke and Manuel get here."

Maddy's hands shook as she followed Jason's instructions. She didn't want to think of all the horror stories she'd heard through the years about people drowning when they were caught in flash floods, but the accounts kept spiraling through her thoughts.

"Here they are." Jason lifted himself up to the window ledge and out onto the hood of the vehicle. He waved at Burke and Manuel as they climbed from their truck. Burke was shouting something, but Maddy couldn't hear over the rush of the water and her own pounding heart.

She could see Burke tying something. He and Manuel leaned close together. Burke twirled a rope with something on the end and tossed it toward Jason. Jason stretched up to catch, but the throw fell short. Maddy held her breath, praying Jason wouldn't fall off into the river.

The second toss proved more effective. Jason caught the rope. Maddy watched as he pulled over a chain with a hook on the end of it. Burke shouted more instructions. Jason untied the rope and worked his way back to the window.

"Maddy, can you tie this to the steering wheel post?" Jason held out one frayed end to her. "I'm going to have to go under and fasten the hook to the undercarriage. I'll need something to ground me in case I lose my grip." He grinned. "I don't want to take the fast route to Florence."

"Jason, that's crazy. You can't go down in that water. You'll drown." Panic stole Maddy's breath.

"Such confidence." Jason covered his heart in a dramatic gesture. "You wound me." He leaned closer. "I don't suppose you'd give me a kiss. Just to sustain me." He winked. Maddy sputtered, at a loss for words. Jason's eyes spoke only of merriment, not fear, as he backed out and began to tie the other end of the rope around his waist. She hoped he knew how to tie a knot that wouldn't come undone in the fierce pull of the river.

With a firm hold on the grabhook attached to the chain and with the rope tying him to the SUV, Jason lowered himself over the front into the raging water. His gaze didn't leave Maddy's as he disappeared. She wanted to smile, to be an encouragement as he went under, but fear stole all thoughts of hope. Clinging to the end of the rope tied to the steering post, Maddy could only pray, "Please, Lord, please."

On the bank, she could see Burke and Manuel, their heads close together as they conferred. They didn't look happy about the situation, either. They stood at the very edge of the water, the toes of their boots almost immersed. Maddy thought the two of them wanted to be there helping Jason. From what she knew of Burke and Manuel, they were both used to doing, not waiting for someone else to do the hard job.

The rope across the hood drew taut. Jason seemed to have been under for hours, but Maddy knew that couldn't be right. She tried to sense him through the end of the tie she held, but she couldn't. "Please, Lord." Maddy knew God had to hear her whispered words, even over the roar of the river.

A loud crack made Maddy jerk her head up. The rope leading from the steering post over the hood of the car had snapped taut, but in the wrong direction. It was now leading out the driver's window and downstream. Maddy couldn't breathe. From the corner of her eye, she could see Burke and Manuel both moving downstream. She glanced over to see fear etched in their features.

"Jason." Maddy scooted over to the driver's seat again. She put her hand on the rope and tugged. Nothing happened. "Oh, God, please." Jason had to come up for air. He'd been under too long. Was he already dead and that was why he was swept downstream?

Reaching out the window, Maddy grasped the rope closer to the water. She pulled, allowing herself to fall backward so her weight would be added to her strength. A few inches came out of the water. She pushed with her legs. A few more inches. She refused to give up. Jason's life was at stake here.

She didn't know how long she kept pulling. The rope in her hands was waterlogged now. She knew there was no way Jason had survived, but she had to get him to safety anyway. Tears traced down her cheeks from her closed eyes.

"Maddy. Maddy." Jason's voice sounded so close. "You're going to cut me in half if you don't ease up on the rope."

Maddy's eyes flew open. Jason, bedraggled, with enough debris in his hair that he could pose as a monster, leaned in through the window.

꩜

"Jason." Maddy released the rope as she surged up and toward him. Jason almost lost his hold on the frame of the SUV. He hooked one hand around the steering wheel to keep from falling back in the water.

The fear of almost drowning had been chased away when he saw the look in Maddy's eyes. She wouldn't admit it, but she did care for him. He'd seen the tears, the struggle she'd been going through when she thought he was dead.

Now, with her arms around his neck and her warm kiss on his cheek, he thought life couldn't get much better. If he were to get serious with any woman, this would be the one. She was just about perfect.

"You might want to let me in so Burke and Manuel can pull us out." Jason couldn't resist getting in a quick return kiss on Maddy's cheek before she backed off. Her eyes sparked with fire as she moved over to the passenger side.

"How dare you do that to me, Jason Rondell."

"Huh? Do what?" Jason halted halfway in the window and stared at the riled woman who had been kissing him a moment earlier.

"Scaring me like that. You had no right. If you'd listened to me, we wouldn't be in danger in the middle of the San Pedro. We both could have drowned." Tears sparkled in Maddy's eyes. Jason knew she was on the verge of a crying jag. He'd seen the signs often enough in his sister.

He finished climbing inside and waved to Burke and Manuel to pull them out before he turned to her. "Hey, beautiful. How else was I supposed to get you to break the two-foot rule twice in one day?"

"You. . .are. . .awful." Maddy faced forward, her arms crossed over her chest, chin jutted out. She was so beautiful. Jason turned to watch the winch turn as they were eased from the grasp of the water. Maybe Maddy had a point about staying away from one another. The more time he spent with her, the more he wanted.

"We're going to have to tow you back to the ranch." Burke slapped his hand on the side of Jason's SUV. "There's no way you can drive this now. We'll get you back, let everything dry out, and do some work on it. You should have it up and running in another day or two."

"Hey, Mad Girl. If I'd known this was a swimming party, I'd have wanted to come along." Manuel's jibe met a stony glare.

"Manuel, don't you start in on me. It wasn't my idea to try to be macho and drive through the river." She still refused to look at Jason.

Manuel grinned and winked at Jason. "Hey, you need a warm jacket. You're wet, and the temperature is subzero in that car."

"That might be nice." Jason began to struggle with his wet jacket. "Even if I could turn on the heater, I'm not sure it would overcome this chill."

Glancing outside, Jason asked, "Hey, do you think I could get some pictures before we go? This might be good to include. I can show the readers how the river looks in flood stage and normally."

"I've seen times this crossing is dry for months on end." Burke adjusted his hat. A trickle of rain dripped off the edge. "Hard to believe when you look at this torrent."

By the time Jason finished getting the photos he wanted, Maddy had disappeared and Manuel was waiting in the SUV.

"Hey, I hope you don't mind this." Manuel waited until Jason had stowed the camera.

"No problem." A twinge of guilt rippled through Jason. That was almost a lie. He wanted to spend the time with Maddy and maybe get her past being upset with him.

Once they were on the highway, the ride was smooth. Jason kept a close eye on the truck pulling them. "So, Maddy says you two used to date."

"Yeah, she and I were pretty close at one time." Manuel rapped his knuckles on the window. "I can see she's really taken with you. She's pretty special. I hope you realize that."

"I know." Jason glanced over to see Manuel watching him. "If you still care so much, why aren't you together?"

Manuel shrugged. "She moved away with her aunt. We tried to see each other still but finally realized we were better friends than anything else. Maddy's the one who introduced me to Cassie, my wife. Maddy is like a sister to me."

They were quiet for a few minutes. Manuel cleared his throat. "I don't want to say too much, but I will tell you Maddy had a rough time growing up. She moved in with her aunt when her family left here. They didn't care so much what happened to her. Her aunt is okay, but she doesn't care so much about Maddy, either."

Jason could feel the weight of Manuel's gaze. He wondered what point the man was getting to.

"Not long after Maddy moved away, I became a Christian. I've been praying a long time for Maddy. So have Burke and Blaire and my mom. She's special, and we would love to see her find someone to love her like she needs to be loved."

"If you think I'm the one, you're mistaken." Jason frowned as he watched Burke put on his turn signal for the driveway leading to the ranch. "I like Maddy. A lot. But with my job, I can't become involved. It won't work out."

Manuel's jaw tightened. Jason thought the man was struggling with what to say. "Then don't trifle with her." Manuel's gaze bored into Jason. "She's had too much heartache. Don't add to it."

Jason didn't reply. He couldn't. The picture of Maddy's fear turning to joy as she saw him in the window after thinking he'd drowned came to mind. The feel of her in his arms. The sweet kiss they'd shared before she pushed him away. Her feistiness and the fun of their verbal sparring.

He wasn't sure he could make any promises to Manuel. No matter how much Jason insisted he wasn't the one for Maddy, he couldn't help wishing something would work out between them. He didn't have any idea how he would be able to turn his back on her when this assignment was over.

Chapter 10

I saw that." Burke's eyebrows drew together. The twins exchanged glances as if wondering if their father could possibly be talking to them. Jason bit back a grin. Those boys were such a handful, maybe more like a roomful.

"I saw you flip those peas at your sister." Burke continued to glare as the twins' innocent expressions took on a shadow of guilt. "There will be no more throwing food. Understand?"

"But, Dad, she likes it." Jed pointed at his sister, who was shoving one of the green missiles into her mouth. "It's a game we play."

"Mealtime isn't the place for games. This can get out of hand and make a lot more work for you."

Jason could see everyone struggling not to laugh. Maddy began to cough and picked up her water glass, pretending to take a drink.

"For us?" Ike glanced around.

"Yes, for you." Burke continued to glower, although Jason thought he was having trouble keeping up the facade. "If there are peas all over the floor, you will not only clean them up after supper, you will have to mop the floor, too."

Jed's mouth dropped open. "Mop the floor? That's Mom's job."

"Not if the mess is an intentional one that you make." Burke's mouth twitched. "Besides, there's nothing stating that guys can't mop a floor. I've done it sometimes."

Blaire snorted. Burke shot her a glance. Maddy hiccuped. She pressed the glass to her mouth.

"You got peas all over the floor?" Ike's tone held a note of awe. "Were you throwing them at Mom?"

"I did not get peas all over the floor or throw them at your mother. I'm just saying there isn't a job that's for only one person. We all live here; we share in the work." Burke set his fork down by his plate. "Now, if you two are through, perhaps you can go out and play. We're going to start some boring conversation in here."

The scrape of chairs followed as the twins raced each other from the room. Blaire lifted Caitlin from her high chair so she could leave, too.

When they were gone, Blaire turned to Burke, a sweet smile on her face, her voice coated with sugar. "You've mopped the floor?"

"Don't give me a hard time. I was trying to teach them a lesson." He picked up a pea and flicked it at Blaire, hitting her on the nose.

"I'm telling." Maddy threw down her napkin. "I have witnesses to what you just did, and I'm telling the boys."

"You don't have a thing." Burke turned to Jason. "Did you see anything?"

"See what?" Jason widened his eyes and blinked, his imitation of Jazmyn when she was trying to act innocent. Blaire and Maddy both began to laugh. Jason and Burke joined them. "I'm thinking if I had those twins, I'd be locked up in the loony bin by now. They have more schemes than any kids I remember."

"They just keep life interesting." Blaire smiled at Burke. Regret stabbed through Jason. He wanted to have a relationship like that. One where they could speak just by exchanging a glance.

"I wanted to ask." Burke turned to look at Jason. "Are you limited to Dudleyville in your book or can you include the surrounding area?"

"What did you have in mind?"

"I was thinking Maddy could take you to the petroglyphs. They're off the beaten track. Most people around here don't even know about them."

"Burke, I don't know how to get there." Maddy folded her napkin into halves and pressed the crease with her finger. "Maybe you could take Jason."

"I would, but I can't take the time off. I'll give you directions. I know you've been out in the hills around here enough times that you should be able to find them with no problem." Burke reached behind him into a drawer and pulled out a sheet of paper and pencil. "Here, I'll draw a little map."

Burke glanced over at Jason. "There are also a few ghost towns in the area if you're interested."

Jason shook his head. "A lot of books have dealt with ghost towns. The petroglyphs sound interesting, though. They're more unusual." Jason watched as Burke sketched a crude map to the place. He thought he'd be able to follow the directions to the cliffs where the old Indian drawings were without Maddy, but he didn't want to try. For some reason the idea of going without her left him empty. Although he knew they could never have a relationship, he couldn't help wanting to be around her as much as possible for this short time.

"How long does it take to get there?" Jason asked.

"Well, the roads aren't the best." Burke rubbed his jaw. Blaire snorted again. This time Burke winked at her. "I'd say it might take an hour or two depending on whether you get lost or have to take any detours."

"Have you ever been on any of these roads?" Jason turned to Maddy.

She leaned over to study the map. "I've at least been part way. I've gone out in the hills around here quite a bit with Manuel years ago." Her face flushed, and she didn't look at Jason.

"By bad roads are we talking worse than the road leading up to Thor's place in the mountains?" Jason raised one eyebrow as Maddy finally glanced up at him.

"Do you mean now or before he fixed up the road when he and Jazmyn moved up there?" Maddy asked.

Jason shook his head. "I feel like I'm getting the runaround here. I don't care which it is; just give me an idea."

"Part of the road is like any dirt road." Maddy tilted her head to one side and stared off into the distance. A strand of hair fell across her creamy cheek, the tip brushing the corner of her generous mouth. Jason's breath hitched. He longed to brush the lock away.

"There are places that make Thor's road look good, even before he fixed it up." Maddy met his gaze and grinned. "It's a challenge and a lot of fun. Are you up for it?"

$\mathscr{D}$

"I think we're going to have to go back and find a way around this." Jason leaned forward, peering through the dirt-smeared windshield.

Maddy knew she couldn't laugh. From what Jazmyn said, even when they were camping in the mountains, Jason did his best to keep his SUV clean. She said on their way home they always had to stop and go through a car wash. Jason wouldn't park his vehicle at his house if it was covered in mud or dust. Right now, mud coated the lower half of the car and spattered the rest.

"I went up Thor's road before he had it worked on. He had a washed-out place almost this bad," she said. Maddy didn't add that Jazmyn told her about the time Jason had frightened her almost to death when he went around the spot. She'd been sure they would end up rolling down the mountain. Maddy had spent enough time on back roads that she knew better.

"The operative word being 'almost.' I think we should back up." Jason's green gaze turned to Maddy. She swallowed hard. *Maintain distance*, she thought.

"You are such a city slicker." Maddy gave him a saucy look, hoping he didn't see her true feelings. She threw open her door, turning to slip out as she watched for Jason's reaction. "Out here, we just throw in a few rocks to fix the washout and drive over it."

"Wait." Jason lunged across the seat to grab her arm as she started to step out. "Look." He nodded outside the car.

The first step would have lasted for about fifty feet. From there the slope was more gradual but still would have a person tumbling end over end. She swallowed hard. She knew better than to hop out without looking first. If only Jason didn't make her lose her train of thought all the time with that hypnotic grin of his.

She glanced over at the object of her thoughts and wrinkled her nose. "I've decided to get out your side instead of mine. Move it, city slicker. I'll show you how we do things here in the sticks." Maddy hopped out, crossed to the slope, and picked up a fair-sized rock. She carried it to the place where the road needed repair. Glancing at Jason, she raised one eyebrow, waiting for him to get the idea.

"There." Jason moved the last of the rocks into place. Sweat beaded on his brow despite the cool, overcast day. "That should do it. I think we can drive across."

Maddy wanted to laugh. The place had been filled in enough twenty minutes earlier, but Jason insisted on building it up more. She couldn't help wondering why he was being so careful. She would have to tell Jazmyn about this when they got back to town. Tossing a smaller rock into the crevice at the edge of the road, Maddy took back that thought. She refused to give Jazmyn any ammunition toward furthering a romance between Jason and herself. Wedding bells were not ringing in her future.

"Getting in?" Jason held the door open. "Or do you want to wait out here while I drive across?"

Maddy lifted her chin. "I was thinking you might want to let me drive while you wait. If the road doesn't hold, you can rush to my rescue."

"Ah, the White Knight." Jason grinned. "I like that."

Her face heated. Maddy ignored his comment. After the unexpected thought about weddings, she'd wanted to bait Jason. Maybe if they were both angry, they wouldn't have this attraction to deal with. Instead, he'd turned the tables on her—again.

The rest of the trip to the petroglyphs went quickly. Jason parked near the edge of the path leading down to the rock drawings.

"Is this close enough?" Jason's intense gaze stole Maddy's breath. They hadn't talked much since crossing over the washed-out spot in the road.

"Fine." Maddy pointed out the windshield. "The trail down starts right there. Burke was right. I have been here before, but it's been years."

Runoff from the rainy seasons had wreaked havoc with the steep, rocky path. Maddy could see where rivulets of water had run in recent weeks. The ground still held a lot of moisture. She glanced at the menacing clouds overhead, hoping they wouldn't get wet today. They exited the car and started down the path, attempting to skirt the slick spots.

"Look." Jason's command had Maddy swiveling as she brought her gaze back from the clouds. Her right foot slipped into one of the soft, muddy places. Her ankle turned. Maddy cried out as she skidded down the trail. She reached out to grab something to stop her fall. Her hand connected with the dirt of the embankment. Pain shot up her arm.

"Maddy!"

She heard Jason's cry as if from a distance as she hit hard. More pain lanced up her leg. Her hip ached. She skidded to a stop, her eyes closed, certain she was going over the edge.

"Maddy, are you okay?" Jason knelt next to her. She cracked one eye open, then the other. Something hard dug into her hip.

"Your hand." Jason lifted her fingers. "You're bleeding." He pulled a clean handkerchief from his back pocket. She bit her lip as he wrapped her torn finger to stop the blood. His forehead was etched with concern. "Are you hurt anywhere else?"

"I don't know." Maddy tried to sit up. Her head was downhill, so movement was hard. "Can you help?"

"I don't want to move you if you're hurt too bad."

Maddy crossed her eyes. Jason smiled. She forced herself to return the smile. "I'll be fine. I think there is a boulder the size of the Empire State Building poking into my hip. I need to move."

Jason helped her sit up. They both looked down at the offending rock. Jason's lips twitched. "I think the Empire State Building shrunk."

Maddy made a face. "Well, I didn't squash it, if that's what you're thinking."

Jason laughed and stood. "Let me help you up. We need to see if your ankle is all right."

Putting her hands in his, Maddy tried to ignore the connection sizzling between them. As she came to her feet, her ankle began to throb. When she tried to step down, she gasped as pain shot up her leg. She lost her balance again and fell forward. Jason's arms came around her. He pulled her close, steadying her.

For a moment Maddy leaned against him, enjoying his strength and the feeling of being close to him. She looked up. Concern and caring mingled in his expression. Jason brushed the hair from her face. She couldn't breathe. She couldn't speak. He lowered his head. His lips brushed hers. She moaned.

"No." Maddy shoved him away, falling back against the embankment.

She could see the hurt in his eyes.

Chapter 11

Costa Rica. I like that one." Jason's death grip on the phone made his fingers ache. He closed his eyes, picturing the various assignment possibilities his agent had suggested were available. He refused to consider why he'd chosen the one farthest from Arizona. Staying in town was not an option.

As he hung up the phone, Jason closed his eyes. The picture of Maddy falling on that steep path wrenched at him. He could still recall his helplessness as he watched her tumble. In that moment he'd known something had changed. He couldn't ignore his feelings for her anymore. Maddy would always be in his heart, whether she wanted to be or not. There wasn't a thing Jason could do about it.

After Maddy pushed him away, letting him know she didn't return his feelings, he knew he had to stay as far away from her as possible. The only way he could handle these newfound emotions would be through distance. Seeing her would be too hard.

So he'd cut short his trip to Dudleyville, come home, and called his agent. Jason had begged to be sent on a job in a remote location, even though there were more lucrative and appealing assignments closer to home. This urgency to get away was driving him mad.

Heading for the bedroom, Jason began to plan what he would pack. This trip would be in the humid, warm jungles of the equator. No cold weather clothes needed. He could pack light. Stuffing what he needed in a duffel bag, Jason opened his nightstand drawer to fish out his passport.

Lying on top was the candid photo he'd taken of Maddy at T. L. Enterprises before Christmas. His heart leaped at the sight of her face alight with emotion as she talked with some of the other employees. When he'd come home from Dudleyville, Jason had stuffed the picture in the drawer, knowing he wouldn't be able to look at her visage every night without dreaming of them being together.

His hand trembled as he touched the frame. Part of him wanted to grab it out of the drawer and toss the photo away. Another part wanted to sit here and gaze at her, wishing with all his heart she was here in person. Why didn't she want anything to do with him? Was there something wrong with him? Knowing he would find no answers here, Jason fumbled out his passport and shoved the picture farther into the drawer.

His cell rang as he started to open the door. Digging it from his pocket, he noted that Jazmyn was calling. Guilt surged through him. He hadn't given a thought to telling his sister he was leaving. He was so caught up in himself and his troubles that he hadn't stopped to consider anyone else.

"Hey." Jazmyn sounded a little strained. "I wondered if I could ask a favor?"

"Only if it doesn't involve dirty diapers." Jason smiled at Jazmyn's laugh.

"Not dirty ones, clean ones." In the background Jason could hear Caleb fussing. "Caleb has an ear infection. I'm almost out of diapers, but I don't want to take a cranky baby to the store. I should have asked if you're busy first. Sorry."

"That's fine. Is he okay? Do you need medicine for him or a ride to the doctor?"

"I already took him in. They want me to give him decongestant to help his ears drain and something for the pain. Hold on." Jason could hear her rummaging through something. "I'm almost out of decongestant. I thought I had another bottle, but I don't. Could you pick one up when you get the diapers? I'd ask Thor, but he had to run up to the cabin this morning for some paperwork he left there."

"No problem." Jason scribbled down the diaper size and the name of the medication. "I'll be there as soon as I can."

Caleb was nearly asleep when Jason arrived at their house almost forty-five minutes later. Jazmyn held her finger to her lips. She was gone for a few minutes and came back without the baby.

"Finally." Jazmyn took the bag from Jason. "I thought I'd never get him down."

Jason could see the dark circles under his sister's eyes. Once again, he felt guilty for running off when she might need him here. "I'd better go so you can lie down and rest while he's sleeping."

"Come on in the kitchen. I'm going to have a glass of juice first. Do you want some?"

"No thanks. I'm heading off on an assignment." Jason hesitated before following Jazmyn through the house.

"Where you going?" Jazmyn pulled a pitcher from the refrigerator.

"Costa Rica."

"What?" Jazmyn turned, a frown creasing her brow. "Why? I thought you planned to stay close for a while. Isn't that what you told me?"

"It's an assignment." Jason fought the urge to squirm as his sister stared at him.

"You're running away, aren't you?" She set the pitcher on the counter with a sharp snap. "Maddy told me some of what happened in Dudleyville. You can't leave, Jason. I promised I wouldn't say much, but you can't leave right now. Okay?"

Jason stared out the window to the huge backyard. He thought of the assignment his agent wanted to give him and another one he'd mentioned in passing.

Maybe he was giving up too easily. "All right. I'll call and see if I can get the local photo shoot. It's not much of a job, but at least I'll be in town if you need me." Jason wanted to add something about Maddy needing him but knew that was too much to hope for.

✍

"Hey, Maddy."

"Hey, Erik. You're back in town." Maddy paused, saving her document on the computer while she talked on the phone. "How was the trip?"

"Fine." Erik's tone held some reserve.

"Just fine? Not great, fantastic, all that you've ever dreamed?" Maddy sensed Erik needed something from her.

"Maddy." Erik's breathing came through the receiver. She could tell he was struggling with what to say. For once, Maddy held her tongue and waited.

"Maddy, I have to talk to you. I've gotten in such a mess. Please, can you meet me at the deli for lunch in an hour?" The pleading tone was unusual for Erik.

"Hey, I can meet you now if you want." Maddy leaned forward. "I'm sure Kirsten will let me take an early lunch."

"No, I just got back. I have to shower and change before I can come. An hour will be fine." Erik sounded tired, his voice strained.

"I'll be there. Do you want me to describe what I'm wearing so you'll recognize me?"

Erik laughed, as she'd hoped he would. "No, just tell me what color your hair is today."

The next hour dragged by as Maddy watched the clock, wondering what had Erik so upset. Before he left on this last trip he'd told her he would be seeing Zuria. He'd been as excited as a schoolboy getting ready for his first date.

The comforting scent of fresh-baked bread wafted over her as Maddy pushed open the door to the deli. She breathed in the smell, ignoring the way her stomach rumbled. Erik waved from a booth toward the back. She wound through the tables to reach him.

"I hope you don't mind that I already ordered for us." Erik's gaunt face worried her. "You always have the same sandwich and chips when we come here, so I figured it was safe."

"And here I planned to be different today." Maddy put her hands on her hips, then grinned. "Maybe I'll take your sandwich, and you can have mine."

"No way." Erik grimaced. "I'm a meat man. I couldn't eat just veggies."

Laughing, Maddy leaned over to hug her friend before sliding onto the seat opposite him. She waited until they had prayed and were eating to ask again about his trip.

Erik finished chewing, took a long drink of his soda, and put the sandwich down as if he wasn't hungry anymore. "I asked Zuria to marry me."

Maddy almost choked. She coughed, swallowed, and sipped some water. "You did? Erik, that's wonderful!" She noted his dour expression. "Isn't it?"

"She said yes, but. . ." Erik held up his hand, cutting off Maddy's excited exclamation. "We went to her parents' house. I'd never met them, or I would have asked her father for her hand in marriage. Anyway, her father was very upset. He refuses to give us his blessing. Zuria says that she can't possibly marry me until he changes his mind."

"What?" Maddy stared at Erik. "Did he have a reason?"

"Yeah. A good one." Erik twirled the straw in his cup. "He's heard of my reputation from some mutual colleagues. You know, the way I was before I became a Christian. He says it's not right for someone as pure as Zuria to marry someone as tainted as me."

"He called you tainted?" Anger welled up in a ball in Maddy's chest. She wanted to have a talk with Zuria's father. Erik nodded as he poked at his sandwich.

"Erik, does he know you're a Christian now, that you don't live that lifestyle anymore?"

"Zuria tried to talk to him, but he refused to listen. He doesn't believe I've changed."

"So Zuria, who loves you, said good-bye just like that?" Maddy now wanted to have a talk with Zuria.

"Maddy, are you getting ready to tilt at windmills for me?" Erik's sad smile almost broke her heart. "Zuria said to give him some time. She'll try to talk with him. When I return on my next trip, we will discuss this more. That was two weeks ago."

"Have you talked with her since then?" Maddy sipped water, hoping to wash away the lump in her throat.

"She won't answer my calls." Erik's gaze lifted to the plate glass window at the front of the deli. "Maddy, I love her so much. What will I do if I can't marry her?"

"Have you thought about talking to Thor or Kirsten about this?" Maddy asked.

"No, I wasn't even sure I wanted to talk to you, but I had to confide in someone. I can't sleep. I'm having trouble eating." Erik fell silent.

"Erik, we'll pray about this. I think you should talk to your family, too. They love you and will stand with you." Maddy felt the vibration of her phone in her pocket. She pulled it out, praying this wasn't Kirsten needing her back at the office right away. With Jazmyn off because Caleb was sick, the work had been heavy today.

She frowned. "Sorry, Erik. This is my friend Blaire. Do you mind if I take it?" He shook his head, and Maddy flipped open the cell. "Hey, Blaire."

Maddy could feel the color leeching from her face and could see the concern in Erik's eyes as Blaire spoke. "Maddy, we're on the way to the hospital. Caitlin swallowed some paint thinner. I hate to ask this, but is there any way you could get the boys? Isabel and Manuel went to Phoenix today, and we didn't have anywhere to leave the twins."

"I'm sure I can. I'll call Kirsten. Where do I meet you?"

"At the Northwest Hospital. We'll be there in fifteen minutes." Her voice broke off in a sob. "I've got to go, Maddy. Caitlin is throwing up. Please pray for her." The phone clicked off.

"What's up?" Erik reached across the table and took Maddy's hand. "Something's wrong. What is it?"

"It's Caitlin, Blaire's three-year-old." Maddy swallowed hard, willing away the tears. "Erik, I have to get to the hospital and take the twins so Blaire and Burke can focus on their daughter. Will you come with me? I know this is a tough time for you."

"No problem." Erik pulled out his phone. "I'll call Kirsten while you get the sandwiches wrapped up. We can take the boys to the Desert Museum. From what I've heard of them, they'll need to run off some energy and be distracted from what's wrong with their sister."

Maddy turned away and swallowed hard, fighting back tears. She had to be strong, but all she could picture was Blaire's agony if her daughter didn't survive this.

Chapter 12

W
hat we really want is to revamp our Web site and brochures." The man from the Arizona-Sonora Desert Museum stood outside talking with Jason. Concentration seemed to be a major problem for Jason today. He leaned forward, trying to see if the man had a name tag, since Jason couldn't recall what he'd said when he introduced himself. "You're the professional. I wanted to be able to go around with you, but I can't, so take the pictures you think will best display what we have here."

"The view is incredible." Jason gazed south into the Sonoran Desert, wondering how far he could see.

"Looking out this way, the vista includes part of Mexico. Those mountains you see in the distance are across the border." The man, Toby something—that was it—gestured at the purple-blue peaks far to the south.

"The horizon is always deceptive out here." Jason tried to focus his thoughts, pushing away the picture of a pert redhead.

Toby's cell phone chimed. He glanced at the readout window. "I'm afraid I have to go. Busy day. If you need anything, feel free to come in the office and ask."

"Thanks." As Toby walked away, Jason turned his attention to the map he'd been given with the list of suggested photo subjects. He hadn't realized how many animals, reptiles, and birds were housed at the Desert Museum. He'd tried to bring Jazmyn here after he'd moved to Tucson from the Northwest, but she hadn't been good at getting out at that point. He'd have to talk her into bringing Caleb out to see the exhibits once the baby was a little older.

The morning flew by as he went from one display to the next setting up shots. The work proved to be slow as he dodged energetic youngsters who raced from one place to the next. Their parents often appeared bedraggled, one mother in particular whose youngsters reminded Jason of Burke and Blaire's kids.

At lunchtime Jason headed toward the Ocotillo Café with the voucher Toby had given him. Toby suggested the Ocotillo but assured him the voucher would work at the Ironwood Terrace also if the other was full. When he stepped inside, Jason noted an abundance of winter visitors, people who fled the colder climates to come to Tucson for the frigid months. Since the skies were clear and the sun out, he chose to go to the Ironwood Terrace. With his light jacket, eating outside would be fun.

The Ironwood was crowded with more children clamoring for hot dogs or hamburgers. Jason joined the queue for sandwiches, ordering a marinated chicken breast with prickly pear plum sauce. He carried the tray outside, choosing a small table away from the busiest areas.

All morning he'd been struggling with thoughts of Maddy. Jazmyn had nailed it when she suggested he was running away to his out-of-the-country assignment. Every night he awoke in a sweat with the image of Maddy falling jerking him from sleep. No matter how hard he tried, he couldn't forget her or the feeling of having her in his arms. He ached to have her there again yet knew with his job that wasn't a practical desire. He couldn't ask any woman to wait for marriage until he'd satisfied his wanderlust. Plus, he couldn't ask a woman to marry him, knowing she would have to be the head of the household while he was away for weeks at a time.

The sandwich, delicious at first, turned to dust in his mouth as he realized how difficult his dilemma would be to solve. Maddy had already stolen his heart. At the same time, she deserved better than he. There must be some man out there who would be perfect for her, but it couldn't be he.

Putting his refuse in the trash, Jason headed back out to continue his work. As in the morning, he found concentration a chore. He would catch a whiff of a perfume or scent and think of Maddy. Several times he jerked around thinking he'd heard her voice, only to find some other woman, who didn't really sound like Maddy at all, laughing or talking.

"Ah, Lord, what do I do?" Jason hid behind his camera, not wanting people to see his struggle. He hadn't taken the time to pray and seek God's will, but then he'd known for so long that the Lord didn't want him to marry yet. He was sure that wouldn't change until he changed his working arrangements. *Lord, please help me to understand Your will. I keep thinking I know what You want for me, and I forget to ask.*

✦

"And we were just helping her clean out her innards."

Maddy lifted an eyebrow as Erik glanced at her. The twins had been talking nonstop since they left the hospital. At least Jed had been talking. Ike put in a comment now and then but didn't talk as much as his brother.

"Clean out her innards?" Maddy turned to look back at the twins.

"That's what Grandpa always told us paint thinner would do if we drank it." Jed nodded at Ike. " 'Member?" Ike nodded.

"Caitlin got all dirty. We used the hose to clean her up, but she ate some of that mud. Ike and I thought maybe she should have her innards cleaned out, too, so we took her in the workshop." His little brow furrowed in concentration. "Do you think it worked?"

"When she threw up, I didn't see any mud," Ike said. "It sure smelled bad, though."

294

"Dad said something about if we'd light a match we could fly to the hospital, but Ike and I didn't have any matches." He frowned. "Mom won't let us have them."

Maddy cleared her throat. From the corner of her eye she could see Erik holding back his laughter. At the hospital, the doctors were sure Caitlin would be fine, but they wanted to take an X-ray of her lungs to make sure they were clear. Blaire told Maddy that when Caitlin threw up she could have gotten some of the paint thinner in her windpipe, which could cause problems. Maddy had given Blaire a key to the house in case they got out of the hospital before she and Erik were back with the boys.

"Here we are." Erik turned off the winding road into the Desert Museum parking lot. "You boys ready?"

"Is this one of those places with pictures on the wall and people shush you when you try to say something?" Jed asked.

Maddy laughed. "Nope. This isn't like most museums. You know what they have right out front where you buy the tickets?" Jed and Ike shook their heads. "They have lizards."

The boys' faces lit up. "We have a lizard in our house—Mr. Smarty."

"In your house?" Maddy glanced at Erik to see him hiding a grin as he climbed from the car.

"Yeah, I brought him in to show Mom. She screamed and scared him," Jed said. "We call him Mr. Smarty because he keeps getting away so we can't catch him. Mom keeps saying he's going to end up in bed with her some night and give her an attack." Jed exchanged looks with his brother. "We thought if we could catch Mr. Smarty, we would stick him under her covers for a surprise."

"Oh, that would be fun." Maddy saved her laughter until the boys had raced ahead to the lizard exhibit.

"I'm thinking it's an amazing thing that Burke and Blaire are still sane." Erik wiped his hand down his face. "I'll buy the tickets while you corral the crew."

"Gee, thanks. Give me the hard job." Maddy made a face at Erik. She scanned the area.

The boys were petting a family of very realistic bronze javelinas. Her throat locked up as memories of the morning she and Jason were startled by the peccaries washed over her. She couldn't breathe, could only stand there and stare. She missed Jason so much. Everywhere she went there were reminders of him. At work she saw him taking pictures for the employees' album. At the deli she could picture the two of them sharing a coffee or lunch. Of course, every time she talked with Jazmyn, Jason's twin, it was like watching Jason talk. They shared so many traits and features.

"Ready to go, or do you want to stand here and daydream a while longer?" Erik stood next to her, his gaze questioning.

"I'm ready." Maddy forced a smile. "Did I tell you about seeing the baby javelina a few weeks ago when we were in Dudleyville?" She continued to fill in Erik on her adventures as they gathered the boys and passed through the entry gates.

"Hey, a snake." Ike tugged at Maddy's hand. "Can we hold it?" He pointed to a table set up at the edge of the walkway. A docent was talking to a group of people about the snake winding around her arm.

"You might be able to touch it. See what the lady says." Maddy watched the boys worm their way through the group. The docent listened to Jed's inquiry and leaned over to allow the boys to pet the snake.

"I don't suppose you noticed the car in the parking lot?" Erik asked.

"I rarely notice cars unless I'm afraid they'll run over me." Maddy rolled her eyes. "What was it? Some sports car you're dying to have?"

"Nope, just an SUV parked up front." Erik's eyes sparkled as he watched her. He seemed to think she should find this significant.

"Okay. I didn't know you were into those. I thought you preferred something racier."

"I do, for myself." Erik chuckled. "This SUV happens to belong to someone I know."

"Okay." Maddy waved to the boys, who were racing back. Didn't they ever walk anywhere?

"The lady says there's a place down here where you can find pretty rocks. Can we go there next?" Jed almost jumped up and down in his excitement.

"There's a cave, too." Ike's blue eyes glowed.

"Then we'd better get going." Maddy glanced at her map before pointing out the right path. "I want to see the mountain lions."

"Mountain lions?" The boys spoke in unison. "Way cool." They raced off. Erik and Maddy quickened their pace to keep up.

"So, who do you know at the Desert Museum besides me?" Maddy's breath huffed. She was glad they were going downhill, not up.

"Jason." Erik's announcement halted Maddy in her tracks. "When he took pictures for T. L. last December, I used to see his car there all the time. I recognized it out front. I can see you didn't know he would be here."

Maddy glanced around, wondering why and where Jason would be. She didn't want to see him. She was dying to see him. A thousand emotions and thoughts sent her brain into overload.

"Maddy, you're as in love with him as I am with Zuria." Erik laughed as he watched her. Maddy wondered if he could read the panic in her face.

"I'm not in love. You of all people know why I can't be." Maddy gripped Erik's arm.

"I know nothing of the sort." Erik loosened her grip and began to walk again.

"We'd better catch up with the boys. Who knows what they'll do. Probably let all the animals loose and be digging for buried treasure somewhere."

"Erik, Jason is. . .is. . .well, it's complicated." Maddy couldn't find the words to explain how she felt about Jason. She wasn't sure she knew.

"Maddy, you're trying to convince yourself, not me." Erik squeezed her hand before bending down to examine a rock Jed was trying to show them. He straightened as the boys took off running in the direction of the cave. "Any man would be blessed to have your love. I think Jason is one of the few I believe might be worthy of you. Since Jazmyn and Thor married, I've gotten to know Jason a bit."

"But you know why I can't be good for him." Exasperation made Maddy want to shake Erik.

"I know nothing of the kind." Erik bent down to enter a tunnel. "You're sounding a lot like Zuria's father, you know. Think about how upset you were with him and the comments he made about my past."

Maddy jerked back as if she'd been slapped. She didn't want to sound like that. Erik didn't understand this was different. Her situation didn't compare to his. Their pasts might have similarities, but Erik was a man, and men were allowed to be that way. A promiscuous female was not as acceptable—it was more shameful, dirtier somehow. Even as the thought crossed her mind, she knew it wasn't true. This was something she would need to ponder.

They came out into the sun and directed the boys to the path leading to the enclosures for the big cats. Once again the twins raced away at something resembling the speed of light.

"You'd better get ready." Erik's warning had Maddy looking in the direction he indicated. Jason was taking pictures. She stopped, her hand grabbing Erik's arm. She opened her mouth to call the boys back before Jason spotted them. They could all go a different way and avoid talking with him.

"Hey, it's Jason. Jason!" Jed and Ike raced away to their new friend. Jason swiveled around at their excited calls. His gaze slid from theirs to Maddy. She couldn't move, mesmerized by the longing she read in his eyes.

Chapter 13

For a moment he'd thought he was going crazy. Absolutely bonkers. Reality was colliding with the dream world, and he wasn't sure what was fact and fiction anymore. He knew there was no reason for her to be at the Desert Museum, but her presence was so close he could feel her next to him.

When he heard the twins yell his name, he'd turned to see them racing toward him. Jason couldn't help smiling. After spending nearly two weeks at their home, he'd come to enjoy the pair. Slipping his camera into the case, he prepared for the onslaught. As he stretched out his arms, Jason looked behind the boys, searching for Burke, Blaire, and Caitlin. Instead, his gaze fell on Maddy.

The look on her face told him she wasn't sure she wanted to see him. That hurt. He'd thought so much about her, he'd forgotten how she pushed him away. All he could think about today was seeing her again, finding out why she kept him at arm's length. He could see the longing for more in her eyes sometimes. Other times, she acted as if he was the last man on earth she wanted to be around.

His breath whooshed out as the twins slammed into him at the same time. "Jason!" The boys gave him a huge hug. "Are you taking pictures? We found some treasure and got to touch a snake." Jed hopped on one foot, gesturing behind him while Ike still clung to Jason.

"Treasure, huh?" Jason dragged his gaze from Maddy.

"Yeah, we're here with Maddy and Erik. Caitlin's getting her innards cleaned." Jed jumped in the air and did a one-eighty before dropping to a crouch when he landed.

Erik? Jason sought Maddy again. Sure enough, there was Thor's brother standing close to Maddy. They were walking toward Jason and the boys. Jealousy spiked through Jason. He swallowed hard. Maddy had the right to choose whom she wanted to be with. Just because he wanted her with him didn't mean she wanted the same thing.

"Jason." Erik released Maddy's hand and reached out to shake. "Good to see you. You on assignment or just enjoying a day out?"

"Assignment." Jason released Erik's hand and looked at Maddy. He smiled. "Hi." He wanted to drag her close and kiss her senseless. He wanted to pull her away from this madhouse and ask her why she didn't care for him like she cared for Erik. They seemed so comfortable together, something he and Maddy had rarely shared. Jason shoved his hands in his pockets.

"How did you end up here with the boys on a workday?" Jason tried to keep from staring at Maddy but couldn't seem to focus on anything else. "They said something about Caitlin and her innards."

Maddy's full lips twitched. "It isn't funny." She pointed at the enclosure behind Jason. "Jed, Ike, why don't you two go over and see what everyone is staring at? I think this might be where the Mexican wolves are."

The boys whooped and raced over to wiggle through the people. Maddy waited to turn back to Jason and tell him what she knew of the events that had occurred at the Dunham ranch this morning until the boys were pointing and talking. "I'm thinking Burke and Blaire have no idea the boys were trying to help Caitlin get clean. I'm sure their grandpa will be horrified when he finds out his offhand remark, which he probably intended for good, ended up being the catalyst for Caitlin's trip to the hospital."

"No doubt." Jason shoved his hands deeper in his pockets. "Have you heard how she's doing?"

"They were waiting for X-rays when we left. Blaire said she'd call as soon as they found out anything." Maddy reached into her own pocket. Jason wondered if she carried her phone there. She must be almost as worried as Burke and Blaire since they'd been friends for so long. When they'd visited the ranch, Caitlin often sat on Maddy's lap in the evening, cuddled there while the adults talked.

"Hey, someone said Cat Canyon is this way." Jason glanced down to see Jed tugging on his hand. "I want to see the coatis and the pumas."

"They're ring-tailed cats." Ike leveled a solemn gaze at his brother.

"Coatis." Jed's chin jutted out.

"Whoa. Halt." Maddy smiled down at the boys. "You're both right in a way. Where you're from, people often call the coatimundi a ring-tailed cat, although they aren't the same. They're not really even a cat, more like a raccoon."

Jed nodded. "They like oranges."

"They do?" Jason glanced at Maddy. She nodded.

"Some friends of Dad's live in a canyon and have orange trees." Jed stood straighter. "We went up there to pick some, and I found one still on the tree, but the orange had been eaten. Dad said the *coatis*," Jed's gaze drifted to Ike, "like to climb the tree and eat the inside out of the orange, but leave the outside hanging on the branch. The peel was all mushy when I tried to pick it."

"Ring-tailed cat."

Jason could see from the corner of his eye that Maddy had heard Ike mutter the name, too. He avoided looking at her and held his breath to keep from bursting into laughter.

"Well, why don't we go find these ring-tailed coatis?" Erik cleared his throat. Jason could see the sparkle in his eyes and knew he'd heard the exchange, too.

"Don't get too far ahead," Maddy called out to the boys as they raced off down the path.

"I just hope they don't mow anyone down." Jason hesitated. He wanted to go with Maddy and Erik, but he had a job to do.

"You may as well come along if you have the time." Erik grinned at Jason. "The entertainment value is priceless. You should have heard them on the way out here."

"After spending a couple of weeks at their house, I can only imagine." Jason gave an inner shrug. "Sounds good. I haven't photographed the coatis yet anyway."

When she'd first seen Jason, Maddy had wanted to run. Now she couldn't remember why. Walking down the trail beside him, she longed to slip her hand in his. Despite the crowds, the boys, and Erik, this togetherness brought back the companionship she felt with him on those cold January mornings in Dudleyville. No, companionship didn't leave you tongue-tied, unable to think of anything to say.

A chattering group of older people was coming toward them. Erik stepped ahead so Maddy could move to the edge of the path. Instead of getting behind her, Jason moved closer until their arms brushed. Maddy's heart raced. She could feel the back of his hand touching hers. She glanced over as the tourists came even with them. Jason was watching her, his green eyes intent as if he were trying to read her thoughts. She hoped he couldn't.

Before the path opened up again, Jason wrapped his fingers around hers for a moment. The caress of his thumb across her palm left her weak. She almost groaned aloud when he stepped away. She wished they were alone. She wished she'd never come here today. Her emotions were on a roller-coaster ride that she couldn't take much longer.

"Look. Look." Jed's wild gestures told Maddy the boys had found their coatis. "They have long tails."

Maddy leaned down to peer into the enclosure at the same time Jason did. Their heads bumped. Maddy pulled back, turning to look at Jason. She couldn't seem to turn away.

"Are you gonna hit him?" Jed asked.

"What?" Maddy straightened. The boys were staring wide-eyed. "Why would I hit him?"

"That's what I do to Ike when he bumps into me like that. I stare at him; then I hit him." Jed nodded as if he'd imparted some important piece of wisdom.

"I'm thinking your mom and dad don't approve of you doing that." Maddy bit her lip as Jed dug his toe in the dirt beside the path. "I don't think I'll hit Jason. This was probably an accident."

"What if I hit you?" Jason rubbed his head. "That hurt. You may have done it on purpose."

"Then I might have to step in and defend Maddy." Erik slipped his arm around her shoulders. " 'Cause that's what boys do for girls, isn't it, Jed?"

Ike's mouth opened in a perfect O as he stared at Erik. "You can get in big trouble for fighting, even if you're fighting for a girl. We did that at church when Barry pushed Caitlin. He's in third grade, so Jed and me both had to fight. Dad got awful mad."

"Yeah, but Barry never did that again." Jed's smug smile and Ike's echoing one told Maddy the twins didn't regret hitting the bully. She'd heard tales about Barry.

"Well, we're not going to have a fight here," Jason said. "I'm thinking we should see the mountain lions and then go have ice cream. What does anyone else think?"

Erik's phone chimed as the boys began to jump up and down. He stepped away to talk. Maddy directed the boys' attention back to the coatimundis to give Erik the time he needed.

"I'm sorry, Maddy. Something has come up. I have to get back to town." Erik shoved the phone back in his pocket. He turned to the boys. "Maybe we can come back here again sometime and finish seeing everything."

"We don't want to go yet." Jed frowned. "Maybe you could leave us here and come back later."

"I'm afraid that won't work." Erik looked at Maddy. She could see the regret in his eyes.

"Let's go, boys. We'll have Erik drop us off at my house, and we can bake some cookies for when your dad and mom get there with Caitlin." Maddy couldn't look at Jason. She wanted to mirror the boys' disappointment because she wasn't ready for the day to end, either.

"Why don't you let me take you home?" Jason asked. "I have to take some more pictures. If I don't get everything done today, I can come back."

"Please?" Jed and Ike, their eyes as wide as the coati's, watched Maddy.

"Are you sure?" Maddy met Jason's gaze. She couldn't read what he was thinking and wished she could. The last time, they'd parted with her hurting him. She wanted to explain but hadn't been able to find the words.

"I think that's an excellent idea." Erik's eyes twinkled. Maddy knew he was enjoying this. He wanted her to be with Jason. If she didn't know better, she would almost accuse him of setting this up.

"Then it's settled." Jason held out his hand to Erik. "I'll be sure to get them back after we have ice cream and see some more animals. Right boys?" The twins gave vigorous nods.

For the next hour, Maddy laughed with Jason over the boys' antics. They didn't seem to ever wear down. "I'm beginning to think children are alien beings." Maddy grinned at Jason as they prepared to enter the hummingbird enclosure.

"That's not a new thought." Jason winked, setting her heart thumping.

"I think they draw their energy from the adult caring for them. That's why they keep going while we wear down."

"That theory makes perfect sense to me." Jason touched his palm to her back as she passed him, guiding her to the next door. The boys were already gazing in wonder at the tiny darting birds inside. Maddy wanted to stop and lean back against Jason.

The song on Maddy's phone began to play. She dug it from her pocket, motioning to Jason that she would step outside to take the call. When she returned, Jason had his camera trained on the twins. Behind them hummingbirds flitted and darted though the foliage.

"Hey." Jason smiled down at her. Maddy took a deep breath, trying to recall what she'd been about to say.

"That was Blaire. Caitlin is okay. She may have some, um, effects as any residual paint thinner moves through her system."

Jason grimaced. "I can imagine. Tell Blaire not to light a match while Caitlin's using the bathroom for the next few days."

Maddy began to laugh at the picture. The relief that the young girl would be okay swept over her. Even though she'd been distracted, in the back of her mind concern for Caitlin had always been there.

"Can we light a match?" Ike was staring with wide eyes. "Will Caitlin make the bathroom explode?"

Jed began to make sounds of detonation.

Maddy could see from Jason's expression that he hadn't meant for the precocious twins to hear his comment. She bit her lip and leaned close. "I think we may be wise to warn Blaire."

Chapter 14

Maddy, I am so glad Kirsten and Jazmyn allowed you to come up here for a few days to help me out. I don't know what I'd have done without you." Blaire shoved a large bowl of potato salad into the refrigerator before sinking into a chair at the table where Maddy sat with Caitlin on her lap.

"I'm feeling guilty holding Caitlin while you're doing so much work." Maddy gave the toddler a light squeeze. "Of course, if anyone tried to eat my potato salad, they'd be running off before the party got started."

Blaire smiled. "Now, Maddy, I've eaten your cooking. Besides, no one is as bad as I was when I first moved here. Before coming to the middle of nowhere, I thought if you wanted to fix supper, you picked up prepared food at the deli and put it in your own bowls."

Maddy laughed. "I do remember Manuel telling some funny stories about your meals." She grinned wider as Blaire grimaced. "What else is left to do before everyone arrives?" Maddy glanced out the window, wishing for the hundredth time she could see the driveway.

"All that's left is for people to arrive. Burke and Manuel will wait to cook the meat until everyone is here."

"Well, Jazmyn, Thor, and Jason will appreciate the cookout. You didn't have to do this." Maddy kissed Caitlin's soft cheek.

The doctors hadn't kept Caitlin at the hospital. The X-ray showed her lungs were clear, so they said to watch her for any other problems. So far, other than a little diarrhea and being extra cranky, she'd been fine. Maddy hadn't minded being here to help out. She'd welcomed the opportunity to be away from the possibility of running into Jason.

At the Desert Museum, Jason had kept a running patter to amuse the twins and Maddy. He'd decided to finish his photographs later so he could accompany them around the museum. By the time they had climbed back in the car, the boys were so tired they fell asleep within ten minutes. Jason hadn't said much on the drive home. He'd been deep in thought, and Maddy was too tired to think of anything to say. Several times Jason's hand had brushed against hers. Each time an electric awareness coursed through her.

When they had arrived at her house, Burke and Blaire were there with Caitlin. Thor and Jazmyn had stopped in, and Burke had invited all of them up to the ranch for a barbecue on the weekend. Noticing the panic on Blaire's face,

Maddy had asked Jazmyn if she could take a couple of days and go up to help out. That's how she had ended up with alone time with her friend.

"Jed, Burke's dad, called last night to see how Caitlin is doing. He feels so bad, like this is all his fault." Blaire brushed the hair back off her forehead. "I keep assuring him you never know what the boys will do or how their minds work."

"Poor guy. As if he doesn't have enough on his mind. How's his brother?" Maddy asked.

"He's doing better. He has one more radiation treatment. Jed plans to come home in a couple of weeks. He says he's had enough cold weather in Montana to last him several lifetimes." Blaire chuckled. "I asked him if he's ready to move up there."

"What did he say?"

"I think he threatened me." Blaire reached for Caitlin, pulling the toddler onto her lap. "He said something about me not being brave enough to say that to his face." She laughed. "For Christmas, I sent him sunglasses to help with the white glare from the snow. He says he owes me for that one, too."

"I can sympathize. I don't even like to go to the mountains around here to see the snow. Viewing it from several miles away is close enough for me." Maddy jumped when the kitchen door swung open. She hadn't realized how much of her was attuned to listening for anyone coming.

"They're here." Manuel winked at Maddy as she swung around. She could feel her face warming. "I'm off to get my family. I'll be back to help Burke with the cooking in a few minutes. He said to get the meat out of the refrigerator and ready to go."

"I'll do that." Maddy jumped up. She wanted to stay busy to have an excuse to avoid talking to Jason. Maybe he would be out with the guys doing cooking and talking about animals or sports. He'd be away from her. That's what she hoped. Keeping her distance was imperative. Right now her defenses against falling for Jason were at a low ebb.

"Blaire, do they want both of these trays of meat?" Maddy bent over to lift one of the wrapped cookie sheets.

"Yes. One of them is steaks, the other is ostrich. Burke promised Thor he would cook him some ostrich meat to try." Humor tinged Blaire's tone. She was probably thinking that most people turned up their noses at the thought of eating ostrich meat. Thor, being a hunter, was used to an unusual variety of foods. Jazmyn had mentioned some of the dishes Thor prepared for her that Maddy wasn't sure she'd be able to stomach.

"Sounds good." Maddy lifted the heavy tray and turned as she straightened.

"Hey." Jason stood by the open refrigerator door. His forest green gaze captured her. Maddy lost her grip on the meat tray. Jason's hands whipped up to catch the cookie sheet before the food ended up on the floor. Maddy's cheeks burned.

"You don't have to throw things at me." Jason's mouth quirked up in a crooked grin.

"Oh, I don't know." Blaire winked at Maddy. "When I first met Burke, I threw things at him all the time. I gave a whole new meaning to jalapeño bombers."

Maddy struggled for something to say. If she could just catch her breath. Why did Jason have this effect on her? "I. . .I'll just grab the other tray." She gestured back into the refrigerator.

"Maybe you should do it before summertime." Blaire began to giggle.

Maddy flushed again. She bent to retrieve the smaller platter of meat. She followed Jason out the back door, glad to be away from Blaire. Her friend would give her a hard time after that scene in the kitchen. She'd assured Blaire she didn't feel anything for Jason, but now Blaire would have seen the truth.

∽○

"That's the last of them, I think." Jason watched as Maddy let the dishwater out of the sink. He dried the last few plates before hanging the towel up to dry.

"Thanks for helping." Maddy's shy smile brightened the afternoon.

"Do you want to listen to Burke and Thor discuss their businesses, or would you prefer to go for a walk with me?" Jason leaned forward to peer out the window. The sky was clear, which meant cool weather. They'd need jackets, but he bet Maddy would be all for the walk.

"Hmm. Let's see." Maddy tapped her index finger against her cheek. "Meat and marketing or fresh air. Although I love M&M's, I'll take a hike this time."

Jason grinned. "If I'd known your weakness for chocolate candy, I'd have been up for bribing you."

"It's not too late." Maddy wrinkled her nose at him as she pulled her jacket from the coatrack beside the back door.

Jason stuck his head in the living room to let the others know they were going and followed Maddy outside. He'd been right. The warmth of midday had spiraled down to chilly. "I don't remember winter being so cold before." Jason pulled the zipper of his jacket halfway up.

"The city is warmer than here." Maddy stuck her hands in her pockets. "I think the river being close or maybe the elevation is a little higher—anyway, I've noticed that this area is cooler than Tucson."

They walked in companionable silence for a while. Maddy led him past several ostrich pens to a path through the desert. The fresh, clean smell of the desert, devoid of any trace of car exhaust, had Jason drawing in deep breaths in enjoyment.

"Did you get back out to the Desert Museum to finish the pictures you needed?" Maddy didn't look at him as she spoke.

"I did. I'm done with that assignment and ready for a new one." Jason studied her profile. Her nose turned up a bit on the end. Her hair had black spikes today instead of the usual red and blond combination.

"Where are you off to next?" Maddy glanced up at the almost cloudless blue sky.

"I'm not sure. I'll have to talk to my agent this next week and see what's come in."

"I always wanted to travel, but I've never been out of Arizona." Maddy's whimsical tone portrayed a trace of regret or sadness. "Do you like the traveling?"

"Most of the time I love it. That's why I keep doing this job." Jason watched a long-legged jackrabbit bound away from them. "Seeing new places, meeting new people can be pretty exciting, but when I'm gone for a long time, all I think of is getting back to Arizona. I think this state has the most varied scenery and the prettiest spots in the whole world. There's so much to see here you really don't need to go anywhere else."

"Well, I'd still like to go someday." Maddy grimaced. "Maybe it's just the grass on the other side and all that."

"Maybe." Jason shoved his cold fingers in his pockets. "I wanted to talk to you, Maddy." He paused, trying to figure out how to say what he needed to say. He'd thought about this for the last two days but still didn't know how to phrase his story without sounding pathetic.

"What is it?" Maddy stopped, her huge doe eyes trained on him for the first time since they started walking.

"I feel I owe you an explanation of sorts." Jason took a deep breath. "Has Jazmyn ever talked to you about our childhood?"

"She said she lived with your mother and you lived with your father. She told me about the abuse she suffered and how much you helped her after you were both grown up. Your parents are both gone now, right?"

"Yeah, they died within a few months of each other." Jason gave a derisive laugh. "They hadn't seen each other in years, yet it was like one knew the other was gone." He shook himself, trying to dislodge unpleasant memories.

"Anyway, I started out with the thought that my mother left because of me. Maybe she was unstable because of something I'd done."

"Jason, no." Maddy stopped and put her hand on his arm. Jason took her hand in his, and they continued walking.

"I'm over that now, I think. In college I had a girlfriend. I was crazy about her. We made all these plans." Jason ran his thumb over the back of Maddy's hand, loving the feeling of their fingers entwined.

"That's when I got my first assignment. It was a big break in the type of photography I wanted to do. We were both excited. At least, that's what I thought. I was gone for three months, traveling from place to place. I called when I could, but many of the locations were so remote I had no way to contact anyone."

"Let me guess." Maddy squeezed his hand. "When you came home, some-one wasn't waiting for you."

"You got it." Jason swallowed hard, amazed to still feel the hurt after all this time. "She'd already married someone else."

"After only three months?" Maddy gaped at him.

"She admitted she'd been seeing him while we were dating." Jason rolled his eyes. "She told me she wanted to tell me in person, that's why she waited to say anything until I was home again."

"Nice girl," Maddy said.

"Yeah, well, I hear from her now and then. She's been married three times so far and is now working on divorcing her third husband."

"Wow. I'm thinking God protected you." Maddy glanced over her shoulder. "We should probably head back. Thor and Jazmyn wanted to leave before too late."

"Yeah." Jason tugged her hand until she stopped and faced him. "What I'm trying to say and doing such a poor job is that I need someone willing to wait for me. Someone I can trust to be there when I get home."

"I have this picture of coming home to a house that smells wonderful, a wife who smiles when she sees me, and kids who run to meet me when I walk in the door. I haven't dared to hope in a long time. Until you, Maddy. . . " Jason found he was holding his breath, watching for her reaction, too uncertain to verbalize all his desires. He felt like he was teetering on a brink about to fall off a cliff. He wanted Maddy to fall with him.

"I. . ." Maddy gazed back toward the ranch house, her face filled with emo-tion, but Jason couldn't tell what she was thinking. "I have to get back." She released his hand and began to hurry away.

Chapter 15

Fumbling the key to his front door, Jason wanted to forget getting inside, curl up in a ball on the front porch, and go to sleep. After the fiasco with Maddy at the barbecue, he'd taken the first available assignment that would take him out of state. He'd been gone for three weeks. The whole time had been a war within. He'd wanted to be home where he could see Maddy, but he also believed she didn't want to see him. This constant battle was wearing him down. The lock clicked, and he stepped into his empty house.

A scent of lemon polish wafted in the air. His cleaning service must have come today. Jason had realized about a year ago that he didn't like coming home to an air of abandonment, so he'd hired a service to clean his house once a week when he was out of town and someone to keep up the yard work.

The message light on his phone pulsed. Jason called in every other day to check his messages, so he only had three: one telemarketer, one hang-up, and a message from Jazmyn. He listened to that one while he grabbed a bottle of water from the refrigerator.

"Jason, I know you're getting home late, but could you call me? I'll be up until about ten thirty. Hope you had a good trip." The machine clicked off. Jason deleted the messages, dropped into his favorite chair, and dialed Jazmyn's house. He only hoped his brain would work well enough to process whatever his sister had to say.

"Hi." Jazmyn's soft tone told him Caleb must be asleep, maybe Thor, too. "How was the trip?"

"Exhausting." Jason let his head fall back on the soft recliner.

"Really? I thought you loved traveling to the East Coast."

"Yeah, I do. These particular lodges were all in spectacular locations." Jason hesitated. He didn't want to give away too much to Jazmyn. She was perceptive enough to catch on to why he hadn't enjoyed the trip. "They were all crowded, though. Sometimes I have trouble getting the shots I need with so many people around."

"Hmm." Silence from Jazmyn. Jason almost drifted off when her next words startled him awake. "I need to talk to you about Maddy."

Shock had Jason surging up in the chair. "What? Is something wrong? What's happened?"

Jazmyn's low laugh had him wanting to bite his tongue. "That tells all, brother dear. She's fine. I wanted to know how you felt about her."

Jason groaned. His tired brain caused him to blurt out more than he'd wanted to.

"Can you meet me for breakfast tomorrow morning at the little café down the street from my office? Thor said he would take Caleb so we could have some time alone."

Glancing at the clock, Jason sighed. "I'll be there." He hung up the phone, then ran his hand down his face. Draining the last of the water, he headed for the bedroom. If he intended to talk with his very perceptive sister, he had to get some sleep. The problem was he hadn't been sleeping well for the last three weeks. Why would this night be any different?

The early morning air held a chill with a promise of warmth to come. Jason hunched his shoulders as he walked from his SUV to the café. He refused to glance toward the T. L. Enterprises building, although the pull to watch for Maddy entering those doors was almost more than he could resist.

Jazmyn waved from a booth in the back of the room. The clink of dishes and the low murmur of conversation accompanied him through the room. He breathed in the scent of fresh-brewed coffee, wishing the aroma alone would help him wake up. Last night hadn't been any better than the previous nights for sleeping.

"Good to see you." Jazmyn stood up to give him a hug and a kiss before they both slid into the booth. "You look like you've been hit by a train."

"Gee, thanks." Jason wiped at his face. He didn't want to tell his sister he felt as old as Methuselah.

The waitress arrived to take their order. Jason mumbled something, hoping a few minutes later that he'd ordered something he liked. Jazmyn chattered about Caleb and Thor, catching Jason up on everything he'd missed while he'd been gone. When the food arrived, he ate without tasting, savoring only the warmth of the coffee.

". . .Maddy." Jazmyn leaned close across the table. Her breakfast plate had been pushed to the side, most of her omelet eaten. She cradled her coffee cup in her hands.

"What?" Jason stared at his sister, lost to what she'd been saying.

"Jason, I don't think you've heard a thing I've said in the last few minutes. You're a zombie."

"Sorry." Jason lifted his cup to take a sip.

"I said you're as bad as Maddy."

Jason choked. He coughed and gasped for breath. "What?"

"Both of you are like zombies. What happened at the barbecue? I can't get Maddy to talk to me. She's just wandering around the office, not saying much. That is so unlike her. Jason, I couldn't even convince her to go shopping with me." Jazmyn's wonder made Jason realize how concerned she was for the assistant she shared with Kirsten. He knew that Maddy loved to go to the mall and browse through the shops. She often dragged Jazmyn along to peruse some sale or another.

"I don't understand." Jason wanted to go—to run away and leave his problems behind. That hadn't helped during the past three weeks.

"She's in a fog. I think it has to do with you. Talk to me." Jazmyn leaned back to sip her coffee. The look on her face told Jason she would wait until he was ready but she wouldn't give up.

"I talked to her about my dreams." He attempted a smile. "No nightmares. Just what I want in life. She didn't stick around for the discussion part. She ran. Then I ran."

"Well, running doesn't seem to be working, does it?" Jazmyn's eyebrow quirked up. "Maybe you should give her another chance. Why don't you call the deli and order a picnic lunch? Take her to a pretty spot that's quiet so you can talk."

"Do you think she'll go with me?" Jason sipped his water to help his dry mouth.

"I think Kirsten and I will tie her in your car if we have to." Jazmyn grinned. "Come by the office and ask. You can order the lunch from there." She reached over to pat his hand. "She'll go. She's missed you a lot."

ᴄᴏ

"Maddy, could you come here?" Kirsten and Jazmyn were both in Kirsten's office when Maddy returned from break. "We're trying to find the paperwork on the Everett account. Would you check and see if it's on Jazmyn's desk and bring it here, please?" The two women were surrounded by paperwork and drawings spread on the desk between them.

"Sure." Maddy pushed through the door to Jazmyn's office, muting the noise the two women were making. Crossing to the desk, she sifted through the inbox, locating the account information Kirsten wanted. Turning, she gasped. The papers drifted to the floor.

"Hey." Jason's face was drawn, his eyes circled with darkness as if he hadn't slept the whole three weeks he'd been gone. Maddy knew he'd gotten home last night. It was all she'd been able to think about. She also knew without makeup, the bags under her eyes would resemble suitcases, too.

"I have to talk to you, Maddy." Jason shoved his hands in his pockets. "Will you take the afternoon and go with me? I already have a picnic lunch from the deli packed in my car."

"Work. I have work." Maddy's mouth was so dry she couldn't swallow. She wanted to run, but her feet were rooted to the spot.

"Jazmyn and Kirsten seem to think it's okay for you to take the afternoon off." Jason's hesitant smile broke her heart. More than once she'd run from him with no explanation. She couldn't face what she needed to tell him. The last three weeks had drained her to the point where she realized she had to be open with Jason. She'd prayed about this last night, asking the Lord to provide a time. This must be His answer.

Maddy blew out a quiet breath. "Let me give this to Kirsten. I'll grab my purse and meet you at the elevator."

Silence stretched between them as Jason drove out of town. Maddy's throat ached as she thought of the wall they'd erected. This was her fault. She had to put it right. Maybe, just maybe, when Jason understood why she'd done the things she had, he would be able to forgive her. Deep down she knew her sin was unforgivable.

"Here we are." Jason shrugged his jacket on as he rounded the car to open her door. "Jazmyn assured me this is a beautiful spot for a picnic." He glanced up at the overcast sky. "Looks like it's clearing up. When the sun comes out, we probably won't need these jackets."

Grabbing the basket from the backseat, Jason led the way down a well-trodden path. A shallow stream meandered through the low hills. A few trees, their trunks gnarled and twisted, dotted the banks. Green grass grew along the edges. Blue lupines and orange and yellow poppies colored the hillsides.

"It's beautiful." Maddy breathed in the clean, spicy scent of moisture-laden desert air. "I love the smell of the desert after a rain. There's nothing like it."

"You're right. Here." Jason held up his hand to assist her down from a rocky ledge. Opening the basket, he pulled out a blanket, which he spread on the ground. "I'm not sure what all is in here, but Jazmyn says the deli packs the best lunches." He flashed a smile. Maddy's heart leaped.

"Well, I could eat an elephant right now." Maddy sank down on the blanket. "Any of those in there?"

"Hmm. I do believe. Yes." Jason lifted out a large sandwich. "I'm pretty sure this is the elephant special. It even comes with the hay."

"Jason, I'm not sure alfalfa sprouts and hay are the same thing." Maddy bit her lip to stifle the laugh. She hadn't felt this carefree in weeks. Until this moment, she hadn't realized how much she missed Jason.

"Don't they make hay from alfalfa?" Jason's wide-eyed innocence made her grin. "See, point proved. They are the same thing." He grinned back at her. "Enjoy your elephant sandwich. Here's some condiments." He rummaged a bit more. "Ah, here's a tray of sliced veggies and pickles."

His eyes twinkled as he looked sideways at her, his hand still in the basket. "And if you're a good girl and eat all your hay, there might even be a treat in here for you."

"Yum. I love hay. See?" Maddy pulled loose a few alfalfa sprouts and stuck them in her mouth.

The rest of the lunch eased the strain between them. Jason described the lodges he'd been photographing. Maddy talked about some of the new projects at T. L. Enterprises. The ripple of the water soothed her until she almost forgot they'd had a falling out.

"Maddy, we have to talk." Jason leaned back on his elbows, his legs stretched out.

She felt as if her heart stopped; then it began to race faster than a jet. "I know." She licked her lips. "Jason, I didn't mean to hurt you. I have things to say to you that are hard. I'm sorry I didn't tell you this before."

"Maddy, you don't have to explain anything."

"But I do." Maddy's eyes burned, yet she refused to cry. She would not use tears to garner sympathy. "Please, this is hard enough. Just let me say it."

Maddy flicked an ant from the blanket, unable to think of any funny comment to make about the insect and the picnic. She swallowed to ease the ache in her throat. "I'm the oldest of seven children. My parents both had to work, so I was the caretaker for my younger siblings. I did the laundry and most of the cooking, besides going to school." She held up her hand as Jason started to say something.

"I'm not telling you this so you'll feel sorry for me. Most of the time I loved my life. I know some people disagree, but my parents were great people. Not perfect, but I'm sure they must love me. They were busy much of the time. Money was short, so they did extra things to earn a little here and there."

Plucking a blade of grass, Maddy began to peel it apart. "When I was a teenager, my parents had to move back East. I only had two years left before I graduated. I didn't want to leave my friends, so I begged them to let me stay with my aunt. She wanted me to stay, so my parents agreed. I didn't understand their reluctance until the last few months. I'm sure what I'm going to tell you is why they don't have anything to do with me anymore." Her voice tapered off.

She lifted her gaze to meet Jason's. "You see, Aunt Amelia is a free spirit. She believes in doing whatever you want as long as you don't hurt anyone else. I loved her and adopted her beliefs for years, never realizing that I was hurting someone—myself."

Maddy went on to explain to Jason about the lessons on birth control and safe sex. She couldn't look at him as she glossed over the part about all the boys and men whose names she couldn't even remember.

By the time she finished, Jason's eyes were dark with anger, his jaw tight. He threw the leftovers back in the basket, grabbed up the blanket when she stood, and headed for the car. Maddy followed, her heart aching so bad she wanted to die.

"Jason, I'm sorry." She gasped at his cold gaze.

And knew he'd never forgive her.

Chapter 16

Standing on the sidewalk outside the church office building, the cool morning breeze ruffling his hair, Jason fought going inside. He had to talk to his pastor, yet he didn't want to. Since he'd heard Maddy's story a week ago, he hadn't spoken with anyone. He couldn't eat, sleep, or focus on work. He wanted to push all thoughts of Maddy away, but the picture of her stricken expression when he'd turned so cold haunted him.

The offices were quiet. No chatter. No phones ringing. So different from Sunday morning when the whole building was filled with laughter and excitement.

Jason rapped his knuckles on the frame of the pastor's office door. Brendon Marsh glanced up from where he'd been jotting notes. His pleasure at seeing Jason radiated from his broad face. Brushing a hand over his short, graying hair, he stood and extended his hand.

"Jason, it's always good to see you. Have a seat. Would you like some coffee, water?" Pastor Marsh sank back into his chair as Jason shook his head. "We haven't seen much of you lately. Been doing lots of traveling?"

"Almost nonstop since last December. I love seeing new places but am always relieved to get home."

Brendon laughed. "I can only imagine. I'm gone once or twice a year to a pastors' conference or men's retreat. That's always enough for me. I guess I'm a homebody. Give me my family, a picnic table, some meat to throw on the grill, and I'm satisfied."

"Right now that sounds pretty good." Jason rubbed his thumb on the smooth arm of the chair. He'd wanted so much to talk with Pastor Marsh, but now he had no idea how to begin or if he even wanted to anymore.

"So, what can I do for you?" Brendon asked.

"I don't know." Jason stared down at his shoes, noticing how scuffed they were.

"You look as if you've been having some trouble sleeping, Jason. Are you struggling with something?"

"There's this girl." Jason started to glance up at the pastor but couldn't meet his gaze. "I. . .she. . ." He cleared his throat. "She's not right for me, but I can't seem to forget her. Besides, she works with my sister, so I know I'll be coming in contact with her."

"Why isn't she right for you?" Brendon asked.

Jason tried to find the words he needed. He opened his mouth, closed it. His mind was a blank. Why wasn't she right for him?

"Is she a Christian?" Pastor Marsh leaned forward to put his elbows on his desk.

"Yes." Jason cleared his throat. "She's wonderful, perfect, except for one thing." He licked his dry lips. "I've always wanted to marry a woman who is pure—a virgin. That's important to me." He hesitated. "I even realized I might be expecting a bit too much. Today many women aren't pure."

"Most men aren't, either," Pastor Marsh said.

"True." Jason rubbed his hands down his face. "I think I could take her not being a virgin, except that she's been very promiscuous." Jason glanced up, then hurried on. "She lived with her aunt, who is very liberal. The aunt encouraged her to live for herself."

"Has she continued this behavior after becoming a Christian?"

"No." Jason shook his head. "She doesn't even date. My sister told me that Maddy said she's afraid of returning to that lifestyle, so she stays away from men."

"I see." Pastor Marsh folded his hands together. "So the problem is that she's been with more than one man when she wasn't a Christian. Is that right?"

The anger he'd felt when Maddy had first told him of her past burned through Jason again. He'd always prayed for a wife who had saved herself for marriage. He'd been so sure that God would answer that prayer—that this was God's desire for marriage—that Jason hadn't considered he might fall in love with a woman who wasn't a virgin.

Love? In love? The thought hit Jason hard enough to steal his breath. He didn't love Maddy. He couldn't love her. Couldn't.

"My agent called last night about an extended assignment. I'd be gone for four months. I'm thinking I should take it. By the time I return, this will be resolved." Jason spoke with forced finality.

"You think running away is the answer?" Brendon tented his fingers, tapping them against his lips.

"I'm not running." Jason allowed the anger to cloak him. "I'm giving us time and distance. Sometimes you have to do that when you resolve problems."

"Possibly." Brendon nodded. "Tell me this, Jason. Why did you become a Christian?"

"What?" Jason stared at his pastor.

"Why did you become a Christian? What prompted you to ask Jesus to become your Savior?"

Jason frowned, recalling the time when he'd been weighed down with guilt for the anger and hatred he felt toward his mother. She'd not only turned her back on him and his father, but kept him from knowing his twin sister. "I couldn't take the sin anymore, the awful anger I felt. I had to be rid of it."

"What happened when you gave your life to Christ?"

"I became a new person. We all do." Jason tipped his head to the side, studying Brendon. "Why?"

"I was wondering what happened to all your sin," Brendon said.

"God removed it. The Bible says as far as the east is from the west. Right?" Jason asked.

Brendon's smile lit the room. "Right." He paused, his gaze direct and intent. "So if you were made new, washed clean from all you'd done wrong, what's so different about Maddy?"

The words slammed into Jason with the force of a physical blow—the truth. He'd been cleansed of hatred. Was sexual sin any worse than hatred? Not according to the Bible. Maddy hadn't continued her sinful ways. She'd been very careful. If God had forgiven her for what she'd done, who was he to hold her past against her? Dropping his head into his hands, Jason couldn't hold back the tears.

Brendon came around the desk. He and Jason knelt by the chair, and they prayed together for Jason, for Maddy, for their relationship if this was God's will.

"Jason, a word of caution." Brendon put his hand on Jason's shoulder as they stood together at the door. "If you do continue seeing Maddy, be aware of the damage her past may have done. Just as you wouldn't offer an ex-alcoholic any liquor, be cautious about pushing any physical closeness on Maddy. She may not have the defenses. From now on, purity in the relationship is your responsibility."

⁂

Hitting the key to send the document to the printer, Maddy pushed back her chair to stand and stretch. Before she shut everything down for the day, she wanted to ask Jazmyn if they could go for a latte or something. She had to talk to someone. This past week had been a worse nightmare than when Jason was out of town. If this kept up, she could write a book on becoming a zombie. Little food, less sleep made a person a brain-dead zombie.

Jazmyn was on the phone. She gestured Maddy to come on in the office. Maddy waited near the door, her thoughts on what she would say to Jazmyn.

"Maddy, I'm so glad you're still here." Jazmyn clicked the phone off and flung the cell in her purse. "Caleb is running a high fever. Thor called. I have to get home right away, but I haven't finished this paperwork. I promised Kirsten I'd have it ready for the meeting tomorrow." Jazmyn fumbled at a pile of papers on her desk, scattering them even more.

"Stop." Maddy hurried over to her friend. "Go home." She squeezed Jazmyn's hand. "Take care of your son. I'll get this all together. I don't mind."

"Are you sure?" Tears glittered in Jazmyn's eyes.

"Hey. He'll be fine. Babies get fevers all the time. He's probably cutting teeth or has an ear infection." Maddy forced a smile. "I didn't have any plans for tonight. I'll get this all together and ready for the morning."

"Maddy, I don't know what I'd do without you." Jazmyn hugged her. "Call in an order from the deli for your supper. Put it on my tab. They'll deliver. Thanks so much."

Watching her friend hurry down the hall, Maddy wanted to cry. She'd finally worked up the courage to talk to someone, and now she couldn't. The ache in her chest seemed to expand until she wanted to curl up and die. Maybe Jason had been right to turn his back on her. Maybe she wasn't worthy to be a Christian.

Quiet settled over the building as workers called good-byes to one another and left for the evening. Maddy stayed in her office going through the paperwork she'd taken from Jazmyn's desk. She couldn't concentrate. Thoughts of Jason flitted through her memory. Pictures of their time together in the early morning hours, the overwhelming fear when she thought he'd drowned, the sweetness of his kiss. Maddy shook her head. "Girl, you gotta forget the man. He made it clear he's outta here."

"Talking to yourself is a sign of madness. That why you're called Maddy?"

Maddy squeaked. "Erik, you could make some noise instead of scaring a girl to death." She sat back in the chair, waiting for her heart to quit racing.

Erik dangled a deli bag from his fingers. "A little bird said you needed to eat so I picked up some comfort food."

"I don't need comfort." Maddy narrowed her eyes.

"Maybe not, but I do." Erik twirled a chair around and plopped the bag on the desktop, scattering a pile of papers. He scooped them up from the floor looking so sheepish that Maddy couldn't do anything but laugh.

"What's up, Erik? Aren't you getting ready to head out again?"

"Tomorrow morning." Erik began to pull out sandwiches, potato salad, and plasticware. "I need some advice."

"You've come to the right place. Madame Mad at your service. Have you considered my rates, though? You may not be able to afford such an expert."

"I did think about that." Erik lifted a wrapped slice of lemon cake with creamy frosting from the bag and held it out of Maddy's reach. "Will this do?"

"Ooh, you are so bad. You know I'll do anything for that cake." Maddy grabbed at the sweet and missed.

"Uh-uh. Not until you've eaten and I've gotten my advice, Madame Mad."

Laughing, they opened their sandwiches. Maddy waited until they'd prayed and eaten enough to take the edge off their hunger before asking, "So, what's up?"

"It's Zuria." Erik set his food down. "I can't stop thinking of her. I've tried to convince her to meet me, but she won't go against her father's wishes. He still thinks I'm too much of a scoundrel to be good enough for her."

"What does her father do?" Maddy asked.

"He runs a clothing shop, very upscale, geared toward younger women. In fact, he has several shops and is trying to expand again."

"Well." Maddy leaned forward. "As a buyer, you have something in common. Go visit Zuria and her father. Focus on him, not his daughter. You can let her know beforehand that you want to get to know him." Maddy reached across the desk to touch Erik's hand. "Once he sees who you are, he won't object to you dating his daughter."

"Madame Mad, I think you might have hit on the solution." Erik winked at her. "Now, how can I help you? You're looking a little peaked tonight."

The lump in her throat kept her from swallowing for a few minutes. Maddy blinked back tears. She refused to cry anymore. For the next few minutes she filled Erik in on all that had happened between her and Jason. When she finished, she was so drained she couldn't even eat more.

"Maddy, do you love him?" Erik reached over to clasp her hands in his. "Do you?"

Maddy closed her eyes for a moment. "Yes, I do. But Erik, I'm so wrong for him."

"Why?"

"Because he's so good. He's been a Christian for so long. He's never done the horrible things I've done." Her eyes burned. She bit her lip to stifle the things she wanted to say.

"Maddy, I thought we were all sinners saved by grace. Isn't that what the Bible says?" Erik's blue gaze bored into hers.

"Yes, but—"

"No buts, Maddy. He's a sinner, just like you and me. No difference." Erik squeezed her hands. "If he can't see the treasure he has before him, then he isn't worthy of you. Picture this, Maddy. Jesus died for you just like He died for Jason. There is no difference to Him, and there shouldn't be to us, either."

Tears trickled down Maddy's cheeks. What Erik said sounded so right, but would Jason ever see the truth?

Chapter 17

"Hey." Erik leaned over the desk to wipe a tear from her cheek. Maddy sniffed. She pulled open her drawer and tugged a tissue from a box. "Maddy, I'm serious. If he passes up the chance to love you as much as you love him, he's a fool."

"Maybe he's the one who isn't a fool, Erik." Maddy wiped her nose. "Think about it. If we married and had kids, what would they think if they found out what their mother had been like? My past could affect how they grow up."

"Why is that?" Erik brushed the crumbs from his sandwich into his hand and dropped them in a trash can. "Would you teach your daughters the same things your aunt taught you?"

Maddy's eyes widened. Her face heated. "No. You know that. I would tell them how much you suffer for having lived that kind of lifestyle."

"Then I guess you're right. Your past would affect the way they grow up. They would be well-informed, raised with a scriptural upbringing, and able to make positive choices. Your background doesn't have to affect them in an adverse way."

"But..." Maddy wrapped the rest of her sandwich and put it back in the bag. "What if it does?"

"I've heard about a lot of kids in church. Some of them come from great Christian homes with godly parents who have taught them biblical truth from the time they were babies. Most of them turn out to be great Christians, but there are a few who make other choices. There is no guarantee, Maddy. You can pray for your kids to choose God, but you can't make that choice for them. Do your best, and give them to God. That's what I've heard my pastor say more than once.

"You know my past is similar to yours. We've both lived very promiscuous, ungodly lives. I've struggled with this, too. Zuria and I talked at length about kids and choices. I'm not just saying this off the top of my head." Erik pulled the wrapped piece of cake from where he'd hidden it from her. "Enough serious discussion. Let's eat cake." He grinned.

Maddy couldn't help laughing. "Zuria is one lucky lady. I know her dad will love you, Erik. When are you going to bring her over here to meet the family?"

"So far, you're the only one who knows of my interest in her. I haven't said anything because my family can be so..."

"Family-like?" Maddy winked.

"Yeah, I can see Thor climbing on the first plane available and confronting

318

Zuria's father. Kirsten would be right behind him. They've always wanted to fight my battles even though I'm now considered a big boy."

Maddy giggled at the thought. Erik was well over six feet tall with shoulders so broad she wondered if he had to turn sideways to enter an elevator. "I'll keep mum about this, but I want to meet Zuria soon."

"Well, enjoy that cake." Erik stood. "I have to finish packing and get a little sleep for an early takeoff tomorrow. I'll call Zuria about visiting her father. Pray for us."

"I will." Maddy stood up to give Erik a quick hug. "Thank you, Erik. You're the best brother a girl could have. Maybe you could give mine lessons." She listened to Erik's laugh as he headed for the elevator.

Her eyes were still gritty as Maddy walked into her office the next morning. She'd spent some time in prayer last night after Erik left, then stayed late finishing the paperwork for Jazmyn. The scent of the hot peppermint latte she carried drew her on. She'd decided to splurge in order to stay awake during the meeting this morning.

"Maddy, you are a gem." Jazmyn gave her a hug. "You finished everything, and it's all on my desk ready to go. I'm here to give you a warning."

"Warning?" Maddy's sleep-deprived brain fumbled to think of what she'd done wrong.

"Yes. If you ever try to leave here, I'll tie you to your office chair and hold you hostage." Jazmyn grinned.

"Hmm. I think that is more of a threat than a warning." Maddy tapped her lip with her finger. "I'm thinking this might be some leverage for a raise."

Jazmyn laughed. "I'll put in a good word with the boss. He and I are pretty close, you know."

"So I've heard." Maddy laughed. "Oh, how is Caleb this morning?"

"We took him in last night. Thor insisted we had to. He did have another ear infection. He's taking decongestant and something for the pain again. He was sleeping when I left. I'll probably cut my day short after the meeting."

"I can present your ideas this morning if you want to get back home," Maddy said.

"That's okay. Thor will call if Caleb wakes up. We don't have too much on the agenda, so the meeting won't take too long."

Maddy was glad Jazmyn had been right. She couldn't have sat through more than an hour of discussion and presentations. Even with the latte she had trouble staying alert.

"Well, I'm heading home. Time to take care of baby and daddy." Jazmyn shook her head. "I don't know which one is worse—Caleb being sick or Thor worrying about his baby boy."

"That's one I don't envy you. Give that sweetie of yours a kiss from me."

319

Maddy raised an eyebrow at Jazmyn's look of surprise. "I meant Caleb, not Thor."

They shared a laugh as Jazmyn headed out.

The knock on her door a few minutes later startled Maddy. She looked up a the door swung open. Jason stood there, his blond hair tousled as if he'd been in windstorm. He took her breath away, but she couldn't let him see that.

"Jazmyn left a few minutes ago. Caleb isn't feeling well, so Jazmyn will b at home the rest of the day." Maddy tried to keep her tone even, hoping Jaso couldn't hear her heart pounding.

"Actually, I wanted to see you." Jason's intense green gaze held her fas Maddy couldn't move if she wanted to. And at the moment, she didn't want to.

✍

Palms sweating, Jason waited for Maddy to say something. Anything. He knew she had every right to toss him out of her office without an explanation becaus of the way he'd treated her the last time they were together. He prayed she' show lenience and allow him to apologize for his behavior.

Her hair had grown out some. The windswept red with blond tips glistened i the late morning light. Maddy's brown eyes were huge and dark with emotion, he full lips thinned a bit as if she were biting back words that shouldn't come out. H could only imagine what she was thinking; he could see the hurt in her face.

"Maddy, please." Jason cleared his throat. "I need to talk to you. Will yo take a short break? We could go for a quick coffee or something." Jason stoppe short of getting on his knees and begging. He hadn't realized the depth of hi love for Maddy. He'd been denying those feelings before. Now they washed ove him in a deluge reminiscent of the flood they'd experienced.

Her eyes glittered as she gave a short nod. "I'll let Kirsten know. I can onl be gone twenty or thirty minutes. With Jazmyn out, I have a lot of work."

"Thanks." Jason wanted to say more but kept quiet as she called her bos and they made their way to the coffee shop down the street. "What would yo like?" Jason asked.

"I think an iced coffee. I've had enough hot coffee today." Maddy stared a the menu. "How about the orange cream?"

"Sounds good. My treat." Jason wanted to touch her but refrained. "Why don you grab a table while I order?" He watched while Maddy chose one of the ta tables with the high stools. She'd told him once those were her favorite becaus they made her feel taller than her five foot four.

He carried the iced drinks to the table and climbed onto the stool opposit Maddy's. The desire to hold her, touch her, was almost overwhelming. Wit Pastor Marsh's warning ringing in his heart, Jason sipped his drink.

"You said Caleb is sick. What's the matter?"

Maddy explained about the ear infection. Her expression as she talked of th baby softened. Jason couldn't help smiling.

"Maddy, I have to apologize to you. I was wrong to treat you the way I did. I'm so sorry."

She stared at her drink, not looking at him. Her thumb rubbed the moisture from the outside of her cup. Jason thought he could see the glitter of tears in her eyes. He didn't know what to say. *Lord, please give me the words to mend the hurt I've caused Maddy.*

"I want to say that I didn't mean to suggest you weren't good enough for me, but that wouldn't be true." Jason halted when Maddy's tortured gaze met his. "I have to be honest. I spoke with my pastor. He pointed out that I was being a self-righteous Pharisee. What you did was no worse than any of the sins I've committed, yet I acted like I was better than you. I can't undo my actions, but I'm asking for your forgiveness."

He met Maddy's gaze as she studied him. He waited. Brendon had warned him that Maddy might not want to forgive at first. Jason prayed she would be able to.

"I understand why you would have trouble with my past. I do, too." Maddy bit her lip. She took a sip of her drink. "I've already forgiven you, Jason. I have to get back to work." Maddy slipped off the stool and picked up her drink.

"I'll walk you back," Jason said.

"You don't have to." Maddy attempted to smile. "I think I know the way."

"That's okay. I still have more to say to you." Jason took her elbow as they crossed the room. Maybe he shouldn't, but the need to touch her overwhelmed him.

"I'm listening," Maddy spoke as the door closed behind them.

"Maddy, I can't stop seeing you." Jason pulled her close to the building, out of the way of foot traffic, and she looked up at him. "I want to spend time with you and see where this leads. My feelings for you won't go away. Trust me, I've tried to ignore them. I can't sleep thinking about you."

"Sleeping pills might be easier." Maddy's attempt at humor and her sad smile tore at his heart.

"Look, I have this assignment coming up. I'm supposed to go to a dude ranch and take pictures. I've cleared it with the owner if I bring an assistant. He's providing cabins for both of us. Will you go with me?" He held his breath, waiting for her answer.

"I don't know if I can get away from the office."

"It's only for a long weekend. We'll drive there on Thursday after you get off work. We'll be back by Sunday night, so you'll be able to show up Monday morning." He brushed his fingers over her cheek. "I can put some pressure on one of your bosses."

"I don't know." Maddy stared down.

"If you're worried. . ." Jason hesitated, not sure how to say what he needed to say. "I'll agree to keep the relationship completely platonic." Maddy's cheeks reddened as she met his eyes. "I understand some of the struggles you might be facing now. I promise not to do anything that will compromise you. Will that help?"

Maddy swallowed hard. She blinked. A tear dropped from her lashes. Jason caught it with his thumb.

Maddy closed her eyes. "Okay. I'll go."

Jason wanted to shout. He wanted to grab Maddy up and twirl her around. He tilted his head until their foreheads met. "Thanks, Mad Girl."

Chapter 18

Jason opened Maddy's door and took her elbow as she climbed from the car. Her awestruck expression as she took in the secluded ranch in the Tucson foothills mirrored his own wonder. "I didn't even know this was here. Did you?" he asked.

"I'd heard there were dude ranches around, but I've never seen one of them." Maddy took a step and swiveled to look down a lane that must lead to the barn and paddocks. "If we hadn't just driven through the rush hour traffic, I wouldn't believe there was anyone close to here. These trees are amazing. They must be almost as old as the hills."

She was right. Some of the mesquite trees growing around the buildings were larger than any Jason had ever seen. There were also green-barked paloverde trees. The hills leading off toward the east were dusted with stately saguaro cacti. He knew the ranch bordered the Saguaro National Forest, which explained the abundance of the old cacti.

"I have to take plenty of pictures, but we'll also have time to take in some of the activities offered." Jason smiled as Maddy's eyes lit up.

"You mean we'll get to ride the horses?"

"If you want. They also have hiking trails, swimming, mountain-bike trails, a sauna, and that's just what I remember from the brochure." Jason chuckled as her eyes widened. "Shall we go in and find out where we're staying?"

Jason's focus was drawn to the old wooden beams when they stepped inside. This place would photograph well. He almost missed the introduction to the manager when she approached. He tuned in to what she was saying.

"This is our busy season, especially right now. A lot of schools in the north and east are on spring break. The parents want something a little different where there's warm weather, so they come to a dude ranch." The manager's smile as she escorted Jason and Maddy through the lodge could have given the power company a boost. "We have a lot of repeat customers."

They stopped outside a door. "We saved you this suite so you could see what our best accommodations are like. The writer who is covering the story was here last week in the same room." She slid a key card through a lock and opened the door, stepping back to allow Jason and Maddy to enter. "I'll have your bags brought from your car." The manager stepped inside to flip on more lights. The spacious sitting area contained a couch, two recliners, a coffee table with a vase of fresh flowers, and a couple of end tables, all done in a Western theme. "The bedroom is through here." The manager led the way to a recessed door.

"Um. I think there's a mistake here." Jason could see the upset in Maddy's expression. "We need two rooms, not one. This is a beautiful suite, but we can't both stay here."

The manager cocked her head to one side. "You and your wife want separate rooms? I'm so sorry. I didn't understand that."

"We're, uh, we're not married." Jason could feel the heat in his face. He couldn't look at Maddy.

"Oh, I see." The manager plucked her cell phone from her pocket and flipped it open. "Let me check on what else is available. As I said, this is our busy time right now. Excuse me a minute." She crossed the room with rapid steps, exiting as she began to speak into the phone.

"Sorry." Jason turned to Maddy. Her cheeks were dark with embarrassment. "We could run out and get married real quick, you know. Mexico isn't that far away. We could even make it back before midnight." He wiggled his eyebrows to let her know he was joking, although there was a part of him willing to consider the notion.

"I would never elope to Mexico." Maddy crossed her arms and glared at him. "It would have to be Vegas with an Elvis impersonator or nothing."

"Oh well." Jason heaved an exaggerated sigh. "Vegas is too far. We'd never have time to get back here and take the pictures I need. Too bad."

"You are awful." Maddy leaned close to speak as the manager's footsteps sounded outside the door. Jason was glad to see his joking had relieved the tension. Maddy's eyes twinkled with suppressed mirth now.

"Once again, I apologize for the mix-up." The woman's perfect brows drew together as she crossed the room to them. "I don't have any other suites available. The only room I have is a single that is on the other side of the lodge from here. It does have a queen-size bed."

"You know." Jason studied the exceptional room with the rounded beams in the ceiling and the wide fireplace. "Perhaps there's someone in one of the single rooms who would like to upgrade to a suite. I could take some pictures tonight and be done with this room."

The manager pursed her lips. "We have a couple who have yet to check in. They are coming for an anniversary and could only afford the smaller room for the weekend. I'm sure they would be delighted at the trade. Their room is close to the other one available. Would you have the pictures done by, say, seven o'clock?"

"No problem." Jason winked at Maddy, happy the dilemma could be solved so easily. He whispered to Maddy as they left the room. "Whew. Saved us the quick trip to Vegas."

"Not to mention the Elvis impersonator wedding." Maddy's lips thinned as if she was trying not to giggle.

*

"This place is incredible." Maddy slanted a look at Jason as they rounded a hill on the foot trail they were following. "I think I may have said that before."

"No more than five hundred times." Jason stopped again to lift his camera and focus on the mountains in the distance. Maddy knew this would be a great picture. The foothills, green from the spring showers and dotted with cacti, stood out against the taller, darker Santa Catalina Mountains.

"I get the feeling we're alone in the world out here." Maddy sucked in the clear air. "No exhaust. No horns blaring. No sirens or helicopters. We aren't that far from town, but it's so quiet. Almost as quiet as Burke and Blaire's place."

She jumped as something jerked her hair. "What are you doing?" She tried to glare at Jason, but his adorable grin had her fighting not to smile.

"You reminded me of the time I took your picture at the Dunham ranch. I was pretending to be an ostrich." Jason lifted his camera and clicked a quick picture.

"Okay, buster. I want that film. I did not sign a waiver for you to take my picture." Maddy put her hands on her hips.

"You can't have the film. This is a digital camera." Jason chuckled and held out his hand. "Come on, let's head back. It's almost time for lunch. After that we're scheduled to go for a horseback ride. They've arranged for a guide to take us to some exceptional spots that I can photograph."

"How many pictures of this place will be used with the magazine article?"

"Only a few, but since I'm here already, the ranch is getting a cut rate on pictures. They decided to make up a new brochure. There are a couple of other possibilities my agent is working on, too. One is a book about unusual vacation spots." They stepped into a spacious dining room.

"Oh my." Maddy breathed in the aroma of fresh-baked bread. "I hope they have something to lift me up on that horse, because I won't be able to climb on after this meal. Will you look at that dessert table?"

"This way, Maddy. You're supposed to get the fresh bread, salad, and soup first." Jason's green eyes sparkled. "No dessert unless you clean your plate. And certainly no dessert first."

"You are the worst ogre. I am taking notes. I plan to report back to your sister."

"I am trembling in fear." Jason widened his eyes, clapping his hand to his chest.

"Good. I'm heading for the sweets." Maddy laughed over her shoulder at the look of surprise on Jason's face.

"I can't believe you're doing this." Humor tinged Jason's tone as he caught up to her as she perused the extended table laden with goodies. "Think of the example to all the kids in this room."

"You, for instance?" Maddy quirked up an eyebrow at him.

"Yeah." Jason grabbed a pair of tongs to pluck up something gooey with cherries on it. "See, I'm ruined for life."

"You can't fool me. Jazmyn told me about the time you had s'mores for breakfast in the mountains." Maddy took a couple of small dessert items and turned away from the table. "Besides, I was only letting the line get down at the salad bar."

"Incorrigible." Jason's muttered word almost didn't reach her ears.

When they arrived at the corrals, Jason eyed the horses with trepidation. "Isn't there a rule about waiting an hour before riding?"

"I always heard thirty minutes, and it applies to swimming."

Two of the wranglers came over to help them choose mounts. Maddy chose a chestnut mare. The other wrangler talked to Jason then led out a buckskin gelding for him.

"I'll be taking you out." A tall cowboy with a long face led his horse over to them. "My name's Dan." He shook hands with Jason then Maddy. "Would you like me to pack your cameras until you're ready to use them?" At Jason's nod the man stowed the equipment in one of his saddlebags. "Let's mount up. We've got a bit of ground to cover. I have a list of places they want photographed this afternoon."

Maddy had only been riding once or twice since she moved to Tucson. She'd forgotten how tall a horse could be. She didn't take long to get acclimated. Her horse was more spirited than Jason's. His tended to plod along after the other two, while her mount pranced down the trail eager to run and stretch her legs.

Jason held on to the pommel with both hands, his face a study of concentration.

"Have you ever ridden before?" Maddy asked. "I'd have thought with all your travels riding horses would be old hat."

"I've ridden a camel and an elephant but never a horse." Jason grimaced as the gelding stumbled. "The other two had someone leading them at the time, and it wasn't an experience I wanted to repeat. I almost got seasick on the camel."

Maddy laughed. "I've never heard of that happening, but then I've never met anyone who's ridden a camel before."

"Here I am, at your service." Jason tried to give a bow, but tightened his hold on the saddle as the horse picked up his pace. "How do you stay on when she keeps dancing around like that?"

"She's just a little frisky. I used to ride a lot in Dudleyville." Maddy couldn't resist a little teasing. "When we reach the next open area, maybe we can have a race. I think your horse will follow mine."

"Don't you dare." Jason glared at her. "I would end up in the middle of one of these prickly cacti and have to spend all day tomorrow getting the stickers out."

Maddy tilted her head back and laughed. "I could take pictures."

"How generous of you." Jason rolled his eyes.

The scenery was wild and beautiful. Dan explained that the ranch owned more than six hundred acres. The lodge was far enough into the land that there wouldn't be any close neighbors. With the longer side bordered by the national forest, the dude ranch was assured they wouldn't have intruders building close to them. Privacy was important to the guests who came here.

"Oh, what a beautiful little creek." Maddy pulled her mare to a stop at the top of a hill overlooking a tree-lined stream.

"Most of the year this doesn't have much water. We've gotten enough rain, and with the snow melt from the Catalinas, there's a fair amount running through there." Dan's drawl was almost classic cowboy. "After you get a couple of shots, we'll cross and go to one more place before heading back. I don't want you to be too sore tomorrow." Dan's grin reminded Maddy that her muscles weren't used to this type of exercise.

"Are you sure this is safe to cross?" Jason looked a little pale as he leaned forward to study the bank.

"It's not too deep. Maybe eight inches at the most." Dan rubbed his jaw. "Of course, with the snow factor, the water is a bit chilly." He leaned over and grabbed the reins of Jason's mount. The pair eased down the bank into the stream.

Maddy waited until they were almost across to urge her mare forward. Instead of following the others down the short bank, the chestnut leaped forward, landing in the middle of the creek. The unexpected jump sent Maddy backward. The mare hopped to the right. Maddy slipped sideways, spilling into the frigid water. She gasped at the shock of the cold.

"Maddy!" Jason splashed into the stream and helped her up. Maddy couldn't believe he'd gotten off his horse so fast.

"How did you get down?" She glanced at the bank to see Dan grinning widely.

"I just fell off. It seemed the easiest way to do it in a hurry." Jason held her close. The warmth of his body helped but didn't keep away the chill. Jason cupped her cheek. "Are you okay?" His breath fanned across her face. His mouth was mere inches from hers. Maddy could see he wanted to kiss her. She leaned closer longing for his touch.

Jason stepped back, breaking the connection. "We'd better get out of here before we freeze."

Maddy stared in stunned disbelief. Jason had honored his word. Even when she'd been willing to break a promise, he hadn't.

Chapter 19

Standing in the middle of the stream, cold water sluicing off him, Maddy warm in his arms, Jason could think of almost nothing but kissing her. Almost. Pastor Marsh's warning words whispered through his conscience. Jason listened. He didn't want to, but something told him this was a critical moment in their relationship. Before they could go further, Maddy had to trust him. He stepped back.

"This may be the desert, but snow melt off the mountains makes for cold water. Let's go." Jason grabbed Maddy's hand and led her from the water. They were both shivering.

"You all right, ma'am?" Dan took Maddy's free arm to help her up the bank.

"A little cold. A lot wet." Maddy flashed a grin. "And majorly embarrassed."

Dan laughed. "Even the best of us can end up in the drink once in a while. I forgot to warn you about the mare's idiosyncrasy when she's crossing water. I apologize."

"No problem. It isn't the first time I've fallen." Maddy twisted her shirt to get some of the excess moisture out. Her hair clung to her scalp in wet clumps. Droplets trembled on her eyelashes, and Jason knew they weren't tears. She'd never looked more beautiful to him.

"The last place we were supposed to film is on the way back to the stables." Dan pushed his hat back to rub his head. "You may want to skip it now."

"That's all right." Maddy, her shoes squishing with each step, moved over to the mare and swung into the saddle with simple grace. "I'll be fine. Jason doesn't take too long, and he needs to get those pictures. Tomorrow we'll both be too sore to want to get on a horse." She grinned at Dan as if they shared a secret. Jason wasn't sure what she was talking about.

The next morning Jason understood. When he climbed from bed, he almost collapsed. Muscles he didn't know he had ached so badly he wasn't sure he'd be able to walk. Somehow he got through the day and finished the photo session. He'd hobbled around like an old man, his only consolation being Maddy's equal distress.

☙

Two weeks later, Jason whistled as he climbed from the shower, marveling at the change in his life since going to the dude ranch. He and Maddy had been together almost every day. They'd talked for hours, laughed together, eaten together, worshipped together. His love for her had deepened to the point that he didn't want to be apart from her at all. Every night he called her right before she fell asleep. Each morning he gave her a wake-up call before she left for work. Even the Elvis impersonator wedding was looking like a good option. He wasn't sure he could wait much longer to ask her to be his wife, but he didn't want to rush her and scare her away.

The ringing phone startled him from his reverie. Jason grabbed the handset, thinking only of Maddy calling. "Hey."

"Jason?" His agent sounded hesitant, as if he thought he'd gotten the wrong number. Jason rolled his eyes, wishing he'd taken the time to look at the readout and see who was on the phone.

"Yeah, it's me," Jason said. "What's up?"

"Listen, I need you to go on a last-minute assignment. Brad Walker was supposed to do this job, but he was in an accident yesterday and ended up in traction in the hospital. The photo shoot can't be put off."

"Is it local?"

"No, this one's for two weeks out of the country. I can arrange for you to leave this afternoon." The agent paused. "Please, Jason. I've promised to try to fill this one. There's no way Brad can go, and everyone else is already on assignment elsewhere."

A shroud of heaviness settled over him. He didn't want to leave right now. He wanted to be with Maddy. Memories of the last time he'd left town when he'd been serious about a girl flitted through his mind. Maddy wasn't like that. She wouldn't turn her back on him while he was away. He could trust her.

"Okay, I'll be ready to go by late this afternoon. Call me with the details." Jason spent a few minutes discussing the assignment, jotting notes about what he would need to pack and what equipment would be involved. His agent promised to send him an e-mail with all the particulars so he could print what he needed before the flight time.

The drive downtown to T. L. Enterprises didn't take long. Traffic was thinning out since the warmer weather was approaching. Jason pulled into the covered parking garage, waved at the guard, and slipped his SUV into a visitor slot.

Maddy's smile when she saw him would be the high point of the day. Jason stuck his hands into his pockets to keep from grabbing her and kissing her. Keeping the relationship from becoming intimate was up to him. He repeated it in his mind like a mantra.

"Hi. Let me get this e-mailed off to Kirsten, and then I can take a short break," Maddy said. A couple of minutes later, she turned away from the computer. "So, what's up?"

"I have to leave town." Pleasure washed over Jason at the look of dismay on

Maddy's face. She would miss him. He explained the reasons. "I'll only be gone for two weeks. I'll call you every chance I get."

"Blaire called and invited us up this weekend for Caitlin's birthday. I was going to ask you today." Maddy tried to cover her disappointment, but Jason could still see the regret in her eyes. "I'll be going. Sometimes cell reception isn't the best at their house."

"I remember." Jason traced his thumb down her cheek. "Don't go chasing any javelina while you're there. Okay?"

"Not without you." Maddy tilted her head. "I don't plan to swim in the San Pedro either."

Jason laughed. "Maddy, I have to go. I. . ." He wanted to say so much more but didn't know how to verbalize what he felt. "I had something else planned for this weekend. I suppose I should wait until I get back, but I can't." Jason rounded the desk and knelt beside Maddy's chair. Her eyes were huge as she stared at him.

Opening the small box he'd concealed in his palm, Jason asked, "Maddy, I love you. Will you marry me?"

ↈ

Gaping like a fish lying on a riverbank, Maddy stared at Jason. Had he just used the *L* word in conjunction with the *M* word? She couldn't breathe. Her gaze lowered to the glittering ring he was holding now between his thumb and forefinger. Tears burned her eyes.

"Oh, Jason. Yes." She flung her arms around his neck. "Yes, I'll marry you." She sniffed, trying to hold back the tears.

"And why is that?" One side of Jason's mouth quirked up.

"What?" Maddy stared at him openmouthed. Then she realized what she'd forgotten to say. She pursed her lips as if pondering his question. "Well, let's see. You do take the most beautiful pictures." Jason glared at her.

"Um." Maddy tapped her lower lip with one finger. "How about because you're so brave when crossing flooded rivers?" Jason scowled even more. "You're very good at dismounting from horses?" This time Jason gave an audible growl.

Maddy couldn't keep tormenting him. "Maybe because I love you to distraction. I can't sleep or get my work done because I'm always daydreaming about you and wishing we could be together all the time. Will that do?"

Jason grinned. "That's much better." He started to lean forward as if he wanted to kiss her, then stopped. He slipped the ring on her finger, sadness filling his eyes. "I have to go, Maddy. I'll be back in two weeks, and we can discuss everything." Maddy knew the story of his previous fiancée and how hard this must be for Jason.

"If you leave right now, you won't be able to come back in two weeks." Maddy couldn't help smiling at Jason's confused expression. "If you leave without telling your sister, who is in the office right there, that we're engaged, you'll never be allowed to come home. Am I right?"

Jason grimaced. "I suppose you are." He stood and held out his hand. "Shall we brave the squealing and clapping hordes?"

He was right, Maddy noted. Jazmyn did squeal. So did Kirsten and about half the other girls who worked on this floor. Jason didn't get away for another forty-five minutes. She wanted to keep him longer but knew he would be late for his flight. She really wanted to drag him into a corner and kiss him silly but respected his caution and was aware of her own lack of control.

✍

Two weeks stretched ahead like eternity. Maddy tried to keep busy. She treasured the time spent with Jason on the phone, but those times were few and far between. She wished she could just be there with him—that they were already married and didn't ever have to be apart.

"Hey, Maddy." Erik stuck his head in her doorway. "I'm looking for someone to have lunch with me. Kirsten gave you a reprieve and permission for a long lunch."

"Hey." Maddy grinned at her friend. "I haven't seen you since you got back. You have to fill me in on everything that happened." She grabbed her purse from the bottom drawer and put her computer on hibernate. "I'm ready."

The deli was crowded with the remainder of the lunch crowd. Maddy found a table by the window while Erik ordered their sandwiches.

"I hear congratulations are in order." Erik pulled her hand close to examine the ring after they'd prayed over their food. "Are you happy?" His eyes were somber as he studied her.

"Very." Maddy sighed. "I just can't wait for Jason to get home tomorrow." She opened her potato salad. "Okay, enough small talk." She grinned when Erik laughed. "Give me all the juicy details. Did Zuria's dad love you or what?"

"Let me say it wasn't love at first sight." Erik laughed as Maddy rolled her eyes. "Zuria wanted me to visit them and stay at the house. Her mother was all for it, but her father didn't even want to look at me."

Erik took a long drink. "To make the story short, I felt like a fifth wheel most of the time. I couldn't seem to do anything right. Her father was always upset with me over something. Mostly for breathing, I think."

Maddy patted his hand. "I can't imagine it was that bad."

"It was." Erik shook his head. "Zuria finally took me aside and told me this would never work out."

"Oh, Erik. What did you do?" Maddy didn't know whether to be angry or sad.

"Well, it turns out Zuria's mother didn't share her father's feelings. She took me aside, told me he was scared of losing his only little girl. He was afraid she'd move to the United States and he'd never see her again. She also said he had a business problem that had been eating at him, which was making him more difficult to be around." Erik winked at Maddy. "It so happens I knew exactly what to do to solve the problem."

"You did?" Maddy grinned.

"Yep. First things first. The next morning I went to his office. I didn't want to betray a confidence or put him off. I told him about a business problem we'd had. I didn't tell him we'd already solved it, but put the solution to him as a possibility. You could almost hear the wheels turning."

"You are so devious." Maddy took another bite, chewing as she listened.

"After giving him time to consider how well this would work for him, I got down to business. I told him I loved his daughter, and I believed she loved me. I also explained how often I'm in Europe on business, so if we married, Zuria would be visiting often. Then I explained that we were in similar occupations and could share business secrets that might be beneficial to one another."

"I knew he'd love you, and he did, right?"

"It took another day, but the next night at supper he announced that he was giving his blessing if Zuria and I wished to marry."

"Oh, Erik, that's wonderful." Maddy jumped up from her chair. She leaned over to kiss him on the cheek. Erik caught her in a hug as she did. As the embrace ended, Maddy's gaze was drawn to the window. Jason stood outside, staring at them, hurt etched in every line of his face.

Chapter 20

The desperation in Maddy's voice as she called after him echoed through Jason's head as he drove. He hadn't stopped, knowing he couldn't bear her excuses. The pain that knifed through him when he'd seen her embracing Erik had turned to a dull, throbbing ache in his heart. He should have known. He should have learned his lesson years ago. What was the old saying? Something about "Fool me once, shame on you; fool me twice, shame on me"? Well, he was ashamed of being so gullible. Never again. Never.

Turning the SUV onto a dirt road, Jason slowed to accommodate the washboard surface. He'd been so excited to surprise Maddy. The photography job had finished early. Jason had changed his ticket for a day earlier than his scheduled flight, longing to get home to his fiancée. If he'd known how little she cared for him, he would have stayed overseas longer. Maybe forever.

A small turnout came into view as he rounded the next curve. Jason slowed, easing off onto the rutted parking spot. He climbed from his car and locked the door. Not far from where he stood a narrow trail led up the hills to an outcropping of rock. Jason hadn't been here for years, but he used to come here often to pray and have some time alone.

He hadn't been hiking as much. By the time he settled on the point of the outcropping, his legs ached from the steepness of the path. Jason stared out over the vista without seeing the miles of hills rolling out below him. The ache inside was more than he could bear. He didn't want to admit how much Maddy's betrayal hurt. His previous fiancée's jilting was nothing compared to this. She'd had only a part of him. He'd never realized how little he loved her until now. His love for Maddy was so deep that the hurt was almost unbearable.

"Lord, I'm angry. I don't know how You could have allowed this to happen. You know how long it's taken me to trust anyone." Jason stopped, swallowing hard, fighting to keep his emotions in check. "I guess I shouldn't blame You. I knew she and Erik were close. I've seen them together before, but she assured me they were only friends. That embrace looked like more than you would give someone you claimed was like a brother."

Doubt niggled at Jason's conscience. Did Maddy feel comfortable hugging Erik because they didn't have romantic feelings for one another, or had she hugged him because they did? Confusion warred within. Jason dropped his head into his hands, glad there was no one here to witness his meltdown.

Night had fallen by the time Jason arrived back in Tucson. He grabbed some fast food at a drive-through window. He couldn't face seeing people right now. This was Friday night. Party time. Date night. Something he'd hoped to be doing with Maddy. On the return flight that's all he could think about.

As he pulled into his driveway, Jason knew what he had to do. He'd call his agent first thing tomorrow morning and see what was available. Maybe there was an assignment in Nepal or Timbuktu. He would take anything as long as he could leave this town. Everywhere he turned here he could see Maddy embracing Erik. Jason knew he had to get away to retain his sanity.

Jason jerked awake. He'd fallen asleep on the couch. Cold french fries and a burger had spilled onto the floor beside him. He rubbed his face, trying to wipe away the dream. Maddy had been there, laughing up at him, her sparkling eyes dancing with amusement. He'd been so warm with love for her. The ring he'd put on her finger sparkled in the lights of the restaurant where he'd planned to take her.

Swinging his feet to the floor, Jason sat up. His stomach churned. Maybe he'd just get a flu bug and die off. That had to be better than the misery he was living.

A knock on the door startled him. He glanced at the window, surprised to find it was morning. Scooping up the spilled food, he put it back in the bag beside the coffee table before checking to see who was at the door.

"Jazmyn." Jason swung the door open and turned to head for the kitchen. He needed some coffee, not caring how rude his actions were.

"He's here, Thor." Jazmyn's words had Jason groaning. Just what he needed.

The scent of ground coffee filled the air by the time Thor, Jazmyn, and Caleb were inside. Jason couldn't even muster a smile for his nephew, even though Caleb normally delighted him.

"Have a seat." He gestured at the table. "Coffee will be ready in a minute. What brings you out so early?"

"Jason, it's ten o'clock. You promised to come for breakfast when you called from the airport on Thursday." Jazmyn took Caleb from Thor as the baby began to fuss. "What's going on, Jason?"

Rubbing his unshaven jaw, Jason knew he must look like something the cat dragged in from an alley. "I overslept." He couldn't think of anything else to say, and that was sort of the truth. He'd also forgotten about breakfast, but he wouldn't tell his sister that.

"Besides, I have to do laundry and pack. I'm going on another assignment." Jason didn't say he hadn't talked with his agent yet. He knew there was always something available somewhere.

"You can't go off right now." Jazmyn's eyes narrowed as she studied him.

"We're planning a special barbecue next weekend for Thor's birthday. Remember? You promised to take pictures."

"I don't think I'm up to any big shindig right now," Jason said.

"It isn't big. Mostly family. Burke and Blaire will be there with their kids." She waited a beat. "You promised, Jason." Caleb began to cry in earnest.

"Let me take him outside for a walk." Thor held out his hands for the baby. "I think he's getting as upset as his mother."

They were quiet until Thor closed the door. Jason couldn't meet his sister's gaze. She studied him for a long time, making him want to shift in his chair like some schoolboy caught shooting spit wads at the teacher.

"Jason, I know something happened with Maddy. You can't run off like this. You have to stay and see it through. Maddy is devastated."

"Right." Jason could hear the bitterness in his tone.

"Jason, did you ever know why Mom left Dad and took me instead of you?" Jazmyn's hand trembled on her coffee cup. Jason stared at her. He'd always wondered why her, not him.

"She left Dad because of some trumped-up idea that he was cheating on her. She took me because she thought all males were the same, so you would turn out just like your father. Mom told me that many times over the years, but I refused to believe it."

Jason couldn't say anything. He stared at his sister, unable to comprehend what their mother had done. To his dying day, their father refused to date or have anything to do with another woman. His love for his wife was an inspiration to Jason.

"She ran, Jason. Without giving Dad a chance to talk to her or explain. Every time he found us, she ran." Jazmyn touched his arm. "Do you understand what I'm saying?"

Jason could only nod. Jazmyn was wondering if he was turning out like their mother. Well, he wasn't. He couldn't.

"Maddy is devastated, Jason," Jazmyn said. "She loves you. She won't talk to me about what happened, but give her a chance to explain. Please."

It was the please that got him—that and the accusation that he was just like their mother. Jason had never been able to deny his twin anything. He loved her more than he would ever let her know. He knew he wouldn't be making the call to his agent. However, he wasn't sure he'd be able to survive the pain of staying here.

⁂

"Maddy, is the paperwork ready on the Carson file?" Kirsten asked as Maddy entered her office carrying a latte she'd ordered.

"Almost." Maddy set the cup on the desk where Kirsten liked it. "I have to finish the comparison chart and the cost and expense tables. I should have them ready by three o'clock. Will that be okay?"

"Fine, Maddy." Kirsten took a sip of her latte. "Everything okay?"

"Yeah." Maddy tried to smile but figured she looked more like she was grimacing than happy. "Is there anything else today? I'd like to leave a few minutes early if you don't mind."

"Big sale at the mall?" Kirsten smiled. "I haven't had a chance to hear what's happening this weekend."

"No sale. I just need a little time." Maddy didn't want to admit that she had to get away from the office and all the people who still asked when the wedding would be. If one more person asked if the date was set, she would scream.

"I would have said you could take off early, but Thor called a few minutes ago and told me he's calling a last-minute executive meeting. He and Erik will be here at four thirty. He's ordered dinner to be delivered since we'll be going overtime. Can you stay?"

Maddy shrugged. "Sure." At least the other employees would be leaving by four o'clock. She wouldn't have to worry about them saying anything. "What's the meeting about? A new client?"

"He wasn't very forthcoming. I'm not sure what he's got planned. Jazmyn might know. She's been on the phone with him off and on this week but hasn't said what they've been discussing."

"Well, I'd better get the Carson file finished. Is there anything in particular that I need to get ready for the meeting?"

"If so, I'll let you know or Jazmyn will. Thanks for the latte, Maddy." Kirsten's smile was warm, but Maddy couldn't muster much of a response.

The afternoon dragged on. Maddy kept her office door closed as much as possible to keep others out. She hated to appear unfriendly, but since the fiasco with Erik and Jason, she hadn't been very social. Most of the office workers had noticed, but they'd been polite enough not to ask anything too personal.

The Carson file took longer than she thought. Kirsten asked for a couple of minor changes, which Maddy did almost by rote. She'd been having trouble this week getting her work done as fast as usual. Concentration was hard because the vision of Jason devastated and then running kept ruining her focus.

"Hey, Maddy, we're ready to start." Jazmyn had rapped on the door before sticking her head inside. "Thor and Erik are here. Can't you smell the Chinese food they brought up?" She grinned. "I thought my stomach would beat me to the conference room. I'm starving."

"I smell it now." Maddy didn't want to tell Jazmyn she hadn't been too hungry this past week. Besides, the food did smell good. Maybe with friends to distract her, thoughts of her dilemma with Jason wouldn't ruin her appetite.

"Let's eat." Thor held out a plate to her as Maddy entered the conference room. "I'm thinking we need to be full before we start talking. Otherwise we'll just hear stomachs growling and won't get a thing accomplished."

"Sounds good to me." Erik shouldered Thor aside to reach one of the trays. "I'm thinking I should try everything first to make sure it's good."

"Generous." Thor rolled his eyes. "That's my baby brother."

"Where are the babies?" Maddy asked.

"In the other room." Thor gestured with his head. "We already fixed Martha a plate. The kids aren't quite ready for Kung Pao chicken."

"You could give Caleb one of these little red peppers to suck on. That might be entertaining." Erik grinned as he held up one of the hot peppers.

"Don't even try it." Jazmyn and Kirsten faced Erik, a united front protecting their children. Maddy almost smiled. She loved the way this family bantered, knowing they cared so much for one another. She wanted this in her future. Since her parents and siblings moved back East years ago, they hadn't been close at all. Even though she lived with her aunt, she rarely saw her.

Maddy stayed quiet as they ate. She enjoyed the repartee of the others but didn't add much. She did eat since the food was light and tasted so good.

"Well, we need to get this meeting under way. Everybody ready?" Thor sat at the head of the table, his hands folded in front of him. "Maddy, I'd like you right here beside me." He patted the table at his left. Jazmyn sat at his right. Erik took the chair beside Maddy, and Kirsten was next to Jazmyn.

"Do I need to take notes?" Maddy asked. "Kirsten wasn't sure about the meeting agenda."

"Nope, no notes." Thor turned to look at Maddy. She could feel the others watching her, too.

"What's going on?" Panic tightened her chest. "Did I do something wrong? Look, I know I've been a little slow this past week, but I've had some extenuating circumstances. I promise I'll do better next week." She fell silent, not wanting to break down and cry. Were they planning to feed her and fire her?

"Maddy, we love you." Jazmyn's smile eased some of the fear. "This company would fall to pieces without you." She glanced at Thor then winked at Maddy. "Just don't tell the head man I said that. He thinks he's the indispensable one." They all laughed.

"We're here to help you, Maddy." Erik reached over to put his large hand over hers.

"You mean you called an executive meeting to help me?" Maddy sniffed.

Thor took over. "We know what's happened with Jason. You two are both miserable. This meeting is a planning session on how to get Jason to wake up and realize what is going on without you swatting him with a baseball bat and dragging him off."

Maddy swallowed hard. "I've never been very good at baseball anyway."

"So, this is what we've been thinking." Jazmyn flashed a grin at Kirsten, and they both leaned closer across the table. "We've been talking all week while you've been moping." Maddy grimaced, and Jazmyn made a face at her. "Well, you have. Anyway, we'll lay out our plan and see if you're agreeable. I think it just might work."

Maddy looked from one to the other. If the whole executive team at T. L. Enterprises was behind this, poor Jason didn't have a chance. She smiled. She couldn't wait to hear what they had to say.

Chapter 21

Staring at his reflection in the mirror, Jason was amazed to see that his inner turmoil wasn't reflected on his face. He looked normal. Maybe a bit tired, but if he relaxed even that wouldn't be noticeable. How could he have so many questions and hurt so much inside without anything showing on the outside?

He opened the cabinet behind the mirror to get a couple of pain relievers for the tension headache lurking at the back of his neck. If he didn't stop it now, the family get-together at Jazmyn's wouldn't be any fun at all. Of course, he doubted he'd have a good time anyway. Maddy and the uncertainty of what he should do about her still clouded his thoughts.

The warm smile on Jazmyn's face lifted his spirits when she opened her front door. "Jason. I'm glad you came."

"Didn't think I would?" Jason stepped into the entryway, not even paying attention to the size and opulence of the mansion anymore. This was just his sister's house now.

"I wasn't sure." Jazmyn stretched up to kiss him on the cheek. "What I said about Mom. I knew it wouldn't apply to you, and I'm sorry I said anything."

"I'm not." Jason gave his sister a hug. "Dad made light of all that happened between them. He probably didn't want me to hold anything against her." He blew out a short breath. "Anyway, thanks for setting me straight."

"Come on in." Jazmyn grabbed his arm and led him down the hallway. "Most of us are here. Erik's on his way from the airport." She must have felt him tense at the mention of her brother-in-law. "Jason, please keep an open mind. Okay?"

He nodded. "I'll try." Pushing away all doubts and fears, Jason strove for a lighter tone. "Did you get the delivery from the bakery?"

"That was wicked." Jazmyn glared at him, her slight smile telling him she was teasing. "A whole box of goodies that I had to keep until this evening. Wicked, brother."

"Are there any left?" Jason chuckled as her eyes widened in mock innocence. "I know you, sis."

"I have enough left to put them out on a small saucer. We can all fight over them." She grinned. "That is, if Kirsten doesn't find them in the kitchen."

"Did I hear my name?" Kirsten sat in a rocking chair, snuggling Caleb against her shoulder. Peder sat on the floor near her feet chewing on a block.

Blaire Dunham sat in a chair across from her. "That wouldn't have been in reference to what used to be a full box of goodies from Ekaterina's, would it?"

Jason groaned. "Don't say I didn't try. At least the ladies of the group enjoyed my contribution to tonight's feast."

"Don't worry," Blaire said. "There's plenty of meat for the men." She glanced over her shoulder. "At least there might be. You should probably check on Burke, Thor, and Wes. They're taking a long time to cook everything. By the way, Caitlin and the twins are out there somewhere, so be forewarned."

"Point taken. I'll leave you with your sugar highs and oversee the barbecuing. They may need an expert's advice." Jason wiggled his eyebrows at the women. The three of them all made faces as he headed toward the patio.

Outside Thor, Burke, and Wes, Kirsten's husband, were all standing beside an immense outdoor cooking area. The gas grill was surrounded by marble-topped counters. Underneath were cabinets with all the necessities for outdoor cooking, including a refrigerator. Jason had fallen in love with the setup the first time he'd been invited over for a cookout.

"Hey, Jason. We'll be ready to eat soon." Thor waved a meat fork in the air.

"Smells good." Jason sniffed the smoky aromas drifting past him. "What's cooking?"

"Almost anything you want." Thor grinned. "We aim to please. I have boneless, skinless chicken breast fillets for the ladies. Burke brought some ostrich burgers for the kids. Wes contributed some marinated pork, and I brought an elk roast that we started earlier."

"Is the grill large enough for all this?" Jason knew that was laughable since the grill could almost hold a whole cow.

"We do have one side reserved for vegetables." Thor shook his head. "Meat should be enough, but they insisted."

Burke chuckled. "But just wait until they try the dish Wes cooked up to go with the pork." Burke, Wes, and Thor all grinned widely enough to let Jason know something was up. Wes was known for experimenting with unusual foods. "He made some applesauce with fresh grated horseradish root in it. The stuff is good but guaranteed to make your eyes water. He did bring a bowl of plain applesauce for the kids."

Jazmyn opened the patio door. "Thor, Erik's back. Can you guys come in for a minute?"

"Sure, be right there. Let me check the meat first." Thor lifted the lid. Smoke billowed up. Jason's mouth watered at the smell of meat cooking. He watched as Thor moved the meat to a cooler section so it wouldn't burn while they were inside. Wes and Burke headed inside, but Jason waited for Thor, hoping no one would see this as avoidance. He'd prayed hard this past week about Erik and Maddy so that he wouldn't harbor any ill feelings, yet he was still reluctant to have this first face-to-face.

"Ready?" Thor clapped him on the shoulder and led the way across the patio.

Jason blinked at the dimness of the room after the bright afternoon sun outside. Everyone stood in a group around Erik. He towered over the others. Only Thor would be taller. As Jason's eyes adjusted, he could see Erik had his arm around a woman. Her long, dark hair shone as it fell in waves down her back.

"Here they are." Jazmyn spoke, and everyone turned to face Jason and Thor. "Come and meet Zuria," Jazmyn said.

Erik gazed down at the exotic beauty beside him with so much love that Jason halted. The cad. Just a week ago he'd been embracing Maddy. Now he had another woman on his arm, acting as if she was the love of his life. Jason couldn't imagine how hurt Maddy would be. Anger began to burn inside him. While he'd been standing there, Erik had introduced Thor. Now Erik and the woman were closing in on Jason.

"Jason, I'd like you to meet my fiancée, Zuria Olivier. Zuria, this is Jazmyn's brother, Jason Rondell."

Zuria held out her hand, several expensive rings adorning her long, delicate fingers. "I am so happy to meet you. My Erik says you are twins." Her low, throaty voice was thick with an accent Jason couldn't identify.

Turning to Erik, Zuria gave him a radiant smile. "Now, where is Maddy? I have to thank her for all she has done for us."

"Good idea." Erik leaned close to kiss Zuria's temple. "She's been so eager to meet you."

Jason couldn't breathe. He stared dumbfounded at the happy couple. "You mean Maddy knows about this?"

Erik's gaze held Jason's. "Jason, without Maddy's friendship and advice, Zuria and I wouldn't be engaged. Maddy helped me figure out how to win over my future father-in-law when he only thought the worst of me. He believed I was defined by my past, the lifestyle I used to live."

"I told Erik I would not marry without my father's blessing. Maddy gave Erik the idea of how to win my father's trust and my heart." Zuria's adoring gaze trained on Erik sent longing through Jason. He wanted Maddy to look at him the same way. In fact, before he'd been so pigheaded, she had looked at him that way.

"I'm sorry. I have to go." Jason pulled his keys from his pocket.

"Where are you going?" Jazmyn asked.

"I have to find Maddy." Panic made Jason's heart thunder in his ears. He had to find her and try to make this right.

"Jason, she's here. Outside with the twins and Caitlin." Jazmyn's hand on his arm settled him for the moment. "Let us get the kids, and then you can go talk with Maddy."

Settling on a bench in the midst of the rose garden, Maddy bowed her head. "Lord, I know You've forgiven me. My past is wiped clean. But I don't feel clean all the time. I don't feel made new. How can I ever hope for Jason or anyone else to see me that way?"

She squeezed her eyes closed. This whole plan wasn't right. What if Jason felt forced to marry her? Later he might regret having a wife with such a sordid past. That could ruin a marriage. He had to make this decision on his own, yet she would never be sure he had.

"Lord, help me know for sure that he loves me." There was the problem, Maddy thought. How would she know for sure? This simply couldn't work. She glanced around. No one was in sight. She'd work her way around to the front of the house, slip inside, grab her purse, and be gone before anyone knew the difference. Once Jason had time to consider, he'd realize how he'd been tricked into thinking he loved her. Maybe someday they could be friends, but Maddy doubted it.

As she hurried around the end of the rose garden, Maddy slammed into Jason so hard she knocked him back a step. She gaped. He looked so good. His eyes shone with excitement. She had to get away fast.

Jason grabbed her and swung her around before setting her down. He pulled her close and began to trail kisses over her cheeks and brow. Maddy couldn't move. She had to hold on to him to keep her shaking legs from folding under her. She needed to tell him to stop but couldn't.

"Maddy. I'm so sorry." Jason's kisses halted at the corner of her mouth, and he began to work his way back up to her temple. Maddy held tighter, her hands fisted in his shirt.

"Maddy, I can't believe I thought those things. Erik and Zuria told me what you did for them. How could I have doubted you? Please, forgive me. Please."

"Jason. Please." Maddy tried to push away. She couldn't help that her traitorous arms only slipped farther around Jason's waist.

"Sweetheart, I've been going crazy this past week. I love you so much. I missed you. I couldn't eat, couldn't sleep, couldn't work. Please, forgive me."

Maddy intended to remove the engagement ring and give it to Jason—she did. Instead, his mouth settled on hers. The kiss was so sweet, like nothing she'd ever experienced. She didn't want it to end.

When Jason pulled back, she could see the love in his eyes. All her doubts washed away. "Tell me you'll still marry me." Jason caressed the side of her face. "I love you so much. I can't imagine life without you."

"We're only eight hours from Vegas and the Elvis impersonator." Love rushed through Maddy in a heady wave.

Jason laughed. "I want to live for a long time with you as my wife. If we did that, my sister would make that life miserable." He stepped back, his hands enfolding hers. "I'm still going to keep my promise to you, Maddy. We will wait for our wedding night, no matter how hard it will be. Okay?"

"I love you so much, Jason Rondell." Maddy squeezed his hands. "I have no idea how I'll survive those times when you're out of town on assignment."

"Well, now, I have an idea about that." Jason grinned. "Of course, it may get you in trouble with your bosses. We'll have to discuss the proposition with them."

By the time they arrived back at the patio, the meat was cooked. Two tables were piled with food. Jazmyn, Kirsten, and Blaire hugged Maddy when they heard she and Jason were okay. Maddy met Zuria, who regaled them all with stories of Erik's intelligence and charm as he won her father's blessing.

"Mom, can we go play? This talk is boring." Jed and Ike stood in front of Blaire. Caitlin, resting on Burke's lap, wiggled down.

"Be polite." Blaire glanced around, winking as she caught Maddy's eye. "Stay close."

The boys turned to Thor. "Can we play with your dog Loki?"

"Sure. He'd love it. Don't get him too excited or he might knock your sister down," Thor said.

"Wait." The children all halted at Blaire's command. "Jed, what are you going to play?"

Jed dug the toe of his shoe into the grass. He grinned. "Loki's going to teach us to fish at the pond." The boys raced off before their mother could even open her mouth.

"Caitlin." The young girl danced in place as she looked at her mother. "How does Loki teach you to fish?"

"Like this." Caitlin mimed sticking her head in the water, opening her mouth, and snapping at something. She galloped off as Blaire shot Burke a look.

"All right, I'm on it." Burke chuckled. "I'll do my best to keep all the fish safe and the kids dry."

"Like that's going to happen." Blaire sighed. "Knowing Burke, he'll be right in the pond with the rest of the kids and dogs." They all laughed as they watched Burke amble after Caitlin.

"I have an announcement." Jason clinked his fork against his glass. Conversation halted as everyone turned. Maddy bit her lip, watching Jason, praying this would go well.

"As you know, Maddy and I are getting married." Jason grinned as the other guys whooped and the women clapped. "I've thought a lot about how hard it will be to go on photography assignments when I'm married. I won't want to leave Maddy, and I'm hoping she won't want to be separated, either." Everyone laughed. Maddy's face warmed as Jason smiled down at her.

"Anyway, I think I've come up with a solution. I've decided to take on a partner." Jason winked at Maddy.

"Oh, Jason, that's wonderful. Are you getting someone you know?" Jazmyn sat forward, excitement making her eyes sparkle. "This means you'll be around more, doesn't it?"

"Well, not exactly." Jason rubbed his jaw. "In fact, I'm hoping I won't get thrown out of here."

"What do you mean?" Jazmyn's brow furrowed.

"You see, I've had several hints from Maddy about how much she would love to travel and see new places. I've asked her to go with me after we're married. We'll do the photography shoots together. After all, she's helped me on a number of jobs around here." Jason's arm tightened around Maddy. Everyone she worked with looked shell-shocked.

"Jason, you can't."

"You can't take her."

Kirsten and Jazmyn spoke at the same time. Their faces mirrored their horror at losing their assistant.

"Now, wait a minute." Thor held up his hand. "This might work. Most of the places Jason goes have electricity. Right?" Jason nodded.

"If Maddy agrees, we can send her with a computer specially equipped to keep in touch with the offices here. We can put security on it for protection. Most of her work is done by computer anyway. She can send the files to an assistant who will be in charge while she's gone, and that person can do the printing, etc. I've been thinking Maddy needs help anyway. Kirsten and Jazmyn are working the poor girl too hard."

Maddy gaped at Thor's announcement and held her breath, waiting to see what Jazmyn and Kirsten would say. Her heart raced. If they agreed, this would be the answer to a longtime prayer of hers.

"Well, I guess that would work." Kirsten frowned as she glanced at Jazmyn.

Jazmyn shook her head. "Nope. Won't work. There is no way to send our special lattes in an e-mail."

"True." Kirsten pursed her lips. "Besides, how would she get those wonderful French pastries for our meetings? I agree. This simply won't do."

They both started laughing and came over to hug Maddy and Jason.

Chapter 22

I can't do this." Maddy sank into the chair and buried her face in her hands. She couldn't hold the tears back any longer. Blaire sat in the chair next to Maddy, rubbing her back. Jazmyn knelt on the floor at Maddy's feet. Kirsten pulled up another chair.

"What is it, Maddy?" Jazmyn squeezed her shoulder. "What's wrong?"

"I don't know." Maddy sobbed. "The last few days have been so hard. I have all these doubts. Jason is so wonderful. How can I saddle him with someone like me?"

"Is this my brother we're talking about?" Jazmyn shook her head as Maddy peeked between her fingers. "And here for the last couple of weeks I've been feeling sorry for you."

"For me?" Maddy hiccuped.

"Yeah. I only have to put up with Jason's tormenting once in a while. You're in for it for a lifetime." Jazmyn put on a sad face. "Poor baby. Want me to sneak you out the back way?"

Wiping her eyes, Maddy tried not to smile at her friend. "And what if I'm the one torturing your brother for a lifetime?"

"Yes." Jazmyn patted Maddy's arm. "Maybe I can give you some pointers. He deserves whatever he gets. Did I tell you about the time we were camping and he pretended to be a bear outside my tent?"

Maddy couldn't stop the giggle. She covered her mouth.

"If there had been a bear handy, I would have fed Jason to him. Poor thing would have gotten a stomachache, too." Jazmyn grinned. She leaned up to hug Maddy. "Seriously, my brother loves you to distraction. I don't think I've ever seen him so happy, Maddy. You'll be a wonderful wife."

Tears filled Maddy's eyes again. "Then why do I have so many doubts?"

"I think it's pretty normal," Jazmyn said. "Remember when I married Thor? You commented as I was getting dressed that I needed a bit more eye makeup." She grinned. "You were so tactful. To tell the truth, I was terrified. All I could think about was becoming like my mother. What if I ran out on Thor and took one of our kids? What if our children grew up apart like Jason and I did?"

"How did you get past that?" Maddy asked.

"I remembered I have something my mother didn't have." Jazmyn's eyes held a trace of sadness. "I have Jesus. He's the strength I need. He's my example and my source of love. I can do all things when He's strengthening me."

"Well put." Blaire spoke up. "You were there when I married Burke, too. I kept thinking I was signing up for a lifetime with a cowboy and a bunch of giant chickens. I even dreamed about them the night before my wedding. Those stupid ostriches were chasing me all over, yanking at my hair and nipping at my dress no matter how fast I ran."

Maddy started to laugh. "I can picture that happening."

"Me, too." Blaire chuckled. "I realized my fears were only that. When I looked to Jesus and kept my eyes on Him, my fear evaporated. Luckily, it was in time for me to fix my makeup after the crying jag and walk down the aisle without looking like a raccoon."

"Do I look that bad?" Maddy glanced around for a mirror.

"Don't worry," Blaire said. "You have plenty of time to fix your makeup before the ceremony starts." She checked her watch. "I do think it's about time to get busy."

"Thanks." Maddy blew her nose. She looked at all her friends.

Kirsten stood and held out her hand. "Come on, assistant. You wait on me all the time. Now it's my turn to help you out."

"So, did you cry at your wedding, Kirsten?" Maddy asked.

"Nope." Kirsten gave a sly grin. "But I'm told Wes did." Maddy laughed until her sides ached.

With Kirsten, Blaire, and Jazmyn helping her, Maddy prepared for her wedding. When she stood before the mirror in her wedding gown, she just stared. Would Jason find her beautiful? She forced the niggle of doubt away.

"Maddy, you are gorgeous." Jazmyn stood behind her arranging the veil. "Jason will drop his teeth."

"What! I have to marry some toothless guy?" Maddy grinned at Jazmyn as they shared a memory of a time when Jazmyn said something similar to Maddy on the way to a party at Thor's house before she'd met him.

"At least he won't bite you then." Jazmyn winked.

"Wait a minute. You didn't tell me he bites." Maddy put her hands on her hips.

"Too late." Jazmyn grinned. "I'm not taking him back."

"That was the pastor's wife. It's time to go. Everybody's waiting for the bride." Kirsten crossed the room to them. Jazmyn was Maddy's matron of honor. Kirsten and Blaire were the other attendants.

"Where's Caitlin?" Maddy realized the young girl was nowhere to be seen.

"With her daddy." Blaire took Maddy's hand. "He'll be ready with her when it's time for her to do the flowers. I think we should pray before we go out there." The four of them bowed their heads. Blaire led the prayer. Peace settled over Maddy. Some of her shaking eased, and she couldn't wait to see Jason.

PICTURE THIS

The music filled the church. Maddy waited outside the sanctuary. Her parents hadn't come for the wedding. Deep inside she'd known they wouldn't. Manuel was probably right about them, but she couldn't help hoping that they really did care about her. Instead of her father giving her away, Maddy had asked Burke if he would. He'd gotten tears in his eyes as he told her it would be an honor to stand in as her father.

Now Burke took her hand, placed it on his arm, and squeezed her fingers. "You're the most beautiful bride since Blaire." He winked. "Jason's one blessed guy. Don't you ever doubt that, okay?"

She didn't remember much about the walk down the aisle. Jason caught and held her gaze from the first moment. She could see the anticipation and excitement in his eyes, even from the back of the church. Maddy had trouble breathing when they stood next to each other, hand in hand. The shakes returned.

✍

The vision drifting down the aisle stole all thought from Jason. Maddy was beyond beautiful. She was his bride. She would be the mother of his children. He couldn't wait to start their life together—the most exciting journey he could imagine.

When he took her hand in his, he could feel her trembling. Even with makeup expertly applied, he could tell she'd been crying. Second thoughts? Doubts? Knowing Maddy, she'd been thinking he may have changed his mind. Well, he would show her.

Leaning close, Jason spoke low from the side of his mouth so no one but Maddy would hear. "As soon as they're not looking, I'm going to kiss you."

Maddy blushed. She squeezed his hand hard. Cutting her eyes toward him, she shook her head. Jason grinned. She wasn't shaking now.

When the pastor had them face each other to exchange vows, Jason started to lean forward and lift the veil. Everyone chuckled. Pastor Marsh cleared his throat and shook his head. Jason released the veil and straightened. Maddy's lips twitched.

When the vows were over, Brendon opened his mouth to begin speaking. Once again, Jason leaned forward and lifted the veil. He pursed his lips. Tittering laughter rippled through the audience. Brendon and the groomsmen snickered. Maddy giggled. Jason affected disappointment as he let go of her veil.

"Now, Jason." Humor tinged Pastor Marsh's words. "Now you may kiss the bride."

Jason grinned. He flipped the veil over Maddy's head. She started to lean forward for a sweet kiss. Instead, he grabbed her, lifting until her feet were clear of the floor. Once the kiss started, he didn't want it to end. Again Brendon cleared his throat. By the time Jason released Maddy, the whole congregation was clapping. Maddy, pink-cheeked, turned with him so Brendon could present them to their family and friends as husband and wife.

"Do you realize all I want to do is get out of here and be alone with you?" Jason spoke softly so no one but Maddy would hear. "Whose idea was it to have all this hoopla after the wedding?"

"Hoopla?" Maddy raised one eyebrow.

Jason grinned as he got ready to pose for the next picture. "Yeah. First we had to shake hands and hug every person in the state of Arizona. Now we have to take enough pictures to fill ten albums. Next we have to go eat, talk to people, and then get stuff thrown at us when we leave. What's with that?"

"Maybe it's because they don't like the meal or their shoes are pinching by the time everything is done." Maddy winked.

"No doubt." Jason grinned. "Maybe we could slip out the side door or I could pay the limo driver to let us out somewhere else."

"No way, buster." Jazmyn punched Jason on the arm. "This is your turn, and you'll stay for the whole deal."

"This is torture." Jason groaned.

"You might be exaggerating just a bit." Maddy giggled. "Besides, with the cost of a wedding, you want to get the most out of it."

"Listen to your bride." Jazmyn kissed Jason's cheek. "At least you only have about one hundred guests. Thor and I had a few hundred."

The afternoon wore on. Despite his complaints, Jason enjoyed the joking, the stolen kisses, and being with Maddy. God had blessed him well with her as a wife.

"Hey, time to leave pretty soon?" Jason asked. Maddy looked as if she was ready to drop. "We have an early flight to catch. You ready to travel with me?"

Maddy sighed, snuggled next to him, and looked up, her warm brown eyes full of love. "For the rest of my life."

A Letter to Our Readers

Dear Readers:

In order that we might better contribute to your reading enjoyment, we would appreciate your taking a few minutes to respond to the following questions. When completed, please return to the following: Fiction Editor, Barbour Publishing, Inc., P.O. Box 719, Uhrichsville, OH 44683.

1. Did you enjoy reading *Painted Desert* by Nancy J. Farrier?
   ❏ Very much—I would like to see more books like this.
   ❏ Moderately—I would have enjoyed it more if _____
   _____
   _____

2. What influenced your decision to purchase this book?
   (Check those that apply.)
   ❏ Cover   ❏ Back cover copy   ❏ Title   ❏ Price
   ❏ Friends   ❏ Publicity   ❏ Other

3. Which story was your favorite?
   ❏ *An Ostrich a Day*   ❏ *Picture This*
   ❏ *Picture Imperfect*

4. Please check your age range:
   ❏ Under 18   ❏ 18–24   ❏ 25–34
   ❏ 35–45   ❏ 46–55   ❏ Over 55

5. How many hours per week do you read? _____

Name _____

Occupation _____

Address _____

City_____ State_____ Zip_____

E-mail_____

If you enjoyed

Painted

DESERT

then read

UNDER THE BIG SKY

by KELLY EILEEN HAKE

A Time to Plant
A Time to Keep
A Time to Laugh

Available wherever books are sold.
Or order from:
Barbour Publishing, Inc.
P.O. Box 721
Uhrichsville, Ohio 44683
www.barbourbooks.com

You may order by mail for $7.97 and add $4.00 to your order for shipping.
Prices subject to change without notice.
If outside the U.S. please call 740-922-7280 for shipping charges.